ASHES DON'T TELL EVERYTHING

SOME SECRETS REFUSE TO STAY BURIED

NORMA JEAN RICHARDS

NEXT CHAPTER LIFE PRESS

Publisher: New Chapter Life Press

Cover Design: Created By Norma Jean Richards

ISBN: (eBook): 979-8-9999940-1-1

First Edition: 2025

For more information, visit: Next Chapter Life Press

https://coachnextchapter.com/about-ncl-press

❀ Formatted with Vellum

She buried the past—until it came
back breathing.

ASHES
DON'T TELL
EVERYTHING

Some Secrets Refuse
to Stay Buried

NORMA JEAN
RICHARDS

A woman's story never ends with her,
  it echoes through daughters,
  through losses,
  through the things left unsaid.
  — *N.J. Richards*

DEDICATION

*To my mother, **Naomi Richards**,*
who taught me that even in silence, there is strength.
A woman who prioritized books in a home of eight children,
she gave me the love of reading, and with it,
the ability to make words come alive.
Though she has gone, her legacy breathes in these pages.
She was my first example of how a woman can survive what's unspeakable
and still show up with beauty, faith, and grace.
She wore her struggles like her perfume, subtle but unforgettable,
with the right shade of lipstick, her hair styled perfectly,
and a voice that never shouted, but always moved mountains.
She showed me that ashes don't tell everything,
and that some stories deserve to rise from the ashes.
This is for her.

ACKNOWLEDGEMENT

While this novel is lovingly dedicated to my mother,
   I would be remiss not to acknowledge my husband,
   Bishop Ben Washington.
   Without his unwavering belief in my voice,
   this story may never have reached the page.
   When I questioned my ability, he answered with belief.
   When I made excuses, he offered support.
   And when I claimed I didn't have the time, he created the space.
   His faith in me never wavered;
   even when mine did.

CONTENTS

PROLOGUE
HAWKS LANDING - 2009

THE WILDFIRE devoured everything in its path: homes, headlines, and history.

From the edge of the chaos, Madison Jackson Winter watched her life go up in flames. Smoke blurred the sky, sirens pierced the air, and somewhere behind her, the mansion she once called home crumbled like a lie finally told.

Tonight, she was supposed to be dead.

The news would report it that way.

A bishop's wife, lost in the fire.

A tragedy.

But Madison didn't run from the flames.

She ran from the life that trapped her: the arranged marriage, the mistress, the polished sermons that masked control.

From the weight of a stillborn child who cried in her dreams.

From the cage of silence that her title demanded.

In the ashes, she buried Madison.

In exile, she became someone else; someone freer.

Autumn Nina Storm.

But the past doesn't burn so easily.

PART ONE
THE BEGINNING OF THE END

CHAPTER
ONE

AUGUST 14, 2017

Pendleton Women's Federal Prison
3:14 a.m.

"WAKE UP, convict! Get up now, bitch!"

The voice sliced through the dark, yanking her awake, heart pounding.

This wasn't the usual wake-up. Something in her tone cut colder than routine, the sharp edge Madison hadn't heard since the night of that lockdown two years ago.

BAM... BAM... BAM!

The baton slammed against the bars again, harder each time. Clatter echoed down the tier, met with groans and curses. But there was no roll call. No breakfast carts squeaked. Only the voice, that baton, and the uneasy silence between each strike.

Madison sat up, bare feet hitting cold cement. Her eyes strained against the dim light as her mind scrambled to catch up. The voice outside her cell grated, sharp and venomous.

"QUIET DOWN!"

This wasn't just a rude awakening. Something was off, the *off* that made the air feel charged, like the moments before a fight or a fire alarm. And in prison, when the script changed, it rarely meant freedom. More likely: blood, transfer, or ghosts clawing their way back.

She exhaled sharply, running a hand over her face.

They didn't drag inmates out of bed at this hour unless something had gone very wrong.

"Jesus. Really?" she muttered, slumping onto the steel-framed bed. The foam pad barely muted the bite of steel beneath her. On nights like this, when cold crept through the walls, it felt like sleeping on raw steel. She'd give anything for one more night on that five-grand Kluft mattress she used to mock.

Outside her cell, the chaos intensified. Fluorescents snapped on, harsh, unforgiving. Groans. Metal clanged as fists pounded on doors, voices rising in anger and frustration.

"Heffa! Yo' ass got a visitor, NOW!" Sgt. Janet "The Bull" Wallace's voice was unmistakable, deep, raspy, and authoritative.

Madison's teeth clenched at the sound of the baton striking the bars.

She knew the drill. But that wasn't happening now.

Sgt. Wallace bellowed. "22!"

The locks released with an ominous snap, the heavy steel door sliding open with a groan. Unnerving possibilities raced through her mind: had something happened?

Was someone dead? Was she being transferred?

Beneath the fear, a petty truth nagged her: they'd woken her up.

Three years ago, she stood at the defense table, hands clasped in front of her, as if stillness might shield her from the weight of the verdict. Her lawyer reached for her hand, but she gently pulled away, her eyes fixed on a single crack in the courtroom wall slightly above the jury box. "Madison Jackson Winter, also known as Nina Autumn Storm," the judge read, voice flat, almost bored. "A jury of your peers has found you guilty of involuntary manslaughter, and you are being sentenced to three years in Pendleton Women's Federal Prison."

Three years. Long enough for headlines to quiet, whispers to dull, and both names to fade. Not Madison Jackson Winter, the polished First Lady with a past wrapped in privilege and scandal. Not Nina Autumn Storm, the alias she clung to like a life raft.

Here, she was only inmate #39178, a number stitched into her collar and forgotten enough to stop mattering. A whispered cautionary tale passed from cell to cell of the woman who didn't bow her head when the verdict came down. She stood tall, chin lifted, as if the courtroom owed her something.

And maybe it did.

Each night, as the Quad Commander announced, "Lights out in five," the air filled with boos and groans. Inmates cursed, laughed, and created their nightly racket. But not her. It was her escape from guilt, from the relentless whisper of her actions, and the crushing reality of loss. In the dark, she was the woman she had fought to remember before everything burned.

As the chaos outside her cell calmed, Madison pressed her hand to her chest, steadying her breath. "I've got a no-visitor order… so who the hell is here?"

Before the words could form, she had entered the cell. Sgt. Wallace moved quickly, too quickly. She slammed Madison against the cold cinderblock wall with practiced force. Pain exploded behind her eyes, a white-hot flash that left her ears ringing. Her knees buckled, her breath stuttered out of her lungs, and for half a second, she thought she might vomit.

Wallace's voice boomed, sharp and relentless: "Boogie! Where the hell do you think you are? This ain't no damn resort, and I'm sure as hell not the help!"

Madison winced, swallowing the cry. She wouldn't give them the satisfaction. She slid down the cold, hard concrete wall after the blow, the impact echoing in her ears, but it wasn't the physical sting that truly stunned her.

It was an echo of a memory.

She was eleven again, crouched in a dark closet, hearing a monster's footsteps creaking the floorboards outside. Back when silence meant survival, and disappearing was the only way to keep breathing.

The old cold rose again: powerlessness. But something shifted. Her body remembered fear. But her soul, her soul remembered surviving.

That was the difference.

Now, something sparked inside her, not just the fear of who was waiting, but defiance. "I'm not eleven anymore," she thought, "trembling in that closet, waiting for the monster to leave."

Sgt. Wallace yanked her by the arm, dragging her upright before Madison could fully find her footing. "You deaf now?" she snapped. With one swift motion, she shoved Madison back onto the bunk, hard enough for her spine to slam against the metal frame.

"Need I remind you? You're still a convicted felon. You belong to the system until you're processed out. Now get your ass in gear."

Madison moved slowly, deliberately. She stepped into her pants slowly, like molasses, as if the clock had stopped just for her. Her gaze stayed fixed on the wall, a quiet refusal to look rattled, while she smoothed her shirt and brushed away imaginary dust. Each motion was a silent protest: *You don't get to rush me.*

"Let's go, inmate," Sgt. Wallace barked, her voice sharp with impatience, lingering in the doorway with arms crossed and baton in hand. A silver chain with a dove charm hung around her neck, strangely gentle for someone issuing orders like a drill sergeant. Her piercing gaze scrutinized Madison's slender figure, a smirk on her lips.

Still, Madison didn't rush, standing with a quiet elegance that only irritated Sgt. Wallace more.

"You wanna test me tonight?" Sgt. Wallace hissed, stepping forward.

Madison finally turned, leaving the cell with a cool, unreadable gaze. "I'm moving, Sgt. Wallace," she said evenly. "Just not dancing."

Wallace's jaw clenched. With a rough grip on Madison's elbow, she gave her a shove down the corridor.

"Move."

Madison stumbled a step but didn't look back. Just kept walking, slow, steady, on her terms.

The walk felt longer than usual. The air was thin, tinged with the scent of bleach and sweat.

Her throat tightened. She wasn't sure which prison had devoured first: her softness, her voice, or her belief in mercy.

From somewhere behind her, a voice hissed low: "*Dead girl walkin'.*"

Another muttered, "*Somebody's in trouble.*"

The whispers slithered along the tier, sharp as razors, feeding the dread she tried not to show.

Whispers continued:

"*Had it all.*"

"*Liar. Murderer.*"

She wanted to scream: "*You don't know me. You'll never understand what I gave up protecting a lie that was never mine.*"

But she swallowed it whole. Sometimes, silence weighs less than the truth.

Her pulse spiked, but she kept moving.

At the first checkpoint, the officer's voice cut through: "Hold still."

The metal detector's low hum buzzed against her ears as she extended her arms, like a ghost reenacting the routine of the living.

"Clear."

She exhaled slowly, noticing how her fingers wouldn't quite stop trembling; not fear, not anger, but anticipation.

Who was waiting?

No letters, no calls, no visits, since Mister Mayor, now deceased.

Could it be an attorney? A reporter? Someone from her buried past?

Her mind drifted back to her trial, where an unreadable yet familiar face watched intently from the gallery, calm, piercing, and patient, constantly watching and observing, silently judging every word and movement. That face haunted her thoughts, an enigma wrapped in calm, a constant reminder of the scrutiny she was under.

An icy shiver ran down her spine.

Next checkpoint, her pulse racing.

A guard gestured forward.

"Keep moving."

The corridor stretched, each step dragging her closer to the unknown. The air thickened, charged with something unspoken.

Mister Mayor, her only visitor in three years, had come six months ago, unannounced, as if time hadn't dimmed his presence. The faint hiss of the oxygen tank filled the room before his voice did, but when she saw him, his eyes still carried that same mischievous spark, like he might ask her to sneak him pie before he left.

She wanted to weep but didn't.

She wanted to reach for his hand, but didn't.

Instead, she crossed her arms, her face a mask, like in foster care, marriage, or court.

"Autumn," he whispered, voice frayed but steady.

"I'm fighting... but lung cancer's not a fair fight." He caught his breath.

"They gave me six months. I had to say goodbye. But I have a request."

She trembled inwardly.

He asked her to be someone again, more than a number, a mugshot, a secret.

It wasn't the request that cracked her, but the name.

Autumn.

That was her resurrection, her deceased best friend's name, her second chance, her secret.

But now, the system resurrected Madison, assigning her #39178, in prison orange, with her hands cuffed and stripped bare.

And Mister Mayor, dying yet dignified, asked her to become Autumn once more.

That was six months ago.

But now, someone else waited in the visitors' area.

Nameless. No note, no request, no warning.

The kind of visitor who made guards mutter and inmates fall silent.

A whisper of possibility.

And the question returned, sharp as broken glass: *Who do they want me to be this time?*

For the first time in years, Madison felt the old fear crawl back up her throat, the kind you can't swallow, no matter how hard you try.

CHAPTER
TWO
AUGUST 14, 2017

Pendleton Women's Federal Prison
3:24 a.m.

SOMEONE WAS WAITING. Only one name rose like a bruise in her mind.

Bishop Jacob Winston Winter III.

Her husband's name alone. The man who held a Bible in one hand and her silence in the other. Her stomach turned, and her pulse quickened. *"Please, Lord,"* she whispered, voice cracking under the weight of memory. *"Not him. Not now."*

"Speak up, bitch." Sgt. Wallace shouted fiercely as she shoved her into the tunnel, ominously known among inmates as "The Gauntlet."

This was no ordinary passage; it was a dark, foreboding tunnel of steel and shadows where no surveillance cameras monitored and the rules of conduct were murky and undefined, creating an atmosphere of danger and chaos.

Sgt. Wallace marched ahead, silent now, her boots echoing on the cold concrete.

But this walk was different. Colder. More final.

Unexpectedly, Sgt. Wallace's voice dropped to a mere whisper, its gravity wrapping around Madison like a shroud of dread.

"Madison Jackson Winter."

Madison froze, the name hanging in the stale air like a heavy weight. Her heart pounded, a frantic drumbeat against the silence, as she tried to grasp the significance of those words. The full name felt like an accusation.

"Listen. Don't react." Her voice was strained, laced with a sense of urgency. "You won't see me again."

The pause that followed stretched endlessly, like the shadows in the tunnel, thick with unspoken words.

"So, I'm saying this now. I'm sorry." Her words hovered on the edge of silence, burdened by unspoken tension. Madison turned to her, stunned, a swirl of disbelief and confusion swirling in her chest like a storm.

"Keep your eyes looking ahead, Madison," she said, not as an instruction, but with unease. "You think I was hard on you? I was. But if I hadn't been, you wouldn't have survived in here."

Sgt. Wallace's voice cracked, emotion thickening in her words. Each phrase carried the weight of their shared struggles, echoing through the tunnel and sinking deep into Madison's soul.

Madison's shoulders slumped as if the question had been holding her upright. Her breath slowed. Looking down at the hand, gripping her arm, then back up, eyes glistening but hard. "Why me?" she whispered, her voice trembling, vulnerability seeping through, sharp as a knife cutting through darkness.

Sgt. Wallace's voice broke, the words spilling rough and reluctant.

"Because I owed someone."

She didn't say who. Didn't say why.

Madison's steps faltered, just a hair, but enough to betray the shock under her calm.

Wallace's jaw tightened. "Your visitor will explain," she said finally. A beat.

Then, lower: "If they tell you the truth."

Parting her lips as if to say more, then shutting them tight again. Madison caught the crack, the faint crack in the mask. Sgt. Wallace didn't know everything. Maybe she never did. And that uncertainty-the unknown, was the real warning.

Just like that, they stepped out of The Gauntlet, beginning the descent into the unknown.

Reaching the next checkpoint, the heavy door loomed before them like a gate to an uncertain fate. Sgt. Wallace pressed Madison against the cold metal, the force of her grip almost a formality.

"Bougie Brat Bitch, haven't you learned yet not to ask questions?" she sneered, her tone dripping with disdain.

Another guard chuckled, dark amusement flickering in his eyes. "That half-breed bitch ain't learned yet."

As Sgt. Wallace uncuffed her with a quick flick of her wrist, their gazes locked, and an unspoken understanding passed between them. In that moment, Madison felt the warmth of a bond that defied chaos. Sgt. Wallace gently squeezed her hand, her voice a tender whisper beneath their circumstances.

"Live on your terms," she breathed, not a suggestion, but a charge. Then, softer, almost fragile: "You gon' be alright."

Sgt. Wallace turned back toward the gauntlet, glancing over her shoulder with hesitant eyes. "Tell your visitor..." she started, then shook her head. "Never mind."

CHAPTER
THREE
FEBRUARY 6, 2014

Pendleton Corrections Office
8:50 a.m.

SHE ASKED, so she protected Madison, even though she didn't fully understand why.

Didn't need to.

No explanations. A name. A favor.

The voice on the other end of that call, one she hadn't heard in years, was soft with memory, heavy with something unspoken.

She'd returned from vacation, a rare escape from concrete, cold steel beds, and the never-ending hum of tension, only to step back into whispers in the breakroom and a flagged file waiting on her desk.

No priors.

No visitors.

Sealed juvenile record.

Murdered parents.

A paper trail that vanished every time it was supposed to begin.

In the intake's file margin, a single handwritten note:

"High-profile. Do not assign to the general population without contact with the prosecutor's office."

Sgt. Wallace stared at it, the handwriting all too familiar.

She grabbed the phone and dialed.

"Janet," came the voice, calm and practiced.

"You got her?"

"I did."

A pause.

"I appreciate this, Janet."

"I didn't say I agreed to anything."

A longer pause this time

Then the voice on the other end dropped, low and real, saying, "She's important to me. I can't explain why yet. But if there's still a part of you that cares…"

Hearing the familiar echo of that voice, Sgt. Wallace removed the phone from her ear and gazed at it quietly, not with surprise but with guilt, still, Morgan. The same girl she had envied, who lived in a mansion that felt too white, who always sat tall with her curls pulled into a perfect ponytail, her clothes pressed, and her voice practiced.

The one she wronged and never stopped owing.

Back then, she was Janet Wallace, the street-smart granddaughter of Morgan's nanny, Miss Lovie. Summers meant staying in the guest room off the kitchen, watching Morgan glide through that white-pillared mansion with the ease Janet pretended not to envy.

She hated how her grandmother called Morgan "*my baby*," a phrase Janet herself rarely heard.

But resentment softened. Eventually.

Now they were grown. They didn't talk often. Didn't need to.

History in that house bound them tighter than friendship ever could.

So, when Morgan Marie Bennin-Alcott called after all these years and asked for a favor?

Janet didn't ask why. And Morgan didn't explain.

"Alright," she'd whispered into the phone.

Three years ago, that had been enough.

She had kept her promise and guarded the secret without knowing its shape, only its weight.

CHAPTER
FOUR
AUGUST 14, 2017

Pendleton's Visitors Room
3:33 a.m.

MADISON'S WRISTS ached from the handcuffs as she walked down the visitor's room hallway, the sound of locks snapping behind her like a warning. The linoleum floor shined, and the overhead light buzzed harshly, feeling too bright and sterile.

The steel door to the visiting room buzzed.

She stepped in.

Only one woman waited at the far end.

Tall. Elegant. Black. Dressed in a muted blouse and sharply pressed slacks, she was restrained in every line of her clothing. But the hair betrayed her: a platinum pixie cut, bright, defiant, like one part of her refused to be managed.

Madison stopped, pulse quickening.

There was something about the jawline. The posture. The stillness.

The courtroom.

That's where she'd seen her before; in the back row every day, silent, composed, watching. Not judgment. Not pity. Something else.

Concern.

The guard shifted behind her, the scrape of boots breaking the still-ness. Madison sat, chin lifted, and nodded for the woman to take the opposite chair. Her hands curled beneath the table, hidden.

"Madison Jackson Winter," the woman began, voice even, though tension ran under it. "I don't have long. My name is Morgan Marie Bennin-Alcott. I work in the District Attorney's office. I got permission from the Governor to be here."

Madison's brows lifted just slightly. Her shoulders remained square, but her eyes narrowed.

District Attorney. Governor. This wasn't a visit. It was an ambush.

Damn.

What kind of stunt was this? Only seven days left... now what?

"I recused myself from working on your case," Morgan continued.

Madison said nothing, but suspicion gave way to a thread of curiosity.

"What do you want?" she asked, almost annoyed.

"I couldn't," Morgan said again, voice cracking despite the control she fought to maintain. "Because three weeks before jury selection... I found something out. Something that unraveled everything I thought I knew about myself."

Madison tilted her head slightly.

Morgan paused, swallowed. "I discovered... you're my mother."

Madison's breath hitched, but her face stayed still.

"No," she whispered, almost to herself. Her eyes flicked over Morgan's features again, searching for anything wrong, anything that would make this a mistake. The jawline? The eyes? A scar that should be there but wasn't?

"Who told you that?" she asked sharply, a note of defense slipping through her usual calm. "Who sent you?"

Morgan didn't flinch. "The truth did."

Silence stretched.

Madison's hand curled under the table, her nails digging into her own palm. She wanted to dismiss it and push the claim back across the table like poor paperwork.

But then, there it was.

The sharp line of her jaw, along with the stillness in her posture.

A familiarity she'd never named until now.

Something within her yielded. A small shift, almost invisible. The calculation stayed, but disbelief cracked.

"You're my mother," Morgan said again, softer now.

Madison's breath snagged. Her throat tightened.

She finally asked, almost whispering, "What hospital?"

"County General."

Madison nodded once, almost imperceptibly.

"They told you I was dead," Morgan said, restraining her anger.

"They told me I imagined it," Madison answered, voice barely audible.

The room faded, the walls, the table, and she was thirteen and a half again, drowning in white sheets and gloved hands. Nurses moved like ghosts. A doctor's voice, flat as tile: *stillborn*.

Now the child behind the muffled cry sat across from her.

"They lied," Morgan said, voice cracking. "I survived."

Madison's gaze dropped to Morgan's trembling hands.

"You didn't get to hold me. Or name me. Or even say goodbye." Morgan's tone hardened. "They stole from you. From us."

Madison stayed silent, but the weight of it pressed into the table like lead.

"I should have told you sooner," Morgan added. "I didn't want you to find out like this."

Silence again. Not the safe kind. The kind that bruises.

"Time!" the guard barked from across the room.

Morgan leaned forward, urgency breaking through her composure. "I know you're being released next Tuesday. Could I... come for you?"

The guard stepped closer. Madison stood, cuffs waiting. Her eyes stayed on Morgan, sharp, steady, as if memorizing the shape of her face, or proving to herself it was real.

Before the cuffs snapped closed, she spoke.

"M&M," she snickered. "See you Tuesday."

Morgan blinked. "What?"

Madison didn't explain. She turned and let the steel bite into her wrists.

No more words. No promises.

She walked out carrying one fragile, dangerous truth pressed tight against her ribs:

The word *"mother"* belonged to her again.

PART TWO
HAWKS LANDING

CHAPTER
FIVE
JUNE 12, 2009

Hawks Landing
5:30 a.m.

EIGHT YEARS before the prison walls and the silence of the visiting room, there was a house on fire.

Lady Madison Jackson Winter woke at 5:30 am, expecting an ordinary day, unaware that by nightfall, Hawks Landing and she would be gone. Each morning, she wrestled with the weight of his memory, making it hard to breathe. Sitting up, stretching as the cool satin sheets brushed her skin. The faint scent of jasmine from the diffuser filled the air, an old habit to mask the discomfort of waking in a house that never felt like home.

For years, she had perfected her morning routine, each step curated to maintain the illusion of the perfect wife. Bishop Winston Jacob Winter III enforced expectations without ever needing to raise his voice; rules unspoken but deeply understood. The house reflected him: pristine, measured, exacting. Even the thermostat never wavered from 68 degrees, his ideal temperature.

One morning, Madison crept downstairs early and nudged it up to 72 degrees.

To feel something warmer.

He noticed at breakfast.

"Too warm in here," he said, loosening his tie. "Feels... off."

"I thought it might be nice for once," she said, her tone light.

Ignoring her, he instructed the maid to turn the dial down again.

"Consistency is comfort," he said. "Especially in a house like this." Smiling with that calm, arrogant smile which always implied, *I know what's best.*

Madison rarely argued, instead quietly returning to buttering her toast and settling into his version of home.

With that memory, a rare smile crossed Madison's face as she put on the silk slippers, grabbed her robe, and descended the spiral staircase. Echoes of creaks made it feel more like a museum than a home. Since the coffee wouldn't start brewing for another half hour, she instead went to the den, her private escape. This was the only place in the past two years that offered comfort without judgment when her grief was unbearable.

Crossing the threshold of her peace and sinking into the depths of the oversized Natuzzi leather armchair, Madison let her eyes drift to the life-sized family portrait above the fireplace. Commissioned for their twentieth wedding anniversary, her mother-in-law curated it... down to the last button.

"You should wear the pearl," she'd said, laying the dress on Madison's bed with a finality that left no room for opinion.

Madison had run her fingers over the icy fabric. "It's... cold," she murmured.

Her mother-in-law smiled tightly. "It's dignified. A First Lady should never look too warm."

So Madison wore the pearl. The photo was perfect. They looked perfect.

Now, staring up at it, the gloss of that day appeared to mock her.

A still life of a woman who learned to smile on cue, hold her husband's hand like a prayer, and dress the part. Always.

Bishop standing beside her in tailored perfection, his suit crisp, smile practiced, hand resting lightly on her shoulder like a prop. He looked every bit the devoted husband, the dignified Bishop; even if the truth had long since unraveled beneath the seams.

And Coby... their last family portrait. She brushed away the memory like smoke irritating her eyes. Coby, with that half-smile, deliberately placed to hide amusement during formal events.

He hated the photo, saying, "We look like statues, Mom."

"That's the point," she'd joked.

He was a ghost in every room.

She couldn't recall the last time she wandered through this house without expecting him. Occasionally, wind in the vents echoed his laughter.

The ache remained, but today, the portrait, usually comforting, felt like reopening the wound.

The wound haunted her, causing her to spend countless mornings trying to make sense of her life.

In these quiet moments, she faced a harsh truth: her life in Hawks Landing was a carefully maintained act she no longer wanted to keep up. The house's lavish decor and opulence felt restrictive, like a gilded cage.

The wealth and curated social image were overwhelming, like humidity before a summer storm, heavy on her chest.

Pulling herself up from the chair, she reached over and paused before opening the drawer. Inside: the worn pack, half full, and a matte gold lighter tucked beside it like a secret. She didn't smoke for the nicotine. It was a ritual. The pause. The control.

One cigarette between her fingers, then a flick. Click. The flame flared briefly, lighting her face, then vanished into the inhale. The first drag was slow, deliberate.

Her shoulders softened.

Smoke curled upward in defiance past the family portrait, as if standing in camaraderie with her resentment at still being called "Lady Winter" at church, functions, and charity events, an illusion, hiding her erosion behind lipstick, pearls, checkbook donations, and hollow smiles.

She once thought being indispensable was power, but now even Bishop no longer needs her, not since Coby.

After Coby died, Bishop never spoke his name to her again.

Madison grieved in silence. Tidy and composed. Expected.

Two years ago, she almost left for good. A storm raged outside as she packed her passport and her father's old photo album, complete with recipes, into a weekend bag. She reached the highway but then turned back, overwhelmed by the idea of someone else sitting in the front row while Bishop spoke of redemption.

But now she would leave, packing nothing, without saying goodbye.

Anything to feel alive again.

Putting her cigarette out in the ashtray, she went to the kitchen, expecting the comforting aroma of freshly brewed coffee from Lena's nightly routine.

But there was no coffee. The kitchen was unkempt, with dishes in the sink and an empty wine bottle on the counter.

Lena must have forgotten, she thought, amused by the idea of her housekeeper having a late-night drink, until she saw Lena's note on the refrigerator. The note explained she wouldn't be coming today due to evacuation concerns from the wildfire. It also mentioned Nina had arrived the night before and was staying in the guest room upstairs.

That explained the mess.

Nina's late night, not Lena's.

The landline on the wall blinked with a new voicemail. Madison pressed play as she opened the fridge to get the pitcher of water.

A man's voice filled the kitchen, low and rough, like he hadn't slept.

"Uh, hi, this is Cole. I'm a friend of Nina's… She, uh, mentioned she'd be staying there. I've been calling her cell all night, but she hasn't picked up. I'm… worried. If you see her, could you tell her to call me back? Please."

The message ended with a hollow click, making the silence feel even heavier.

Madison poured water into a glass slowly.

Cole?

Nina had finally revealed the name of her mystery lover last week, offhandedly, like a tether to someone beyond this house.

Her gaze drifted to the ceiling, to the guest room upstairs. The house was still. Too still.

Madison took a deep breath and sipped the water slowly as she leaned against the counter. Something about today didn't sit right.

Maybe it was the potent smell of smoke seeping through the air vents.

When she retired last night, the forecast showed the wildfire in the distance being ninety percent contained, so she wasn't too worried.

However, the smell of smoke prompted her to turn on the TV for updated news.

Almost at the same time as a news anchor announces an immediate mandatory evacuation of Hawks Landing, there is a loud knock at the front door.

Then another one.

Startled, Lady Winter moved to the security monitor in the den.

As the screen flickered to life, her breath caught in her throat.

Police officer.

She clasped a trembling hand over her mouth, a chilling sense of déjà vu.

Nearly two years ago, she stood in this very room, gazing into the solemn face of another officer. She didn't know she would get news that would change her life forever.

And now, as she looked at the uniformed officer outside, an icy wave of dread washed over her.

History was knocking at her door, and she wasn't sure she had the strength to open it.

Her first instinct was to run. To hide.

But she knew it wasn't an option.

Her heart pounded as she headed to the door.

She opened the door slowly.

The officer shifted slightly back as the door groaned open. His uniform bore streaks of ash, and his eyes showed exhaustion mixed with warmth.

"Ma'am," he began gently, "we're under mandatory evacuation. The wildfire changed direction. It's moving faster than expected. You'll need to be out as soon as possible."

Behind him, the sky had changed; no longer dawn-blue, but a smoky, rust-tinged haze. Ash drifted like snowflakes through the still air. Somewhere in the distance, the deep wail of a siren howled like a warning.

Madison's fingers tightened around the doorframe. She nodded once, slowly. "Understood."

"Do you need help to evacuate? Anyone else in the house?"

"One guest," she answered. "I'll alert her."

He gave her a polite, professional nod.

"Please, don't wait too long."

"I won't."

He hesitated for a moment, as if sensing something more profound in her stillness, then turned and walked back to his cruiser.

Madison stood in the doorway, watching him disappear into the smoke.

She didn't close the door right away. She stood there, breathing in the scent of scorched earth, letting the moment settle into her skin.

Beyond the rolling hills of Hawks Landing, in the distance, the wildfire blazed.

Within herself, a different fire had already started.

The end was coming to what had started twenty-two years ago.

CHAPTER
SIX
MARCH 23, 1981

The Winter Family Outreach Center
10:00 a.m.

THE SPRING '87 wedding of Madison Jackson Malone and Bishop Winston Jacob Winters III was the spectacle gracing the covers of polished church bulletins, society newsletters, and even *JET* and *Time* magazine, elegant, lavish, and thoroughly planned.

Yet it was far from being like the fairytale it seemed.

Madison, 22, radiant in an ivory gown chosen by another, stood beside the 31-year-old heir of a religious dynasty. Lady Cora Winston, the matriarch of the family's spiritual and political legacy and Madison's future mother-in-law, had meticulously crafted her for this moment. She designed the marriage with calculated precision, not passion, orchestrating it like a chess game to ensure the family's continued success through influence and wealth.

Reporters from around the globe were in attendance, vying for the coveted interview. Still, the story that did not hit the news was how Madison came to be a part of the Winter family saga. Cora, on a routine visit to the *Winter Family Outreach Center*, first noticed 17-year-old Madison, a court-referred teen with wary eyes, a sealed juvenile record, and whispers of a stabbing involving her foster father and a ten-year-old boy.

The file was thin.

The potential was not.

On the pivotal day, as Cora prepared for the intake interview, she watched the girl through her office door's glass, arms crossed, attentive. Madison arrived ten minutes early, suggesting she was either smart, nervous, or both. She was attractive, but beauty doesn't guarantee safety. Too many beautiful people sabotage themselves through loud laughter, sharp words, and rushing too quickly.

Not this girl. She sat too straight, eyes too still. Posture wasn't taught; it came from waiting for the next blow, the next loss.

Cora sensed something but couldn't quite put her finger on it.

Smoothing her blouse, adjusting the sleeves of her dove-gray suit, she flipped open the door and smiled at the girl just warm enough to disarm, but not so soft she would be mistaken for kind.

"Come in, Madison."

Entering the office, Cora gestured for her to take a seat opposite her desk.

"You understand what this program is?"

"Yes, ma'am."

There was neither a "like" nor hesitation.

Good.

"You're not here for punishment," Cora continued. "You're here for redemption. Do you know what it means?"

Madison blinked. "A second chance."

"No," Cora corrected. "A second name."

Cora saw the spark in Madison's eyes.

She was listening.

Not out of obligation. Out of hunger.

That's when Cora decided. She didn't announce it.

Leaning back with her arms crossed, Cora studied the girl in front of her like a delicate thread waiting to be woven into the right story.

This girl.

Beautiful, bruised, and unspeakably lonely.

She wasn't loud or entitled. She didn't wear privilege, but she could. Given time, training, and the right rooms to walk into.

Cora could mold her into something unforgettable. Something powerful.

She would be perfect for the role. But Cora hadn't yet spoken aloud.

Even her son would learn to adjust.

Across the desk, Madison sat stiffly, her posture too poised for a girl who'd spent years in and out of courtrooms.

Her fingers twisted in her lap, a slight tremble betraying the wall behind her eyes.

Cora softened her tone.

"You deserve better than what the system handed you, baby. I see what others miss. And I'd like to take you under my wing... if you'll let me."

Madison hesitated, eyes flickering.

It wasn't trust. Not yet.

It was a cautious expectation.

"All I ask is your effort," Cora added gently, her voice sweet but certain. "The rest we'll shape together."

By the end of the meeting, Madison had accepted the offer. It sounded like rescue.

Cora escorted Madison to the door with a hug, then closed it with a quiet, satisfied click.

Later, to a board member, she'd confide:

"She's not polished, but she's got fire. She'll clean up nicely."

A beat.

"And she'll be loyal. She's starved for a place to belong."

Another pause, darker now.

"And she won't question the role I give her... not yet."

And with that... Cora had made a quiet phone call. And then another.

Whatever juvenile record Madison had, sealed or not, ceased to be a barrier. Judges persuaded. Paperwork disappeared. Someone abruptly allowed the girl with a violent past to leave the country under the *educational exception*.

Cora presented it as a rehabilitation opportunity.

However, the reality was that she was moving her project elsewhere.

So, for the next five years, Madison vanished into Paris.

Not to escape, but to reinvent herself.

Cora not only funded her education at a prestigious university in the 7th arrondissement; she engineered it. Sociology by day, social engineering by night: etiquette coaches, language tutors, posture drills, fashion consultants. Dinner parties with dignitaries, afternoon tea with benefactors, someone was always watching, correcting a gesture, softening a tone, sharpening a smile.

Paris was the classroom, but Cora was the true architect.

By the end of the first year, Madison could order wine without hesitation, discuss Voltaire with ease, and glide through galas without a single misstep. She learned how to dress for power and listen with intent, skills that owed as much to survival instincts from Mama Pearl's foster home as to Cora's vision.

And every night, she wiped away the lipstick, stared into the mirror, and wondered if the woman looking back still belonged to her, or Cora.

Nothing was accidental. Every relationship, silence, and glance was intentional.

Including Madison's return to the States, and the evening Cora Winston's Circle welcomed her. Madison entered the Winston estate through a marble archway, causing the room to fall silent.

A dozen influential women, elegant, authoritative, and strategically reverent, turned to face the entrance, their chatter fading away like a weak radio signal.

Cora didn't announce her. She didn't have to.

Madison wore a sleek black Dior sheath, understated yet unmistakable. Her hair was in a low knot, a single pearl at her throat. Her posture conveyed the confidence Cora had taught her: poised without apology. Extending a soft *"Good evening,"* she took the empty chair at Cora's right, not offered, but understood.

Later that evening, Madison and Cora retreated to the study, the door shutting with a soft click behind them.

Inside, the world dimmed to velvet shadows and lamplight.

Madison stood near the window, arms loosely crossed, the faint hum of the evening party still drifting down the hall.

Cora poured herself a glass of white wine. She didn't offer Madison one; she never did.

"You carried yourself well tonight," Cora said, settling into her wingback chair.

Madison turned slowly, uncertain if it was praise or a test.

"You didn't tell them who I was," she said.

"I didn't need to." Cora sipped. "They saw enough to know you weren't the help."

"You said I was coming home."

Cora rose, crossing the room with a deliberate grace that always felt like control. She adjusted the fall of Madison's sleeve, the gesture maternal but possessive.

"You are," she said, assured, taking a seat in the plush leather wingback chair behind the oak desk.

"But home isn't comfort. It's a calling."

Madison's voice sharpened, quiet but edged.

I'm not here to be anyone's… creation."

Cora's smile thinned, sharp as glass.

"You're not a creation, Madison. You're an investment. One that's about to pay off."

Madison flinched, barely. Cora saw it.

She set her glass down on the desk and leaned back, tone softening, but not losing its steel.

"My son is a complicated man. He requires… presence. Grace. Loyalty. And the right woman by his side."

"You mean someone you approve of?"

"I mean someone who can withstand what power demands."

The pause stretched long, heavy as the oak desk between them.

Finally, Madison asked, her voice low:

"Why me?"

Cora stood, closing the space between them until Madison had nowhere to look but up. "You have what others don't," she said, each word precise. "Silence where they'd scream. Stillness where they'd beg. The world was never going to give you anything."

Her hands hovered an inch from Madison's shoulders, deliberate, withholding.

"So I gave you the chance to take it. Now take it."

She left Madison alone in the dim light, staring at her reflection in the rain-streaked window, unsure if she'd been crowned... or branded.

The uneven trails of rain carried her back to a Paris café, stirring an espresso she didn't even like, the silver spoon clinking against porcelain.

Looking like a woman who belonged there.

Elegant, polite, and measured, like the fine porcelain she held.

But there were days like this, when the rain hit just right and an ache rose in her chest. Days when she missed her friend so fiercely it hurt.

Nina Autumn Storm.

The girl who shoved her into a closet, whispering, "Be quiet. Be nobody. He'll go away."

The girl who braided her trembling fingers and vowed, "We're more than this place."

The girl who climbed into a hospital bed when the social worker lied about the baby being stillborn, holding her as if she wasn't broken.

That was family.

Now here she sat in the life they once dreamt of, drinking espresso she couldn't bear.

She kept telling herself she'd reach out to Nina. But as time stretched, excuses piled up, and the thread between them went slack.

It wasn't betrayal. Not exactly. It was survival.

Still, the guilt lingered.

Through the window, Paris life looked beautiful.

Madison pressed her fingers to the glass and thought, not for the first time:

This won't last.

CHAPTER
SEVEN
JUNE 25, 1986

Hawks Landing Country Club
5:45 p.m.

MADISON'S first encounter with Bishop Winston Jacob Winter III was after her return to the States, a meeting shrouded in subtlety. That evening, at Lady Cora Winston's exclusive quarterly "who's who" dinner, she found herself seated at the far end of a sprawling mahogany table. Fifteen guests filled the room, among whom eleven were men, and each held influence as judges, deans, legacy donors, politicians, and bishops. The evening's subtle power plays and silent tensions hinted at secrets waiting to be uncovered.

Name did not introduce Madison, dressed in Cora's carefully chosen navy silk dress, but by her potential.

"She's someone I believe in," Cora had said. "Someone you'll all want to watch."

Bishop Winter arrived late.

The room changed the moment he stepped in. Not loud or flashy, but completely confident. He moved like a man unchallenged, dressed in a tailored charcoal suit, no tie, collar open just enough to reveal the fine line of his clerical chain. His smile was subtle but purposeful, given only to those he considered worth the effort.

When Cora introduced them, he looked her up and down, and offered a hand, not to shake, but to hold, palm up.

"Madison," he said, the name like a sermon warm on his tongue.

Then, almost teasing, but not kind: "I don't believe all the good things, of course. I prefer to learn the truth myself."

She placed her hand in his, fingers cool against his warmth. His grip was firm and confident. Her breath fluttered briefly, but she remained unwavering. "It's an honor, Bishop Winter," she said, voice steady, neither timid nor overeager.

Just right.

He watched her a moment too long.

"She's been through fire," Cora added, sipping from her glass. "And came out polished."

Madison smiled at that, practiced and pleasant. But deep in her stomach, something tensed.

She had not known this meeting was coming. Cora had only said, "Tonight is important. Wear confidence. And the navy."

Throughout dinner, Bishop Winter asked questions, soft ones with sharp edges. On faith, loss, and loyalty. And then, without looking up from his plate, he added one that stilled her fork halfway to her lips:

"How do you decide who deserves your silence?"

He never raised his voice, but his presence filled every quiet.

When dessert arrived, he leaned in and said low enough that only she could hear,

"You know how to carry silence well. That's a rare thing."

Madison nodded with a polite smile, though internally, an old pain clenched her ribs.

She had learned to remain silent, not as a virtue but as a defense. Yet here, others appreciated and wanted it.

By the end of the evening, Bishop Winter rested his hand briefly at the small of her back as they said goodnight. It was a gesture measured and mechanical, as if he were checking a box, not touching a person. Not inappropriate, but not innocent either. More like someone agreeing to a deal he didn't need to believe in, just one he intended to control.

In the car ride home, Madison stared out the window, the city lights blurring into streaks.

Cora didn't speak until they were nearly back at the estate.

"Well?" she asked.

Madison answered without looking away from the window.

"He doesn't miss much."

Cora smiled. "That's why he leads."

Madison didn't answer.

But her silence, as always, said plenty.

CHAPTER
EIGHT

JUNE 25, 1986

Bishop Winter's Estate
9:15 p.m.

BISHOP WINSTON JACOB WINTER III had little control over his destiny. From birth, the blueprint was there: inherit the pulpit, head the international non-profit organization, marry the woman chosen not for love, but for optics.

His heart, unfortunately, had other plans. That heart belonged to Elise.

Beautiful. Complicated. Undeniably wrong in Cora's eyes.

"She's a distraction," Cora had once snapped. "You cannot mold a mistress into a First Lady."

And now, Madison.

Later that evening, Bishop Winter stood in the study with a bourbon and a cigar, eyes fixed on the fireplace. Cora entered without knocking, as always.

"She's impressive," he said. His tone was careful, neutral.

"She's ready," Cora replied, placing a thin dossier on the desk with a soft thud. "She listens. She learns. She doesn't embarrass you."

Winston turned slowly, brow furrowed. "She's not Elise."

"No," Cora said, unyielding. "She's better."

Cora saw herself in Elise, the passion, the independence, the unwillingness to bow, and she couldn't tolerate it in someone she couldn't shape.

"I've dealt with women like Elise before," Cora once muttered. "Smart enough to charm a man, too stubborn to serve a legacy." Elise may have been Winston's love, but Cora was the architect of his calling. No one, especially a woman from the wrong side of the tracks, would threaten her empire.

He laughed once, dry. "You keep grooming these girls like they're horses."

"I prepare women," she corrected, folding her arms. "You need someone who knows how to walk beside you without stepping on your shadow."

Winston swirled the bourbon in his glass. "You ever think maybe I don't want shadows anymore?"

"You want a legacy," Cora said firmly. "Don't confuse desire with destiny."

He looked down, jaw tight. "Fine. I'll play along."

Cora raised an eyebrow. "You'll thank me one day."

He didn't answer. Just took another drink.

The silence between them was thick with all the things he couldn't say aloud.

CHAPTER
NINE

MAY 2, 1987

The Winter's Wedding and Reception

AS THE WORDS "I DO" left her lips.

Something sharp twisted inside her, a quiet, aching betrayal, not of him, but of herself.

She remembered the promises she'd once whispered into the dark:

"I will only marry for love."

"I will only say yes to someone who sees me, who chooses me."

"I will find a man like my father, strong, kind, steady."

Those promises disappeared, erased by years of silence, Cora's relentless grooming, and the appeal of belonging. Expectations had swallowed whole the girl who made those promises and rebranded as Lady Winter before she could even protest.

The pastor's voice boomed, "I now pronounce you husband and wife..."

In Madison's ears, those words echoed faintly off marble walls, filled with memories of her father's gentle voice, laughter around the kitchen table, and the naive hope of choosing love.

The guests erupted in applause, the organ swelled, and Madison's smile stayed fixed, her face a perfect mask of serene joy.

As the couple turned to face the crowd, the cameras flashing in a blinding storm of light, Madison whispered silently, beneath her breath, where no one could hear,

"You were supposed to choose me."

And with that, she let the world take its picture.

The reception blurred by in a shimmer of clinking glasses and forced smiles.

The ivory-and-gold ballroom held dignitaries from churches nationwide, city officials, politicians, wealthy donors, and curious elite. It looked like something out of a dream. Madison moved through it like a spectator.

From the corner near the grand staircase, Cora stood back, her eyes gleaming with quiet pride. Watching Madison glide through the crowd, poised and untouchable, Cora saw her reflection in that practiced grace. This was the moment she had orchestrated, the unveiling of the perfect First Lady, her polished creation. And in Cora's mind, it wasn't just Madison on display. It was proof that Cora's vision, her sacrifice, had all been worth it.

But even as Cora soaked in her triumph, Madison felt the weight of the gold brocade clinging to her skin, each laugh and compliment another layer of silk-wrapped suffocation. The applause, the whispered praises, they weren't for her. They were for the mask. The one Cora had taught her to wear, the one she couldn't take off.

Greeting strangers who called her "First Lady" with reverence complimented her poise and gushed over the elegance of the ceremony. Thanking them all, as Cora had trained her to do, never letting her smile slip. When they mentioned "how lucky" she was, she nodded and even laughed when one woman whispered that she and Bishop Winter were the "Black Camelot."

But inside, she was crumbling.

She'd just excused herself from a group of city council wives when something caught her eye.

Near the edge of the ballroom, partially hidden behind a towering floral arrangement, a catering attendant in black and white stood utterly still, holding a silver tray of hors d'oeuvres.

Their eyes met.

The tray trembled.

Time slowed.

"Nina?" Her voice was barely a whisper.

The woman blinked. Recognition cracked across her face like glass under pressure. "Maddie…?"

Neither moved for a second.

Madison then moved ahead as Nina placed the tray down.

They met halfway, no words, just an embrace that cut through years. The kind of hug that envelops you in a memory, stitching shut the wound of absence.

Not caring who saw, she buried her face into Nina's shoulder, breathing in the scent of vanilla lotion and warmth.

"You're here," she murmured.

Nina pulled back, her voice thick. "I didn't know… until I saw your name on the wedding program. Maddie, I've been looking for you."

Tears welled in Madison's eyes. "I thought I'd never see you again. They, Cora, she kept me isolated."

"I know." Nina nodded, squeezing her hand. "I figured. But I never stopped trying. I even came to a church service once, to see if you were real."

Madison laughed. "I'm not sure I am."

They lingered for a moment, unexpressed pain and affection flowing between them like static electricity.

A catering manager cleared his throat deliberately, catching Nina's attention as he signaled for her to return to her duties.

"Gotta go," Nina whispered. "I'll be here all night. Find me."

"I will."

Nina brushed a tear from Madison's cheek. "I never stopped being your sister."

Madison stood breathless, watching her friend disappear back into the blur of trays and white-gloved hands.

The rest of the night, Bishop would dutifully appear by her side whenever the cameras demanded it, holding her waist as if he were steadying a podium and kissing her cheek, as if offering a benediction.

Cora's carefully designed reception was perfect until…

As the guests leaned in and the cameras clicked, Madison turned to face her new husband with a practiced smile, the small slice of cake trembling slightly in her hand.

They had choreographed the cake exchange down to the angle of her wrist. But just as she lifted the fork, her fingers slipped.

The cake tumbled, landing unceremoniously at their feet.

Flickers of gasps echoed through the ballroom.

While his hand tightened briefly at her waist, not a squeeze, not quite pain, but enough for her to feel the reprimand in his stillness, his face didn't change, not for the cameras, but she felt it. And then he let go, smiling as if nothing had happened.

For a moment, Madison remained still, her mind caught on a distant Sunday evening, sitting at the kitchen island, her father frosting a cake while she licked the spoon, laughing, with no cameras and no expectations.

Just cake and joy.

Before the silence could stretch, Cora appeared with a polished laugh and a fresh plate in hand, seamlessly restoring the scene. "Even perfection makes room for a little sweetness," she joked to the crowd, her smile tight but sparkling.

The room relaxed, and the show went on.

Curated perfection unfolded for the rest of the night.

But when the last guests left, and the car arrived to whisk them off to their honeymoon suite, Madison exhaled for the first time all day.

She thought they could drop the act.

In private, something genuine might emerge.

She had been wrong before. But she still hoped.

CHAPTER
TEN

MAY 2, 1987

Madison and Nina, Again
9:20 p.m.

THE BALLROOM HAD EMPTIED. The chandeliers dimmed. Final glasses clinked in distant bins as catering staff shuffled through cleanup, their laughter and exhaustion echoing quietly in the marble halls.

Madison walked barefoot through the empty halls, her reception gown's hem gathered in one hand: no flashbulbs, no smiles, no Cora.

Just silence.

She walked down a side hallway to the service entrance, her steps feeling oddly familiar. She didn't know why she went there instead of being in the limo, only that something inside her needed to feel real again before the final act of the night began.

Outside the kitchen, beneath the glow of flickering fluorescents, she found her.

Nina was seated on an overturned milk crate, her heels off, her white server jacket unbuttoned. A piece of leftover wedding cake, vanilla chiffon with lemon mousse, sat between them on a cardboard box repurposed as a table.

"You came," Nina said, offering her a fork.

Nodding her head and whispering. "You still eat dessert first?"

"It's the only part of life you can count on being sweet."

They chuckled, like in the middle of the night when bunk beds and foster rules governed their world.

Neither spoke for a long moment.

"Do you remember what we promised?"

Nina glanced at her. "That we wouldn't let the world erase us?"

Madison nodded. "I think I am."

Nina reached out and took her hand, thumb brushing across the gold band that felt heavier now than it had at the altar.

"Erased?" she said. "No. Just hiding. But I see you."

The words cracked something open.

Madison blinked away tears, but one escaped, trailing down her cheek like a thread come loose.

"I needed this," she said. "I needed you."

"You always had me," Nina replied. "Even when they tried to take everything else."

They sat like that, two women in silence, one in silk, one in starch, sharing leftover cake and an unspoken truth:

They had survived.

Apart.

Yet together.

Still.

CHAPTER
ELEVEN
MAY 3, 1987

Honeymoon Suite
12:15 a.m.

WHAT MADISON HAD NOT ACCOUNTED for was the woman he had already chosen long before her. Elise wasn't a scandal. She was a quiet heartbreak.

Forever there, never loud.

Appeared on holidays, dressed modestly, sat near the back during services, and vanished before the final benediction.

Didn't chase Bishop. Didn't need to.

Her presence hummed through the sanctuary like an old hymn that had never been sung but never forgotten.

Elise wasn't a secret.

Madison could never escape the ghost of her marriage. It was clear in Bishop's distant eyes during their first dance, his hands moving to the rhythm but without emotion, and his vows spoken like rehearsed lines without feeling. He smiled at the cameras, yet never truly looked at her. The painful truth was undeniable on their honeymoon night.

Awaken to silence. The bed was still warm beside her, but empty.

He had stepped out hours ago, claiming a call.

No return. No note.

Just the untouched wine sweating on its silver tray.

Two empty glasses. Shining. Waiting.

She wrapped the hotel robe around herself like armor and stepped out onto the balcony. The endless silver of the sea shimmered below. Unbothered. And then movement.

At first, she thought it was nothing. A shadow. Her mind.

But no.

Two silhouettes walked the shoreline.

His stride is unmistakable.

Her presence is undeniable.

Elise.

Not touching. But close.

Not speaking. But communicating in the way their bodies leaned, in the stillness between them.

Madison didn't cry or gasp. Instead, she gripped the iron railing tightly, feeling the cold bite into her palms, anchoring her firmly in the moment. Her gaze remained fixed, unwavering, refusing to look away despite the turmoil inside.

That was the true love story, unfolding under moonlight, uninterrupted and unhidden.

A soft knock startled her. She flinched, breath catching.

"Room service," a voice called gently through the door. "Your champagne, ma'am?"

Madison froze, fingers still clamped on the railing. For a moment, she considered answering, letting them in, allowing someone, anyone, to witness the hollow in this room.

Instead, she stayed silent.

The knock came once more, then faded, footsteps retreating down the hall.

Only when the quiet settled again did she let go of the railing. She didn't know how long she had stood there, ten minutes, an hour, only that something had ended before it truly began. Going back inside and closing the sliding door as if sealing a tomb, she caught her reflection in the glass and whispered, "Why does it have to be flaunted?"

This wasn't about betrayal; it was about dignity.

Why not allow her that? Even if the love wasn't genuine, couldn't he have honored the illusion?

Let her believe, at least on their honeymoon.

But no.

She poured the warm wine and lifted the glass. She took one swallow, then another, each one a bitter surrender.

A silent toast to everything she'd never be.

The tears rose but held.

Her tears had discipline.

They waited for locked doors. For running showers.

And under her breath, she said: "*Even my tears know their place.*"

Later, that morning, the light hit the honeymoon suite with merciless brilliance.

Soft, golden beams spilled across the marble floor, illuminating the untouched breakfast tray someone had wheeled in at dawn, fruit wilting, croissants drying at the edges, and a silver carafe of coffee now lukewarm beneath its polished lid.

Madison sat at the vanity, her back straight, hands folded neatly in her lap.

Her eyes looked tired but not swollen. She had a soft, nude gloss on her lips. Her silk robe was replaced by a graceful blush dress, modest and snug at the waist, adorned with delicate pearls. Appearing complete, yet empty inside. No signs of last night, no trembling in her hand.

Entering the suite, sunglasses on, jaw freshly shaved, Bishop paused only briefly at the sight of her.

"You're ready," he said, more of an observation than a compliment.

Madison turned slightly toward him; her face composed. "I thought we had brunch with the ambassador and his wife."

He nodded, adjusting his cufflinks. "I told them we'd be there by eleven." He avoided her gaze, merely checking his reflection in the hallway mirror. "Make sure you smile today," he added.

Madison stood, slipped on her heels, and they walked out the door without a word.

Publicly perfect.

Two months later, she stood in the lobby of the North Central

Regional Women's Retreat, her hands sweating inside designer gloves. Cora chose her perfectly tailored lavender dress. The matching hat sat tilted atop her fresh, strawberry-blond bob, while her "Soft Orchid" lipstick was just as Cora described, mature yet inviting. Not a hair out of place, no line in her stockings.

Except for the tremor in her fingers, Cora designed everything about her for her first public appearance as "Lady Madison Jackson Winter." Thousands of women from chapters in ten states, some of whom had only seen her name in newsletters and others who had waited for years to see who the new bishop's wife would be.

She was the moment.

And she was terrified.

Standing behind the curtain of the arena's stage, she could hear them, women clapping, laughing, praising. Music from the praise band faded into a soft organ hum, followed by a speaker's voice.

"Now, let's welcome our beautiful First Lady for this morning's word of encouragement, Lady Madison Jackson Winter!"

The applause was thunderous. She stepped onto the stage, her heart pounding and her smile fixed. The spotlight warmed her skin, but the cold of exposure ran deeper as she gripped the podium.

Her voice trembled at first, a faint whisper against the microphone. Still, she and Cora rehearsed cadence late into the night, alongside the girl she once was, the survivor of foster homes, courtroom benches, and correctional facilities. Drawing from that strength, she shared Ruth's story of loss, faith, and rebuilding, using her grandmother's cornbread recipe to illustrate how love can rise from broken places.

When she finished, the room was silent for just a second before a standing ovation erupted. Cora beamed in the front row, tears threatening her mascara, as the senior ladies who had previously side-eyed her arrival joined in the applause. Madison stepped down from the stage feeling dazed, guided into a side parlor with comfy seating and a tray of lemon water waiting. Compliments came pouring in from all around her.

"You spoke right into my spirit."

"My God, I felt every word."

"First Lady, you were born for this."

She smiled and nodded. Said "thank you".

She had done it.

She had arrived.

Following her initial *"coming out,"* Madison's daily routine became rigid, filled with commitments that left little space for spontaneity or joy. Her nights were solitary and often lengthy, occasionally broken when Bishop would enter the master bedroom with a bottle of wine and two glasses. His charm and unexpected warmth offered only a fleeting illusion that dissipated by morning.

Occasionally, Cora would show up unannounced, often reminding her of her so-called "purpose." Cora's presence enveloped the house like incense, both sacred and suffocating.

"You need to stop sulking," she said once. "The Lord placed you here for a purpose. You're not here to be loved. You're here to lead."

She always felt the urge to shake her and scream. *"What kind of God do you serve that sentences a woman to lovelessness in His name?"*

But she didn't.

She smiled. Nodded. Poured the tea.

One evening, when the silence thickened like the ashes of everything she'd buried, Madison broke.

Not with a scream.

Not with a slammed door.

But with a tremble in her voice and a truth she could no longer hold behind her smile.

"Bishop," she spoke with desperation, the syllables shaking, "I spend my days serving others, smoothing over everything, making things beautiful... while my own needs sit, unnoticed. Why can't you, as my husband, see my needs? Why can't you treat me like your wife, loved, nurtured, instead of... tolerated? Dismissed like an afterthought?"

Her voice cracked on the last word.

She hadn't intended to plead, but the ache slipped through, anyway.

He didn't move.

He neither offered his hand nor whispered reassurance.

Just silence.

Then, looking at her with disdain, came the words, never spoken:

"I didn't choose you. Mother did." Then, with a sarcastic grin, he said, "But you already knew that."

She did.

But hearing it aloud shattered an unspoken hope she hadn't realized she still held.

The last illusion snapped when she miscarried at eight weeks. She had told no one, but a positive test sparked a fragile hope that vanished.

One morning, a week later, Cora showed up unexpectedly. She let herself in as usual and found Madison in the kitchen, sitting in her robe, staring blankly, with a cold cup of tea untouched. "Well, you look like hell," Cora said, setting her purse on the counter.

Madison didn't respond.

Cora studied her. "You're not pregnant, are you?" she asked with a smirk.

Madison's lip quivered.

Cora's voice softened slightly. "Whatever's wrong, pull yourself together. Don't make me regret my choices."

That's when Madison snapped, her voice trembling with a mix of frustration and pain. "Regret it?" she echoed, her voice cracking as she struggled to keep her composure. "You think this is about your regrets?" she shot back, her tone cutting sharply through the tense air, revealing the depth of her emotions and the complexity of the situation.

Cora blinked, surprised.

"I lost a baby, Cora," she said, voice trembling as she fought back tears. "A tiny sliver of hope, a fragile piece of something that could have given this life meaning, a future filled with promise that now only exists in my memories."

Her shoulders shook with suppressed grief as she shouted in disappointment and heartbreak, "And now it's just... gone!" The words cracked through the air, carrying the weight of her sorrow, as she struggled to come to terms with the profound loss that had shattered her world.

Cora sat up straight, with defiance to the moment. "I am sorry, but we must prepare for tomorrow's luncheon. So, get ready. The caterers are arriving soon for final selections.

Madison jumped up from the table, robe swaying like a storm cloud around her. "Dammit, Cora, STOP!"

Cora's posture stiffened, chin lifting ever so slightly. "You're married to a man of power. He has duties. Expectations. Your role is to support them."

Madison's laugh was soft, dangerously so. "Then maybe you should've married him."

The silence that followed was sharp enough to cut glass.

Cora stood, smoothing the front of her tailored suit as if brushing off the weight of Madison's words. Her eyes lingered for a beat, not soft, not cruel, just… measuring.

Then she turned.

The echo of her heels trailed behind her like punctuation, sharp, final, deliberate. Hand on the doorknob, still facing away, she said without a flicker of hesitation, "You're grieving. But remember, miscarriage doesn't make you special. You ain't the first woman to lose a baby."

She didn't wait for a response.

She didn't look back.

She left.

Madison stood in the thick silence, her breath lodged somewhere between fury and devastation, the ache in her chest louder than Cora's heels had ever been.

PART THREE
THE EXIT

CHAPTER
TWELVE
JUNE 12, 2009

Hawks Landing
7:05 a.m.

THE DOOR CLICKED SHUT behind the police officers. Madison stood frozen. Sirens shrieked outside, slicing through the early morning haze. The evacuation order was real. Urgent.

She turned toward the stairs, heart racing. The news anchor's voice blared from the TV: mandatory evacuation, road closures, and power grid failure.

The air felt too thick, the house too still.

She climbed quickly, already bracing for how hard it would be to wake Nina.

After the week she'd had, Madison knew exactly where Nina would be asleep, unreachable, drowned beneath wine, pills, and pain. That was always Nina. Once down, she stayed down, especially when the ghosts came heavy.

But still, Madison had to try.

Nina Autumn Storm had been Madison's only constant since they were eleven. Same birthday, same system. That was all it took.

Madison remembered her first day in foster care after her parents were murdered. Her social worker had smiled too much and promised everything was temporary.

It never was.

Eventually, she landed with Mama Pearl, yet it wasn't Mama Pearl who opened the door. It was Nina.

Tall, dark-skinned, unapologetic. Afro picked, perfect, red dashiki, hoop earrings like weapons. She looked grown. Spoke grown.

"Mrs. Mallory," Nina said at the door. "You got an appointment?"

Madison blinked. Speechless. She questioned grown folks.

That night, Nina sat beside her on the bunk bed and whispered, "Stay close. I'll teach you how to survive."

And she did, because Nina had come from chaos, carried it, and knew how to survive it.

Nina's mother was fourteen when she got pregnant by one of her mother's boyfriends. When she confessed, her mother tossed her out with nothing but a trash bag of clothes.

She found temporary shelter with her older sister until Nina was born. That lasted until one day her sister dumped their things on the curb and handed the baby to a neighbor.

After that: shelters. Motels. Couch surfing. Her mother clung to her until she met a man who promised stability and brought only heroin.

Then, the night that rewrote Nina's life.

She was seven. Sleeping on the floor, wrapped in a thin blanket, when her mother's screams shattered the quiet.

"Please stop! HELP ME!"

Nina froze. Then crawled to the cracked door.

A priest's collar. A knife.

His voice bellowed with rage: *"YOU MUST DIE FOR YOUR SINS!"*

Blood spilled across the linoleum. Her mother's eyes found hers one last time. *"Be quiet."*

Nina watched her mother die. And didn't make a sound.

But later, she told the truth. Her words helped convict a serial killer, one who preyed on women no one cared about.

Unfortunately, she was left alone. Her grandmother didn't want her. The state placed her with Mama Pearl.

Mama Pearl was thunder in stilettos, part preacher, part hustler.

Cooked like she ran a restaurant. Cursed like she ran the streets. She did both.

Nina learned quickly. Loyalty was currency. Secrets were survival.

On her first morning, Mama Pearl floated down the stairs, lipstick perfect. "Good morning, baby. I'll feed you when I get back."

By the time she returned, she'd handled two deliveries, a debt collection, and an emergency hair appointment.

Nina realized fast: this wasn't foster care. This was training.

Later, Mama Pearl summoned her to the kitchen.

"So, you're Nina Autumn Storm." She tied her apron. "That's a hell of a name, baby."

Nina sat straighter. "My mama always said everybody goes through stuff. So what?"

Pearl moved fast. Grabbed her collar. Pulled her nose-to-nose.

"Let's get something straight, heffa, yo' mama dead."

She shoved Nina back into the chair and straightened her apron like nothing had happened.

"This is my house. Talk slick again, bitch, and yo ass is grass."

Nina didn't blink.

She'd already learned: the kind ones didn't always save you.

The hard ones? Sometimes, they loved you enough to fight.

Now, Madison paused at the guest room door. The sirens howled louder outside. Smoke crawled into the vents. She didn't knock yet.

She just stood there, hand on the knob, heart pounding, remembering all the time Nina had kept her alive, and wondering if this time, she could return the favor.

Madison threw the door open to the guest room where Nina slept, coughing from the smoke already seeping through the floorboards.

Nina lay on the bed, completely still.

"NINA!" she yelled. "We need to evacuate!"

Her steps slowed. Something was wrong. Nina remained on top of the neatly made covers, perfectly still and dressed.

Madison froze.

Her eyes dropped to the empty pill bottle, and a knocked-over wineglass was on the floor. Her chest tightened.

"No..." she whispered.

She moved closer and touched Nina's hand.

Cold.

"OH MY GOD!" she screamed, "Nina, no!"

She grabbed the bottle of prescription sleep aids, the kind that left no room for mistakes. This wasn't an accident. Her scream shattered the walls as she collapsed onto the bed, cradling Nina's lifeless body and rocking her like a child. "Why?" she sobbed. "Why would you do this?"

Her tears soaked the blanket as grief ripped through her, raw and loud.

She didn't stop it. She didn't want to.

They had promised to always be there for each other. Always. And now, the only person who had ever truly known her was gone.

Her mind spiraled, replaying the last few weeks like a film reel. Nina had seemed distant but not broken; tired, yet still Nina. Strong. Steady. Or so she thought. She had missed it. Nina had been entangled in a complicated relationship with a married man for the past three years, a situation she believed she could manage.

She'd always kept her heart protected. Kept her feelings in check.

But this time... it was different.

Madison had seen the shift. Nina, usually so composed, had grown agitated when he canceled plans. She started speaking harshly about his wife, something she'd never done before.

And then, the final blow: he was moving out of state to reconcile with his wife.

Just like that, Nina unraveled.

She tried to destroy his marriage, called his wife, and exposed everything.

It didn't work. Worse, the wife forgave him.

Then came the final blow: Madison's public announcement that she was stepping down, not just the church's First Lady duties, but as chair of the organization's global charitable foundation, ending her reign as its most visible and beloved ambassador.

A week earlier, she sat across from Nina at the kitchen table, explaining the transition. It was more than just a change; it felt like a reset. A fresh start. It was a release, not only for her but also for Nina, who had been her loyal personal assistant for years. She had carefully arranged for Nina to receive a generous severance package, which included the deed to her beloved beachfront condo, symbolizing her appreciation and the new chapter ahead.

"Nina, we are free!"

Nina had nodded. Said nothing.

Now, in hindsight, Madison saw what she'd missed.

The tight jaw, the deadpan expression, the sadness behind her eyes.

"Being free," she whispered aloud, "can also mean no longer belonging."

She laid Nina's cold, lifeless body back against the pillows, brushing her hand across her friend's cheek.

There beside her was a small black leather bag.

Stacked inside were bills, $150,000 in cash, and a letter in Nina's handwriting:

My Maddie,

Thank you. You're the only person besides my mom who has truly loved me. I've never doubted that, and I hope you'll never doubt how much I love you.

I'm tired, baby. Exhausted in body and soul. I've carried so much for so long that I've lost the will to keep going. I know this might be hard to hear, maybe even harder to forgive, but I need to be honest.

You've always believed in me and depended on me. You stayed with me through storms no one else saw. But now, it's time for you to rely on yourself. I don't mean to leave you alone; I believe in your strength. You're stronger and braver than you realize, and it's time you see that.

Gambling's always been in my blood. I've chased luck more than peace. But this time, I'm making one last bet, not on a game or cards, but on you.

You're my last hand, my last hope. It's the surest thing I've ever played.

Live big, live free. If missing me hurts, let it. Then, get up and keep going. You've got this.

All my love, always.

The note was still trembling in her hand. "I wasn't supposed to lose you, too," she whispered.

The room was still. Dust particles swirled in the orange light filtering through smoke-tinted windows.

"I don't know how to do this without you. But I will."

Madison stood still. She took a breath and reached down.

With gentle hands, she unclasped the diamond bracelet from Nina's wrist, her one sparkle, her quiet indulgence, a gift she'd once earned in Atlantic City and wore like armor.

"Every woman deserves something that reminds her she's survived," Nina used to say.

Madison slid the bracelet onto her wrist, the clasp clicking shut like a vow.

With deliberate care, she slipped the wedding ring from her finger and placed it on Nina's.

A symbol returned.

A chapter closed.

Or...

Madison's breath caught as her eyes lingered on Nina's still face, so familiar, so much a mirror of who she used to be. There was grief, yes. But beneath it, something else stirred.

This wasn't just a goodbye; it was an exchange of lives. One life sacrificed with a heavy heart, marking an end. Meanwhile, another would defiantly move on with resilience and hope, rising from the ashes.

With determination, she slipped into her worn gardening jeans and fastened a loose blouse, her fingers trembling. She wore no makeup or jewelry, prioritizing speed and simplicity. Standing before the mirror, she confronted her reflection: hollow-eyed and grief-stricken.

Yet there was a flicker of something stirring within her.

It was her hair.

That wild, unmistakable cascade of thick, strawberry-blond curls.

In that moment, she could almost hear Cora's voice echoing in her ears, her spirited declaration ringing true: "This makes you special. Never cut it; a First Lady doesn't change what God has made glorious."

But it hadn't felt glorious. It felt heavy, like chains made of silk.

Now, it felt like a lie.

Taking a deep breath, she opened the vanity, grabbed the scissors, and clenched her hair into a fist.

She cut. The sound was soft, almost gentle, like the tearing of fabric.

Strands cascaded into the sink in thick, coiled masses. Years of sermons, photo ops, and magazine covers, gone in an instant.

When she looked up, her reflection was unfamiliar. A tear slid down her cheek, yet she didn't stop. With trembling certainty, she took one last pass with the scissors, shaping her new silhouette.

She leaned close to the mirror, stared into her eyes, and whispered, "Nice to meet you."

An eerie silence shattered the moment outside. No sirens. No bullhorns.

Barefoot and Nina's black bag in hand, she headed to the back staircase for her gardening flats and jacket. In the hallway, she paused at Coby's fifth-grade certificate for "Outstanding Creativity in Culinary Arts." Despite fading, his bold signature stood out. She smiled, fingers tracing the frame's edge. Passing the linen closet, she caught the subtle scent of lavender and clove, Lena's favorite for peaceful sleep and soothing the soul.

She opened it quickly and took a deep breath.

After slipping down the back stairs and gathering her things, Madison moved through the kitchen, but her legs stopped short, rooted by a sudden, crushing wave of memory.

And just like that, they were all there.

The air smelled of butter and spice, like cinnamon on Sundays and rosemary on holidays.

Coby was taking his first steps and clinging to the leg of her apron while she stirred gumbo.

Nina dancing barefoot and tipsy, singing old Patti LaBelle at the top of her lungs.

Lena, sweet, steady Lena, flipping pancakes and humming gospel while the world outside spun too fast.

And what she had never told a soul.

The night they conceived Coby.

Bishop and her, there on the kitchen tile, with their bodies moving together in a rhythm like strangers sharing grief.

Madison coughed as the air no longer smelled like butter and spice.

The fire was real.

She raced to the den and yanked open the drawer. The lighter was still there. She smiled, leaving the cigarettes behind.

"No need for comfort," she muttered. "Not anymore."

Moving into the dining room, she gripped the heavy drapes and tore them aside. With one flick, the flame danced to life.

Holding the fabric steady, it caught fast, and the flames slithered up like serpents toward the ceiling.

Turing and bolting outside, she slid into Nina's car. The engine roared to life.

Still, she paused at the end of the driveway.

Smoke curled from the roof like a ghost, rising from the house that had echoed her silence for far too long.

She didn't look back again.

CHAPTER
THIRTEEN
JUNE 9, 2009

Wildfire Escape
8:15 a.m.

FRIGHTENED, truly terrified, at the thought of being discovered while sneaking out of town or facing the even worse fate of being trapped by the wildfires.

Still, she drove on.

A frantic pulse thumped in her chest as her ragged breathing pressed against her ribs. The acrid smell of burning wood and scorched earth scraped at her throat, her lungs struggling against the thickening air. Every muscle in her body begged her to stop, but her fear of staying was much stronger than the fear of the unknown.

She wasn't always the woman fleeing into the night. Once, she was a beloved child. Before foster homes, marriage, and loneliness, she had felt safe and wanted. Then, everything changed. In a cruel twist of fate, she lost it all.

So, when Cora presented the proposition of marriage to Bishop Winton Jacob Winter III, promising a life away from her foster care struggles, she accepted without hesitation.

Sacrificing herself on the altar of his ambition, believing silence would shield her. But ashes lie; they don't tell everything.

The smoke was relentless, curling around the car and engulfing everything in shades of red and black. The flickering flames cast an ominous glow in her rearview mirror, symbolizing her tumultuous past burning away.

She fantasized about this moment, the escape. Rehearsed it in her mind, imagining herself walking away as someone new. Her fantasies appeared tidy, but this was chaos. A woman fleeing for her life, desperate and planless, and with nowhere to go. Her hands trembled as she considered how wildfires were part of nature's cycle, their destruction making room for fresh growth.

Maybe she was one of them.

The Jaguar jostled over the dirt road, each bump rattling her spine. She clenched her teeth, gripping the steering wheel. To avoid being traced, she left her SUV behind. Nina's striking black Jaguar had no connection to her.

She could still hear Nina's voice from just a few weeks ago, their last night together.

They'd curled up in the Winters' home theater, watching Mahogany for the hundredth time. It was their ritual. Their foster-care fantasy. Diana Ross and Billy Dee Williams lit up the screen, and like always, they waited for the last scene.

"Hell no, I want my old man back!" they shouted in unison, collapsing into laughter.

It never got old.

"Maddie, you always overthink everything," Nina said, smiling, eyes glowing in the screen's flicker. "Sometimes you just gotta leap. Bet on yourself."

"I'm not you," Madison had whispered.

"Exactly," Nina grinned. "You're smarter. I jump blind. You jump with a plan."

Madison had laughed then, quiet, worn out, but real.

And now here she was, driving Nina's car, carrying Nina's name, guided by Nina's last wish.

She hadn't buried Nina. No ceremony, no last goodbye. Just ash, smoke, fire. Perhaps this escape was her eulogy. Her heart clenched, grief threatening to rise, but she swallowed it. Not now.

She'd grieve later if she survived the night.

A loud bang sounded beneath the car. Her stomach dropped.

Did she blow a tire?

The car skidded, fishtailing wildly as she fought to regain control.

The gravel crunched and snapped under the tires while she wrestled it back onto the road, her pulse pounding in her ears.

"God, please!" she choked, barely able to breathe.

"Please don't let me die out here."

Tears and smoke blurred her vision, but she kept going. The road seemed endless, twisting through the forest like a maze. Her hands throbbed from clutching the wheel too tightly, and her back ached from the strain.

Through the dark, a break in the trees revealed the DEAD-END ROAD sign pointing to the construction site. She eased off the gas, exhaling for the first time since leaving Hawks Landing.

Then something inside her cracked.

A flash of Lena's face, loyal Lena, unaware of what she'd helped cover up, and the girls in community outreach who called her "First Lady," with respect and trust.

Despite her guilt, relief flooded her: "I made it out," she thought, glancing at the black bag in the passenger seat, and a new identity born from tragedy.

She pressed the gas.

The DEAD-END ROAD sign disappeared into the smoke trailing behind her, barely registering in Madison's thoughts as another sign occupied her mind.

Not a warning.

A memory.

MALONE'S JAZZ CLUB

Live Music. Good Food. Family Welcome.

Every night, neon letters buzzed above the lakefront restaurant, casting a warm red glow on the sidewalk. Her parents' laughter echoed in the glow, and she wove her childhood memories into the fabric of that building. That building had been her world, their dream, until someone stole it in an instant.

CHAPTER
FOURTEEN
JULY 20, 1954

Flight Home
2:25 p.m.

WILLOW DANFIELD, a flight attendant, met Sgt. Jackson Malone on his flight home after twenty years of service. They flirted throughout the trip, and when Willow accidentally spilled a drink on him, Jackson took the opportunity as she nervously exclaimed,

"I am sorry, sir!"

"Join this lonely soldier for dinner upon landing, and I will accept your apology, pretty lady."

Encouraged by the cheerful urging of the other passengers, Willow agreed.

They enjoyed deep-dish pizza and a bottle of wine at Jackson's favorite pizzeria.

He laughed, sharing with her a light yet earnest expression.

"While overseas, my comrades focused on their families, while I craved this deep-dish pizza."

Engrossed in conversation, neither noticed they were the last patrons until the waiter informed them.

"Closing time, lovebirds!"

Six weeks later, the couple married in a modest ceremony at the

Lakefront Promenade Chapel. There were no grand gestures or expensive frills, only two witnesses, the hum of waves, and whispered promises between them.

Willow often joked that she had his heart from the first night. She remembered leaving the restaurant with his arm wrapped around her shoulders, carrying the takeout box with the deep-dish pizza he'd eagerly talked about while overseas.

Though he was excited about the pizza, he barely touched it.

What stayed with her wasn't the food but the way he leaned in when she spoke, truly listening as she shared her hopes and fears. There was a gentleness and stillness in him that night and afterward, as if understanding her meant more than satisfying any craving.

Willow Danfield hadn't planned to bring home a Black man.

Not because she doubted love, but because she understood the cost.

From the night when he gently kissed her at her door to the moment in the chapel when she slid the gold band onto his finger, Willow realized something she hadn't before: loving a man like Jackson wasn't a sacrifice; it was a quiet, unexpected gift.

She was raised in Milwaukee in a modest house where dinner was at six and conversations about race remained polite. Her father was an insurance salesman, and her mother, who wore pearls while ironing, also volunteered at the library.

When Willow became a flight attendant, they called it "an adventure," quietly hoping it was a phase. But months later, she brought Jackson Malone home, tall, dark-skinned, impeccably dressed, and calm in a way that unsettled them. Her mother's smile cracked like porcelain.

They said nothing. They didn't have to. She felt it in her father's stiff handshake, her mother's brittle cheer, the laughter that always landed a second too late. When Jackson called her "LoLo," intimacy slid into the room like smoke, and her parents hated it.

But it made her feel unmistakably his.

So, she stopped explaining. Let the silence settle like a shut door.

Jackson, though, was all sound and story, dancing in kitchens, skipping church for matinees, turning basketball games into block parties.

With him, it wasn't rebellion or a statement. Just love. Authentic, steadying, soulful.

She loved how he held a coffee mug like something sacred, how he listened more than he spoke, how he said "ma'am" with a soft Southern drawl. He never tried to tame her, only to anchor her.

In choosing him, she found her voice. The one her parents never heard.

The two had spent their honeymoon night at Cook's House, a dimly lit Blues bar on the waterfront where smoke hung in the air, and whiskey flowed freely, embodying hard-earned joy. William "Cook" Cooper, a retired Army mess sergeant, opened it after World War I. A giant of a man with a raspy laugh and hands that fed half the city, he loved music and Southern cooking.

His passion was as strong as his stature.

Cook greeted the newlyweds with a warm smile and genuine enthusiasm that filled the room, making everyone feel at ease. Willow, brimming with happiness, wore a dress that seemed almost too delicate for the smoke-thick air and worn floorboards of Cook's House, its fine fabric catching the light like it didn't know where it was. Jackson stood tall and proud in his uniform, a symbol of his commitment to both his country and his bride.

Cook watched the two with a smile, then asked warmly, "Just married?"

Jackson replied, "Yes, sir," his voice filled with pride and joy. He gestured grandly, "Let's get y'all to the best table in the house," escorting them through the busy restaurant, where lively chatter, clinking glasses, and the aroma of savory dishes filled the air.

As they settled in, anticipation bubbled within them. The soft candlelight flickered gently, casting dancing shadows on the walls, creating an inviting atmosphere. However, as the evening unfolded, they would soon discover that this so-called "best" table was not the prime spot for a picturesque view of the waterfront or entertainment on the stage,

But the only table that didn't require a stack of cardboard propped under one leg to keep it from wobbling.

Cook returned to the table with three half-filled glasses, deep amber liquid glinting over ice, each rim touched with an orange twist. He set them down gently, his massive hand still surprisingly graceful, the bar's low light caught in the glasses, casting soft golden flickers.

He leaned in, his voice warm and gravel-rich, full of the comfort that came from watching a hundred stories bloom and burn across the bar top.

"Now this right here," he said, nodding at the drink. "This ain't just bourbon and sugar. This is the Lady's Old Fashion."

Jackson raised a brow. "Named after a special lady?"

Cook chuckled, eyes glinting. "Named after the lady of this place. My wife, Clarice. Back in the day, she sang here every Friday. Voice like velvet and fire. Wanted to sing in Paris clubs with feathers in her hair and satin gloves on her hands."

Willow smiled, drawn in.

"My girl hated bootleg whiskey," Cook continued. "Said it burned without giving nothin' back. So even during Prohibition, I made sure she had the real thing. Had to trade ribs and sweet potato pie with a bootlegger out of Savannah to keep her glass right."

He tapped the rim of the drink gently.

"She said a proper Old Fashion should be like a promise, smooth, strong, and made to last."

The aroma of orange peel and bitters mingled with aged bourbon and smoke in the air. Cook raised his glass.

"To beginnings," he said, "and to keepin' yo' promises."

Willow smiled, eyes catching the candlelight. She lifted her glass with admiration, as if holding a story or dream of the love she longed for with Jackson.

"To promises," she whispered, letting the warmth bloom in her chest. Then she looked at Jackson, a small, knowing smile tugging at her lips. Part challenge, part invitation. And in the hush between them, her eyes asked what she didn't dare speak aloud:

"Can you keep building with me, even when our silence is louder than our words?"

CHAPTER
FIFTEEN
JUNE 11, 1955

Saturday Nite at Cook's
10:37 p.m.

JACKSON SPENT ALMOST a year working as a bartender at Cook's House, where he immersed himself in the lively atmosphere and social dynamics. Each night, he skillfully mixed drinks while attentively observing the surrounding interactions, watching not just how people drank, but how they moved, talked, tipped, and remembered. Every detail mattered if he was going to accept Cook's offer to buy him out when he retired.

One evening, as the hum of the saxophone settled into the walls like smoke, lazy, warm, and familiar, Jackson stood behind the bar, polishing glasses, when Otis, one of the old heads with tobacco-stained fingers and a slow way of talking, leaned in with a bottle of rye and a half-smile.

"You ever wonder what the sign *NO BACK DOOR LIVING* over the back door means?" Otis asked, voice low but steady, like it came with the weight of years.

Jackson raised an eyebrow. "Didn't think of it."

Otis poured himself two fingers and slid the bottle away. "That's because back in the day, a back door meant shame. Hiding. Cook didn't build this place for Black musicians to sneak in or out the back door like in white joints. He built it so folks like us could walk right in the front with pride."

Jackson paused in his wiping, watching Otis closely.

"During Prohibition, this place was a speakeasy," Otis said, eyes distant now, like he was back in that time. "It wasn't only the drinkin', though." It was church. Jazz on the stage. Cards in the back. And voices, Black voices, that couldn't be heard anywhere else. No cops came through here unless they wanted music or pay to forget the rules."

"Must've been dangerous," Jackson murmured.

Otis nodded. "Always is, when you makin' something, they think you ain't supposed to have."

He took a sip. "Cook used to say, 'The liquor's just what gets 'em in the door. The music's what makes 'em stay. But the story… the stories that make it home."

Jackson leaned on the counter now, drawn in.

"See all of this?" Otis gestured around the room. "These brass rails, velvet booths, and the piano played by hands long forgotten. Not just decoration, but history filled with sacrifice, blood, sweat, and tax records so clean they could baptize a baby."

That made Jackson chuckle, but Otis didn't smile.

"Don't get too comfortable, son. Just because the law changed doesn't mean the game did. There's always someone waitin' to call it luck when you build something strong."

Jackson sobered.

Otis set his empty glass down with a soft clink. "So, when you take over, and you will, keep your books clean, your ears open, and your mouth shut until you know who's askin'. That's how you protect a legacy."

And with that, he walked off slowly, his back straight, leaving Jackson with more than just clean glasses, leaving him with the burden of knowing he was part of something worth guarding.

And that Jackson did.

He couldn't afford to buy the club outright, so Cook financed the deal, allowing Jackson to take over while Cook retired to Mississippi.

In 1955, Cook's House became *Malone's Supper Club*. With Willow by his side, Jackson transformed Malone's into something legendary.

The kitchen expanded, serving soul food with a jazz rhythm, catfish, collard greens, and cornbread so soft it melted on the tongue. The stage grew wider, the acts sharper. Musicians came from across the country, chasing the sound that only Malone's could hold.

Word spread.

It ceased being just a club and became an institution.

Jackson and Willow poured themselves into it. Long nights blurred into early mornings.

One morning, as Jackson wiped sweat from his brow, Willow leaned against the doorway, kicking off her heels. "We can't keep doing this forever."

He chuckled, dead on his feet. "We won't have to. Just a few more years."

She paused. "Try nine months."

Jackson turned to her, brows lifting.

Willow smiled, hand resting on her stomach.

Silence. Then. "Well, damn," he whispered, grinning. "At our age? Forty-seven?"

"At any age," she said, eyes bright. "A baby's coming."

From the moment Madison Jackson Malone took her first breath, the club became her world.

Her cradle.

Her rhythm.

She toddled through soundchecks, curled up in velvet booths during rehearsals, and fell asleep in the back office to the hum of upright bass and the soft swell of saxophones.

It wasn't just where her parents worked.

It was where she began.

Madison grew up with two names.

At church and school, she was "Madison Malone", light-skinned, with strawberry-blond curls and quiet manners.

Her teachers never asked if she was Black.

They just assumed she wasn't.

At Malone's Jazz Club, she was "Maddy-girl," barefoot between tables, tugging trumpet sleeves, sipping orange juice from a martini glass behind the bar.

The club wasn't just her playground. It was her classroom.

She learned math at the cash register.

She learned rhythm from the cook's nephew, who played the drums.

She learned her mother's fire. Her father's vision.

And she learned the weight of being in between. Some guests complimented her "olive skin" and "good hair" as if they were prizes on display. Others asked bluntly: "What are you, baby?"

By seven, she was asking herself and her parents the same thing.

Willow never flinched. "You're both," she said. "You're everything we are."

Jackson kissed the top of her head and added, "You're mine. That's enough."

And somehow, between the two of them, it was.

Until the morning, everything ended.

CHAPTER
SIXTEEN
OCTOBER 28, 1974

Murder at Malone's Supper Club
9:27 a.m.

THE FIRST BULLET shattered a bottle of bourbon.

The second hit Jackson Malone square in the chest.

Willow screamed as her husband collapsed, blood pooling on the floor while she scrambled toward him, her hands pressing against his wound, whispering, "Stay with me, baby, stay with me."

That was when the third shot rang out.

Willow's body jerked violently, her hand flying to the side of her head where a deep gash bloomed red. She slumped over Jackson, her last breath escaping as a strangled whisper.

"Why?"

The shooter had once been part of their family at the restaurant.

Ronnie "Slick" Bryant, a dishwasher they had hired years ago, had stood at that very sink, night after night, scrubbing dishes while humming along with the music.

Jackson had vouched for him, given him a second chance when nobody else would.

Then he got careless.

Jackson caught Ronnie stealing from the till and fired him immediately. Jackson hadn't pressed charges; he gave him his last paycheck and let him go.

That was two months ago. This morning, Ronnie returned, drunk and high.

And armed with a .38 revolver.

The plan wasn't for it to be a murder. It was supposed to be a robbery, a desperate, last-ditch attempt to get cash for another fix. But when Jackson saw his face, Ronnie panicked. Three shots. Two bodies. And a man running from a crime he couldn't take back.

By the time Madison understood, she could never go home again.

The days after the murder were a blur of polyester couches, whispered phone calls, and casserole dishes that stayed untouched.

Willow's family, including her grandparents, didn't come for her.

Jackson's cousin from New Orleans arrived too late to claim guardianship.

They placed Madison in temporary foster care before the bodies were cold.

No one asked her what she wanted.

The social worker was efficient and kind in a clipped manner that made kindness feel like a chore. She handed Madison a duffel bag containing two outfits, a toothbrush, and a photo album from the club; the one the staff had put together for Jackson and Willow's tenth anniversary.

Madison didn't cry. She clutched the album as if it were oxygen.

She slept with it pressed to her chest in every stranger's home.

At night, she stared at pictures of her parents, her father behind the bar, arms folded, laughing. Her mother was holding a tray of beignets; her eyes crinkled with joy.

She'd repeatedly whisper their names.

Jackson. Willow. Jackson. Willow.

As if speaking to them might open some secret door and let her back in.

It never did.

The life she had known ended in a single morning, replaced by strangers, rules, and an overwhelming loneliness.

She spent the next few years in various homes, shuffled like a file no one wanted to keep. Some families were kind but distant. Others were cold. Some were worse.

Through it all, she learned to survive.

To read moods. To disappear into silence.

To guard her story like it was all she had left.

She never spoke her parents' names aloud. Not to foster parents, not to caseworkers. Saying them would make the loss real.

Then they placed her at Mama Pearl's.

The house was always loud, warm, and full of noise, smells, and people coming and going at all hours. Madison had stood awkwardly by the front door with her caseworker, clutching a plastic grocery bag with all her belongings, unsure if she was being dropped off or thrown away.

And then, from around the corner, came a girl.

Brown-skinned, bright-eyed, barefoot. She looked about her age, maybe a year older, with an afro that had gone half-wild in the summer heat and confidence that didn't ask for permission.

"You new?" she asked, hands on her hips.

Madison nodded.

"I'm Nina." A pause. "You eat red beans and rice?"

"...Yeah."

"Good. Mama Pearl says anyone who turns their nose up at dinner can sleep on the porch."

Madison blinked.

Nina grinned. "I'm joking. Mostly."

She told the social worker, "I've got this."

She grabbed Madison's bag without asking and disappeared down the hallway.

And just like that, Madison wasn't alone anymore.

PART FOUR
PINE RIDGE, WISCONSIN

CHAPTER
SEVENTEEN
JUNE 17, 2009

Pine Ridge, Wisconsin
1:39 p.m.

THE ROAD out of Hawk Landing wasn't a drive; it was an escape.

From one life into another.

From Madison Jackson Winter to someone new.

That road had unraveled behind her days ago, miles of forgotten towns, back-road gas stations, and restless sleep in the front seat.

Now, with each new mile, something else was shedding.

For weeks, she had whispered her new name like a spell.

Finally, she mustered the courage to speak it aloud for the first time:

"Nina Autumn Storm."

As the words slipped from her lips, they carried the promise of change. It was a name that hinted at hidden secrets, untold journeys, and the possibility of discovering peace ahead, encouraging her to embrace this new identity wholeheartedly.

But in the end, she let Nina go, at least aloud. Not out of shame, but reverence. Saying Nina's name too often felt like picking at a wound that had only just scarred. So, she carried her quietly instead, tucked between syllables, held in silence.

The world would recognize her as Autumn, while she called herself Nina in moments of quiet.

The road into Pine Ridge unfolded like a cracked ribbon, gravel worn, faded lines, and brush overtaking the edge. Though it was her first time on this route, it felt heavy with expectations and echoes of unspoken memories. Each curve stirred something, some soft, others sharp as glass.

Tall pines lined the road, their twisted trunks standing like silent guardians. Wind hissed through the pines, their needles whispering in a language she almost understood. Above, the sun filtered through the canopy, casting dappled shadows that danced across her windshield.

It was breathtaking.

It felt unsettling.

And she questioned whether she fit in with either.

She clenched the steering wheel, her fingers aching from the long hours already driven. Her back throbbed with a steady, dull ache, reflecting the emotional weight she carried. The lack of sleep over the last few nights burned her eyelids, and too much gas station coffee, coupled with a lack of meaningful conversation, dried her lips.

When was the last time someone truly saw me? She wondered. She had been fading away for years, long before the wildfire. The wildfire offered a chance to escape, but something inside Madison cracked amid ribbon-cutting ceremonies, galas, photoshoots, and rehearsed prayers.

Her lifelong friend Nina noticed the cracks long before Madison dared to name them.

"You're not breathing anymore," Nina whispered late at night, curled up in a guest room at Madison's estate. The French doors were open, filling the air with the scent of night jasmine from the terrace. The two sat side by side on the velvet chaise, sipping red wine from gold-rimmed glasses and nibbling hors d'oeuvres from Madison's charity dinner leftovers.

"You throw parties like confetti, Maddie, but you're drowning in this house.

Madison offered a practiced smile, the kind that made socialites lean in and nod with admiration.

However, Nina never nodded. Nina saw through it all.

"You think money means freedom?" Madison said quietly.

"No," Nina replied. "I think you think obedience means survival."

Nina never married. She never wanted to, never felt the need.

Love, maybe. Intimacy, sure. But dependency? No. That wasn't her language.

After her mother's murder, covered up, ignored, and then quietly tied to the church, Nina became part of a confidential settlement. The church never admitted fault, but the money spoke enough. Starting at age twenty-one, she received an annual payment of $150,000 for twenty-five years.

She used it well.

Traveling and living as she pleased, eating what she wanted, and never apologizing for enjoying her comfort. She bought diamond studs, vintage leather jackets, and splurged on massages and antique cookbooks. Nina believed in pleasure, as if it were justice.

Still, when Madison married into the Winter family, into all that ice and structure, Nina didn't hesitate. She became her assistant, not because she needed the money, but because she refused to let her best friend walk into that cold, echoing house alone.

The images of the week were still vivid in her thoughts.

The wildfire had painted the sky a dreadful orange. Ash drifted like dying snowflakes past the floor-to-ceiling windows of the formal dining room as she dashed up the winding staircase, calling out to Nina, "We have to evacuate."

Nina was curled on the bed, hands tucked under her cheek like a child. Peaceful. Still.

Running.

Later, alone in Nina's car, watching the flames devour her home and life.

She reflected, "Madison is no more. Nina was the life we shared; now Autumn Storm will be the life we dreamed."

She hadn't picked Pine Ridge on a whim. Not entirely.

There was something about the name in the brochure found at the gas station, Pine Ridge, home to the away-from-home Landing Diner.

It sounded like a place where a person might land after they lost their wings.

Still, she didn't trust 'safe havens' after everything. The car's stuttering and a tremble beneath her seat interrupted that thought.

She frowned. Then came the metallic clunk, sharp and decisive. A hiss. A pull.

And finally... surrender.

A flat tire.

She cursed under her breath and pulled to the side of the road, gravel crunching beneath her tires.

"No, no, no," she whispered, pounding the steering wheel once, then again.

She was alone.

No cell service.

No Map.

Nobody knew where she was.

Which meant... no one would come looking. A terrible gift. A terrifying reality.

She stepped out of the car, breathing in the scent of pine and dust. The forest was unnervingly quiet, too quiet. The surrounding stillness was almost theatrical, like she had stepped into the pause before a play began.

Was this a sign?

Or just another cruel interruption? She couldn't tell anymore.

Then came the sound. The crunch of tires on gravel.

She turned sharply, pulse racing in her chest.

A battered red pickup truck appeared, sunlight reflecting off its dusty windshield. It slowed down next to her, stirring up a gentle dust cloud. She squinted, shielding her eyes from the glare. The driver's door creaked open.

A man stepped out, tall, broad-shouldered, steady. He wore a worn coat and a dark felt hat that shadowed his eyes, but not his warmth.

Something about him felt grounded, as if he were part of the land itself. His movements were slow, yet confident. No pretense. He raised a hand in greeting. "Need a hand, miss?" His voice was low and calm, the kind that soothes your shoulders before your mind can catch up.

Autumn hesitated.

Every bone in her body told her not to trust men who showed up when you were vulnerable.

She had learned that the hard way.

But this man… he didn't leer. He didn't invade. He waited.

"I… I have a flat," she managed, surprised by how small her voice sounded.

He didn't comment, just nodded once and walked to the trunk. Checked the spare, then knelt beside the car. He moved in a practiced, methodical manner as if he'd performed this action a hundred times before and required only purpose, not praise or payment.

She observed. He worked quietly, pausing once to glance up and say,

"Name's Harper Lewis White. Folks around here call me Mister Mayor."

He said it with a wry half-smile, like the title was both a joke and a scar.

She blinked. "You're the mayor?" She thought. Is this man serious?

He chuckled, his eyes crinkling at the corners.

"Not elected. Not officially. I incorporated my land as a town years ago. Bit of a loophole. Appointed myself mayor for life. No one contested."

"It's a unique arrangement, wouldn't you agree?"

She ignored his question, pondering his words with intrigue and apprehension. A battle raged within as she questioned his true nature. He was either the most innovative person she knew, creative and boundary-pushing, or a lonely man clinging to control.

She studied his hands as he tightened the bolts on the new tire.

Large, calloused hands.

A gold band still circled his left ring finger, worn and dulled by time but not removed.

He built with his hands and buried with his heart. A man marked by silence. The way he tightened each lug nut and paused before rising showed the air's quiet presence around him.

Not haunted. Just… marked.

But something about the silence between them felt familiar, as if it were a shared ache.

Neither asked. And neither offered.

Wiping his hands with a rag, he looked at her with a protective tenderness, saying, "There's a diner in town. Small place. Cozy. Coffee's hot. Food's decent."

He didn't ask where she was going.

Just a direction. An invitation.

She looked down the road. Then back at him.

And nodded.

All she knew was that, for the first time in weeks, she felt...

safer than she had any right to.

As she approached the town, she slowed down slightly, not because of the curve ahead, but because of an unfamiliar feeling swelling in her chest. It wasn't fear, exactly, more like a quiet panic fueled by the possibility of what it might mean to be accepted or noticed. Mister Mayor's truck kept moving ahead smoothly, as if he trusted the road and her. Encouraged, she pressed on the gas and followed.

Pine Ridge wasn't what she had imagined.

She was astonished as she took in the vibrant scene of a bustling town, where a cluster of quaint buildings harmoniously nestled at the edge of a lush forest.

The gas station flickered with warm neon, the barbershop hummed with quiet conversation, and the drugstore boasted a painted mural of smiling children beneath bright lettering. The streets buzzed gently, with shopkeepers, bicycles, and a slow-moving pickup with pumpkins in the back.

Dominating the landscape was a church, its steeple reaching ambitiously toward the sky.

And then, the Landing Diner.

The red truck pulled in. So did she.

The diner's exterior radiated cozy warmth reminiscent of her parents' jazz club, inviting patrons to escape the outside world. As she stepped onto the brick pavement, barefoot, summers outside the club, where music and freedom merged, came flooding back to her.

The scent of cinnamon and wood-smoke floated through the air.

Inside, the diner glowed with warm light, wrapping the room in an easy, welcoming hush. Cozy booths hugged the walls, offering pockets of comfort and quiet. A long counter ran the length of the space, its glossy red stools gleaming under hanging lights. Black-and-white photos adorned the walls, capturing moments from a rich, resilient history of Black culture, faces full of music, pride, and memory.

Madison paused just inside the doorway, the scent of coffee and fried apples tugging at something buried deep. It was the sort of place where people arrived as they truly were. Such a place hadn't been part of her life for many years.

Beside her, Mister Mayor stepped forward.

The bell above the door gave one more chime as it shut behind them, and in that instant, the room shifted.

Heads turned.

Conversations dipped, then picked up again, but with a different rhythm.

"Well, now, look who's here," someone near the window drawled.

"Afternoon, Mister Mayor."

"You're late, but I'll forgive you."

"Seat's warm, just like always."

There was affection in the teasing. The laughter contained respect.

Madison kept close to him, suddenly aware of how out of place she must seem, with her unfamiliar face, worn sneakers, and the silence that was all too familiar. But no one stared long. They offered smiles, nods, and greetings spoken just loud enough for her to hear.

She didn't know these people.

But somehow, they didn't feel like strangers.

Mister Mayor gestured toward a booth in the back, one with a good view of the entire room.

She slid into the seat, hands folding in her lap. Still on guard, but not frozen.

He sat across from her, already nodding at the waitress with silver braids and tired eyes, who was pouring coffee before he even asked. "They'll take care of you here," he said, voice low but sure.

And in that moment, wrapped in the warm hum of chatter and clinking silverware, something loosened in her chest.

This wasn't merely breakfast; it was an offering, a quiet, and familiar start.

The waitress smiled and asked, "You must have arrived early for the Jazz Festival. We don't get many pass-throughs this time of year."

Madison just nodded.

"She'll have the special," Mister Mayor said gently. "Meatloaf's good today."

Madison didn't argue; too exhausted to put up a fight or pretend otherwise, feeling too broken even to try to perform.

And somehow, this place, this strange little town, felt like the only place in the world that might not ask her to.

As the food arrived and the clink of forks and plates filled the air, she allowed herself, if only for a moment, to breathe.

She studied Mister Mayor across the table. He wasn't flashy or dominating, but hints of stories, loss, resilience, and hard-earned experience lingered about him. He didn't ask about her past or demand answers, not even her name. His silence, free of intrusion, felt more intimate than any question.

After a while, Mr. Mayor leaned back, saying, "Got to fulfill one of my mayoral duties."

Autumn looked up, unsure what he meant.

"I'm the Pine Ridge Elementary school crossing guard."

The waitress chuckled. "Honey, Mister Mayor is all things to everybody."

He stood, offered to walk her to the car, and suggested that she stop by the Pine Ridge Lodge if she planned to stay.

Outside, the afternoon air felt cool for June as the trees swayed as if they knew something she didn't yet. She stood beside her car, gazing at the illuminated sign above The Landing Diner.

It felt like more than a name... a promise.

Just as she turned to leave, something caught her eye.

A small sign in the diner's window. Faded. Unassuming.

But somehow... meant for her.

HELP WANTED.

That late afternoon, outside the diner, the sky over Pine Ridge had transformed, not merely blue but layered with deepening shades of blue and ash. The town was quiet in a way that felt unguarded. Unsafe in its strange way.

The brochure had caught her eye at a gas station two states back, a folded, half-faded piece of paper wedged between travel guides. A Black-owned town nestled in the mountains of Wisconsin.

Quiet. Safe. Off the radar.

It promised obscurity.

That's why she'd come. Somewhere far enough from questions. Remote enough to vanish.

And yet... now, standing in the parking lot outside the diner, she didn't feel invisible.

That was the problem.

From the moment she'd stepped inside, there'd been warmth. Not the forced kind. Something deeper.

Her silence went unquestioned by the waitress.

The man who fixed the tire didn't ask for anything in return.

Comfort filled the diner's air.

The people laughed without suspicion.

It felt like home, yet it was dangerous. Home was a place where you lowered your guard, allowed others in, but she knew well what happened when people got close: they began asking questions, pulling at threads, and offering safety only to decide you no longer deserved it.

She wasn't sure if she wanted comfort or if she just missed the illusion of it.

Across the lot, the sign caught her again.

HELP WANTED.

She didn't require the money or kindness; she needed a place where she wouldn't vanish, without the threat of being discovered. And perhaps that was the most frightening aspect.

She lingered for a moment, keys in hand, then let them drop into her coat pocket and turned back toward the diner.

Maybe this time, she'd stay long enough to see what it felt like... to stop running.

CHAPTER
EIGHTEEN

OCTOBER 16, 2009

The Landing Diner
7:14 a.m.

AUTUMN HAD SETTLED into Pine Ridge, where the leaves turned brilliant red and gold, painting the world in colors she hadn't seen in years, and now waitressing at The Landing Diner, the warm haven where locals shared stories over biscuits and coffee. The sizzle of bacon, the scent of cinnamon, and the soft murmur of conversation filled the air like a balm.

Each cup of coffee she poured was a quiet offering; each booth she wiped down was a ritual of belonging.

She rented a small room at the Pine Ridge Lodge, decorating it with soft touches, a candle, a quilted throw, and a single jazz record she played quietly at night. It was nothing like the sprawling house she had left behind, but it was hers.

A space of her choosing.

The diner became more than just a workplace and shelter; it was a sanctuary. Each day brought a routine: breakfast rush, laughter from the front booth, someone reading yesterday's newspaper as if it held a new truth.

One morning, as Autumn refilled coffee cups with practiced grace, she paused at a booth where an older man sat reading the same worn paper, flipping through the pages like scripture.

"You ever tire of yesterday's news?" she asked sarcastically, offering a faint smile.

He didn't look up. Just tapped the headline and said, "Yesterday got lessons today, don't always understand."

She nodded, surprised by how much that landed.

Miss Angie, wiping down the counter nearby, chimed in without turning around.

"Folks come in here for more than food. They come to remember who they are."

Autumn swallowed the lump in her throat and returned to the pot, the smell of coffee curling around her like a comfort she hadn't expected to find.

"Check, please," Mr. Weinberg called from his usual counter seat. A portly man with thick white hair and a slow, deliberate way of eating, he came in twice a day like clockwork, six-thirty a.m. and six sharp in the evening. Breakfast was always eggs over easy, grits with butter, and black coffee. Dinner? Meatloaf or pot roast, whichever was hot.

Never once asked for a menu. Never once paid a bill.

"You know it's on the house," Autumn said, refilling his cup.

"It always is," he replied with a wink. "I'm grandfathered in."

She raised an eyebrow playfully. "Then why do you always ask for the check?"

He chuckled into his cup. "Because I still believe in manners and miracles."

Autumn smiled, the kind that stuck with her longer than it should have.

The locals called him Mister Mayor's shadow, but his real name was George Weinberg, supervisor at the Pine Ridge Mill and Mister Mayor's closest friend since 1961. He'd been there when the mayor won Pine Ridge in a poker hand, and stood beside him when they lit the first streetlamp. Helped file the papers that turned backwoods into Pine Ridge.

"He built it," George once said, his fingers curled around a chipped coffee mug. "But we held it. You know what I mean?"

Autumn nodded, even though she wasn't sure she did. Not yet.

One evening, as Autumn wiped down the counters after closing, she felt it again, the hush of stillness that beckoned remembrance. Even now, amid the diner's silence, she could sense that moment she chose not just to run, but to begin again.

That first night in Pine Ridge ended with her walking back into the diner, pulling the torn HELP WANTED sign from the window, and handing it to the gray-haired waitress behind the counter.

Miss Angie.

Mister Mayor's sister, who retired from teaching in Alabama after losing her husband a few years back, had come here to manage the diner.

Miss Angie took the sign and tossed it in the trash, then poured a cup of coffee, set it on the counter, and motioned to Autumn, "Mister Mayor will be back soon."

When he returned, no application.

Didn't demand ID. Didn't question the silence she carried.

All he said was, "What name should I put on your nametag?"

She paused. Heard Nina's voice in her head: *"Bet on yourself."*

"Autumn," she said.

He nodded.

Didn't ask for more.

She didn't offer.

They both knew enough for now.

They both needed help.

Over time, she learned his story, not from him, but from regulars like George Weinberg, and half-whispered tales passed between coffee cups.

Poker's hand. Legal cases. Crosses burned. Disputes. Stubbornness. The Legend.

"Some people build their lives with bricks," Mister Mayor once told her. *"Others with bruises. I built mine with both."*

CHAPTER
NINETEEN
OCTOBER 16, 2009

The Landing Diner
8:24 p.m.

THE DOOR CHIME STARTLED HER. She looked up, realizing she had forgotten to lock the front door. Mister Mayor was standing there with a furrowed brow and his coat slung over one shoulder. "You're exactly who I was hoping to find," he said.

"You've been sleepin' in your car?" he asked next, no judgment, just fact.

Of course, he knew. Nothing happened in Pine Ridge without Mister Mayor knowing.

She didn't answer, but she didn't lie either.

The Fall Jazz Festival fully booked the Pine Ridge Lodge and every campground, leaving her without a room for a week. Instead of disturbing anyone, she curled up in her car to wait it out.

He stepped forward and placed a key on the counter.

"I own this building," he said. "Upstairs used to be an apartment. Mostly storage now, but the heat works. It's yours if you want it."

"Why?"

He looked her in the eyes.

"Because I got the key, and I trust you to use it."

He didn't wait for thanks. He walked out into the night, as if settled.

Later, as she climbed the steps behind the diner, they creaked loudly under her careful steps, the cold brass key pressing into her hand. Every sound of the wood echoed her quickened heartbeat, full of anticipation. The door resisted as if guarding long-buried memories, finally giving way with a reluctant groan.

As she entered, her heart pounded for reasons she couldn't entirely understand as she explored the unknown. It wasn't just the dust covering the deserted furniture or the faint flickering light casting shadows in the room. It was something more profound, a quiet, almost oppressive feeling that wrapped around her and resonated deeply within her.

This was a silence she had avoided confronting since before Coby's tragic death, before Nina's haunting stillness settled like a heavy fog around her, and long before the wildfire she could still see in her rearview mirror, a reminder of chaos now gone.

It felt as though the burden of survival had robbed her of her voice and silenced her thoughts.

Gently running her fingers along the windowsill, she felt the chipped paint flake under her touch like memories shedding their layers. For a brief moment, she imagined Nina behind her, laughing as she shook out a colorful throw blanket, her energy full of life.

"It's small, Maddie, but it's ours. And it smells like possibility." Nina would say, her bright eyes sparkling with unfiltered hope.

But Nina was gone. The silence following her death was not just an absence; it was heavy, filled with unspoken words and unfulfilled dreams. It reverberated through her very bones.

Yet, somehow, this space felt different. Could it hold the possibility of solace? A place where the silence could live out loud.

That first night, she slept little.

She took a blanket from her bag and settled into the armchair, too restless to lie flat, yet too exhausted to do anything else. From the kitchen below, a soft hum from the refrigerator and the creaking of pipes and walls sounded as if the building were stretching. The combination of old wood and cleaning fluid filled the space with its scent. With a hiss, the radiator possessed a personality. Although cold, the air felt gentle.

She found a chipped mug in the cabinet and rinsed it out, filling it with hot water from the tap.

No tea, no sugar, heat.

She cupped it in her hands like a prayer and sat by the window, staring out at the alley below.

It was nothing like the marble-floored master suite she'd once slept in. There were no silk robes, soundproof walls, or hollow silence. Despite that, somehow, it felt more like home.

When the sun rose and golden light spilled through the blinds, Autumn was still awake. Still watching and still holding on.

Pine Ridge stirred below her window. The steady rhythms of the town, the crackle of tires on gravel, the low hum of voices, the rising scent of brewing coffee whispered a quiet invitation.

And slowly, she let herself listen.

She got to know the diner's rhythms in that little upstairs apartment. The click of the coffeemaker before sunrise. The clang of pans. Mr. Weinberg arrived right on time. The bustle of a town that ran on routine, where breakfast orders came before news headlines and nobody asked where you'd come from if you showed up on time.

And then there was Daniel.

The teenage busboy with sleeves always rolled up, apron barely clinging to his hips, and too much energy for the quiet pace of Pine Ridge. Lanky, always in motion, always curious. He reminded her of Coby.

Jacob Winston Winter.

Her son.

The boy who wanted to be a world-renowned chef, who printed business cards at fourteen: Coby Winter, Executive Chef.

The boy killed on the night of his senior prom by a drunk driver.

She never told Daniel. Told no one.

No one in Pine Ridge was aware of Coby. Or about her previous life as *Lady Madison Jackson Winter*.

They knew her as Autumn Storm, a name she guarded fiercely. But memories didn't need permission; they slipped in, especially around boys like Daniel.

One evening, she found him crouched near the storeroom, fiddling with a dented saucepan and a bag of pecans he'd brought from home. Flour dusted the front of his shirt, and his curls stuck to his forehead with determination.

"What are you doing?" she asked, leaning against the doorframe.

He grinned. "Ever make syrup? Bourbon, butter, brown sugar. Figured we could do a test run."

Barely seventeen, already dreaming of owning a restaurant.

Autumn hesitated, then rolled up her sleeves. "Show me."

They stood side by side at the prep table, his voice narrating each step, her hands steady with the heat. The scent of caramelizing sugar filled the air, thick and warm, like a promise.

Hope.

"I want to open a food truck," Daniel said, stirring with care. "Southern fusion, but like, modern. My mom says college is safer, but..."

"She just wants you to be safe," Autumn murmured, the words catching in her throat. "College feels like safety."

He nodded without stopping. "I don't want to be safe. I want to be good." The words hit her hard, echoing Coby's defiant voice from the past. "I want to be more than just someone's idea of security."

She swallowed hard. "Then you go be good."

Daniel beamed like she'd just handed him his future.

Later, after the syrup cooled, and he scraped the last from the pot with a biscuit, he asked, "Think Mister Mayor would like it?"

Autumn smiled. "He'll probably say it's too sweet and then ask for seconds."

Daniel laughed, then turned thoughtful. "He always says this town only works if we make room for people's wild ideas."

She looked at him, this tall, scrappy kid with sugar on his cheek, and something shifted inside her.

Perhaps: She may have been carrying more than just grief. Pine Ridge wasn't erasing her story; it was quietly asking her to write a new one.

That may be enough.

Maybe this town was healing her, or perhaps it was just teaching her how to carry grief without putting it down.

PART FIVE
THE WEIGHT OF SILENCE

CHAPTER
TWENTY
FEBRUARY 12, 2015

OVER HER YEARS IN PRISON, they assigned Madison to various jobs, each putting her in situations that could lead to solitary confinement or, worse, endanger her life. She wasn't a well-liked prisoner, either by the guards or by the inmates.

The news reports and tabloid stories that depicted her as a privileged, cold-blooded killer ensured that.

And she hadn't helped her case. She kept to herself, refused to speak to the press, and never gave the inmates or the guards a reason to believe she needed anyone.

They labeled her before she even set foot inside Pendleton Women's Federal Prison.

"Bougie brat bitch."

That was the name that stuck.

Morning shows, podcasts, true crime blogs, and social media broadcasts dissected, dramatized, and reshaped her story worldwide. The only truth was the version spun by headlines. Since the moment they found her over the body, clutching the murder weapon with trembling hands, *Madison Jackson Winter, aka Nina Autumn Storm*, had said nothing in her defense.

Not one. She didn't explain.

Did not cry, make excuses, or seek forgiveness.

And that silence, heavy and deliberate, had spoken louder than any confession ever could.

An unidentified benefactor hired a top criminal defense attorney. He claimed self-defense, citing emotional distress and describing it as a tragic accident. The legal team tried every argument they could think of, except mentioning her voice.

Because Madison refused to speak.

The prosecution's evidence was damning, but it was her silence that sealed the narrative. It made her unknowable. Untrustworthy. Dangerous.

The jury found her guilty, but her attorneys' skill prevented a capital conviction. Instead, she faced involuntary manslaughter and three years in federal prison, a sentence that outraged the public and intensified her time behind bars.

When the story broke, her face was everywhere. The first photo showed her handcuffed and shoved into a squad car, eyes hidden beneath a baseball cap. Then came the video from her preliminary hearing: an orange jumpsuit, strawberry-blonde curls in a tight pony-tail, and a black eye spreading across her left face from a jailhouse welcome. The black eye served as the first warning; she would find no welcome.

Her defense team understood the importance of optics.

They requested permission for her to wear her clothes to court, subtly attempting to humanize her and counteract the headlines. The judge agreed.

At the trial, she entered wearing a sleek black sheath dress and low leather slingbacks. Only a light layer of foundation minimally made up her face. She carried herself with impeccable posture. When needed, her tone remained calm and controlled.

She looked the part they needed her to play: a composed, respectable, misunderstood woman from a powerful family. But none of it mattered. Public opinion had already judged: entitled, arrogant, guilty. No one cared about the consultants, strategists, or witnesses. They were interested in the story involving a woman with wealth and secrets, a murder weapon, a dead man, and a trial of secrets in the ashes.

For two long weeks, Madison Jackson Winter sat in court wearing carefully chosen outfits, her light-skinned features stressed to highlight her vulnerability. Her long, naturally curly strawberry-blonde hair was pulled back, and her voice remained unheard.

Every day, she watched the jury, twelve strangers with unyielding expressions. One woman at the end frowned each time Madison entered, her arms crossed as if guarding against an uncomfortable truth. In the front row, a man scribbled notes without looking up, brow furrowed as if the case bore the weight of the world. An older man in the middle, with a face etched by experience, had an icy stare. He often glanced at the others, seeking validation before turning back to Madison, his face showing resignation and disapproval.

She wondered if they truly saw her or if they were seeing the story society had fed them.

Sometimes, in the courtroom's stillness, she imagined speaking.

Just once.

She sometimes pictured it in the stillness between objections and sidebar conversations, when the gallery collectively held its breath, and her heartbeat pulsed behind her eyes.

The walk to the witness stand, and the rustle of fabric as she sat down.

The awkward pause as the bailiff swore her in, "*Do you solemnly swear...*" and she raised a trembling hand.

She never made it that far; her lawyers forbade it, claiming her silence made her sympathetic and mysterious. They didn't realize it made her invisible, which was precisely what she wanted.

But in the reel playing quietly in her mind, she leaned into the microphone and said,

"*My name is Madison Jackson Winter.*"

No aliases. No masks.

And someone in the back row would gasp.

She'd clear her throat.

Meet the prosecutor's eyes.

And when he said, *"Tell us what happened that night,"* she'd pause.

Let the silence fill the room, like water rising around their ankles.

She would recount it all: how he had cornered her, how she had begged him to stop, and how his words turned into fists. She fought back, bleeding, crying, and defending herself, not out of hate, but out of fear for them. Then the shot rang out.

She wouldn't cry for the judge, the jury, or the spectators.

Instead, she'd say his name, her son's, and theirs, and perhaps then they'd realize that everything she'd done, the name she changed, the life she disappeared into, and the quiet corner of Pine Ridge she carved out, wasn't a lie.

It was her way of protecting herself and surviving. But that moment never came. No judge called her forward, no lawyer asked her to speak. The truth stayed locked in her mouth like a jaw wired shut. The facts remained. She lived under an assumed name. The life she built wasn't hers to claim. Police found her at the scene, and she took the fall.

When the judge read the guilty verdict of involuntary manslaughter, the courtroom exploded.

Outrage. Gasps.

A woman in the gallery screamed, "She should've gotten life!"

Madison didn't react.

And then she'd see their faces, their laughter, the lives she burned to protect. She wondered what truth might scorch if spoken. So she said nothing.

And that silence? It echoed louder than any confession.

Louder than fire.

Later that day, she arrived at Pendleton with no fanfare, no family waving goodbye, no one waiting to meet her on the other side.

It was a swift, mechanical intake:

Strip search

Uniform issue

Body inspection

Orientation on the rules

Tier and cell assignment

Stiff linens still damp from bleach

The air was heavy with disinfectant and something else: sweat, sorrow, hopelessness. A guard barked orders with all the warmth of a blade. Madison's palms stayed flat at her sides, her spine erect, her eyes low.

Guards marched them down the corridor, single file.

The moment she stepped onto the tier, it began.

"Look at her! That's her!"

"Boogie Brat Bitch."

"Miss High-and-Mighty got herself locked up!"

"How much they pay to keep you alive, princess?"

The air seemed thinner here, with lower ceilings, as if the building itself resented her presence. She kept her gaze straight ahead, one foot following the other. Keep moving. She sensed the walls watching her.

Reaching her assigned cell, a guard glanced at his clipboard and snapped, "Cell 22. Bougie Bitch." Laughter echoed through the tier. Madison paused, even though she hadn't spoken during the intake. This, she knew, required correction. She turned and said evenly, "Are you referring to me? I am Madison Jackson Winter." The instant she finished speaking, a sudden blow sent her crashing against the wall, her arms twisted painfully behind her, and sharp rib pain shot through her.

Cold cuffs locked around her wrists.

"Take her ass to solitary for 72."

They dragged her away, boots echoing off the walls.

The jeers continued, "Bet she got champagne in her veins!"

"Welcome to hell, Snow White!"

She didn't flinch. Didn't cry. Didn't ask why.

She knew better now.

The guards didn't need a reason. But now, they had one.

Verbal assault of an officer.

Her first lesson came hard and fast: Even politeness was a punishable offense.

They threw her into solitary confinement.

Her time in solitary confinement turned out to be unexpectedly valuable.

It wasn't redemptive. Not cathartic.

Informative.

It was there, in that dim, narrow box of cement and steel, that Madison learned the first unspoken rule of surviving prison:

Nothing here is fair. And no one is on your side.

The exception to the rule?

Officer Katrina Johnson.

She didn't wear kindness like a badge; it clung to her in sharp, quiet moments, glimpsed only when she thought no one was watching.

"If I show kindness to inmates," she said one day, her voice low, her face unreadable, "maybe somewhere, someone will show kindness to my son."

The words came with a wry smirk. But Madison heard the fracture beneath them. The truth vibrating between syllables.

"You learn working in prison that everyone's 'innocent,'" she said with a shrug. "But my son..." Her voice faltered briefly. "My son was innocent."

Madison didn't ask. She didn't have to. Officer Johnson was already speaking, unprompted, like someone who'd held the story in too long.

Her son had been seventeen, a good kid.

Wrong place, wrong time.

He held a gun for a friend, unaware of its use in a robbery. That friend cut a deal to save his skin and testified, naming names.

In exchange, he received a five-year sentence.

Officer Johnson's son got twenty-five.

"He was just a kid," she whispered. "If he were white, they would've called it a mistake."

A year after Madison began her sentence, she learned that Officer Johnson's son had committed suicide. The following day, Officer Johnson resigned.

Her seventy-two hours in solitary blurred like a fever dream. A six-by-eight-foot cell, barely wide enough to stretch out in, held her. The thin, uneven mattress pressed against the wall near a stained steel toilet and a tiny sink. The air reeked of sweat, bleach, and a sourness she couldn't identify. Silence was so thick it felt almost tangible. The toilet gurgled intermittently. All sounds, distant coughs, and electrical hums felt amplified and intrusive.

The only light entered through a narrow slit in the door, long enough to cast distorted shadows but too narrow to see outside.

Time didn't move. It dragged.

At some unknown hour, the metal slot scraped open with a jarring clank.

"DINNER!"

A brown paper bag dropped through. The rattle of a cart echoed down the corridor, and then, silence. She opened it. A peanut butter sandwich wrapped in wax paper, a carton of milk that was already warm and bruised, and brown apple slices.

The smell turned her stomach.

With a flare of frustration, she flung the bag at the door and slumped onto the mattress, curling into herself, willing her body to fade into the icy walls. She shut her eyes and thought of a booth in a diner. The conversation hummed. The smell is of cinnamon and lemon. She chased the memory like a child chasing fireflies, hoping for light in the dark.

"You warm enough, sugar?" Miss Angie had asked that night, topping off her coffee with steady hands.

Madison had nodded, fingers wrapped tight around the chipped ceramic mug.

"You ain't said more than two words all week."

"I don't have much to say."

"Then just listen; that's half the talkin' anyway."

Madison remembered how Miss Angie sat across from her, sipping her tea like the world wasn't burning outside. No pressure. No questions. Just presence.

Now, the memory flickered behind her eyelids like a film reel. Still, she could hear the gentle scrape of Angie's voice, the clinking dishes, and the shuffle of old men playing dominoes by the window.

She exhaled slowly, feeling detached. For a moment, the memory kept her.

Moments later, the door creaked open.

Officer Johnson stood there, baton in hand, eyes tired.

She looked down at the untouched food on the floor and let out a sigh.

"That's the usual reaction," she said dryly. "But I suggest you pick up that bag and eat it. If you're lucky, you'll get another one in twelve hours."

She turned and walked out.

Madison sat up slowly. Picked up the crumpled bag. Unwrapped the sandwich with trembling fingers. Took one bite. Dry. Stale.

But it filled the hollow ache in her stomach. Barely.

Madison's second night was thick with unease. She thought she heard footsteps halt at her door, the faint squeak of the slot opening, and then a cough. Amid the fog of wakefulness, a voice emerged, familiar yet cast in confusion.

"You're still here. Keep your mind intact."

Johnson returned the next morning, this time opening the door.

"Eat and listen."

Madison glanced toward the window.

"You're the first wealthy prisoner we've had here since Pendleton went private," Johnson said. "Most of the women here are poor, come from broken homes, commit non-violent offenses, stupid shit, just trying to get by, and often receive ridiculous sentences.

A pause.

"Kickbacks, the more bodies they send here, the more money they make.

"An empty bed means empty pockets."

Madison said nothing. She took another bite. Chewed slowly.

"These women watched your trial like it was daytime TV," Johnson went on. "And you? You weren't the tragic heroine. You were the villain."

Madison gave a faint, bitter smirk. Of course.

It wasn't new

The women in her husband's congregation secretly disliked her, their disdain hidden behind manicured nails and fashionable church hats. They exchanged shifty glances and whispered judgments about her origins, presence, and poise.

To them, she was:

Not religious enough.

Not humble enough.

Too pretty and poised.

Too much.

A constant reminder of all the ways they felt inadequate.

Same judgment, only with a different choir.

She muttered, mostly to herself, "Thought I left this behind."

Officer Johnson caught it. "What was that?"

Madison looked into her eyes through the slit. "I'll be fine. I've been in prison before. It just didn't have bars."

Johnson didn't flinch. She nodded, just once.

"Yeah," she whispered. "I figured as much."

Her tone softened. "But be careful. They see you as a rich person who doesn't understand struggle. Some of them sold drugs to feed their kids. Some stole to pay rent. And here you are, convicted of murder, and still got less time than half of them."

Madison realized why they despised her so much. She also knew that the truth was irrelevant, that it had always been that way.

Three days later, the cell door unlocked. Officer Johnson stood outside.

"Time's up."

She didn't speak as she stepped out.

Her body was sore, her skin sticky, her hair matted.

Three days with no shower.

Two paper bags each day.

One woman she barely trusted.

She followed Johnson toward the showers, the overhead lights buzzing like angry flies.

Officer Johnson spoke one last time.

"Want to leave Pendleton alive?" she asked, already knowing.

"Never turn your back on anyone. Don't trust anyone, no matter how nice they seem. Everyone here has their agenda."

She paused, studying Madison. "Including me." A faint smile. "I treated you decently because I want someone, somewhere, to treat my son decently."

"I believe in karma."

CHAPTER
TWENTY-ONE
FEBRUARY 15, 2015

Pendleton's General Population,
3:30 p.m.

THE GENERAL POPULATION block of Pendleton Women's Federal Prison wasn't a prison. It was a jungle. No bars. No rules. Just stares that dared you to blink first.

Curiosity or caution sparked with every glance. People made judgments with each whisper. Every smirk was a challenge or an invitation.

In this jungle, social dynamics were as intricate and dangerous as the terrain. And Madison was brand new.

As soon as Madison stepped onto the floor, she felt it.

Some looked at her like prey. Some like a punchline. A few... like a challenge.

She remembered Officer Johnson's words: "Never turn your back on anyone. And don't trust a soul, no matter how nice they seem. Everyone here has an angle."

And she clung to them like a lifeline.

Her new cell was smaller than solitary, but louder. A narrow bunk. A chipped metal sink. The faint smell of sweat and bleach permeated the cinderblock walls. A rusted vent wheezed in the corner, blowing more dust than air. The mattress was a thin slab of foam stretched too tightly over steel, stained with the sleepless nights of others.

Her cellmate, a thick-shouldered woman with cornrows and tired eyes, didn't speak when Madison arrived, just nodded once and turned back to the wall. Headphones jammed deep, humming something low and sad.

They exchanged no names. In here, silence was safer than small talk.

Still, when the lights dimmed and Madison tried to ease herself onto the bunk, her movements stiff and quiet, the woman muttered without turning around,

"Don't let 'em see you crack, Church Lady. That's all they waitin' for."

It wasn't kindness exactly… just a warning wrapped in secondhand mercy.

Madison didn't answer.

That first night, she curled onto her side and shut her eyes. And for a fleeting moment, she saw Coby. In the kitchen. Laughing. Singing off-key and pouring syrup with both hands while she told him to slow down. She could hear his voice like a whisper from another world.

"You're tougher than they think, Mom. You don't like to show it."

Her throat tightened. Not from crying. From *not* crying.

From the pain of holding in everything, she wanted to scream.

Morning came too early, announced by a shrill buzz and the clank of doors sliding open. Madison sat up slowly, her back aching from the unforgiving bunk. Her cellmate was already lacing up her boots, moving with the practiced rhythm that said this wasn't her first stint.

"Showers before chow," the woman muttered without looking up. "Stick to the left wall. Don't make eye contact. Drop nothing."

Then she was gone.

Madison followed the stream of women filing down the hallway, their faces blank with routine. The shower block was a humid chamber of fog, mildew, and noise. Showerheads hissed and dripped; the drain coughed like a dying machine. Steam curled around the cracked tiles, and the stench of mold mingled with the scent of cheap soap.

She picked a stall near the back, no curtain, just a broken bar where one might've hung once. She kept her eyes down and washed quickly and efficiently. The water was lukewarm at best, but it was clean, which was better than nothing.

"Look at this one," a voice murmured behind her. "Boogie Brat Bitch still got that better-than-them look."

Madison turned her head just enough to catch two women watching her, both wrapped in thin towels, tattoos peeking out from under damp skin. One of them smirked.

"Is she the preacher's wife or the killer? I can't keep it straight."

The other laughed. "Same difference."

Madison said nothing. She wrapped her towel tightly and walked away.

CHAPTER
TWENTY-TWO
FEBRUARY 16, 2015

General Population Breakfast
7:32 a.m.

THE CAFETERIA LINE WAS LOUD, shuffling, unforgiving. The noise that made you feel small if you weren't careful. Madison stood still, waiting her turn, trying not to let the smell of powdered eggs and burnt toast churn her stomach.

She carried her tray across the floor, eyes scanning for a place to sit. Most tables were full or had trouble. She finally dropped into an open seat across from a girl named Ty, a wiry kid she remembered from the intake line before she went to solitary.

Ty just watched her eat. Quietly. Then it happened.

A tall, broad-shouldered woman with a knotted scarf holding back her braids sauntered by, slowed, and reached for Madison's banana like it was hers, a casual swipe. No warning.

Madison didn't raise her voice. She didn't curse.

"Put it back," she said, her voice level.

The woman froze, hand still hovering over the tray. "Excuse me?"

Ty's eyes widened. A fork paused midair at a nearby table.

The woman let out a low laugh. "You must be new."

Madison didn't flinch. "And you must want to find out if the rumors are true." She leaned in slightly, her voice cool and even. "Take what's yours. Not what isn't."

"I said, put it back." Looking at the woman square in the eyes.

A long second passed. The woman studied her like a puzzle with one missing piece. Then, with a scoff and exaggerated flair, she dropped the banana back onto the tray.

"Didn't want it anyway," she muttered, walking off.

Ty smirked, half-impressed. "They're gonna start watching you now."

"They already were," Madison replied, stabbing at her eggs like it was any other morning.

No one said anything else. But a shift had happened.

She hadn't thrown a punch. She hadn't lost control. But the cafeteria wasn't the only battleground.

The laundry was a dangerous place filled with knives and rumors. Though simple, laundry duty was risky, ranking just after the chaotic kitchen as one of the building's most perilous areas. The air was thick with the scent of detergent and a sharp chemical odor. Dimly lit and cramped, the space vibrated with the hum of machines, blades sparkling ominously in shadowy corners where secrets lurked.

She stayed alert, never turning her back. Pressing against the cold, vibrating machines, the hum constantly reminded her of lurking dangers. Every movement was deliberate; she moved like prey in a predator's den, her gaze steady and watchful, like a hunter stalking, ready for anything that could come out of the shadows.

She paused near the industrial dryer, loading damp sheets, when a hiss of tension sliced through the hum.

Two inmates, Red and Trina, stood shoulder to shoulder by the folding table, voices low, faces tight.

"You ran your mouth," Red growled, her fingers curling around a folded bedsheet like it was something sharper.

"I didn't say your name," Trina muttered, eyes darting.

"You didn't have to."

Madison stilled, one hand inside the dryer. No one else moved. The machines thudded on, oblivious.

Then, in a blink, Red slammed the sheet down, and a blade flashed beneath it, no bigger than a box cutter, but bright as vengeance.

"Keep my name outta anything," Red said flatly, not raising her voice. "Next time, I won't warn you."

Trina swallowed hard and stepped back.

The entire exchange lasted seconds, but Madison's pulse roared in her ears. She turned back to her work, head low, movements smooth.

Rule #4: *Witness everything. React to nothing.*

Madison never suspected that Sgt. Wallace was secretly working behind the scenes to get her transferred to the kitchen.

CHAPTER
TWENTY-THREE
MARCH 23, 2015

Pendleton's Kitchen Assignment
5:30 a.m.

AT FIRST, it felt like punishment. It became something else entirely.

On her first day in the kitchen, they gave her a dull knife and instructed her to "make herself useful." Her hands hovered over the chopping board, unsure. The weight of the blade brought back memories, not of violence, but of Salmon Croquettes.

Coby's favorite.

She chopped slowly, onion first, then celery, her motions deliberate, precise. The aroma rose, sharp and earthy, curling into her nose and stinging her eyes. For the first time in months, she felt it: control. Not over her sentence. Not over the rumors or the whispers. But over something.

Heat.

Flavor.

Memory.

She had once hosted charity galas in silk gowns, paired wine with oysters, and corrected plating on hors d'oeuvres beside private chefs flown in from France. Now, she stirred dented pots with warped spoons, using powdered seasonings and dull knives on a broken stove.

Still, they lined up.

From the corner, a voice murmured, "You taste that sage?"

"Girl," another woman replied, mouth full, "whatever she made? I'd fight somebody over seconds."

There was laughter, low and surprised.

Madison didn't smile. But she stirred a little slower, savoring the hush that followed.

They didn't like her. But they ate every bite.

And in prison, that was its kind of power.

Each day, the kitchen felt like it belonged only to her. Madison had rituals to stay grounded, tying her hair, humming jazz, and washing her station twice. She remembered preparing ten-course galas with expensive floral arrangements. But this? This was real. Here, every chopped onion and pinch of salt reminded her she was alive and had choices, even if limited to flavors.

She started exchanging recipes with another inmate known as "Mama Jo," who had previously owned a soul food shack near Detroit. With a hearty laugh and scars on her arms hinting at untold stories, Mama Jo commanded attention. She was serving a fifteen-year stint for killing a man with a cast-iron skillet, though she'd always said, "*He had it coming, and I seasoned it first.*"

Madison never asked for details.

Some recipes were better left untold.

Though the two women lacked genuine trust, they shared a profound understanding of flavor.

That was enough.

One day, Mama Jo leaned in and muttered, "You ever make biscuits with no buttermilk? Prison magic."

Madison smirked. "Show me."

A silent partnership developed based on survival rather than friendship or alliance. They competed: who could make the most out of the few ingredients? Who could extract the most incredible comfort from the smallest rations?

Madison never discussed her past, and Mama Jo never inquired. Their unspoken rule was clear: it didn't matter where you came from, only what you could create with a pot and a burner.

Some days, Madison cooked with muscle memory alone. Other days, she let herself feel, really feel, the crack of an egg, the sting of steam, and the smell of rosemary crushed between her fingers.

She began mentally jotting down notes, as if she were still crafting a menu or composing recipes that would never see the light of day: Cream of corn soup with chili flakes and garlic powder. Substitute powdered milk for cream. Add cayenne when no one's looking. Serve hot with an apology.

Fried cabbage with onions, sugar, and vinegar. Remember to taste before you serve. Remember to smile.

She had just finished stirring a vat of chili when she caught the tail end of a conversation.

It drifted in from the corner of the kitchen, near the dish pit where two women scrubbed trays with too much force and not enough soap.

"She's real quiet, huh?" one said, her voice low but cutting.

"Too quiet," the other replied. "You know what they say about the quiet ones."

Madison kept her back turned, with her hands instinctively ladling, stirring, and adjusting the heat, while her ears remained sharp.

"She don't talk cause her bougie ass did it," said a third voice, closer now.

"Murdered her husband."

Someone else scoffed, "That's not true!"

"She's crazy, that's why they gave her such a short sentence. PTSD or whatever rich folks get."

She shook her head, her fingers gripping the ladle's handle, and dared not say aloud, "All wrong."

But silence had a way of inviting others to fill the gaps. And they invariably did. Loudly, eagerly, with style. Her jaw remained tight, her back straight as a rod. She stirred the chili carefully, as if it might burn her if she wasn't careful.

Mama Jo appeared beside her a moment later, drying her hands on a towel.

"They talkin' shit again?" she asked, not bothering to whisper.

Madison gave a slight nod.

"Good. Means they're scared of you." And with that, Mama Jo walked away.

Madison took a breath, then sampled the chili, tweaked the spice level, and continued cooking.

Her act of rebellion.

When cursed at, she kept cooking. When doubted, she served her dishes with pride. She didn't aim to deliver justice, retribution, or solutions. Instead, she offered comfort food, which held significance in this cold, concrete place. People mocked her while licking their fingers.

They were sure of one thing: despite her stubborn silence, she handled a knife in the prison kitchen like a master chef.

But before Pendleton.

There was another silence.

Another knife blade.

CHAPTER
TWENTY-FOUR
JANUARY 18, 1981

Foster Home
9:38 p.m.

AT SIXTEEN, she desperately fought for her freedom, leaving behind a permanent bloodstain. It wasn't a thought-out choice but a primal survival instinct driven by intense fear. In a spontaneous act of protecting innocence, Madison thrust a blade into the back of the man who was supposed to be a protector of children in his foster care.

Instead, he had been the predator lurking among them, a shadow weaving itself into the fabric of their fragile world.

The foster father, the one with the devout smile and dark, clutching hands, had trapped the smallest of them, a quaking ten-year-old boy whose fear saturated the atmosphere like spilled ink. Madison recalled the boy's silent cries, with his tiny fists pressed against his mouth to stifle them.

And then everything shattered.

She noticed the knife's glimmer on the kitchen counter, the very knife she'd used to peel apples earlier that day. Instinctively, her hand grasped it, the blade becoming an extension of her rage and fear.

She hadn't intended to kill.

She hadn't even aimed to engage in a fight.

But the moment his hands gripped that child's shoulder, something inside her broke. A cord of restraint stretched too thin for too long.

The blade plunged between his ribs with a wet sound like splitting wood. His gasp, half surprise, half rage, still haunted her sleep. His body crumpled forward, dragging the child down with him. Madison pulled the boy free, shoving him into Nina's arms.

"Run," she whispered, her voice shaking. "Don't look back."

The aftermath of that night lingered in the narrow, shadowy alleys of her mind. Every memory was as sharp as the blade she had used, etching itself into her bones like an unshakeable scar. The metallic scent of blood, the heavy silence following his fall, and the tremor in her hands. These details remained vivid.

Yet, it wasn't the cold steel that had ultimately saved her. No.

It was the intervention of the local outreach program for troubled youth that became her lifeline. Seeing not just a violent past but a future worth redeeming...

So, she thought.

They instilled in her the belief that she was more than the sum of her mistakes, that she could reshape her narrative. It was a lifeline she had clung to during that time, whispering promises of hope in the darkness that threatened to engulf her.

"I escaped it once," she muttered one night, chopping vegetables for the next day's soup. "I thought I was buying myself a better life.

Instead, I bought a delay."

PART SIX
STORMS PASS

CHAPTER
TWENTY-FIVE
AUGUST 14, 2017

Madison's Cell,
4:21 a.m.

THE MOMENT the cell door clanked shut behind her, Madison crumpled. The breath she'd held through Morgan's visit shattered into sobs she couldn't control. Her palms pressed against her face as if she could hold herself together, but it was too late.

The truth had cracked something wide open.

"She's alive. My baby is alive.".

The words pulsed through her like a second heartbeat, jagged and unbearable.

At thirteen, others broke her quietly, lied to her, hushed her into silence, and buried her grief under shame and obedience.

No funeral.

No goodbye.

They expected her to forget the void.

And now that void had a face, a voice, a fury.

Madison shook with the weight of it all: the years stolen, the lies told, the aching thought that her daughter had walked the world thinking her mother abandoned her. Hot tears soaked her hands as a deep cry escaped her throat, one she hadn't allowed herself in years.

Not when they took the baby. Not when they locked her up. Not until now.

Her sobs quieted into shallow breaths, her body hollowed by the storm she'd finally let break. In the silence that followed, memory crept in a little less raw, but no less unsettling.

The visit with Mister Mayor.

His smile had been soft, almost paternal, but behind his eyes she'd sensed something else.

Something calculating.

As her thoughts shifted, so did the weight of his request.

The last time she'd sat across that table.

CHAPTER
TWENTY-SIX
MARCH 10, 2017

Pendleton's Visitor Room
1:30 p.m.

THEY CALLED HER NAME; the guard's voice cracked like a whip, and she didn't resist. She followed them down the stark hallway, each step echoing like a confession. The thought of someone from her past witnessing her in shackles and shame was almost unbearable. Familiar eyes tracing her diminished form, where confidence once thrived, now revealed vulnerability, twisting her stomach.

Her prison-issued garb hung loosely on her frame, a constant reminder of the life she used to lead and the freedom she had lost. The way her hair was pulled back, stripped of any adornment, felt like an attempt to erase the woman she once was, the vibrant individual who laughed freely and loved deeply. Each element of her appearance screamed at her degradation, amplifying her sense of humiliation and despair. She had fought against the tide of emotions, desperate to hold on to a fragment of her former self, yet feeling utterly exposed in such scrutiny.

And as she entered the visitation room, her breath caught, not because of where she was, but because of who was waiting.

Mister Mayor.

Even hunched over, with an oxygen tank wheezing at his side, she recognized him instantly. Though he was stooped and shrunken, she recognized his silhouette instantly; it was etched in her memory like a signature in stone. His shoulders no longer squared with the defiant authority she remembered, and his once-bright eyes, which had seen through her silence all those years ago, were dulled by time and illness.

Yet, there was still that spark, dormant, but defiant.

The hiss of the oxygen filled the quiet like a metronome, marking each second they had left. His dark felt hat was the same, though it sagged with age, and his coat hung from his frame like it remembered the stronger man it once embraced.

"You shouldn't have come," she said, her voice cracking beneath the weight of her shame.

"I had to," he rasped, the air slicing through his words.

"I didn't want you to see me this way." She lowered her head as she spoke.

But he shook his head, a faint smile curling his lips. "I didn't come to see who you are now," he said faintly. "I came to remind you who you still are."

His hands trembled slightly as he folded them on the cold metal table, and when he reached for her, his touch was light but insistent. His thumb brushed her knuckles as if to say, I see you beneath this.

"I don't know why you didn't defend yourself," he murmured, voice heavy with sorrow and unspoken questions. "But I know you, and I want you to come home."

She swallowed hard, her throat thick with unshed words. "That doesn't matter anymore," she whispered.

"It does to me," he said firmly.

"Pine Ridge won't want me back," she said, bitterness tightening her chest.

"I built Pine Ridge for people like you," he said, his voice gaining strength despite the oxygen hiss. People, they tried to erase."

He slid a small, weathered business card across the table. The card displayed his attorney's name in crisp black ink.

"Reach out to him when you're released," he said, his voice gravelly but steady.

"I've left a package for you. A lifeline."

His breath trembled, and he leaned back with effort.

"In the meantime," he said, his tone softening but tinged with irony, "think about what I asked. You're no stranger to starting over."

As he rose to leave, his frail hand lingered on the table's edge, as if anchoring himself to her one last time.

"Storms pass," a faint smile curling the corner of his mouth. "You don't have to."

After she met with Mister Mayor and long after the final headcount, as the overhead lights dimmed, she sat on the edge of her bunk with a pencil stub and a sheet from the prison-issued notepad.

It had been years since she had written anything personal.

Not a diary.

Not a prayer.

But Mister Mayor's visit had stirred something too raw to ignore.

So, she wrote, not because she believed it would fix anything, but because, for once, the silence inside her felt like it needed answering.

Letter to herself.

Dear Maddie,

I don't know if I'm writing to the woman I was, the one I might still be, or both.

Here, they call me "Convict." Inmate #39178. The boogie brat bitch. The woman who didn't cry when the verdict dropped.

To them, I'm a ghost. But you and I know the truth.

I cried long before the trial.

Every time I buried a piece of myself to keep a lie alive.

For a long time, I thought silence meant survival.

If I stayed small enough, obedient enough, righteous enough—maybe no one would question the hollowness inside me. Perhaps I could outrun the ache by performing.

I was wrong.

What I did. What I lost. It still wakes me.

Not just Coby. Not just Nina.

You. I lost you, Maddie.

The woman who once believed joy was something more than a sermon or a duty.

And tonight… he came. Harper Lewis White.

Mister Mayor. Frail in body, stronger than I've ever seen him.

He didn't look through me. He looked at me.

Called me by a name I haven't heard since sentencing.

Nina Autumn Storm.

He reminded me I was once a storm.

And not all storms destroy. Some clear the path.

So I'm writing this to say: I remember you. I forgive you.

And I'm not giving up on you.

Not now. Not after everything.

Love,

Me

Days later, the letter to herself stayed unread, carefully folded under the thin mattress. It offered some relief, but not healing. What remained now was Coby. Sometimes, she could almost sense his presence in the early dawn or hear the gentle clink of a breakfast tray in the corridor.

This time, the words arrived not as a reflection but as a confession, a letter to the boy she lost and the part of herself she buried with him.

Letter to Coby

Written three days after Mister Mayor's visit.

Dear Coby,

I don't know where to begin.

Not because I lack the words, but because they come too fast.

Too loud.

I failed you. Not just the night you died, long before.

I let myself become a woman who smiles in pictures, and drowns in private.

Who let grief disguise itself as faith.

You were the last thing I ever loved out loud.

And I'm scared I've forgotten how.

I think about your laugh more than your voice.

Isn't that strange?

It filled every corner of a room before your footsteps even got there.

How you danced through the kitchen, music blasting, seasoning flying, swearing your pineapple upside-down cake could make a Food Network judge weep.

And it would've, baby. It would've.

Sometimes I hear you in the clatter of dishes, the shuffle of feet in hallways that don't exist.

And I wonder... would you recognize me now?

Would you forgive me?

They told me to find peace. That you're "in a better place."

But I never wanted you in a better place.

I wanted you here. Just one more night.

One more argument about pie crust or Kendrick lyrics.

One more call that starts with, "Hey, Ma," and ends with "Love you."

I remember the last thing you cooked, shrimp and grits.

You wiped the plate, bowed, and said, "Presentation is everything."

God, I hope you knew I saw you.

All of you.

Even when I didn't know how to say it.

I didn't just lose a son that night.

I lost the last piece of me that remembered how to live without apology.

But maybe that's why I have to try again.

Not to replace you, never that.

But to become the woman you would've been proud to know.

Love,

Mom

No envelopes or stamps needed.

Mailing them wasn't the plan, and when she folded them both and tucked them away, something inside her settled.

Not healed. Not yet.

But clearer. Steadier.

The next day, an undeniable anticipation filled the air as she made a daring request.

Her first phone call in three long years from the Pendleton Women's Federal Prison. With shaking fingers, she dialed the numbers written on the business card Mister Mayor had given her, each ring amplifying the uncertainty of what awaited her on the other end.

Holding the receiver and nervously tugging the cord from the phone attached to the cement wall, she waited for someone to answer, whispering to herself, *"Ok, Mister Mayor. I am coming home."*

In that quiet moment, her thoughts returned to that corner booth at the Landing Diner a year after settling into Pine Ridge. The morning sun cast a long shadow on the linoleum as they shared pecan pie and strong coffee. Mister Mayor made the offer that would change her life and solidify her place in Pine Ridge.

CHAPTER
TWENTY-SEVEN
SEPTEMBER 26, 2010

The Landing Diner
7:15 a.m.

"AUTUMN, have you ever thought about taking over this place?"

She blinked. "Taking over?"

"The diner. The whole thing. I've been leasing it to people for years. It's been profitable and has a good system. But you..." He paused, spoon in hand. "You belong to this place."

She didn't answer right away.

"I know you came here to start over. Not to stay. However, Pine Ridge has a way of selecting individuals. Have you ever noticed that?"

She looked out the window. Snow was falling in soft, slow flakes.

"I gave up owning things," she whispered, shaking her head.

"Maybe. But things still want to belong to you."

During her years in Pine Ridge, she never shared details of her past. The residents may have been curious initially, but a heavy, respectful silence lingered. Glances exchanged held questions, yet nobody asked directly.

Not after witnessing Mister Mayor's calm, strong, and protective demeanor. It was clear: If she had something to say, she'd say it when she was ready.

However, shortly after his offer, she revealed something.

She disclosed, her voice quivering and hands shaking, that she possessed $150,000 in cash with her.

"I want to buy the diner and stay," she said, urgency clear in her tone.

A wave of anxiety washed over her as she worried about the implications of her confession. What if he asked her about the money's origin? What if he suspected she stole it? Or worse, what if he saw her as a fugitive, running from something terrible?

To her astonishment, Mister Mayor remained unmoved.

A week later, while they were enjoying pie and coffee after closing, he quietly pushed her plate aside and placed a document in front of her.

PURCHASE AGREEMENT

"Ultimately, you, Autumn Storm, consent to buy The Landing Diner, which includes the building, equipment, and all furnishings, for a selling price of one dollar," he said with a laugh.

"Fair deal?"

She stared at him, speechless.

Tears filled her eyes, surprising, warm, and abundant.

He leaned closer, pressing his palm against hers, and whispered words that shattered her composure completely.

"Baby girl."

That voice. The tone. The timing.

Not just her father's, but someone else's. Someone from long ago.

Suddenly, she was age ten again, standing at the edge of her parents' funeral.

The cemetery smelled of wet leaves and mud. Two caskets rested beneath a sagging velvet tent. Adults whispered around her, but none met her gaze.

Her tears had dried hours earlier. Her mother's lace gloves swallowed her fingers, still faintly scented with rosewater. Patent leather shoes pinched her toes. She stood still, trying not to feel anything.

Then, a hand on her shoulder.

She turned.

A man knelt beside her. Graying beard. Soaked coat hem. Breath like bourbon and cigarettes.

No scripture. No sermon.

Just this: *"Even this, baby girl... even this gets better."*

Something inside her, tight as wire, unwound.

He looked at her and saw her. Not the orphan. Not the grief. Just... Madison.

She opened her mouth to speak, but the social worker's hand closed over hers like a trap, yanking her away. She stumbled through the grass, her tights ripping at the knees, her head twisting back to find him.

He stood still, hand raised in quiet blessing, cigarette between two fingers, coat flaring in the wind like wings.

She never saw him again.

But she never forgot.

And now, hearing those exact words, *baby girl*, after all these years, something deep inside her shifted. Mister Mayor never questioned the money's source. Instead, he proposed she invest it in expanding the diner to include a bakery.

"Any pie that tastes that good has a story," he told her. "And each bite feels like home."

During the town's celebration of *The Landing Diner & Bakery's* first anniversary, amidst the laughter, clinking glasses, and the smell of cinnamon and sugar, Madison felt a rare stillness settle over her. Surrounded by joy and echoes of hard-won memories, she found herself unexpectedly vulnerable.

In a quiet moment, away from the speeches and smiles, she turned to Mister Mayor. And for the first time, she invited him past the polished storefront and curated recipes, into the part of her life she had once tried to outrun, the girl she used to be, the family she lost, and the legacy baked into every pie crust and handwritten menu.

"You know, Mister Mayor," Madison began, her voice softer than usual, "people think I built this place on pie and cake, but it's more than flour and sugar. It's a legacy. It's memory."

She glanced out the small window, her expression distant but steady.

"When we started expanding the diner's offerings, when the demand for Papa's Pecan Pie and NaNa's Lemon Coconut Cake took off... it felt like something long gone was being reborn."

Tears welled in her eyes as she continued, her voice low. "You were there, steady, committed, helping me test recipes, keeping me calm when it all got overwhelming. But for me, it wasn't just business. It felt like pieces of my family were coming back to life."

She paused, fingers tracing the faint scar on her wrist as she unfolded a few carefully wrapped items. Her voice softened. "My parents ran a steakhouse and jazz club, full of music, food, and laughter. That place was everything to us. Then, when I was ten, someone murdered my parents. They were gone. And before my tears dried, so was the club, the house, the life I knew."

She swallowed hard.

Besides a trust fund I couldn't access until I was twenty-one, I only had a leather-bound photo album. Inside were grease-stained notes, black-and-white photos, and recipes written in my grandmother's hand. That book was my only reminder of who I was before the system reduced me to a case file.

Her eyes met his now, filled with both warmth and a warning not to pity her.

"I smile every time someone buys my Papa's Pecan Pie. They're tasting sweetness, but I'm basking in the meaning. Comfort. Family. Sunday nights that smelled like sugar and safety."

She had worried that sharing too much would give her away. But now? In the presence of Mister Mayor, she felt no threat in remembering.

"Mister Mayor, my momma had three dishes she could cook, and one was always the main dish on Sunday. Chicken and dumplings, spaghetti and meatballs, or salmon croquettes, but dessert was my daddy's. He'd toast whole pecans in butter, never pieces. Said broken nuts didn't belong in a perfect pie."

Then, almost out of habit, she glanced over her shoulder, as if expecting someone to be watching, and lowered her voice.

"Daddy would sneak a look around the kitchen, put a finger to his lips, and whisper, 'Shhh…'" She smiled faintly. "I'd whisper back, like it was a secret just for us."

The memory hung in the air for a moment. Her smile lingered, then faded, just slightly like a light dimmed by a passing shadow.

Whenever he mixed the pie filling, he would wink and say, "Baby girl, the butter for the savor, but now go get the flavor!"

Her body moved as if muscle memory took over, shoulders shifting, hands miming the rhythm of old motions.

"That was my cue," she said, a quiet smile tugging at her lips. "I'd hop down from the stool, race over to the bar cart, and grab the bourbon. Just a splash for the pie…"

She paused, eyes flickering with something softer.

"…and a full shot for Daddy. That was the mystery ingredient."

Bourbon.

Strangely, Madison never drank bourbon.

To her, it wasn't just liquor; it was a line. A warning. A memory that split sweet from sharp.

She remembered that night clearly, the one tucked behind every version of "Papa's Pecan Pie." It had started like so many others: chicken and dumplings, laughter in the kitchen, the scent of brown sugar rising from the oven. Her father had been soft-spoken that day, humming as he cooked, sneaking her a spoonful of filling like they were sharing a secret.

Then the phone rang.

Short. Tense. Angry.

She could still hear the clatter of the receiver slamming against the wall.

Her mother asked what was wrong.

He shoved her.

No warning. No shouting. Just a shove. And then he walked out the door like nothing had happened.

The next morning, they drove Madison to school, her mother's hand on the wheel, her father quiet beside her.

A few hours later, they were dead.

She was too young to understand the details.

But she remembered the bourbon.

And she remembered making herself a promise.

No bourbon. Ever.

Years later, when customers at the diner raved about Papa's Pecan Pie, she smiled politely. Let them savor the sweetness. Let them think it was just a recipe.

They didn't know that ashes don't tell everything, or that silence can hide the cost of making bitterness taste like home.

PART SEVEN
THE MUGSHOT THAT CHANGED EVERYTHING

CHAPTER
TWENTY-EIGHT

DECEMBER 11, 2014

Minnesota District Attorney's Office
9:20 a.m.

JUST SIX MONTHS had passed since Morgan Marie Bennis-Alcott had returned to Minnesota following a painful divorce, a stretch that drained her emotionally and mentally. Driven to revive her career, she took on a demanding role in the District Attorney's office, hoping it would offer a clean slate and renewed purpose.

She did not know that her first major case would soon arrive with a powerful impact: the infamous case file of The State vs. Madison Jackson Winter, widely known to the public as the mysterious Nina Autumn Storm.

This case garnered statewide and national attention for its sensational nature, turning into a media spectacle. The defense team argued that relentless media coverage had poisoned the Wisconsin jury pool and pushed for a Minnesota venue. Every ADA wanted it, as it could make or break their careers, with the trial unfolding live for millions to see.

In the bullpen of the DA's office, chatter buzzed louder than the fluorescents.

"The entire country's watching," muttered ADA Lin, sipping cold coffee as he scrolled headlines on his tablet. 'Winter Woman: Killer or Martyr?' blared one title.

"Everyone wants it," replied Taylor, adjusting her blazer and glancing toward the corner office. "You land this case; you don't just make partner. You make headlines."

"Or you crash and burn on live TV," Lin said, smirking. "No pressure."

Morgan Marie Bennis-Alcott walked past them, a file tucked under her arm, face unreadable. The room quieted, just for a beat.

"She's got it," someone whispered.

Taylor rolled her eyes. "Of course she does. Queen Morgan. Perfect for TV."

Lin nodded. "Yeah. But the thing is, she's not here for the spotlight. She's here for blood."

Rumors of book deals and movie adaptations buzzed through the courthouse, energizing the scene. Producers watched closely, eager to profit from public interest. Reporters bombarded the office with interview requests, hungry for a story or exclusive insights.

Amid the frenzy, Morgan quietly approached her supervisor to request formal recusal from the case just days into preparation, leaving her colleagues in shocked disbelief. They gaped, unable to understand why she would willingly forfeit such a monumental opportunity that could propel her into the spotlight. How could she turn her back on a career-making trial that others would kill to join?

Morgan had her reasons, a truth she wasn't ready to face. When she opened the file, her breath caught. The mugshot. Staring back was a face too familiar, a tilted head, full lips, arched brows. It was like looking in a mirror. *"Why did nobody else see it?"*

She had seen blurry glimpses of the defendant on the evening news, always half-hidden behind security guards or camera flashes. But this was the first time she had seen her.

Clearly. Unfiltered. She shut the file, trembling, then approached the window, gazing at the void. Her stomach twisted. No, it couldn't be just a coincidence, a resemblance, nothing more.

She hesitated before reopening the file and studying the names:

Madison Jackson Winter, alias Nina Autumn Storm, maiden name Madison Jackson Malone.

That name "Malone" hit her like a wave, familiar, encoded in her blood, a whisper from a past she never fully understood.

Over the next few days, she delved into the archives, working late after the office closed. Her fingers moved swiftly across the keyboard, navigating a hospital's outdated database.

And then there it was.

A redacted file appeared.

Jane Doe.

Thirteen and a half years old.

Admitted: August 12, 1978.

Diagnosis: Labor.

Outcome: Stillbirth.

No burial record. No next of kin.

And scribbled in the margin... M. Malone.

The date of her birth. Her breath hitched, hands cold. She stared at the screen.

She sank into her office chair, her knees folding as if someone had kicked them out from beneath her. Her fingers trembled over the mouse, but the screen had already blurred, her vision tunneled to the echo of a single thought, *"Who am I, then?"*

Her life centered on a straightforward narrative: adoption, loss, and gratitude. She felt chosen, believing her mother had died during childbirth, and that she was the phoenix emerging from someone else's tragedy.

Now? She wasn't even sure her name was hers.

She closed her eyes, trying to summon her childhood bedroom. Pink walls, books alphabetized, trophies lined meticulously on the shelf. Dusty called it "The Museum of Morgan," a testament to their proud, precious daughter, our miracle, our diplomat. Yet, beneath the memories, a question lingered: was it all a carefully crafted deception?

Minnie told her, after a high school breakup, that she was "born to lead, not bleed."

There was a photo of Dusty's campaign featuring them together, smiling like the ideal American family. Even then, she sensed that something lingered just beyond the edge of every frame; something unspoken.

And now she understood. Madison, her mother, had always been present in her life. Yet, someone had decided she wasn't fit to raise her. A wave of anger washed over her, feeling slow and unfamiliar. This wasn't the courtroom anger or righteous fury she knew; it was a deeply personal, raw emotion.

How many times had she looked at her reflection in the mirror, wondering why her smile felt strange? Why did her sadness seem to have no apparent cause yet never entirely go away?

The answer stayed hidden in a folder beneath a redacted line for all these years. Concealed like a wound, everyone preferred to ignore it. And now?

She wasn't merely an attorney working on a high-profile case. She was also a daughter, lost, and seeking answers. Morgan traced her finger over the mugshot as if she could feel the truth through the glass. She whispered, "I found you."

Someone had torn her away from her mother; she had spent thirty-seven years living a beautiful, polished falsehood.

Morgan always knew she was adopted; it wasn't a secret or something to hide. It couldn't, considering her adoptive parents were white. They explained that her birth mother died in childbirth and her father's identity was unknown; this story, meant to protect her, explained her family's different appearance.

Minnie, her adoptive mother, lost the ability to have children because of a childhood illness. After years of unsuccessful fertility treatments, she and her husband, Dusty, opted for private adoption.

On August 12, 1978, the call came early in the morning. A woman had died giving birth, leaving behind a healthy baby girl with no relatives. They rushed to the hospital. In the nursery, Minnie immediately identified a beautiful, brown-skinned baby with thick, curly black hair and claimed her as theirs. Dusty stood quietly nearby, accompanied by his best friend and longtime driver, Uncle Dunk, who later told Morgan, "I knew you were special when you opened those big eyes and didn't cry."

Morgan Marie Bennis-Alcott.

Her adoptive parents were not just a political couple; they were a machine. Dusty Alcott, the outsider turned Governor of Minnesota, and Minnie Bennis-Alcott, the real strategist behind every headline. Their ambition wasn't loud, but it was relentless, forged in back rooms, polished in press conferences, and cemented in campaign wins.

But in private, their partnership was something else entirely, sharper, more transactional, sometimes tender, always calculated.

One evening, as Dusty prepared for a televised address with Minnie adjusting his tie, he casually mentioned with a hint of sharpness, "They'll never say it out loud, but I'm still the California transplant. Even after the governorship."

Minnie stepped back, gently grabbing both his hands and shaking them. "Then stop trying to win their affection and focus on what truly matters."

He responded, "And what's that, Min?"

She met his eyes. "Legacy."

He laughed, low. "Easy for you to say. You were born into this machine. I had to build my spot from scratch."

"You married into it," she said pointedly, crossing the room. "And I made sure you didn't waste it."

Dusty exhaled, softer now. "You ever wish it wasn't all strategy?"

She smiled thinly. "No. Power is protection. I learned that young."

He looked at her, studied her face. "You think I would've made it without you?"

Minnie tilted her head, voice cool. "Not a chance."

A familiar voice from outside the door said, "Governor, it's time."

Uncle Dunk.

He wasn't blood, but he was family in every way that counted, a steady, unshakable presence. His bond with Dusty stretched back to sun-soaked Southern California: Dusty, the winemaker's privileged son; Uncle Dunk, the preacher's kid, raised on hard truths. Their friendship sparked in high school over basketball, jazz, and loud political debates shared over milkshakes.

For a while, Uncle Dunk looked headed to the NBA. Scouts called. Highlights dazzled. Then a drunk driver shattered his pelvis and his future.

Dusty never treated him like a broken promise. When he moved to Minnesota to start his law career, he hired Uncle Dunk not out of pity, but loyalty. Gave him work as his driver and security, a cottage on the property, and more than anything, dignity.

In return, Uncle Dunk gave him unwavering loyalty and gave Morgan something rarer: the truth. Honest, unvarnished, and real. In a world of performance, Uncle Dunk never played.

To Morgan, Uncle Dunk was more than a fixture; he was her compass. He faced uncomfortable truths head-on. Teaching her love could be solid without being soft. He called her out, challenged her doubts, and celebrated her wins, constantly reminding her of her roots.

His affection, sharp-witted and wise, pulled her back to clarity amid pressure. Not with grand gestures, but a look, a word, a timely, "Nah, baby girl, that ain't it."

And that was enough.

One evening, after a grueling debate tournament in high school, where Morgan had taken first place but stormed out before the applause, she found Uncle Dunk leaning against his truck, arms folded, waiting.

She didn't speak at first. Just crossed her arms and kicked at the gravel.

"You win and still mad?" he asked, one eyebrow raised.

She sighed. "They only clapped because of my last name."

He snorted. "No, they clapped 'cause you carved that smug little Harvard boy up like Sunday brisket."

Morgan looked away. "Doesn't count if I had to become someone I'm not, just to get through it."

Uncle Dunk nodded, slow and steady. "Then stop pretending to be someone you're not. But don't you ever shrink for folk who don't know how to carry your light."

She blinked.

Then he added, "You lead, baby girl. Even when it's lonely up front."

CHAPTER
TWENTY-NINE
JUNE 5, 1986

Bennis-Alcott Estate
1:37 p.m.

FOLLOWING UNCLE DUNK'S ADVICE, Dusty persuaded Minnie to hire his aunt, Miss Lovie, as Madison's caregiver. Since all the house staff were white, it was crucial to have someone who could meet Minnie's care needs while also building a cultural connection with Morgan.

Miss Lovie's granddaughter, Janet, often visited. Although she and Morgan were the same age, they couldn't be more different.

One afternoon, Janet, who had been suspended from school and was furious, destroyed Morgan's dollhouse.

"You're not white. Why you tryin' to be white?"

She shoved Morgan to the floor and, without warning, began hacking away at her thick, curly hair with dull scissors. Tears streamed down Morgan's cheeks, silent and hot, as dark coils fell around her like pieces of herself.

When it was over, she looked up, past the jagged edges of her ruined hair, at her shattered dollhouse, shattered across the carpet like it had meant nothing at all. At that moment, something in her broke. Not just the toys. Not just the hair.

The trust. The innocence. The safety.

Dusty and Minnie rushed in, sending it into chaos. Adults screamed at one another over the incident and what actions to take, but Morgan would always recall Minnie's shriek,

"This is unacceptable! Look at her!

How is she supposed to go to school looking like this?"

"SHUT UP!" Dusty shouted. "Do you hear yourself?"

"Why are you shouting at me?" she snapped back. "What do you mean, do I hear myself?"

"DO YOU SEE HER?" she shouted!

The silence that followed cracked through the room like lightning after a storm.

Dusty had never raised a hand before, not to Morgan, not to anyone, but the sight of his daughter sobbing on the floor, surrounded by curls and broken pieces, had pushed something too deep to hold back.

He scooped Morgan into his arms, her small body trembling against his chest. Then, towering over Minnie, his voice low but seething, he jabbed a finger into her forehead.

"You selfish bitch," he said, each word sharp, controlled. "I've loved you enough to excuse your issues, but don't you dare project them onto this beautiful little girl."

Minnie stumbled back, wide-eyed but silent.

The room froze. The air went thick.

No one moved. No one spoke.

That moment didn't end. It just settled into the walls, into the silences that filled the house afterward, tight-lipped breakfasts, hollow I-love-you's, and doors closed a little harder than before.

Morgan never asked if things went back to normal.

Because they didn't.

They just went quiet.

Miss Lovie's granddaughter, Janet, didn't return to the Bennis-Alcott home for what felt like an eternity to Morgan.

When she finally did, it was as though she had crossed some invisible threshold. Unspoken words, thick with tension, hung between them like ghosts. Their eyes met, and in that silent exchange, they both knew they were walking on the jagged edge of a memory neither dared to voice.

It was the memory of that one fateful day they had buried so deep beneath shared laughter and protective lies, they'd almost convinced themselves it no longer existed.

Almost.

Something had shifted between them that day, a fracture that had never truly healed, no matter how fiercely they held onto their friendship.

And yet, Morgan and Janet had emerged from those shadows not just as friends, but as soul sisters, a bond tempered by fire, unyielding and unbreakable. Their friendship wasn't delicate. It was a fortress, scarred and steadfast, built on years of shared secrets and silent understanding.

So, when Morgan's voice trembled, just slightly, but enough for Janet to hear the urgency buried beneath the request, when she said,

Keep an eye on her. Madison Jackson Winter.

Janet didn't hesitate.

She didn't ask questions. Didn't press for explanations.

She understood the weight behind Morgan's words.

Morgan didn't need to explain why.

Janet already knew that if Morgan was asking, it mattered.

And when something mattered to Morgan, it became a sacred duty to Janet.

So, she pulled on her uniform, Sergeant Janet Wallace, and she made it her mission to protect,

Convict Madison Jackson Winter.

Not because she fully grasped the truth or truly knew who she was. But Morgan's faith in this woman was enough to steady Janet amidst the chaos. She would protect Madison not only with her badge but also with the quiet resolve of a vow made long ago.

A vow that, whatever ghosts Morgan faced, Janet would stand as a barrier between them and what the future held.

CHAPTER
THIRTY

JUNE 7, 1986

Ride to Lady Shay's Salon
9:20 a.m.

AFTER THE DOLLHOUSE was destroyed and Morgan's hair chopped off, Uncle Dunk took Dusty and Morgan to a hair salon in what Dusty called the "inner city," a phrase that Morgan would later discover was coded language for the neighborhood where most Black people lived.

That morning, as they rumbled along cracked streets under a sky streaked with gray, Morgan pressed her forehead to the cool window glass. Outside, murals stretched across brick buildings, bold faces with halos of color, fists raised, eyes full of fire. They clung to weathered walls like memory. Below, laundry fluttered between balconies like prayer flags, and street vendors arranged their tables with incense, beaded jewelry, sweet mango, and roasted peanuts, the air humming with scent and rhythm.

Music pulsed from open doorways, bass-heavy and alive. On a street corner, a group of teens lounged near a corner store. Their boom box blared a Marvin Gaye track, the bass vibrating in the soles of Morgan's shoes. One boy tossed a basketball between his hands while another picked at a bag of chips, his laughter rising above the beat.

As their car slowed to a stop in front of the store, a girl in cutoff jeans leaned toward the street and nudged her friend.

"That's a whole Bentley," she said, smirking. "Bet they lost."

The others laughed, but it wasn't cruel. Just curious.

"Nah, that's Uncle Dunk's people," one of the older boys said, nodding toward the car. "Respect. Don't front."

The girl looked again, her eyes landing on Morgan, who quickly looked away.

Uncle Dunk turned from the wheel. "Stay put," he said, climbing out and heading into the store.

Morgan and Dusty sat in silence. The heater hummed. The music outside shifted to something slower, something full of longing.

Dusty cleared his throat. "You okay, sweetheart?"

Morgan didn't answer. She just watched the group on the corner as the girl caught her eye again, this time not with judgment, but with something like recognition. A nod. A small one.

Morgan returned it before turning back.

For the first time in days, she didn't feel like a broken doll.

A few minutes later, Uncle Dunk reappeared, carrying a small brown paper bag. He climbed back into the car, handed the bag to Dusty with a knowing grin, and said,

"Here you go."

Dusty laughed, pulling out a bag of M&M's, then passed it to Morgan.

"You're my M&M," he said with a smile.

Morgan tore her gaze from the window and looked at him, confused but curious. She listened, though her mind still buzzed with the sights and sounds outside, so different from the sterile, silent world of the Bennis-Alcott house.

"You see, all these candies are different colors on the outside, but they're the same sweet chocolate on the inside."

She listened, but truthfully, she was more caught up in the rare thrill of eating candy in the morning, something Minnie would never approve of. Still, Dusty's following words would return to her often throughout her life, especially when she encountered people's prejudice.

"M&M, you'll understand this later. Never let how people judge your outside change who you are on the inside. Because the inside is where the genuine goodness is."

He laughed and popped an M&M in his mouth.

Back then, she didn't pay it much mind.

She just thought it was funny that he'd started calling her "M&M and she was eating candy in the morning. Minnie would be furious.

Later in life, they would joke that if people knew how she got the nickname, someone might try to twist it into something offensive or racist. But for Morgan, the name held a sacred significance. It meant her "knight in shining armor" had rescued her that day. It meant someone recognized the treasure inside her, even if others couldn't.

Her thick black hair, which had once grown down to the middle of her back, well, what was left of it, was trimmed that day into a short pixie cut. The stylist explained to Dusty that the only way to fix the damage was to start fresh.

"At the rate this child's hair grows," the stylist said confidently, "it'll be back down her back in no time."

The woman who turned out to be the salon owner, Lady Shay, gently lifted Morgan's chin and smiled.

"Baby, a face as pretty as yours needs to be seen."

The salon buzzed with life. Hair dryers roared like jet engines in the background. The air smelled of coconut oil, Blue Magic grease, flat irons, and hot combs. Women talked over one another, laughing, debating politics, complaining about their exes, and trading recipes for Sunday dinner. Music floated in through an old radio in the corner, Aretha Franklin's "Rock Steady" pounding out a steady, joyful beat.

Lady Shay leaned in as she parted Morgan's hair with her wide-toothed comb.

"Let me tell you something, young queen," she said, low enough just for Morgan.

"Every Black woman got a crown.

Thick,

Tight,

Long or,

Short and sassy.

Doesn't matter.

It's yours.

And don't you ever let this world make you ashamed of it."

Morgan blinked at her reflection, blurred in the giant gold-framed mirror in front of her. Her face looked unfamiliar with the cropped cut, but there was something regal about it, something bold and exposed.

She touched her freshly styled curls and smiled.

That day at Hair by Lady Shay became one of her best childhood memories.

The women in the salon treated her like royalty, complimenting her new short hairstyle and doting on her with kindness. Dusty and Uncle Dunk couldn't pick her up immediately, so after her haircut, the salon gave her a pedicure and manicure with bright pink polish.

Minnie flipped out when she got home.

Minnie insisted on neatly manicured nails with a clear or neutral gloss. French tips were the only exception, and only for "special occasions."

And that wasn't the only rule Morgan broke that day.

Lady Shay had ordered lunch for the salon from the diner across the street, and Morgan had eaten everything from fried chicken to sweet potato pie.

Minnie's strict house rules banned fried food and limited sweets.

Somewhere in all the excitement, she'd fallen asleep.

When she woke up, they were driving home, and it felt like she was leaving her birthday party.

For Morgan, it became her favorite place, almost every Saturday, for the next ten years.

It was the space that accepted her unconditionally and nurtured many of her contradictions.

Like on her thirteenth birthday, when she began the day sitting under a hood dryer with a magazine and foil strips in her hair. Her sneakers barely skimmed the floor. She felt tall and small, grown-ish, as Miss Trina liked to tease.

Across the room, Miss Shirley argued about church politics while her stylist, Cam, rolled her hair with pink rods.

"They put Sister Claudette over the choir again?" Shirley snorted.

"Lawd, help us. That woman couldn't carry a tune in a bucket if it came with a handle."

Laughter erupted, and Morgan giggled too, though she barely knew who Sister Claudette was.

"Don't mind Shirley," Cam said. "She's just mad cause Claudette said her banana pudding was 'runny.'"

"It was!" Shirley shouted.

Lady Shay walked past and winked at Morgan. "You'd better take notes, baby girl. These women will teach you everything school forgot."

Just then, Loretta rushed in, her hair covered by a scarf and wearing sunglasses. "Hey, Lady, can you get me in?"

"Girl, yo' appointment next week, and I'm trying to leave here early." Getting Morgan from under the dryer to adjust the foil. "This is my last Queen today."

"Come on, Lady Shay, Mister Willie is taking me to the club tonight."

Laughter rang out, and someone joked, "Wife must be out of town?"

"Mind yo' business, bitches. I told y'all he's leaving her soon, just waiting on the right time to tell her."

"Ok, ladies, enough of that in front of Morgan," she said while cupping her ears with her hands.

Morgan smiled and leaned back in the chair, absorbing the room's rhythm, the rise and fall of gossip, the thrum of Rhythm & Blues on the radio, the pop of flat irons, and the scent of coconut and cherry oil drifting through the air like a memory.

A woman she didn't know turned to her, eyeing her legs stretched out in long jeans.

"You growin' taller and prettier by the week. Stay away from dem boys."

Morgan didn't know how to respond, but she said thank you.

Lady Shay placed Morgan back under the dryer and adjusted the hood above her.

"Next time you come, bring me some birthday party pictures," she said. "I want to see you in that emerald dress. Remember, it's yo' day and yo' damn world, Queen."

Morgan grinned. "That's cause I do."

Everyone laughed, and someone clapped.

And in that moment, under that dryer, with foils in her hair and warmth on her skin, Morgan felt exactly what she craved from that place:

Enough.

She was enough.

Not too light or too dark. Not too polished or too bold. Not too white for Black spaces or too Black for white ones.

She was M&M. She was Morgan. She was magic.

And she didn't need anyone to validate her crown.

She already wore it.

She never grew her hair back out.

The pixie cut became her signature, sometimes spiked, sometimes smoothed, dyed or frosted, but always short.

Years later, she wondered: was her short hair a rebellion? If so, it wasn't aimed at Minnie. Maybe the pixie cut was more about identity than defiance.

Wearing that style became her silent declaration, a badge of honor, a symbol that, even though she didn't know her birth parents or her whole story, she belonged.

She belonged in the world of Bennis-Alcott Estates…

…and she belonged in the warmth and welcome of Hair by Lady Shay.

She'd arrived at that salon feeling broken, like she was being sent away to be fixed.

But the women in that space, with their smiles, their laughter, and their affirmations, never asked her to fix a thing.

They accepted her exactly as she was.

They told her she was beautiful.

And she believed them.

CHAPTER
THIRTY-ONE
AUGUST 12, 1991

Country Club Ballroom
6:30 p.m.

MINNIE NEVER APPROVED. She wanted Morgan's hair long and flowing, elegant. She believed Morgan was rebelling, but Morgan's defiance was about belonging, not rebellion. Morgan loved Dusty and Minnie, proud of her life of wealth and privilege. She tolerated public stares and learned to explain herself to strangers without rolling her eyes. Yet, what truly hurt was the insinuation that she should be grateful.

That word came into sharp focus on her thirteenth birthday.

Minnie had thrown her a massive party at the country club, where all her private school friends held their celebrations. Minnie, in true fashion, had "gone over the top." Dusty would later call it extravagant.

The highlight of the day was a surprise performance by New Kids on the Block.

But that wasn't what Morgan would remember most.

What she would remember was the sneer on a parent's face and the comment they made, intended to sting.

"I hope that spoiled little nigga is grateful they took her in."

She was sure she was meant to hear it.

She had heard the word before.

"But never from an adult, never aimed at her, never with such venom."

She ran outside, holding back tears, and headed straight for the family's Bentley.

She prayed Uncle Dunk hadn't locked the doors.

Just as she reached for the handle, his large hand grabbed it first.

"M&M, what's wrong?" he asked, handing her a tissue as she climbed inside.

"I can't tell you. Please, take me home," she whispered.

"Tell me what happened, or do I need to get Minnie?" he teased. "You know she'll get to the bottom of it. Nobody messes up her parties."

In one breath, she blurted it out. "One of the parents called me a spoiled nigga. She said I should be grateful my parents took me in."

Uncle Dunk threw his head back and laughed like it was the funniest thing he'd ever heard.

"M&M, child, you should be back in that party holding your head high like the little princess you are," he said. "They're just jealous Minnie did something for you they couldn't or wouldn't do for their kid."

He turned around in the seat to look at her squarely.

"Your parents love you. That's not spoiled. That's loved."

"But she called me a nigga," Morgan snapped, her voice trembling.

"Morgan Marie Bennis-Alcott," he said in a tone that silenced her.

"This won't be the last time someone calls you that. But let it be the last time you cry about it."

He stepped out of the car, opened her door, and added, "Now get yo' lil bougie ass out of this chauffeur-driven car and go show them white folks how a rich nigga lives."

She nearly died laughing.

If Minnie ever found out he spoke to her like that, she would be livid. But Uncle Dunk always made her feel better, maybe because he was one of the few people in her world who kept it real, along with the women at Hair by Lady Shay's.

PART EIGHT
LADY SHAY

CHAPTER
THIRTY-TWO
AUGUST 22, 2017

Pendleton Women's Federal Prison Release Gate
7:30 a.m.

MORGAN ARRIVED at Pendleton Women's Federal Prison, clutching a cold coffee cup. The bitter liquid swayed as she walked through the visitor parking lot, her breath visible in the crisp air. Sleep-deprived, her mind raced with contingency plans and imagined dialogues.

The team verified all aspects of Madison's release, including a secured halfway house placement and approved work release at Main Street Bakery, a family-owned shop known for employing ex-convicts. This satisfied the early release criteria and aimed to give Madison a foothold in a world that had moved on without her.

As dawn broke over the horizon, the prison walls remained cold and unfeeling. The squeak of the gate exactly at 7:58 a.m. shattered the silence like a hesitant breath. Morgan froze, heart pounding. Her pulse surged with a mix of anxiety, hope, and disbelief.

And then she saw her.

Madison stepped into the sunlight, her silhouette sharp against the gray concrete and chain-link fence. She wore a thin, pale jacket, over-sized jeans, and worn sneakers. A canvas bag hung over one shoulder, holding her few belongings. She hesitated, blinking into the bright morning glare as if the outside world was too sudden and too bright.

Their eyes met across the distance, the space between them crackling with unspoken words.

"You're on time," Madison said, her voice carrying across the parking lot with its usual measured calm. Yet something in her tone betrayed a tremor of uncertainty wrapped in defiance.

Morgan swallowed the lump rising in her throat.

"I'm forty-three," she replied with a quiet, almost breathless smile. "I've waited my whole life for this."

Madison's expression softened slightly, her shoulders easing and her jaw relaxing. She nodded to Morgan, her gaze steady despite the rawness threatening beneath the surface.

"Then let's go," she said, her voice low but resolute. "I want real coffee and something warm to eat."

As they walked toward the car, the weight of the past and fragile hope pressed on them. The ground crunched beneath their cautious steps, gravel like unresolved pieces of their story. In the quiet between them, the air felt heavy with ghosts, unfinished sentences, and lost years. When they reached the leased vehicle, mother and daughter steadily closed the gap, their distance measured in hope rather than miles.

A while later, Morgan sat across from her mother at the Second Chance Diner, sharing their first breakfast together. A strange, bittersweet nostalgia washed over her as their fragile reunion over coffee and pastries evoked a long-buried memory.

Lady Shay.

The first Black woman to make her feel seen.

She had been the owner of the hair salon, where Morgan's reflection made sense. Where the hum of hair dryers resembled distant thunder, laughter filled the air like a familiar song, and scents of shampoos and pressed hair blended into a comforting perfume.

Lady Shay's hands had been gentle yet certain, shaping her pixie hairstyle while offering quiet affirmations with every snip of the scissors.

Her touch had instilled more than just style.

Confidence.

Assurance that Morgan could exist between worlds without having to choose sides.

Lady Shay's unwavering presence had been the beginning of everything. The beginning of Morgan learning to own her reflection, to embrace her identity in a world eager to define her by its own narrow terms.

Sitting with Madison, the woman who had given her life yet remained absent from it, Morgan realized she was once again trying to bridge a chasm. The chasm lay between who she had become, a polished professional and a survivor of secrets. And where she had come from, a place woven with shadows, silences, and untold truths.

Her mother's face across the table was no longer just a headline or a mugshot.

It was a living story.

A mirror reflecting the pieces of herself she hadn't fully dared to acknowledge until now.

The scent of coffee, rich and familiar, mingled with the sweetness of warm pastries, their flakiness crumbling under her fingers. Each bite felt like a hesitant step toward the connection. Morgan studied her mother's hands as she held the coffee cup, knuckles worn, skin weathered yet steady. Someone forced these hands to let go too soon and denied them the right to cradle a newborn daughter.

Morgan's throat tightened, but she swallowed back the ache. She didn't know where their story would go next. There was too much hurt, too many missing pieces to pretend this was simple. But at least now, they were no longer strangers navigating parallel lives.

She couldn't help but wonder who her mother, Madison, might have been on a Saturday morning at the beauty salon. Legs crossed under the dryer, gossip magazine in hand, chiming in on neighborhood drama between sips of sweet tea.

Would she have laughed loudly, offered sharp one-liners, asked for hot oil treatments, or insisted on rollers?

Morgan tried to envision her mother there, woven into the rhythm of women who spoke their truths during press and curl appointments, and it stung a little, knowing they never had the chance to share that sacred, scented space.

Morgan had loved Lady Shay from the moment she lifted her sad little face and said in a raspy, loving voice,

"Baby, a face as pretty as yours needs to be seen."

Minnie, Morgan's perfectionist mother, made sure Morgan had a weekly salon visit every Saturday until she went to college. When Morgan couldn't attend, Minnie would hire a stylist to come to their home, even paying for travel expenses during vacations. While she couldn't convince Morgan to grow her hair long, Minnie was steadfast in her belief that a woman's hair should always appear "picture ready," no matter the length.

Morgan didn't mind at all.

Over the ten years of Saturday mornings at the salon, Lady Shay grew from a stylist into a surrogate mother, the matriarch overseeing her space of mirrors, hair dryers, and shared secrets. The diverse Black women who visited the salon became her extended family and mentors of silent wisdom, advocates of dignity, and creators of resilience.

After one sharp, lovingly delivered smack to the back of the head, Morgan quickly learned the unspoken rule of respect: you never called adults by their first names. Everyone was "Tee Tee" or "Miss."

No exceptions.

Among those women, Morgan learned to exist in her skin, to laugh from her belly despite external silencing, to cry without shame amid women sharing tissues and glances, and to listen beyond words to the cadence of lived experiences and silent wisdom. She discovered the power of a well-timed side-eye, the weight of a whispered prayer beneath a hair dryer hood, and the magic of transformation, both outer and inner. The inner kind that made a girl stand a little taller, speak a little louder, believe a little more in her worth.

In that sanctuary of sisterhood, she wasn't "Morgan from prep school." She was just Morgan, the girl with thick hair, a quick laugh, and a quiet strength shaped on Saturday mornings in folding chairs beside women who taught her what dignity looked like in motion.

Years later, when she stepped into the polished corridors of the

District Attorney's office, she carried that same calm authority. She knew when to yield and when to press forward. She listened to what people said and what they left unsaid. She could read a witness's silence like a case file.

Once during a pre-trial interview, a teen victim froze under pressure. Her voice faltered, and the room grew tight with discomfort. Without looking up from her notepad, Morgan said gently, "Take your time. Silence doesn't scare me."

The girl exhaled, nodded, and began again.

Morgan made decisions with the clarity that came from growing up learning how to survive spaces that didn't always make room for her. Her work wasn't just legal; it was personal. She fought for the unseen, the unheard, the dismissed. For girls who didn't yet know they had the right to take up space. For women still learning that they deserved to be whole.

It was those lessons from Lady Shay's salon, the ones layered in love and laced with hard truths, that guided Morgan as she sat across from Madison in the *Second Chance Diner*.

She remembered how Tee Tee Janine once told her, between taming edges and setting curls, "Baby, there's two kinds of women in this world: the ones who carry their hurt like armor, and the ones who let it cut 'em open. You gotta learn to be both. Strong enough to survive, soft enough to stay a lady."

That wisdom echoed in Morgan's mind as she studied the woman sitting across from her; a woman stripped of everything but her name. Silence cloaked her like a second skin, and her eyes revealed a battle fought long before prison claimed her. Morgan couldn't help but wonder if anyone had ever whispered that same truth to Madison when she needed it most.

Every decision she made, every carefully crafted argument, every case she pursued, every moment she spoke up rather than stay silent, was a thread woven from those lessons learned at Lady Shay's salon. She often joked to herself that inner-city salons and barbershops were the Black folks' country clubs and the cost of membership was simply the price of a hairstyle and a willingness to share space, story, and soul.

In time, she came to realize Lady Shay's salon wasn't just popular.

It was iconic, welcoming single mothers on assistance, teachers, socialites, and dignitaries. Inside, titles faded; everyone was just a Black woman taking a break.

Courtesy of Lady Shay.

By the time Morgan had met her, Lady Shay had lived a dozen lifetimes.

CHAPTER
THIRTY-THREE
JUNE 13, 1965

Small Town, Mississippi
3:20 a.m.

BORN SHAYLEE MAE JACKSON in a small town in Mississippi. At fifteen, she left home to pursue her dream of singing jazz. She was tall, dark-skinned, and full-figured, "built like an amazon," as she often put it, and she appeared much older than her age.

This led to her being discovered by a band manager, who mistook her sultry voice and full figure for "grown" while she was singing in her father's church and convinced her to join the band. Lady Shay didn't offer a correction but ran away from home in the early morning hours, knowing her religious and strict father would never allow her to join a band. However, the secret's discovery wouldn't be long in coming, and "religious and strict" would soon feel like welcome life advice, not rules.

Though her voice drew applause, it rarely paid the bills. Lady Shay wasn't earning much from singing with the band, especially as the youngest and least established. She made extra money on the road by styling hair and applying makeup for backup singers, transforming tired faces into stage-ready stars. With a gift for glamour and fashion, she made every woman she touched feel radiant.

Her "make-do" beauty station in the dressing rooms on the road became dual spaces, housing her salon. But no matter how dazzling she made others look, nothing could shield her from the dangers that came with being a young girl in a grown woman's world.

One night, after a packed show in a dimly lit juke joint off the highway, the dressing room buzzed with post-show chatter and cigarette smoke. Lady Shay had just finished touching up a girl for a photo-op when the others drifted out. Some headed to the bar, others toward waiting cars, while she stayed behind, packing up her things and missing home.

She didn't hear the door open at first.

Didn't register the slurred voice until it was too close.

"C'mon now, don't play shy, sweetheart. You sang all that heat, now let a man warm up with you."

Her spine stiffened. She turned slowly, heart lurching.

A drunken, large, red-faced patron with his shirt unbuttoned too far blocked the exit, his breath heavy with whiskey.

And just like that, the danger she'd always tried to outrun had found her.

She froze.

Her stool scraped back. She stood, her breath caught, fists clenched at her sides.

The man stumbled forward.

But he didn't make it far.

Rhonda was suddenly there, slipping through the door like a blade.

All hips and attitude, but tonight, her voice was steel.

"Back the hell off," she snapped, stepping between them. "You drunken, slimy bastard."

"Bitch! Who the hell are you?"

"The woman who's gonna make sure you leave here with yo' teeth still in yo' mouth."

Seeing Rhonda's eyes and the bat in her hand, the man sneered, opened his mouth to speak, then stumbled back down the hallway, cursing under his breath.

The door slammed shut. Lady Shay collapsed into the chair, her chest rising and falling in silent heaves.

Rhonda watched her through the mirror. "You okay?" she asked, gentler now.

Lady Shay nodded, but her eyes were glassy. Silence.

Then she spoke.

"I'm fifteen."

Rhonda blinked. "What?"

"I'll be sixteen next month."

Silence. Rhonda walked over, crouched down until they were eye level. No judgment. Just a quiet, knowing gaze. "You're just a baby," she whispered.

Shay said quickly, fiercely, "I'm not," but her voice cracked. "I can sing, been singing my whole life. Couldn't stay in that house, in that town, waiting for nothing."

Rhonda exhaled slowly. "And now you're out here with grown men thinking yo' ass is one of them. You know how lucky you are that I came back?"

Shay didn't answer. She just stared at her reflection, mascara smudged, mouth trembling.

"You don't gotta explain," Rhonda said, standing. "Just don't lie to me again."

Lady Shay nodded slowly, tears slipping free. Rhonda handed her a handkerchief and stood by the door like a sentry.

From that night on, Rhonda never left her alone after a show.

And Lady Shay, for the first time, didn't feel so alone in the world.

She would tell Morgan the story years later, her voice low and steady, after she caught her slipping a small pistol back into her purse. The man had stormed into the salon, wild-eyed and shouting, demanding to know where his wife was.

Lady Shay didn't shrink.

Just stepped between him and the door leading to the hidden apartment above, the one they used to shelter battered women.

Her hand shot straight to the gun, her stare as cold as steel until he backed out the door.

Later, when the chaos had cleared, Morgan asked her why she had risked her business and her life. Lady Shay said, "Because Rhonda once did the same for me."

She looked at Morgan then, her eyes soft but fierce.

When I see a woman hiding from a storm, I don't question her. Sisterhood is about safeguarding each other's beauty in a harsh world, regardless of the danger.

By the age of twenty, Lady Shay had made significant strides in her music career, performing widely across the country and building a dedicated fan base. Her hard work resulted in a record deal with a major label, propelling her into the spotlight with her hit single, "Take a Break." The song showcased her unique style and vocal talent, earning her two Grammy Awards: Best New Artist and Jazz Record of the Year, thus solidifying her position in the jazz genre.

Amid her newfound fame, she married the band manager who first saw her potential, Willie James, twenty years her senior, who discovered her singing in a Mississippi church and introduced her as "Lady Shay." His unwavering belief and support inspired her affection and respect, giving her the freedom to pursue her dreams without apology.

When she discovered she was pregnant, her heart swelled with hope.

It felt like the divine confirmation her father had often preached: that her leap of faith had not only carved a place for her on stage but might also fill the aching void of family within her. Although her father had never forgiven her for leaving, maybe now she could begin again.

Maybe this child would be her way back to love.

Once in the quiet of the closed salon, while Lady Shay and Morgan waited for Uncle Dunk, who was running late to pick her up, Morgan, in her innocent and childish manner, asked:

"How did you get the name Lady Shay?"

She reached into the worn leather clutch she kept tucked beneath the counter. From inside, she pulled a creased photograph with edges curled, and colors faded with time.

She handed it to Morgan without a word.

"That's him," she said with a reverence. "The man who gave me my name... and his love."

Morgan studied the image of a tall man in a crisp suit, smiling beside a radiant, younger Lady Shay, one hand resting protectively on her back, the other on her pregnant belly.

"I was hardly showing," Lady Shay said, a wistful smile flitting across her lips. "I believed the baby was my second chance. A part of me, a part of him. A small family I could call my own."

She paused, her fingers brushing the photo as if it were something sacred.

Some pictures don't fade; they sink deeper with time.

Five months pregnant, Lady Shay collapsed mid-performance, her body buckling under the strain of high blood pressure. Doctors ordered immediate bed rest. At first, the band rallied around her, but as bookings dried up, the atmosphere shifted. Her husband, Willie, worked overtime to keep the music alive, convincing clubs to book the backup singers at cut rates to keep food on the table.

Then came the night everything changed.

She went into labor alone. Willie, who was finishing a show at a club an hour away, felt a pull he couldn't explain. Just after 1 a.m., he quickly packed and hit the road, desperate to arrive on time.

He didn't.

He dozed off while driving, resulting in a severe crash. Although the other driver survived, he could never walk again. In an almost unbearably cruel turn of events, he sued Lady Shay.

Her fame worked against her. The court ruled that her rising public image and earnings bore some responsibility. They ordered her to pay $500,000 in damages. She settled for half, but it cost her everything. The house. Her savings. Her future.

The baby was only six weeks old when Shay packed her Grammy, her gold record, and the last of her dignity into two suitcases.

She couldn't start over here. Not without Willie. Not with whispers in every room and cities full of echoes.

So, she left the country.

She broke the news to Rhonda in the dressing room.

"I thought I could do it without him," she said, adjusting the baby's blanket, her voice trembling. "But too many familiar places without his face in the crowd... they feel lonely."

Rhonda opened her mouth to respond, but nothing came out.

Lady Shay didn't wait.

She pressed a kiss to her son's forehead, grabbed her bags, and disappeared into the night, leaving behind only the perfume of grief and a silence even the music couldn't fill.

They lived in Paris for ten years. She sang in jazz clubs where her skin color didn't matter, her voice flowing through smoky spaces like silk. In Paris, she refined her skills at beauty schools, mentored by women whose hands flowed like poetry. There, she turned her heartbreak into grace.

She raised her son, who didn't speak English until he was five, in a small walk-up near Montmartre, where the bakery downstairs saved fresh beignets for him every morning.

Paris had been her refuge. Her reset. Her reward.

But even peace, she realized, could feel like exile. In Paris, she was at once invisible and adored.

The French saw her in a way America never had. Strangers complimented her skin on the metro, calling her "reine de la nuit," which translates to "queen of the night," after her late-night sets. Here, people celebrated her size as voluptuous and regal; it had once been a source of shame back home. People in boutiques didn't give her side glances. No one clutched their purses. No one asked her to explain herself.

For the first time, she didn't have to translate her soul.

By night, she sang both in clubs so intimate the mic stand leaned against a radiator, and at other times in grand halls glittering with chandeliers. Audiences absorbed her softened voice, rich with jazz and sorrow, as she articulated her grief through breathy notes; they didn't require her narrative.

They felt it.

Yet, for all the praise, for all the fleeting freedom, something remained missing.

One afternoon, it surfaced quietly and painfully as she watched her son, barefoot, dark-skinned, and filled with questions, being teased by boys from the neighborhood. They ridiculed his accent, which sounded too American to them, and his French, which stuttered at times. However, what hurt her the most was their laughter directed at what he lacked: a father.

Lady Shay stood at the window, hands trembling around a chipped teacup, watching him try to laugh it off. But she couldn't ignore the confusion in his eyes, the shame he didn't yet have words for.

And in that moment, something shifted.

Fame had once been her armor. But now, motherhood was her mission. She would raise a boy who knew his worth in any language, in any skin. A boy who wouldn't shrink when the world pressed in.

A strange ache bloomed in her chest.

For all the beauty and sense of belonging that Paris had offered her, it couldn't answer one question that now gnawed at her insides:

"Where does a Black boy go when he wants to learn how to be a Black man?"

She didn't have the answer. She just knew it wasn't Paris.

Not this Paris.

Elegant and seductive, yes, but also a place where race was a polite conversation over café au lait, not a lived truth. They exoticized his Blackness but failed to embrace it.

So, it took little to decide to return to the States in 1978.

The year Morgan was born.

CHAPTER
THIRTY-FOUR
AUGUST 24, 1996

Lady Shay Salon
10:30 a.m.

MORGAN THOUGHT she was coming in for a quick trim, just one last pixie cut before heading off to Harvard. She wanted to enjoy this last moment in her favorite chair before stepping into a world that didn't know her the way this room did.

She should have known better.

The moment she stepped inside Hair by Lady Shay, the air shifted, like someone had opened a door to something more profound. It wasn't the lights, or the music, or the decorations. It was the weight of history. Of love, thick in the walls like memory.

Streamers in Harvard crimson and soft pearl-white lined the walls. Framed photos of Morgan decorated every mirror and counter, from baby barrettes and the first day of school to that asymmetrical bob from eighth grade, her prom-night glow-up, and a wide-laughing snapshot from under the dryer.

A long folding table sat beneath the front window, covered in foil pans of shrimp and grits, sweet rolls, deviled eggs with extra paprika, and peach cobbler still steaming at the edges. Someone had cut watermelon into stars and hearts. Someone else had set up a punch bowl with floating lemon slices and a bottle of sparkling apple cider beside it.

"Don't just stand there, Harvard," Janet teased, clapping her hands once. "Get in here and claim your crown!"

The room erupted in applause.

Morgan's throat caught, eyes already filling. She tried to say something, but Lady Shay was already beside her, taking her face in her hands like a mother and an oracle all at once.

"We've been doin' your hair since before you had edges," Lady Shay whispered, her voice thick. "Now look at you. College-bound and still have good sense. We are so proud, baby."

Janet handed her a paper plate. "Eat first, cry later."

Morgan laughed through her tears and took the plate, moving through the space like a daughter coming home. They were all there, including Janet, Miss May, Tee Tee Char, Geneva, and Patty. Even Miss Millie had made it, settled in her usual corner seat like a queen in quiet observation, her walker parked beside her with a crocheted shawl draped across the top.

Lady Shay guided her into the chair, smoothing the cape around her shoulders like a tailor prepping royalty.

"Now hush," Lady Shay said with a smile. "Let me do your crown right."

As Lady Shay parted and combed, clipping away just enough to shape the new season, the salon hushed around them. The soft clicks of the scissors created a rhythm only women like them knew. An unspoken knowing that Black women were sharing a moment of transformation disguised as a haircut filled the air.

Lauryn Hill hummed lively from the stereo. Somewhere in the back, Miss May fanned herself with a folded horoscope page.

"I know you wanted Spelman," Shay said after a moment, never stopping her hands.

Morgan nodded.

"And I know why you didn't fight harder for it."

Tears fell before she could stop them.

Lady Shay met her eyes in the mirror. "The world will teach you to choose strategy over self. But don't you ever let it make you forget who you are."

When Lady Shay turned the chair and held up the mirror, a cheer went up again. Morgan was radiant. Polished and powerful.

"That's it," said Miss Geneva. "That's our girl right there."

Then, one by one, the women stepped forward, not in any formal line but guided by something older than time.

Janet placed her hands on Morgan's shoulders. "Walk with your head high, even if the wind tries to bend you."

Miss May touched her forehead. "The road ahead sees you coming, baby."

Tee Tee Char handed her a folded slip of paper. "Something for strength. Read it when you need reminding."

Miss Patty offered a pair of hoop earrings. "To remind you, you still got some hood in you, so don't get up there and start talkin' like you don't know us."

Laughter rippled through the room.

Miss Millie took her hand last, not because she was slow, but because she was always last; the closest. The voice you remembered when the room went quiet. She didn't hug Morgan. Instead, she placed both hands on her shoulders and leaned in close, her voice a rasp of wind and weight. "You go out there and earn every title they said you couldn't. Doctor, Judge, Mayor, or whatever you want. But never let your title be all you carry."

Morgan blinked.

You hear me, baby? Titles can be stripped. But who are you underneath? That's legacy. Yo' people's grit in your bones. When the world tries to unmake you, that's what you protect.

Then she reached into her shawl and drew out a warm, smooth stone from a tiny pouch. "Carry this in your pocket when you feel lost. My grandmother held it when her family lost their land as sharecroppers. My mother held it when they marched in Selma. I held it when I buried my daughter. It ain't magic. But it holds memory."

Lady Shay then moved to the small cabinet beneath her station and opened a hidden drawer, one even her regulars weren't aware of. She retrieved a small velvet box from inside.

"I wasn't gonna give you this until the day you got your first job offer, but Miss Millie said otherwise."

Miss Millie waved her hand. "Life doesn't wait. Neither should we."

Lady Shay opened the box. Inside was a delicate gold necklace with a tiny diamond-crusted crown charm. "It's not about being royalty," she said, clasping it around Morgan's neck. "It's about remembering where your power sits."

Miss Millie's voice, cracked with age but clear with conviction, floated across the room like a hymn you didn't have to believe in to feel: "Keep your feet planted and your spirit soft. That's how we survive, baby."

Morgan tried to respond. She couldn't. Her voice was gone, swallowed by love.

Lady Shay wiped the last tear from her cheek and hugged Morgan. "Don't be a stranger."

Morgan stepped to the doorway and pushed it open.

The afternoon sun hit her like a spotlight, catching the crown around her neck and the fresh shimmer in her haircut. The women gathered behind her, arms crossed, proud and wide.

And from the back of the room, Miss Millie called out, powerfully and final, "Now go on and make us proud, Harvard."

"And don't you ever forget where you got that crown."

People filled the funeral home chapel not because Miss Millie was a retired high school principal, but because she had fed people with her hands, her prayers, and her understanding. And that kind of legacy doesn't go unnoticed.

Morgan sat in the third row behind the family, wearing her black dress for moments requiring grace under grief. Her heels were modest, her shoulders squared, and her heart quietly breaking. After five years, she was back in a room with these women, having returned home for the service following a call from Miss May three days earlier.

"Baby," she said, her voice soft with something that wasn't quite grief, but deeper. "Miss Millie's gone. She passed in her sleep."

That night, Morgan pulled the tiny jewelry box from the back of her drawer, the one she had tucked away years ago beneath old appointment books and faded receipts, as if trying to forget the weight it carried. She opened it slowly, reverently, as though the box might whisper secrets she wasn't yet ready to hear.

Inside, the crown necklace still gleamed. Untarnished. Unshaken. A delicate gold pendant crusted with tiny diamonds, each one catching the light like a quiet testament to survival. The chain had twisted itself into a knot from years of neglect, but her fingers worked it free with care, smoothing it like a prayer.

This wasn't just jewelry. It was a promise. A legacy. A quiet rebellion.

She remembered the women who had given it to her, the ones who had whispered over her head while combing her hair, who had squeezed her hand when the world was too sharp. They had called her beautiful long before she believed it herself. They had placed this necklace in her hand with a knowing look and a single instruction:

"Wear it when you need to remember who you are."

And now, sitting in that chapel, surrounded by murmured prayers and flickering candles, Morgan wore it proudly. Not hidden beneath pearls like Minnie might have suggested, not muted into the background. Just the delicate gold crown, glinting defiantly against her collarbone.

A symbol. A memory. A declaration.

The world could try to strip her titles, her history, her name, but it could never take her crown.

The organ hummed as sobs echoed behind her. The minister read Proverbs 31, but Morgan wasn't listening. She remembered: the smell of sweet rolls and peach cobbler, the laughter and sizzle of hot combs, and Miss Lillie's bold call: "Now go on and make us proud, Harvard."

Morgan bowed her head, not in prayer, but in reverence. And whispered under her breath:

"I didn't forget."

She hadn't meant to stay long, just the service, a quick hello, a respectful nod. But walking into the fellowship hall, she no longer felt like the girl in the chair. She was one of them. Feeling the necklace against her skin, she realized it was no longer just an accessory but a reminder and a responsibility.

After the service, when folks were hugging and reminiscing over pound cake and punch in the fellowship hall, Lady Shay walked up and gently took her hand. "Are you going to visit your parents while you're in town?"

Morgan's voice was firm. "No."

Lady Shay heard the steel in her tone and didn't press. She could tell the past was still close enough to sting. What Morgan didn't say, what stayed locked behind her clenched jaw, was that she still wasn't over it.

Not just the fights about college.

Not just Minnie's relentless control.

But the quiet suspicion she carried was like a splinter: that her Spelman rejection hadn't been fate at all, but interference, a silent hand pushing her away from the place she had dreamed of.

A well-placed anonymous donation. A whispered word in the right ear.

Forgiveness may come.

But not today.

Not with that truth still sitting between them, unspoken and unresolved.

PART NINE
THE TARNISHED CROWN

CHAPTER
THIRTY-FIVE
AUGUST 22, 2017

Second Chance Diner – Pendleton City
8:46 a.m.

THE BREAKFAST FINALLY ARRIVED, steaming hot and beautifully arranged, almost too perfect to touch. Madison stared at it as if it were something unfamiliar, a relic from a life she'd nearly forgotten. It had been almost four years since she'd eaten anything that didn't come on a dull aluminum tray, colorless and portioned.

Now, the vibrant plate before her stirred something deeper than hunger.

Nostalgia. Disbelief. Relief.

She took a breath, steadying herself, not just to eat but to enjoy a meal without scanning the room for danger or sitting across from someone she couldn't trust. For the first time in years, she could eat without fear.

The sound of Morgan's cellphone cut Madison's reflection short, ringing. "Excuse me," Morgan said, quickly rising from the table, "I need to take this outside."

"Make it quick; don't let your food get cold," she chuckled. "That's my first piece of advice as your mother."

As she walked away, Morgan replied, "No, you first reminded me to be punctual."

Madison grappled with her thoughts, no longer a convict.

She sat alone, staring into her dark coffee.

The taste of freedom should have been sweet.

Instead, it was heavy. Sharp. Almost bitter.

Although her joy was genuine, an unnamed anxiety intertwined with it. The unknown loomed outside the diner, a shadow between her past and future. It had been years since she felt this unsettled, not since the dreadful day she left Hawk Landing, when wildfires' flames flickered on the horizon, casting an eerie glow in her rearview mirror.

She had driven with no plan. No map. Just grief and adrenaline and Nina's voice echoing in her memory: "Bet on yourself."

Now she found herself free yet still filled with fear. She looked toward Morgan, who was still on the phone with her back turned... her daughter.

The words didn't come easily; it was like trying to hold something fragile. A truth that still seemed like fiction.

Madison traced the rim of her coffee cup with one finger, her thoughts drifting somewhere between memory and miracle.

"She didn't make it."

No baby. No name. No swaddle.

She remembered hearing a baby cry... just once. Then silence.

For years, she convinced herself it was her imagination.

But now. Morgan. Alive. Educated. Brilliant.

That cry hadn't been her imagination.

It had been her Morgan.

The woman sitting across from her now, with her eyes, her cheekbones... her fire.

Madison had endured a loveless marriage, public disgrace, and imprisonment. But this? This was the moment that shattered her. Yet, it was also the moment that mended her.

Not entirely, but enough to attempt it.

When Morgan returned to the table, she smiled with a slight, cautious curve of her lips that felt more vulnerable than any words could. Madison offered no grand gestures. Just reached across the table and slid the coffee creamer toward her.

A quiet offering. A beginning.

Morgan accepted it with a nod.

And they ate, mother and daughter, neither knowing what would come next.

Sunlight spilled through the diner window, warming the table where pancakes sat half-eaten and coffee cooled between them. Breakfast had drifted into lunch, and neither of them noticed.

Morgan looked at her mother across the table. That word still felt strange. It wasn't a conversation, just fragments, tossed back and forth, trying to fit a lifetime into this fragile moment, as if that could erase the years between them. So many things left unsaid and impossible to put into words.

"What time are you expected at the halfway house?" Morgan asked, deflecting from the eerie familiarity she felt as she sensed the weight on her mother's shoulder and the calmness in her mother's face.

This was an echo of silence.

Her mother disappeared to shield someone, and Morgan has done the same. Maybe history doesn't just repeat itself; perhaps it's passed down like an unspoken inheritance. The realization struck Morgan suddenly: the woman everyone saw on trial, cold, unreadable, notorious, was her mother.

But now? Sitting here? That myth was unraveling.

She wasn't a villain. She was a woman who had bled quietly, dressed her wounds in pearls and lipstick, and kept going. What struck her most wasn't just her mother's words about her husband as she idly caressed the cold cup of coffee, but the way she delivered them.

Not anger. Not even pain. But a protective love.

"He wasn't perfect," her mother said, adjusting the lace doily under the coffee cup. "But he carried the weight of too many people's expectations. And I stayed as long as I did because I loved him too much to let the world see him break."

Then, as if to end the conversation, her eyes drifted to the window, and with a faint smile, she said, "So I learned to break in private."

That's what finally broke Morgan..

The quiet, persistent love for a man who never deserved it. And Morgan could see the toll it took on Madison's body. The way she sat, as if her muscles had memorized pain. Like her spine remembered flinching.

She didn't say the worst of it; she didn't have to. But what did that cost her? Once, her world glittered with couture, galas, and Michelin stars.

As Morgan listened from across the diner, which felt like a chasm between them...

Something shifted.

This wasn't a woman who walked away; she escaped a prison of expectations, performance, and quiet devastation.

Morgan knew that kind of prison.

She had found pieces of herself in the sisterhood at Lady Shay's.

Now she saw it here too, in her mother.

Now she knew what it was.

She, like all the other spectators, had judged her.

Now she saw it differently.

Madison's designer life? *Was self-medicating.*

The shopping? *Therapy.*

The luxury? *Rebellion.*

Her mother had had nothing truly hers, not her voice, not her choices, and not her child.

So she did the only thing she could.

Almost simultaneously addressing Morgan's wandering thoughts, Madison set down the coffee cup and said sarcastically,

"And so, I ran. But not before one last performance."

Morgan studied her.

"Really," she said cautiously, "your last big performance."

Madison's eyes lit up.

She straightened in her seat, as if her spine remembered the spotlight.

"I wore a dove-gray silk gown," she said. "Not white, too bridal.

Not black, too mournful. Hair perfectly styled in a low chignon with a delicate pair of earrings. Elegant. Understated."

Giving Morgan a wink. "That was always the goal, according to Cora."

Morgan leaned back, intrigued. "And the Bishop?"

"He was in fine form," Madison said, the edge of a smile tugging at her lips. "All smiles. All charm. His hand was on my back as if I were a prized possession. Which, in his world, I was."

She didn't need to elaborate. Morgan had seen enough men like him to understand the weight of that possession.

"While lifting my gracefully held champagne flute, and with a practiced smile in response to a donor's praise," Madison went on, "when a moderator on stage murmured, '*Lady Winter makes misery look elegant.*' Was she unaware her mic was still on, or did she know?"

The audience chuckles.

Morgan blinked. "What did you do?"

"I smiled tighter," Madison said.

"And five minutes later, I was in a bathroom stall, weeping into silk and making sure not to smudge my makeup. I had five minutes. Then I went back out and raised $5 million in thirty minutes. That's what I did best. Disappear into the role."

Silence fell again.

"You were good at it," Morgan said.

There was a gleam in her eye, not just of memory, but of mastery. For a fleeting moment, she had held an entire room in her hands and made them believe exactly what they needed to.

"I had to be."

CHAPTER
THIRTY-SIX
AUGUST 22, 2017

Morgan's Apartment in Pendleton City
1:45 p.m.

MORGAN DROPPED Madison off at the halfway house just before the 1:00 p.m. check-in deadline. Since no visitors were allowed during the first week of orientation, she said a quick goodbye and then went back to the townhouse she was leasing for the six months Madison would be living in Pendleton.

The DA's office had approved her request for a leave of absence, with the condition that she remain available for consultation on active cases. Morgan didn't mind because this time was about something more important.

She wanted space to breathe, to reset.

But more than anything, she wanted to get to know her mother and support her through the long, complicated process of starting over.

As Morgan spent the next few hours with a bottle of wine, immersed in Madison's story and the insights gained at breakfast, every piece of her past brought her closer not only to the truth but also to her self-discovery.

It became increasingly clear: fate had always destined them to meet, or perhaps meet again, in a way neither could have imagined.

Some invisible threads had bound their lives long before they knew the other existed. It wove itself through shared pain and buried secrets, threading Morgan's carefully constructed life back to a woman she was never supposed to find.

Morgan had spent her life inside a narrative built on achievement. She had risen through the ranks of justice, fortified by a desire to fix what had once nearly broken her. She believed in fairness.

In truth.

In protecting others from falling through the cracks, she once teetered on the edge.

But as she delved into Madison Jackson Winter's life, her mother, once known as Nina Autumn Storm, Morgan found herself not just investigating but also unraveling. Each revelation about Madison tugged at Morgan's hidden fears and unresolved issues. The more she uncovered, the more her carefully built facade frayed, exposing long-buried emotions.

The search for Madison's truth compelled her to confront her own.

She returned to Minnesota after a heartbreak that shattered her carefully built life and tarnished her crown.

Betrayal.

Infidelity.

Divorce.

A word that echoed like a curse, sharp and final, unraveling years of shared dreams and mutual promises. It was not just the dissolution of a marriage, but the shattering of the image she had built for herself, the poised, accomplished woman who always knew the next step.

Her divorce had been quiet, but only in the way storms are silent when they move underground. On the surface, she had appeared composed: a graceful exit from a ten-year marriage that had once seemed like a fairy tale. But beneath the surface, a woman was unraveling.

Morgan encountered Marcus James in her second year at Harvard. He was brilliant and driven, coming from modest beginnings. With no family legacy or connections, he relied solely on a scholarship, a strong will, and a chip on his shoulder large enough to sustain him.

She saw it first.

Crafting his resume and preparing him for interviews, she connected him with political figures who once addressed her father as "Governor" and her mother as "Kingmaker."

She helped him with fundraisers, law school, and a position at a leading Boston firm. Her love was the initial step on his ladder to success.

At one of their first political fundraisers, Morgan adjusted his tie just before they stepped inside.

"Don't talk too much about your background," she said, smoothing his lapel. "Lead with your ideas. Make them forget where you didn't come from."

He gave a nervous laugh. "I don't belong in rooms like this."

She looked him squarely in the eye. "You belong because I said so. That's all they need to know."

Later, at the valet stand, he slipped his hand into hers and whispered, "I'd be nothing without you."

She smiled, but even then, something inside her whispered back.

"Let's hope you remember that."

Then, just as they had discussed starting a family, something she had never needed but had shared his desire for, he slipped.

She entered the study without knocking.

An open file blinked on his screen.

Her name in the subject line.

Below was a scanned maternity plan.

Then, an ultrasound image.

And the name: *Danielle Carter, Age: 24. Paralegal.*

He didn't bother closing the window.

Just swiveled in his chair, calm. Almost smug.

"Whose baby?" she asked. Her voice didn't shake, but her hands did.

Marcus stood slowly, straightening his tie as if this were a court. "Mine."

She laughed. Once. Dry. "You weren't even man enough to pass-word-lock your betrayal."

"No," he said, "I just didn't need to."

He stepped toward her. No apology. No retreat.

"You made me into something so powerful," he said, voice low, steady, "I forgot I wasn't born that way."

The betrayal did more than break her trust; it destroyed her confidence in her judgment. Over the weekend, she packed, leaving him, the condo, the practice, and the housekeeper. She let him enjoy the shine.

Revenge wasn't what she wanted.

Silence was what she wanted.

And a place to polish what remained of her crown.

A place where women like those found at Lady Shay's would remove the tarnish from her crown with words of wisdom, *"Baby, don't you let that man leave with yo' crown. His no-good ass don't have that kind of power."*

PART TEN
NO TIME FOR COFFEE

CHAPTER
THIRTY-SEVEN
1955 - 2009

Lena's Story

LENA HAD BEEN the Winter family housekeeper for 17 years and would say those were the best years of her life. She never expected to be a housekeeper or nanny, nor did her life turn out as she imagined. Yet, through every trial, she learned that life unfolds regardless of how much you plan.

Before meeting Madison, she had endured more trials and tribulations than most in a lifetime, but she concealed all that pain behind a warm smile and a hearty laugh. She "never met a stranger," and everyone she encountered felt like an old friend, especially when she hugged you instead of shaking hands.

Her mother, Rosa, discovered she was pregnant with Lena two months before finishing high school and pursuing her dream of becoming a nurse. The news upset Rosa's Sicilian mother, especially when Rosa decided to keep the baby, graduate, and take night classes at the local community college. Her mother feared the situation would destroy the family once her father learned of it.

Rosa knew the consequences of deciding based on "young love" and didn't want her daughter to miss out on their dream of her becoming a pediatrician.

From the time Lena could remember, her mother had constantly reminded her of how she came into the world. "I love you more than anything on this earth and wouldn't change a thing, but I work hard so that you don't have to make the decisions I did."

Lena was born in 1955 to Rosa Russo, a Sicilian girl who had earned a full scholarship to medical school and had a future mapped out in ambition. Her parents ran a small pizza parlor, where Rosa often worked after school. Rosa had been valedictorian, and a women-in-medicine program had already accepted her for the fall.

Then came Felton.

He was twenty-one, a Black saxophone player who made deliveries for her father during the week and played jazz on weekends. Rosa was seventeen when she fell for his easy smile and soft-spoken charm.

They tried to be careful. Love wasn't safe where they came from.

When she got pregnant, her parents gave her an ultimatum: give up the baby or face disownment.

She chose the baby.

After moving into Felton's brother's house, Rosa held onto a fragile plan, night classes, savings, and enough love to build a life.

But Rosa's father had a reputation. And the scandal of his daughter bearing a Black man's child? Too much for him to bear.

On the same day Lena Maria Russo was born, they pulled Felton's body from the river.

At the hospital, as nurses cooed over the golden-skinned baby with thick curls, Rosa sat still, her arms wrapped around her daughter, numb.

The young nurse paused at the doorway.

"You okay, hon?"

Rosa looked up, voice low. "My daughter just came into the world."

She looked back down. "And her father just left it."

The nurse said nothing. Just quietly adjusted Rosa's blanket and slipped back into the hall.

Just hours after giving birth, the creaking door swung open and woke Rosa from her nap. A nurse entered, followed by a tall man,

Felton's brother. He wore his cap pulled low and fiddled with an envelope in his hands.

"Rosa," he mumbled, avoiding her eyes. "I'm sorry. You can't come back to our place. They're threatening my family now. Said what happened to Felton... might happen to us if you stay."

He set the envelope on the nightstand.

"Felton wanted you to have this. It's all he had, three hundred dollars. I hope it helps."

Before Rosa could respond, he slipped out the door.

Moments later, another knock. This time, it was Uncle Marco, her father's longtime enforcer. Not blood, but close enough to carry shame like a family name.

He removed his cap.

"Rosa," he began, voice quiet, "I'm here on behalf of your parents."

He laid out the offer: return home, finish school, pretend none of this happened, if she gave the baby to the Sisters of St. Peter's for adoption.

"You can still have the future they wanted for you," he said.

Rosa clutched her baby tighter. Her eyes filled.

"I can't give up my baby," she whispered.

Uncle Marco's tone sharpened. "Your father loves you, but he's got no choice. A Sicilian family raising a mulatto child? It'll destroy everything he's built."

That word. Mulatto.

Something in her cracked.

"You tell my father," Rosa said, voice trembling, "he's dead to me and my baby."

She turned away.

Outside the room, a nurse had been listening. She stepped in, her face gentle.

"I've heard enough," she said with decisiveness. "You're coming home with me and my husband. Finish school. Keep your daughter."

And just like that, Rosa stepped into the unknown. One suitcase. One baby. Three hundred dollars.

No Felton. No Family.

But somehow, she made one.

Lena lived with the nurse for four years while Rosa attended nursing school, believing she had a scholarship with a small weekly stipend. That stipend covered Lena's daycare, which was run out of a storefront church by community outreach workers who charged families what they could afford.

It wasn't until a month before graduation that Rosa learned the truth.

She went to the finance office to collect her final stipend. The clerk hesitated.

"It hasn't arrived this month," he said. "Contact the donor."

"Donor?" Rosa asked. "I thought this was a scholarship."

The clerk flipped through a folder. "It's from Miss Veronica Romano. No mailing address, she uses the Nuns of St. Peter's Catholic Church as her contact."

Rosa stood there frozen. That name, Veronica Romano, was her mother's maiden name.

Her legs weakened beneath her. Her mother… had been paying for her education and living expenses all along. Four years. Silent. Unseen. But present.

Rosa left the office in a daze. She picked up now-five-year-old Lena from daycare and made a decision.

It was time for Lena to meet her grandparents.

Rosa headed across town toward the family restaurant, heart pounding with a complicated blend of hope, relief, and fear. About to graduate, she wanted to show her mother the woman she had become and the granddaughter she'd never met but always loved.

Rosa pushed open the door of the family pizza parlor, hand-in-hand with five-year-old Lena, who wore a new dress and shiny patent leather shoes. The warm air smelled of garlic and baked dough, scents Lena would later associate more with dread than comfort.

At the counter, Rosa's father sat reviewing paperwork, glasses perched low on his nose. For a moment, Rosa was ten years old again, small and uncertain, except now she had her own daughter clutching her hand.

"Hi, Papa," she said happily.

He looked up. His face froze. Then hardened.

"What the hell are you doing here?"

Rosa steadied her voice. Even if you didn't want me to know, I know you and Mommy helped me. I just thought you'd like to meet your granddaughter. Next week, I'm graduating from nursing school.

He slammed his folder shut.

"I did nothing for you," he spat. "Clearly, your mother was sneaking behind my back. God rest her soul; we buried her a week ago. Died of the flu."

Rosa's breath caught. "What? Papa, why didn't you tell me?"

He stood, voice rising with fury. "You think I wanted you showing up at her funeral with that mulatto bastard?"

The word hit the air like broken glass. Lena didn't entirely understand it, but she felt it. The heat. The hate.

Rosa's grip on her daughter's hand tightened. Without another word, she turned and walked out.

No apology. No embrace. Just rejection.

That moment would become a scar Lena carried in silence. But it wouldn't be the last.

The first time she knew she was different wasn't at the pizza shop; it was at school, when classmates whispered behind cupped hands, asking, "Are you white or Black?" One girl called her "mud." A boy laughed and said, "You don't belong anywhere."

She didn't understand the cruelty, only the ache it left behind. Her mother tried to shield her with affirmations and fierce love, but kids often believe the worst before they can accept the best.

So, Lena learned how to smile through pain. How to survive by being useful. By being kind. How to find joy in small victories.

But nothing ever quite erased that first, sharp sting, that moment when her grandfather looked at her and saw nothing but a mistake.

By the time Lena joined the Winter household, she was a 35-year-old widow raising teenage twin sons. Her mother, Rosa, had tried to dissuade her from marrying so young, but Lena followed her heart. She'd known James Theodore Jackson, J.T., since daycare at church. Best friends turned high school sweethearts, he had always been her quiet protector, especially when kids whispered about her mob-connected grandfather and blamed her father's death on race and rumor.

Rosa never left the neighborhood, committed to her nursing job at the local hospital. And whenever Lena came home in tears, Rosa would say:

"If all they can throw at you is 'mud' and 'bastard,' baby, then you just need more words."

Every morning, she'd kiss her forehead and whisper, "La figlia, my daughter, go to school and out-learn them all. The worst name you can ever be called is 'stupid.'"

Then, with a grin: "And it wouldn't hurt to hit back."

Lena and J.T. got married the day after graduation, quietly in the church office with only the janitor and secretary as witnesses. A week later, J.T. enlisted in the Army. Lena attended night classes to become a physician's assistant and worked as a supermarket clerk during the day.

She gave birth to twin boys while J.T. was deployed, and she lived in her mother's small townhouse until they could afford a place of their own. When he returned four years later, they bought a modest home in the suburbs. J.T. joined the fire department as a paramedic, using his military training. Lena finally had the life she dreamed of with a home, a family, and stability.

Then it shattered.

One night, near the end of his shift, J.T. and his partner stopped to grab dinner after dropping a patient at the ER. They walked in on a robbery in progress. Shots were fired.

Both men were pronounced dead at the scene.

May 5, 2007
Hawks Landing, 6:07 a.m.

Standing at the top of the staircase that morning, watching Madison head toward the den, where Lena knew only bad news waited, her thoughts drifted to how she'd become part of the Winter family.

When Lena first met Madison, she had been a widow for six years, raising twin boys who were now high school juniors with football scholarships lined up. Lena worked as a physician's assistant at a free clinic funded by one of Madison's charities.

One afternoon, after a meeting with potential donors, Madison asked Lena to join her for lunch. Over the meal, she quietly shared her secret: she was pregnant and explained that her mother-in-law insisted on hiring a nanny. Her husband had agreed. So, Madison made her own condition:

"If I must have a nanny, it will be someone of my choosing."

She leaned across the table, voice steady but sincere. "Lena, I hope this doesn't offend you. You were the first person I thought of. I've seen how you are with the children at the clinic; it's more than a job to you. I need someone I trust around me. Someone with no agenda."

Lena was deeply moved. The offer came with a generous salary and a three-bedroom guesthouse on the estate. What Madison didn't know then, and wouldn't know for years, was that Lena's mortgage had defaulted three years earlier. She'd been surviving on grit, giving up her bed to her growing sons and sleeping on the couch of a one-bedroom apartment.

To Lena, the offer was more than a job. It was an answered prayer.

Madison arranged transportation for Lena's sons, ensuring they stayed eligible for their scholarships. Initially, Lena agreed to remain until Coby started school. But by then, she and Madison were more than employer and employee. They were a chosen family.

Even after the boys went off to college and Lena remarried, she continued to come to the estate every weekday morning. She managed the kitchen, watched over the house, and most importantly, stayed a steady presence for Madison.

And for Coby, she was "Auntie Lena."

Now, two years before the wildfire, on a quiet morning at the Winter estate, Lena descended the staircase just behind Madison, who was headed to the den, where her husband and a police officer were waiting.

Without turning fully, Madison called over her shoulder, her voice carrying down the hallway, "Bring some coffee to the den."

But Lena didn't move. Her hand gripped the banister. Her heart knew before her mind caught up: this was the kind of morning that rearranged a woman's life. She'd felt this weight before, and knew that ashes don't tell everything—they only whisper what's been lost, never the price paid to survive it.

Not from years of working in this house. Not even from watching other women stumble through grief. No, it came from her own marrow the night two officers stood on her doorstep, hats in hand, voices thick with pity.

"Ma'am, there was a shooting."

She remembered her knees giving out before they finished the sentence, how the mug of tea slipped from her hands and shattered across the tile. Her boys, still young and wide-eyed, had come running.

All she could do was whisper one word: "J.T."

That kind of grief never left. It slept inside you. Until one morning, it woke with a chill and stood beside you on the stairs.

So, when Madison called again, lighter this time, "Lena? That coffee?"

Lena didn't answer.

She just watched her friend walk toward the door.

And thought,

"No time for coffee."

Madison walked past the officer standing in the doorway of the den and straight to her husband, who was already at the desk. He wrapped his arm around her shoulders.

With calm authority, he said, "Officer, this is my wife. What did you need?"

The officer nodded politely, his voice gentle but clipped. "Mrs. Winter, would you like to sit down?"

"No, thank you," she replied, her tone firm. "Just tell us."

The officer's eyes didn't waver. "Early this morning, a head-on collision killed your son, Jacob Winston Winter. The other driver had been drinking. He survived with minor injuries."

Madison didn't scream. She didn't collapse.

She stood there, frozen, breath caught somewhere between that sentence and the next. Her husband's arm held her upright as seventeen years of joy shattered around her in absolute silence.

From that day forward, she returned to the den each morning. Not for closure, she didn't believe in that. To her, closure meant forgetting. And she could never forget.

She returned because it was the last place she had seen him. The last time he turned and said, "Momma, I love you."

It had been the night of Coby's senior prom.

Coby was her light, warm, bright, and irrepressibly kind. In a world that demanded she smile for cameras and pose for power, he was her only refuge. The only thing in her life that wasn't curated wasn't performative.

He made the silence bearable.

His laughter stitched her heart together when everything else unraveled. His hugs reminded her she still existed, not as Lady Winter, not as the Bishop's wife, but as Momma.

As a boy, he was curious and soft-hearted. He danced without music. Cried during sad movie scenes. Asked if God had a favorite color and if stars could hear prayers.

He was the kind of child who gave the love he needed, without asking for it in return.

And now, he was gone.

CHAPTER
THIRTY-EIGHT

MAY 4, 2007

The Winter's Den
7:35 p.m.

LAUGHTER, warmth, and the click of camera shutters once filled the den. The Winter and Dupree families had gathered that night to take photos of Coby and his childhood sweetheart, Jasmine "MeMe" Dupree, dressed for senior prom.

Their story began in kindergarten, with a pulled ponytail and a retaliatory kick, and they'd been inseparable ever since.

Just weeks earlier, they had announced plans to marry after graduation and attend culinary school in France. Some raised eyebrows, dismissing it as young love. But Madison understood: Coby wasn't just in love with MeMe, he was in love with a different life.

Coby's passion for cooking wasn't a phase. Despite his athletic build and the assumptions that came with it, he'd never gravitated toward sports. The kitchen brought him peace.

As a boy, he would sit on the counter with his legs swinging, observing his mother as she cooked. He paid close attention not only to the ingredients but also to her, how her voice became gentle, her shoulders eased, and a rare smile appeared on her face.

Lady Winter would tell him stories while she stirred and chopped, about the parents she lost when she was just a child. Though Coby never met them, he came to know them through the food, through her voice.

"Papa's Pecan Pie was your grandfather's favorite," she'd say, or "Your grandmother couldn't cook worth a damn, but her salmon croquettes? Legendary." His favorite was "Nana's Lemon-Coconut Cake," baked once a year on January 30th, to honor his great-grandmother's birthday, a tradition passed down by his grandfather, Jackson.

Those recipes weren't just instructions. They were memories. Legacy. Grief made edible.

For Coby, cooking became a way to reclaim the family history that someone had stolen. It wasn't just passion; it was purpose.

His and MeMe's plan to marry and leave the country created tension between the families, but Madison understood Coby wasn't simply pursuing love or ambition.

He was trying to escape the dysfunction he'd grown up with.

"I Love You, Momma"

She recalled sitting at her husband's desk that night, watching him help Coby with his bowtie. He joked about reaching up to tie it now that his son had grown taller. Bishop Winter stood at 6'1, while Coby, a lean and handsome 6'3, was the spitting image of his father, except for his long, curly hair, which he kept in a ponytail despite his father's protests.

Madison understood that this was his silent rebellion against what he considered unreasonable expectations.

Madison remembered Jasmine and her mother fussing over last-minute details, though MeMe looked stunning in a form-fitting gown, her bobbed hair framing her face like Cleopatra's. She recalled Tyler Dupree nervously indulging in Bishop Winter's coveted Rémy Martin Louis XIII "Black Pearl" to toast the occasion of the two families blessing the future.

But what she cherished most was when her Coby glanced back at the door of the den, arm-in-arm with Jasmine, and said, "I love you, Momma. You're still my best girl."

She hadn't known it would be the last time she heard his voice.

That night was also the last time she and Bishop sat together without pretense. After the guests left, the house fell into a soft hush, a silence that felt sacred. They remained in the den, the soft glow of the floor lamp casting long shadows against the walls, sipping the last of the cognac and letting the memories wash over them.

He sat on the plush rug at her feet, massaging them gently, and for a fleeting moment, it felt like they were just two distant hearts clinging to the one thing they still had in common, Coby.

They talked about his first steps, the time he accidentally set off the alarm trying to sneak cookies from the pantry, how he'd cry whenever Madison left his sight, and how his laughter could melt the coldest of moods. They remembered how he would dance without rhythm but with uncontainable joy, belt out songs off-key while no one had the heart to tell him to stop, and how their son remained soft-hearted and authentic in a world so often hardened by pride and position.

Bishop Winter chuckled rhythmically, rubbing his index finger over the rim of his glass. "Remember when he swore he was going to be a preacher like me?"

Madison smiled. "Only until he realized it meant getting up early on Sundays."

He laughed. "Said, 'Daddy, I love God… but I also love sleeping in.'"

They both fell quiet for a moment, their laughter fading into something heavier.

"He was always honest," Madison said, her voice just above a whisper. "Even when it hurt."

There was no performance, no image to uphold. The bishop and the first lady fell away, replaced by two parents utterly in love with the boy they had raised and terrified of the world awaiting him. They each, in their own quiet way, shared regrets about the distance that had grown between them, the pressure their son carried, and the times they had chosen duty over presence.

It was a night that stitched together fractured souls, if only for a moment.

Later that night, they made the rare decision to spend the night together in the master bedroom. She would later wonder if it was love, grief, or alcohol. But in the face of her son's death the following day, the reasons no longer mattered.

The death of their son marked not only the loss of the brightest light in Madison's life but also the end of any illusion she had about her marriage. That grief and the subsequent isolation planted the seeds for her decision to leave Hawks Landing and start anew.

That day didn't just take her son. It took her entire world, the life she knew, forever changed. She would never be the same.

CHAPTER
THIRTY-NINE

MAY 11, 2007

The Winter's Den
8:45 a.m.

LENA KNOCKED ONCE on the door of the den, even though it was already open.

She found Madison sitting exactly where she'd been the night before, on the velvet chaise by the fireplace, still in her funeral dress from the day before, shoes off, bare feet curled beneath her like a girl waiting for something to undo the day.

The morning light fell in narrow stripes across the rug, and the room smelled faintly of white lilies and the bourbon Bishop Winter had spilled in his grief.

Lena held a covered cake dish in her hands.

"I made it," she said kindly. "That lemon-coconut cake. The one he loved."

Madison didn't look up.

"I know it's too soon," Lena added, stepping fully into the room. "But when I woke up this morning, I couldn't stop hearing him say, "Nana's cake is sunshine, Auntie Lena. Even when it rains."

At that, Madison finally glanced over. Her swollen eyes, rimmed with the red of silent sobs, finally focused on him.

"You remember that?" she whispered.

"I remember everything about that boy," Lena said.

"He's the only one who ever called me 'Auntie Lena' like I was royalty."

She moved toward the low table and set the cake down gently, as if placing a relic on an altar.

For a long time, they sat in silence. The clock ticked from somewhere in the foyer. Outside, a bird called, too cheerfully for a day like this.

Then Madison said, without looking over, "I don't know who I am without him."

Lena's voice came quietly but steadily. "You're still his mother."

Madison shook her head. "That means nothing now."

"Yes, it does." Lena moved closer, kneeling beside the chaise so they were eye level. "Because being his mother didn't end yesterday. It just changed. Now it means remembering what he stood for, what he loved. What made him laugh and cry and burn bright."

Madison's lip trembled. "He was the only thing I got right."

"You got more right than you know," Lena said, taking one of her hands, chilled from grief. "He was your joy, but also your mirror. All the strength you gave him is still in you."

Madison closed her eyes as a single tear escaped, trailing down her cheek.

Lena didn't let go.

She just stayed silent and steady, the way only a woman who had also buried the love of her life could.

Lena whispered, "I'll cut you a slice."

Madison nodded, barely. "I don't think I can eat yet."

"That's fine," Lena said. "I didn't bring it, so you'd eat. I brought it so you'd remember that the sun does rise, even if it's slower some days."

They stayed like that for a long while, two women sitting in the thick silence of mourning, bound not by duty or title, but by a shared ache no one else could name.

And in the quiet, something shifted.

Not healed. Not yet.

But held.

The next morning, Lena entered the kitchen wrapped in a smell that had become a second skin in the house since Coby's death, lingering on the curtains, in the hallways, and in the creases of Madison's robe.

Onion. Dill. A hint of lemon. Cooking oil and salt.

Madison stood barefoot in the kitchen, pressing patties between her palms with practiced, reverent care. Salmon croquettes. The same dish she had made every morning since Coby's funeral.

She didn't cry when she cooked them. That was the point. It was the only time of day her hands remembered something other than loss. The rhythm of dicing onions, cracking eggs, flaking the salmon, and stirring in breadcrumbs gave her a place to put the pain.

A task. A ritual. A prayer.

She shaped the last croquette and dropped it gently into the hot oil, watching it sizzle like a secret.

Lena entered the kitchen slowly, pausing in the doorway as if she weren't sure if she was intruding.

"You're doing it again," Lena said with a touch of irritation.

"I know," Madison replied, not turning around.

"Baby, it's been over a week."

Madison flipped a patty with the edge of a fork, her movements precise. "8 days."

Lena stepped closer. "You haven't eaten them."

"They're not for eating," Madison whispered.

Lena watched her in silence. The counter beside the stove held a plate covered in foil, yesterday's batch. And next to that, a sealed container. The day before that. They were all there. A quiet graveyard of untouched offerings.

Madison finally turned, her hands trembling, glistening with oil. Her voice wavered.

"He loved these. Said they tasted like home."

"He did," Lena replied, her eyes softening. "He told me once that he liked the way you made them better than any restaurant."

Madison looked down at her hands. "I don't know what to do with myself when I'm not making them."

"You don't have to know," Lena said gently. "Just... don't disappear inside this."

Madison reached up, tucking a loose curl behind her ear with a grease-slicked finger. Her voice dropped to barely a breath. "It's the only thing I can still make right."

Lena stepped forward and placed a warm hand over hers.

"No, baby. It's not the only thing. You still have breath in your body. That means there's still time to make peace. Time to forgive. Time to live."

Madison didn't answer.

She just turned back to the stove.

And flipped the next croquette.

The smell of salmon still hung in the air when the doorbell rang.

Madison didn't move at first. She stood there, staring at the stovetop as the last croquette darkened to a perfect crisp. Lena, still in the kitchen, raised an eyebrow.

"You expecting anybody?"

Madison shook her head slowly.

Lena wiped her hands on a towel and moved to the front door. When she opened it, a uniformed courier stood with a weatherproof envelope, his expression neutral but polite.

"Special delivery for Jacob Winston Winter," he said, confirming the name. "Signature required."

Madison's voice floated in from the kitchen. "What is it?"

Lena squinted at the envelope, noting the return address printed in gold script:

Institut de Cuisine et Pâtisserie de Paris.

"It's from Paris," she said, her voice catching. "The cooking school."

Madison's feet moved before her brain could respond. She approached Lena, slow and reverent, like an altar. Trembling, she took the envelope, stared at the embossed crest, and traced its elegant lettering.

Carefully, as if afraid the letter might vanish, she peeled it open.

Inside were two acceptance packets, one for Jacob Winston Winter, the other for Jasmine Me'Lena Dupree. A formal congratulatory letter and an official notification of scholarship award accompanied each.

Lena watched her, quiet as a breath.

Madison read every word. Twice.

When she finally spoke, her voice cracked under the weight of it. "He got in," she whispered. "They both got in."

A tear fell onto the page, smudging the ink.

"They were going to do it," she said, a choked laugh escaping her lips. "They were going to go. Paris. They were going to start a life."

Lena moved forward and wrapped her arms around her from behind. Madison didn't resist. She leaned into the warmth, accepting the embrace.

In her hands, the letter trembled like a heartbeat. "They didn't even get the chance to know," she murmured.

"But now you do," Lena whispered. "And you'll carry it for them. However long it takes."

Madison nodded slowly, holding the letter to her chest.

For the first time in days, she didn't feel like she was drowning.

Just... floating. On the surface.

Still breathing. Still holding on.

CHAPTER
FORTY
MAY 12, 2007

The Winter's Den
2:05 p.m.

THE DEN WAS DIM, lit only by the late afternoon light filtering through sheer drapes.

Dust motes drifted in the sunbeams like quiet spirits, silent witnesses to the memories soaked into every inch of the room.

Madison sat on the leather settee, the envelope from Paris resting in her lap like a sleeping child. A Coltrane record hummed low in the background, Coby's favorite, what he once called his "thinking music."

She didn't look up when the knock came.

The door creaked open.

Jasmine's mother, Celeste Dupree, stepped inside.

Exhaustion rimmed her eyes, the kind only found after nights of crying yourself to sleep and waking up in the same nightmare.

They hadn't spoken since the funeral.

Too much pain.

Too many words that didn't exist.

Today felt different.

Madison looked up and gently patted the seat beside her.

Celeste hesitated, then crossed the room, smoothing her dress before she sat.

Hands in her lap. Wrung tight.

She didn't speak.

Madison did.

"They got in," she whispered.

Celeste turned, confused.

"To the cooking school," Madison said, her voice catching. "In Paris. The letter came today. They both got scholarships."

Celeste's hand flew to her mouth.

Tears welled.

She leaned forward as if the words had stolen the air from her lungs.

"I... I didn't even know they applied," she said softly.

Madison nodded. "He didn't tell anyone. Jasmine must've helped him. Must've sent it off months ago."

A long silence.

Celeste reached out, fingers brushing the envelope in Madison's lap. Her touch lingered, like she could feel the weight of a future that never arrived.

"It's like they knew," Celeste whispered. "Like the world saw them. Believed in them. Before it was taken away."

Madison's eyes shimmered. "It feels like... confirmation. What they shared was real."

Celeste nodded. "That their love was genuine. That our babies were more than a headline."

Her voice trembled.

Madison turned toward her. Slowly, she reached out.

Their hands met, two mothers, not bound by blood, but by a bond forged in loss. One that could never be undone.

"They were good," Madison said, her voice steady now. "People loved them. And they were going to be great."

"They still are," Celeste said, almost in a whisper. "They still are."

For a long moment, they sat together in silence.

Tears fell freely. Grief breathed between them.

Not church ladies.

Not socialites.

Not "the bishop's wife" or "the real estate mogul's other half."

Just Madison and Celeste.

Mothers of the same flame, wading through ashes, praying that the ashes don't tell everything, only part of the story, not the whole of what was lost or what still burns.

PART ELEVEN
MAMA PEARL AND NINA

CHAPTER
FORTY-ONE
NOVEMBER 9, 1971

Mama Pearl's Foster Home
5:25 p.m.

NINA HAD BEEN fortunate or deeply unfortunate to spend her entire foster care experience in just one home. That was rare. Most kids in the system moved from house to house, family to family, and from one piece of paperwork to another.

But not Nina.

She arrived at Mama Pearl's house when she was seven years old. And she never left, at least not in an emotional sense. Emotionally, parts of her were still stuck in that house.

It was in that three-story home, tucked away in a neighborhood too busy to question, that Nina would meet the people and witness the events that would trigger the PTSD and depression she carried into adulthood, compounded by witnessing her mother's murder.

It started in the kitchen.

Mama Pearl had yanked her by the collar and shoved her into a chair so hard it knocked the wind out of her lungs.

"Let's set the record straight," Mama Pearl snapped. "Yo' mama's dead. I run this house. And I don't tolerate anybody talkin' smart to me."

After that first clash in the kitchen, Mama Pearl didn't say another word to Nina for the rest of the evening. She handed her a plate and pointed to the corner of the table. The house buzzed with activity, kids cleaning dishes, someone yelling from the basement, music playing faintly from a radio on the back porch, but Nina sat still, eating slowly, soaking in the rhythm of it all. This wasn't a home. It was a system. A machine. And she would have to learn how to move with it or get ground up trying.

That first night, Nina didn't cry.

She knew better than to give anyone that much of herself. Not here. Not yet.

After a dinner of baked chicken, fried cabbage, cornbread, and peach cobbler so sweet it stuck to her teeth, Mama Pearl told her to go upstairs and wash up for bed. The bathroom was across from the girls' room, where she'd share a bunk with Marcy, who hadn't spoken all evening.

Nina climbed onto the bottom bunk, still fully dressed, staring at the wooden slats above her. The room smelled of lotion and old books, like heat trapped inside summer sheets. Peeling wallpaper with faded roses covered the walls. A pink plastic fan hummed on the windowsill, barely cutting through the humidity.

Missing the security and warmth of her mother, she refused to cry, her eyes burning with restrained emotion. She knew better than to give anyone that much of herself, to let them see her vulnerability. Not her. Not yet.

She could hear the low rumble of men's voices downstairs. A shuffling of footsteps. Laughter, then silence. Then dice.

Click. Click. Clatter.

The sound echoed through the floorboards like bones rattling in a cup.

She closed her eyes and pretended it was something else, maybe popcorn, or maybe pebbles at the bottom of a stream.

But she knew what it was.

She had heard it before in places where the grown-ups didn't care if kids were listening. She rolled over, facing the wall, her hands curled beneath her chin. The door creaked open.

In a low, clear voice, Mama Pearl warned, "Don't sneak out of bed. You hear me, gal?"

Nina didn't move.

"I'm watchin' you."

The door clicked shut. She lay there a long time, wide-eyed in the dark. She wanted to believe that meant someone cared, that being watched meant someone was looking out for her.

But it didn't feel like safety.

It felt like surveillance.

The bunk above her shifted. Marcy turned in her sleep and mumbled something Nina couldn't make out. A car backfired in the distance, and somewhere a dog barked twice before falling quiet.

In the silence that followed, Nina finally let herself breathe.

Just once.

She reached into her pocket and pulled out the one thing she still had from her mother, a key with no lock. Her mother said it opened the door to their future house, with a porch swing, fresh paint, and no yelling.

She squeezed it in her palm, her fingernails pressing into the soft skin between her fingers.

And in the dark, she whispered to herself, just loud enough to believe it: *"I can do this. I'll survive this, too."*

That was the beginning.

Nina didn't talk back. She watched. She studied everything. Everyone. She learned the rhythm of that house the way other kids learned songs or prayers. She figured out what made people tick, what kept her safe, and, more importantly, what got her favor.

Nina quickly realized there was no space or time to be a kid; Mama Pearl used every part of her house to make money: the basement was a secret gambling den with dice and cards. On weekends, the kitchen bustled as she sold hearty dinners, attracting locals with rich aromas. She used each bedroom as a makeshift haven for her clients, engaging in low-profile madam activities to ensure a steady income.

Even the porch, with its rickety chairs and warm light, became a gathering place for those in need of loans, where Mama Pearl acted as the neighborhood loan shark, offering quick cash solutions at steep interest rates.

Supposedly, the large Samoan man, known only as Teddy Bear, wasn't her husband, but a silent guard she had rescued from something dark and unspeakable. No one knew the entire story, but the way he shadowed her movements and scanned every room spoke volumes. He was equal parts myth and muscle, fiercely loyal, unmistakably lethal. People didn't question his presence; they feared what it meant.

He wasn't just protecting Mama Pearl's empire; he was warning the world what would happen if anyone tried to dismantle it.

Nina would eventually learn precisely why he was needed as a bodyguard and what sort of woman required someone like him.

CHAPTER
FORTY-TWO
NOVEMBER 13, 1971

Mama Pearl's
4:30 p.m.

THE CADILLAC FLEETWOOD purred to a stop at the curb like royalty announcing its arrival.

The engine cut.

Silence settled.

But everyone on the block knew... *Open for Business.*

Mama Pearl emerged first, regal in a tailored two-piece pantsuit the color of deep plum, its gold embroidery catching the porch light like fireflies in motion. Her heels clicked confidently against the wooden boards, each step declaring her authority. Teddy Bear followed like a shadow, his massive frame blocking out half the doorway as he scanned the street with silent precision.

Nina climbed the steps behind them, unsure whether she was more intimidated by the Cadillac or the quiet power radiating from the woman in front of her.

"Don't just stand there with your mouth open, baby," Mama Pearl called back. "Come inside before your questions catch a bullet."

Inside, the air was thick with soul food, stale smoke, and tension, like the house had inhaled too many secrets and didn't dare exhale.

Mama Pearl didn't miss a beat.

She pointed to the hallway. "Teddy, go check the back. I don't like how quiet those dice been rollin'."

Teddy nodded once, then disappeared without a word.

Mama Pearl turned to Nina, her eyes sharp, assessing.

"You ever fry catfish, girl?"

"Y-yes, ma'am," Nina stammered. "Watched mama."

"Well, good. Because my kitchen don't like lazy hands or burnt grease, you can start there. If your hands match your mouth, maybe you'll graduate to something that pays better."

Nina hesitated. "Pays better?"

Mama Pearl raised an eyebrow. "Baby, this house got a hundred ways to make money. But every dollar costs something. You gotta decide what you're willin' to pay."

Nina swallowed hard. "And what about him?" She asked, nodding toward where Teddy had disappeared.

Mama Pearl gave a slow smile, part warning, part pride. "Teddy Bear? He don't talk much, but he hears everything. Ain't my man. He's my shadow. Keeps the wolves at the edge of the woods."

She leaned in, voice low and deliberate.

"He owes me his life. So, if I say 'protect,' he protects. But if I say destroy..." She tapped her long red nail against Nina's chest. "He destroys."

Nina nodded slowly, the gravity of the place settling on her shoulders.

Mama Pearl's voice softened, but not much. "You stay sharp, keep your head down, and remember there ain't no such thing as halfway in this house."

She handed Nina an apron, already stained with flour and stories.

"Now go on. Fish ain't gonna fry itself."

Later that evening, Nina lifted the last piece of fish from the hot skillet with her spatula, then stepped down from her sturdy wooden stool and joined Mama Pearl on the porch.

"Ma'am, I'm finished frying fish."

"Help me with these chairs, baby," she said to Nina without turning her head.

Nina grabbed a chair. No questions. Just obedience.

As they set up folding chairs on the porch and music began playing from the basement, Pearl gave her the rundown.

"This ain't just about money," she said. "It's all about image. When folks see the car, the clothes, and this porch full of pretty people sipping sweet tea, they think we're blessed."

"Safe. Smart. Powerful." She leaned in close, a cigarette dangling from her lip.

"Po folks get robbed. Rich folks get respected.

"Even if you ain't rich, if you look like money, they'll treat you like you're worth somethin'."

It was the first time Nina understood that survival didn't just mean staying alive; it meant shaping how the world saw you... *hiding the truth in plain sight.*

Mama Pearl's house was a theater, with every role cast.

Teddy Bear, silent and looming by the porch, was security.

The girls, some barely older than Nina, helped by flirting just enough, laughing just enough, and walking as if they knew secrets you never would.

Mama Pearl was the leading lady, never challenged or questioned. She raised her voice only when she wanted it to be heard three blocks away.

Nina learned early that even the slightest detail mattered.

A spotless Cadillac, the curtains in the living room perfectly drawn, and the Sunday plates never touched the weekday table.

Mama Pearl tapped Nina on the forehead and said, "Presentation is power."

The words echoed, first in Nina's chest, then across a lifetime.

She carried that lesson into boardrooms, charity galas, and long nights beside Lady Winter.

She learned to wear elegance like armor and hide the cracks beneath the shine.

CHAPTER
FORTY-THREE
OCTOBER 22, 1979

Mama Pearl's
1:30 p.m.

IT WAS A TUESDAY EVENING, quiet by Mama Pearl's usual standards. Rain tapped against the windows like a ticking clock, steady and soft. Teddy Bear was off running an errand. Mama Pearl had gone to the doctor for her "blood pressure and business," as she called it, leaving Nina in charge of the house.

"Don't let nobody touch nothin' till I get back," she'd said, lipstick flawless as she snapped her purse closed. "And if they got somethin' urgent to say... they can say it to you."

Nina nodded. She was fifteen, maybe sixteen. Tall. Observant. But still unsure.

Until the knock came.

She opened the door halfway and eyed the man standing there. Marcus "Skully" Dean. Mid-thirties, known for a bad reputation and an even worse attitude. He ran low-level dice games and sometimes collected from people who owed Mama Pearl. Nina had seen him before, but never this close. He smelled of cigarettes, wet leather, and desperation.

"Evenin', lil Miss Storm," he said, grinning like he'd just smelled blood.

Nina didn't smile. "What you need?"

Skully's eyes slid over her like grease on a skillet. "I came to settle up with Mama Pearl. That last package I picked up? It was short."

"No, it wasn't," Nina replied. Calm. Flat. Pearl had trained her, never apologize when you're right.

He stepped forward, testing the door. "You callin' me a liar?"

She didn't flinch. "I'm saying, Mama Pearl, don't make mistakes, and not here."

"I am." He scoffed, shifting his weight. "You're just a little girl playin' dress-up. You ain't her."

Nina took a breath and stepped into the doorway, squaring her shoulders.

"No. I'm not her," she said, voice cool as steel. "But she left me in charge. So, if you think you can disrespect her name just 'cause she ain't here to hear it..."

She let the silence hang.

Then she stepped out onto the porch, closing the door behind her with a solid click.

"...you better be ready to say it loud enough for the whole damn block to hear."

For a moment, just one, Skully hesitated.

Then Nina added, "And if Teddy comes back and finds out you tried to press up on me while she was gone? You'd better pray Jesus himself is faster than Teddy Bear's right hook."

That was the clincher.

Skully looked her up and down, tongue clicking against his teeth. Then he took a step back. "A'ight. Message received," he muttered, pulling his collar up against the rain. "Tell Pearl I said we're square."

Nina nodded once, then watched as he disappeared into the dark, his bravado melting into the mist. When she walked back inside, heart pounding in her chest like a drum, she didn't collapse. Didn't cry. Sat on the couch like Mama Pearl always did, legs crossed, head high.

Later that night, Mama Pearl returned, said nothing, and just glanced at Nina before pouring two glasses of sweet tea.

They sipped in silence, but Pearl's small, sharp smile said it all:

You did good, baby.

CHAPTER
FORTY-FOUR
SEPTEMBER 18, 1947

Small Town, Mississippi,
2:30 p.m.

"Y'ALL CAME SO FAST, the midwife missed the whole thing," their mother used to say, shaking her head. "Slipped into this world like you had places to be."

Mama Pearl and her sister Mae Lou were born identical but different in every way. Their legal names, Mary Lou and Mae Lou, barely stuck. It was their father, Louis, who renamed them.

"Pearl," he'd say, lifting Mary Lou's chin. "You got quiet strength. Still waters, deep."

Then he'd grin at Mae Lou. "And you, Diamond. You shine even when the world's dark."

They weren't raised like their brothers. While the boys worked the fields, the girls stayed close to their mama and Aunt Cee Cee, learning to read and write by lantern light.

"You see this can?" Aunt Cee Cee once whispered, tapping the rusted lid of a coffee tin hidden beneath the floorboard.

Mae Lou peeked in. "That's a lotta dollars."

Pearl tilted her head. "Enough for something?"

"For your future," Aunt Cee Cee said. "Secretarial school. You two ain't meant for cotton sacks and calloused hands."

Louis agreed. "You're my precious girls," he'd say. "Pearls and diamonds don't belong in the dirt."

And just like that, they set the plan.

Two girls.

One dream.

And a coffee can full of hope.

Unfortunately, hope would fade in the fire.

By the time they were thirteen, the twins were tall, slim, and stunning, the kind of beauty that made people uneasy. Black or white, folks noticed. Diamond soaked it in. Pearl, always watchful, stayed guarded.

Maybe that's why she saw danger before it hit.

That afternoon, Pearl stayed behind after class to finish her test. She told Diamond, "Wait for me on the steps. Don't go wandering."

But Diamond didn't wait.

When Pearl walked out and saw the empty steps, a bolt of panic shot through her.

"Daddy said stay together," she muttered, scanning the horizon. "Don't trust these white folks."

She ran straight into the woods.

Then she heard it.

"You want it, nigger?" The voice twisted her stomach.

She followed the sound and froze.

Diamond lay on the ground, pinned beneath a white boy… the landowner's grandson.

Her dress was torn. Her eyes, usually full of sparkle, were wild with fear.

"Help me," she whimpered.

Pearl didn't hesitate. She grabbed the nearest rock and swung.

Once.

Twice.

Blood. Thick and fast.

He curled up and stopped moving.

The sisters ran. Diamond sobbing, blood trickling down her leg, face swollen from where he'd hit her. She kept mumbling, "He said I wanted it... he said I wanted it..."

Pearl didn't speak. Didn't cry.

She just prayed no one saw.

Because a white boy, dead by a Black girl's hand?

And not just any white boy, Colonel Watts' grandson.

That was a death sentence.

Colonel Watts owned over half the county. Land, the general store, and power. His grandson, raised by the Colonel and his wife, embodied privilege with arrogance to match. Their only daughter, Margaret, had returned home pregnant after a failed affair with a traveling evangelist who had already been married. The Colonel kept the pregnancy quiet, planning to give the baby up for adoption after the birth.

But Margaret died during childbirth, weakened by illness and malnourishment. With her final breath, she whispered, *"I'm sorry. Please forgive me."* The Colonel's wife wept over her daughter's body as the midwife handed over a newborn boy. Plans changed. The baby stayed. "He's all we have left of her," the Colonel said, and they fabricated a story: she had been widowed.

The boy grew up spoiled, untouchable, dressed in knickerbockers, and trained to wield his grandfather's name like a weapon. He learned early how power bent people, especially those who owed rent or needed credit.

On visits to the sharecroppers, the boy noticed the twins, Pearl and Diamond. Though identical, his gaze locked on Diamond, her light, her laugh, her spark. But she dismissed him once, asking innocently, *"Why do you dress like an old man?"*

That question, small, harmless, wounded his pride. And one afternoon, when she waited for Pearl outside the school, he took action.

What he didn't expect was Pearl.

In that single moment, a girl no one expected brought down the spoiled prince of a powerful man.

CHAPTER
FORTY-FIVE
AUGUST 14, 1978

Mama Pearl's Living Room
12:30 p.m.

NINA DIDN'T KNOW all of Mama Pearl's story at first.

But over time, she pieced it together, through whispers, through silences, through the way Mama Pearl held people close but never let them see the cracks.

Teddy Bear once told her, *"That woman's done things you'll never understand, to protect what's hers."*

Nina believed him.

She understood why the doors remained locked, why Mama Pearl dressed sharp, why no one dared speak slick, and why she needed a bodyguard.

That rock in the woods didn't just end a life; it forged one.

It crafted a woman who built her fortress from trauma and survival, a woman who refused to break

And Nina, wise, guarded, fierce, carried those same lessons.

She learned early that the world didn't intend for girls like her to stay soft.

So, she became steel.

But had also understood that even steel bends when the heat rises as she brought a cup of tea that afternoon to Madison on the couch wrapped in a blanket that smelled faintly of hospital soap and stale flowers.

Madison's eyes were raw, her voice thin as she whispered to Nina, "I didn't want to come back to this house."

Nina sat beside her, quiet. Her arm draped around Madison's shoulders, as if holding her together was all that kept her upright.

"You had to," Nina whispered. "We'll figure it out. One step at a time."

"What if he comes back?" she said, clutching the blanket in fear.

Nina glanced around, ensuring no one could hear, and declared, "Teddy Bear said he ain't never coming back anywhere."

The house creaked as an old floorboard shifted. They thought they were alone.

But from the kitchen doorway, Mama Pearl's voice cut through the silence like a blade smoothed on velvet.

"Lemme tell y'all somethin'," she said, stepping into the room, her silhouette framed by the low kitchen light. "You think this here, this moment you're in right now, is the worst it gets? You think the world ain't got bigger teeth than this?"

She lit a cigarette, and the flick of the lighter echoed in the stillness.

"I done seen girls break. I done seen girls run. And I done seen girls turn that breakin' into somethin' that made the world blink."

She sat down across from them, her gaze steady, her voice low and rhythmic, half confessional, half sermon.

"Lemme tell you about fire. Not the pretty kind with marshmallows. The kind that leaves marks. The kind that either takes you out... or teaches you how to be a flame yourself."

Nina glanced at Madison, her eyes wide. They both knew Mama Pearl didn't tell stories for no reason.

Madison wiped her cheek. "What kind of fire?" she whispered.

Mama Pearl leaned forward, elbows on her knees, cigarette balanced between two fingers. Her voice dropped to a hush, thick with memory.

"The kind that started the day my sister Diamond and I ran through the woods, thinking we could outrun a sin the world never forgives. The day we learned survival ain't about bein' strong, it's about knowin' when to run, when to stay, and when to turn yourself into somethin' the world can't swallow."

Her words wrapped around them like smoke and shadow.

And the story began…

CHAPTER
FORTY-SIX
SEPTEMBER 18, 1947

Mama Pearl's Living Room
2:47 p.m.

THE TWINS RAN through the woods, breath ragged, hearts pounding. With every step away from that clearing, the place where Pearl had ended the Colonel's grandson's reign of terror, felt like a countdown. As they reached the edge of their family's land, their father spotted them from the field. He started running. When he saw Diamond's tear-streaked face, her eyes no longer sparkling but shattered, he knew.

This wasn't just bad.

This was life-altering.

The girls fell into his arms, sobbing. He dropped to his knees with them, cradling them both as if his arms alone could protect them from the world.

It was Pearl who finally spoke.

"Daddy... I killed the Colonel's grandson."

He froze.

"You did what?"

Pearl screamed through her tears.

"He raped Diamond. I hit him with a rock. He stopped moving..."

Their father rose slowly, pulling them up with him. Even before they reached the porch of that tiny three-room shack, he knew. This was the last time he held his girls, or the last time he'd see them alive. They needed to disappear before the discovery of the body.

The money hidden under the floorboards, initially intended for their education, would now serve as their escape. Their mother stitched half into the lining of their Sunday quilted jackets. They kept the rest to fund the trip.

Their father asked Pastor Ford to drive the girls to the neighboring town, where they would catch a bus to Milwaukee to visit their mother's sister. This was the only plan they had.

At the bus depot, he handed the girls a sack of fried chicken and biscuits, an envelope with their aunt's address, and two Psalms 23 cards, each with a picture of a lamb.

He led them to the back of the bus. The "colored section."

The girls sat silently, fighting back tears.

He bent down, giving each of them a hug.

"No matter where life takes you," he said, "remember your parents love you. And Jesus is always with you."

A woman sitting behind them, a sweet-faced lady with a little boy in tow, overheard the exchange.

"Reverend, don't worry," she said kindly. "I'll keep an eye on them."

He smiled through watery eyes.

"You're an angel."

As fate would have it, the woman, Mother Daisy, did more than just watch over them.

She became family.

She lived in the same Milwaukee neighborhood as their aunt, attended the same church, and her daughter's husband owned a small grocery store. Recently, she visited relatives down south with her grandson.

When they arrived, her son picked them up and drove the girls to their aunt's home.

The city hit them like a slap.

From the moment they stepped off the bus, Pearl felt it, louder, faster, tighter than anything they had known. Milwaukee was nothing like Mississippi. No acres of green, no dusty roads lined with cotton. No quiet. No sky stretched so wide you could lie under it and feel like it might carry you to heaven.

Here, everything felt vertical and close, steel buildings scraped the clouds, and the air was thick with exhaust and street food. Noise filled the streets: trolley bells, children shouting, radios blaring big band music, heels clicking on concrete. Men in hats shouted from fruit stands, while teenagers sped by on bicycles, laughter and cigarette smoke trailing behind.

The ride to their aunt's was short, but Pearl kept her face turned to the window. She watched graffiti flash across brick walls, nuns herding uniformed children across intersections, a woman in hot pink curlers yelling from a third-story window.

Diamond leaned her head against her sister's shoulder, whispering, "It's so loud."

"I know," Pearl whispered back. "Close your eyes."

"We're her girls," Mother Daisy said excitedly.

Their aunt's apartment sat wedged above a corner tavern, its frosted windows sweating under a crooked neon sign that buzzed even in daylight. As they climbed the narrow stairs, the scent of grease and old beer met them halfway.

Inside, the two-bedroom space smelled like fried fish and gardenia perfume. The wallpaper peeled at the edges, and the lightbulbs flickered every time the jukebox kicked on downstairs.

She answered the door in a gold two-piece housecoat, rollers tight in her hair, cigarette dangling between two fingers.

"Well, look at you two," she said, waving them in. "Tall as ever. Y'all got some of your mama's pretty."

No hugs. No questions about the trip. Just a warning: "Don't sit too hard. Couch springs are goin'."

The kitchen was cramped but full of motion; grease-spotted pans were piled in the sink, a card table leaned against the fridge, and a rooster clock ticked off beat on the wall.

"You'll sleep in the room with the pull-out," she said. "Help in the tavern kitchen after school. Don't ask for nothin' unless it's necessary. You hear?"

Pearl nodded. Diamond stared down at her shoes.

What they didn't know was that the "restaurant" their aunt owned was, in truth, a tavern, and more than that. She'd never told their mama the entire story; that she served whiskey with supper. Her husband hosted dice games and poker nights in the basement. That, folks hinted, their uncle managed *"workin' girls."*

A pimp.

That first night, lying side by side on the pull-out, Pearl stared at the ceiling while Diamond curled beside her, silent.

Below them, laughter. Glass clinking. Cursing. A jukebox changed tracks with a mechanical groan.

"I thought we were escaping," Diamond whispered. "But we're still not safe."

Pearl turned to her. "We're not here to be safe," she said. "We're here to survive."

Diamond nodded. She understood now. Milwaukee wasn't a sanctuary.

It was just a battlefield with different rules.

For the first three months, life was manageable: school, homework, and kitchen chores.

No free rides.

Their aunt wasn't nurturing but practical.

"This life don't owe you nothin'," she'd say, "you only have what you take."

Everything changed the morning Pearl woke to the sound of shouting from the bathroom.

"Heffa, you better not be pregnant!"

Diamond wasn't in bed.

Pearl shot to her feet and ran.

In the bathroom, Diamond hunched, trembling, and vomiting. Their aunt looked down, disgusted. "After all we've done for y'all... you sneakin' around? Who got you pregnant?" Diamond cried on the cold tile, unable to speak.

Pearl stepped in. "Auntie, please, it wasn't like that."

Their aunt turned on them. "My sister sent me her fast-ass daughters, and this is what I get?"

Pearl's voice cracked. "No! A white boy raped Diamond... on her way home from school.

And I... I killed him."

The room went still. Even the house held its breath.

Pearl trembled. "They didn't send us here cause they were tired of feedin' us. They sent us here to save our lives."

Their aunt sat between them on the bed, silence folding around the three of them like a blanket. For a long beat, she just stared. Then quietly, her arms reached out, wrapping them both close.

"Babies," she whispered. "I am so, so sorry."

For the first time since Mississippi, they felt held. Not just physically, but truly seen.

But the next day, when they arrived home from school, they found Diamond's things packed.

CHAPTER
FORTY-SEVEN
JANUARY 6, 1948

Mother Daisy's House
4:15 p.m.

MOTHER DAISY OFFERED to take Diamond in because their uncle didn't want a pregnant girl drawing attention to the tavern. And there was no room for a baby in that two-bedroom apartment above the bar.

Diamond wept.

She and Pearl had never been apart.

Pearl held her tight. "We're just around the corner. I'll come every day."

Diamond nodded, her face crumpled. She wouldn't be returning to school, which broke her heart. She loved learning, but Pearl promised to bring her books, homework, and stories from class.

"Remember what the Reverend said," Pearl whispered as they walked.

"Jesus is always with us. Just don't forget to pray."

Then she leaned close and added, "I have a plan. But you can't tell anybody."

Diamond gave a teary laugh.

"What now?"

"I hid the money we came with. I'm saving everything I make in the tavern kitchen. When the time's right, we're leaving. Far away."

Pearl meant it, but freedom wouldn't come easy. The twins lived a block apart, yet it felt like worlds.

Mother Daisy's house had six bedrooms. Once, it was a boarding house for factory workers. After her husband left, her son-in-law had convinced her to stop renting to single men. Said it wasn't safe.

Diamond noticed them first.

While making the guest bed, she saw them. A pair of men's dress shoes, neatly tucked under the frame.

She didn't ask. But Pearl did.

That evening, sitting at the kitchen table, she watched Mother Daisy dust flour off her hands and asked softly:

"Whose shoes are those under Diamond's bed?"

Mother Daisy didn't look up.

"They belonged to my husband," she said.

"I didn't know you had one."

She smiled. Not sad. Not bitter. Just… settled.

"He left after I gave my life to God. Ran off with a jazz singer. Never said goodbye. Left his shoes like he meant to come back."

"Did you ever try to find him?"

"No. I pray for him sometimes. But those shoes stay right where he left 'em. Not because I'm waiting... but because I needed to remember the day I stopped needing to be chosen."

Pearl didn't speak. She just let that sit.

Mother Daisy handed her a glass of sweet tea, her voice like molasses over iron.

"You don't need a man to prove your worth, baby. You need a place to put your feet… and a God who won't walk out."

First Days

Mother Daisy ran a disciplined yet warm household. She cared for children and took in girls who had nowhere else to go. Someone was constantly in need.

The girls had spent Sunday dinners there before, so the house wasn't unfamiliar.

That first day, she greeted them with a smile and a wave of her hand.

"You two carry those bags upstairs and make the bed in the guest room. Pearl, head home when you're done. Diamond, come see me in the kitchen."

They both answered in unison.

"Yes, ma'am."

In the kitchen, Diamond sat at the table while Mother Daisy placed a plate in front of her: meatloaf, mashed potatoes with gravy, and green beans.

"Hope you got an appetite, beautiful."

Diamond smiled shyly. "Yes, ma'am. Thank you."

Mother Daisy sat down across from her.

"You know why I call y'all 'beautiful'?"

"'Cause we ain't bad lookin'?" Diamond grinned.

Mother Daisy laughed.

"That too. But mostly because life gets ugly. And when life gets ugly, remember your beautiful origins. And no one can take that away."

Diamond's eyes filled. Mother Daisy reached across the table and held her hand.

"I hate what happened to you. I hate what he did. But baby... Jesus can carry you through. You hold on to Him, and He'll hold on to you."

She wrapped Diamond in a hug, whispering, "You're about to become a mama. What happened, happened. You can't undo it. But even at thirteen... with Jesus, you can make it."

CHAPTER
FORTY-EIGHT
JANUARY 6, 1948

Diamond's Bedroom
10:05 p.m.

THAT FIRST NIGHT, Diamond couldn't sleep.

Pearl had hugged her goodbye and promised to come tomorrow. But once the front door closed, something cracked inside her.

It wasn't loneliness or fear but silence.

Back in Mississippi, even in pain, the house had rhythm: Mama clanged pots, Daddy hummed hymns, and even the silence had a heartbeat.

Now? Everything was still; it was as if the world had stopped breathing.

She lay under a lavender and starch-scented quilt, her hands on her belly, weighted with significance. She whispered a name: *"Mercy."* Unsure whether it was a boy or a girl, the name felt like a prayer woven from flesh.

Diamond barely spoke during the rest of the week. Mother Daisy left warm meals, slipped books into her lap, and sometimes just sat in silence. On the seventh day, something cracked. Diamond watched her fry cabbage as the scent of garlic and bacon filled the kitchen. Mother Daisy hummed "His Eye Is on the Sparrow."

Diamond's voice shook as it broke the silence.

"Why didn't he kill me?"

Mother Daisy turned off the burner. Sat down beside her.

"Because God said no."

Diamond wept.

"I didn't fight. Pearl did. I just... froze. I let him. I...,"

Mother Daisy grabbed her hand.

"Stop. Don't ever say that. He did what he did because he was evil. Not because you were weak."

"But I..."

Mother Daisy interrupted. "You survived."

The words dropped like gospel.

"You're still here. You're breathing. And now? You're growing something precious inside you. That ain't weakness. That's power."

Diamond cried until her shoulders shook. Mother Daisy wrapped her arms around her. Whispered scripture. Rocked her like a woman who had held too many broken girls in too many quiet kitchens.

And something in Diamond shifted, a subtle yet undeniable change that lingered beneath her skin. She brushed her hair again, her movements automatic, seeking some sense of normalcy as she helped Mother Daisy with the kids during the day. Her voice was gentle but distant, and she asked for books about childbirth, perhaps searching for answers or comfort in the pages. She even smiled sometimes, fleeting and fragile, like a fragile echo of a past self.

But the sparkle never came back. Not like it had been before, vibrant and full of life. That part of her, which once shined bright, was now buried somewhere in the Mississippi woods beneath blood and ashes, a haunting reminder of something irreparably lost.

Something quieter remained instead.

Sharper.

Resolving to show that ashes don't tell the whole story.

CHAPTER
FORTY-NINE
AUGUST 14, 1978

Mama Pearl's Kitchen
1:25 p.m.

MAMA PEARL'S VOICE SOFTENED, her eyes distant, her hands trembling just slightly around a cigarette she'd long since let burn out.

"When it was all said and done," she murmured, "Diamond and I learned that runnin' don't always get you free. Sometimes it just gets you tired. And tired girls don't fight as hard."

She stood slowly, the dim kitchen light catching the lines in her face like shadows on old paper.

"But tired or not, you've gotta decide when it's your turn. To stop lettin' the world choose for you. To stand still, even if your knees buckle, even if your voice shakes."

Her eyes locked on Madison.

"Baby, you've been runnin' too long. From grief. From truth. From the woman they told you to be."

Then she turned to Nina, gaze softening into something maternal.

"And you? You've been standin' still so long, you forgot you've got legs."

The silence was thick, broken only by the hum of the refrigerator and Madison's uneven breath.

Mama Pearl exhaled, a deep sigh that carried the weight of decades.

"I didn't tell you this story 'cause I like rememberin'. Lord knows I don't. I told it 'cause I see you both standin' at a crossroads I know too well. One path keeps you safe, keeps you small. The other's hard, but it's where you get to decide who you are."

She turned toward the doorway, the kitchen light haloing her like a curtain call.

"The fire's comin' for you, girls," she said, voice low. "Whether you outrun it… or let it teach you how to burn, that's up to you."

Later that night, after Madison had gone upstairs and the house had settled into an uneasy silence, Nina lingered in the kitchen. Mama Pearl stood at the sink, rinsing out a cocktail glass. Her movements were slow and deliberate, as if she were washing away ghosts.

Nina paused in the doorway.

"Mama Pearl…" Her voice cracked.

Mama Pearl didn't turn. "Yes, baby?"

"Where's Diamond now?"

The glass clinked gently in the sink. Then a long, quiet breath. "She's gone."

"Gone?" Nina's voice rose, confused. "What do you mean?"

Mama Pearl turned, eyes glassy, her voice low and thick with grief.

"She went into labor. Early. Nobody was home. She tried to call for help, but by the time anyone got there… she'd bled out."

Nina's hand flew to her mouth.

"Oh, my God…"

"She was only thirteen." Mama Pearl's voice broke. "Too young. Too scared. Her body wasn't ready."

She paused, her chin trembling.

"But my nephew, her baby, he made it. He was a fighter. Just like his mama."

Nina's voice shook. "What happened to him?"

A bittersweet smile flickered across Mama Pearl's face.

"Mother Daisy raised him. Loved him like her own. And I… I hustled to give him every chance Diamond didn't have. Paid for school, for books, everything."

She blinked back tears.

"He's a doctor now. Runs a clinic in the city. Helps mamas and babies who remind him of his own beginning."

Tears rolled down Nina's cheeks.

"I didn't know," she whispered. "I never knew."

Mama Pearl stepped closer and gently brushed Nina's hair back.

"Baby, 'course you didn't know. It wasn't yours to carry."

She paused. Her voice dropped.

"That boy. He's the best of her. The best of all of us who loved her. His name's Mercy. Just like the name Diamond wrote in her diary."

The word settled between them like a prayer.

"She named him Mercy?" Nina asked, voice trembling.

Mama Pearl nodded slowly.

"And Mercy's still here. A reminder that even when life takes the most from us… love can survive."

The silence was full now. Grief. Gratitude. Grace.

Nina wiped her face, her voice barely a whisper. "Thank you for telling me."

Mama Pearl squeezed her hand.

"Now, Nina, yo' ass got enough grief. Don't go borrowin' more."

They stood like that a moment longer, two women, two generations, held together not just by loss, but by the knowing. The sacred understanding of what it means to carry the memory of those who didn't make it… and the responsibility to live for those who did.

PART TWELVE
MISS LUCY'S HALF-WAY HOUSE

CHAPTER
FIFTY
MARCH 13, 1986

Pendleton City, Minnesota
8:27 p.m.

THE WOMEN'S halfway house where Madison was released was a 4,500-square-foot, six-bedroom home with a quiet view of Black Swan Lake. It was owned by Miss Lucy Farrow, sharp-tongued, silver-haired, and stubbornly compassionate. Miss Lucy had served five years for what she called "borrowing" $10,000.

"Wasn't theft," she'd say. "It was survival."

But that *loan*, taken in desperation, had cost her everything, her job, her freedom, and custody of her children. Ten years into her marriage, her husband had kissed her goodbye like any other morning, said he had a haul to make.

He never came back.

He'd moved in with the company's secretary, the same woman who managed his dispatches. Two small children, overdue bills, and a house spiraling into foreclosure burdened Lucy.

She tried everything, from odd jobs to late nights, praying the phone wouldn't ring with another bill collector on the other end.

Then one day, she came home to a dark house. The electricity had been cut off, leaving everything covered in shadows. She stood in the doorway, coat still on her shoulders, eyes scanning the darkness as a wave of helplessness washed over her. With a trembling voice, she cried out, "Lord, why me?"

That night, the weight of her hardships pressed down even harder. She took the kids to a motel, just for one night of light, hot water, a door locked tight, and a moment of peace brought with denial. After rummaging through her purse and finding a crumpled bill, she reluctantly wrote a bad check for pizza and soda, whispering to herself, *"My upcoming paycheck should save me from trouble before the bank catches it."*

Little did she know, this act of desperation was only the beginning of an unraveling mystery, one that would test her faith and resilience in ways she never imagined. At the motel, the kids did homework at the little table by the window. They giggled over soda fizz and greasy cheese. Lucy handed out slices and kept her eyes on the glowing red digits of the clock.

They thought it was an adventure.

They didn't know they were living on borrowed time.

After tucking them in, she sat at the foot of the bed, staring at their sleeping faces in the flicker of a neon sign from the gas station across the lot.

A low murmur escaped her. *"I won't let them lose everything."*

Reflecting on her childhood, she remembered the arguments about money, her father's long hours, and her mother's fervent prayers in the kitchen.

"Did any of her strength rub off on me?" She questioned.

She didn't feel strong; instead, she felt as if she were falling apart. But the motel's light and warmth made the night feel like a palace. In the silence, a firm decision took root: she would do whatever it took to protect her children.

She started withdrawing small amounts from escrow accounts at her real estate office, planning to repay them temporarily until her situation improved.

But things didn't get better.

A property closed early, and discrepancies emerged. The numbers didn't match, and the truth quickly unraveled.

Despite everything, her boss, Mr. Randall Meyers, stood beside her in court.

"Your Honor," he said, "she made a terrible mistake, yes. But it was desperation, not deception. She's worked honestly for years. This... this is not who she is."

The judge didn't blink.

"Intentional misappropriation of escrow funds cannot go unpunished, Mr. Meyers. The law requires accountability."

Miss Lucy sat silent at the defense table, fists clenched in her lap. Her attorney placed a quiet hand on her arm.

"Five years," the judge said. "Parole eligibility after eighteen months."

After court, Mr. Meyers approached her, guilt in his eyes. "I'm sorry. I truly tried."

"Thank you for showing up," she said. "That meant something."

And it had.

Even in her lowest moment, knowing someone saw her as more than her mistake gave her just enough hope to hold on to.

A month into her sentence, Miss Lucy's ex-husband came to visit. Alone.

He sat across from her in the visitation room and said plainly, "I'm denying your visitation rights. I'm getting remarried. The kids need to bond with their new mother. I think it's best they don't see you at all."

Tears streamed down Miss Lucy's face.

"Why are you doing this? Why do you hate me?"

He stood, eyes cold. "I don't hate you. I just needed more."

"You selfish bastard!" she screamed as he walked away.

After that visit, the chance of early release vanished. She fought inmates. Sabotaged herself. Spent more time in solitary confinement than in her cell.

She blamed the system. Her parents. Her ex.

But the truth?

She blamed herself most of all.

She met her husband right after high school, while working at a truck stop diner and taking bookkeeping classes at night. He was older, charming, and made her feel seen and valued. Something no one else ever had.

She fell fast. Fell hard.

Her parents disapproved, especially her father.

"He's too slick," he warned.

Her mother cried. She recognized that look in Lucy's eyes. *Love.*

The kind that makes reason irrelevant.

Miss Lucy packed a bag and left home.

They got married at a courthouse and made their home in Pendleton City. They had twins, so she took a quiet bookkeeping job. For some time, life was straightforward and safe.

Then he vanished.

In prison, she felt forgotten. She wanted to call her parents, but couldn't bear the shame.

"Daddy… you were right," she imagined saying. But the words stayed buried.

She kept asking herself the same question: *"What have I done to deserve this?"*

It wasn't until her last stretch in solitary that something shifted.

Locked inside a room no larger than a parking space, she curled into a ball and sobbed. For hours. For days.

Then one day, she stood up. Started pacing. Started talking to herself.

"Girl, it's over. You're here suffering while the man who left you is out living his life. You're harming yourself for him, for the system, for a world that doesn't care. You're angry at the world, but giving it control. Stop allowing him to destroy you. He broke your heart, but don't let him break your spirit."

That was her turning point.

When she walked out of that cell, she left the old Miss Lucy behind.

She buried herself in books. Attended every group session. Got certified in business administration and peer counseling.

Her release found her a changed woman.

"I found myself in that hole," she would tell new women at the halfway house.

"And when I came out, I promised to dig out every woman still stuck in one."

So, she did.

She opened a home.

Black Swan Lake glistened outside its windows.

But the real beauty lived inside, in the laughter, the healing, the second chances.

CHAPTER
FIFTY-ONE

FEBRUARY 18, 1992

Miss Lucy Halfway House
1:00 p.m.

PAM, Miss Lucy's first resident, arrived at the halfway house with a hard stare and a silence that stretched wider than the lake. She had served fifteen years for killing her husband, a decorated veteran who turned into a violent alcoholic. She confessed the moment the police arrived.

Miss Lucy didn't press. She never would.

She just sat with her chipped peppermint tea mug, waiting.

One snowy afternoon, Pam finally spoke.

"I ain't ever told it straight before. Not to the court. Not to the news. Not even to my sister."

Her voice was low. Flat.

Her fingers twisted the hem of her sweatshirt.

"He told me he'd kill 'em. My babies."

She swallowed.

"Said it like he was tellin' me what time dinner was. Looked me in the eye. Calm. Said if I ever tried to run, he'd make me watch first."

Miss Lucy set her mug down.

Pam's laugh was dry. Bitter.

"I believed him. That's the part folks don't get. He wasn't bluff-ing. The way he looked at them... like they were just props in his game."

She looked at Lucy, eyes burning.

"So, I waited. One night, I packed their little bags. Thought he was at work. But he came back early."

Her voice dropped to a whisper.

"He grabbed my boy by the collar. Said I wasn't takin' nothin' that had his blood. Said I'd die before he let me."

She went quiet.

"I don't remember reaching for the gun. Just the sound it made. And the way he dropped."

Then silence.

She sat back, arms folded tight.

"I didn't kill him cause I hated him. I killed him cause I loved my kids more."

Miss Lucy didn't offer pity. Didn't offer platitudes.

She laid a hand on Pam's knee and said, "They're safe now. That matters."

The court didn't care. Pam had no money for a good lawyer, and no one was speaking on her behalf. Her kids went into protective custody, never to be seen again.

Birthdays became bruises, Christmas, a hollow ache.

Weeks later, Lucy found Pam folding laundry, staring out the window.

"I still don't know where they are," she whispered. "I pray that someone raised them right." That they didn't forget me."

Miss Lucy just reached out and held her hand.

And for the first time in years, Pam let someone hold her pain.

Miss Lucy continued to give space and kindness. rallied.

And eventually, Pam started laughing again. Quiet, cautious laughter that sounded like healing.

She still didn't know if her children would ever come back.

But she hoped that someday... they might come looking.

Ironically, Miss Lucy felt a connection with her first client, believing that as she helped her heal, she was also healing herself.

Three years into her sentence, Lucy received an unexpected visitor: her mother.

She came alone, hands trembling, eyes swollen with grief.

"Your father's gone, LuLu. Massive heart attack."

The words hit Lucy like a punch to the chest.

Even more shocking, he had left her money. A *substantial* amount. Despite their silence, her parents had always known her whereabouts. Her father, with his quiet pride and shared stubbornness, had recently begun making inquiries. He wanted to meet his grandchildren.

That day would never come.

The grief cracked something in Lucy wide open. She reached across the table and took her mother's hands.

"Mom… I love you. I missed you and Daddy more than I ever let myself admit. I let shame and pride keep me from calling when I needed you most."

Her mother opened her mouth to respond, but Lucy gently continued.

"If it's okay with you, I want to leave the worst of our past behind. I want to build something better."

Her mother smiled through tears, nodding slowly.

"My LuLu… I'll see you in a month."

And she did.

Every month for two years, Lucy's mother drove six hours each way to spend two hours with her daughter on weekends. At first, their talks were heavy with grief, guilt, and family news. But over time, they began dreaming again, of life after prison.

After her husband's death, Lucy's mother left nursing, sold the family home, and moved to Pendleton City.

The timing was divine.

Lucy had reached out to her former employer, the man who once stood beside her in court. He mentioned a foreclosed property over-looking Black Swan Lake. The moment Lucy saw the listing, she knew.

She used part of her inheritance to pay restitution. With the rest, she bought the house, renovated it with care, and secured state funding to turn it into a transitional home for women. She appointed her mother as house manager and finance coordinator.

Together, they founded *Miss Lucy's Halfway House.*

In the 25 years that followed, Miss Lucy helped hundreds of women rebuild their lives. She earned awards, grants, and eventually, a televised documentary spotlighting her unique program.

It wasn't revolutionary.

It was *compassionate.*

And it worked.

Miss Lucy eventually tracked down her twins.

They were living with their paternal grandmother, GeGe, in a cramped home in Texas. Their father had disappeared shortly after visiting Lucy in prison, leaving behind nothing but occasional money orders and a mess. GeGe did what she could, juggling hotel cleaning shifts and a whole house. Her common-law partner, a man named Moe Money, was more of a liability than a help.

The twins were raising themselves.

When Lucy regained custody, they were 14, angry, guarded, and full of resentment. They hated Pendleton City. Called it "boring." Therapy didn't work. Trust came slowly.

Still, Lucy tried.

She let them return to Texas for the summers, hoping familiarity would ease the ache. But after graduation, they went back for good.

They never truly healed.

But Lucy never stopped loving them.

"Some people heal slower than others," she told the women at the house.

"That doesn't mean we stop loving them."

She found peace in other places. In the lives rebuilt around here.

In women like Pam.

Sometimes, she and Pam would sit in silence on the porch overlooking Black Swan Lake.

One evening, as the sun melted behind the pines, Pam whispered:

"I wonder if they remember me."

Miss Lucy didn't hesitate.

"I wonder that, too. About my own."

She paused.

"But I believe something, Pam. If we live right and love them from afar, even in silence, it leaves a trail. A trail they might follow back to us."

Pam smiled, eyes misting.

"A trail of love."

"Exactly," Miss Lucy said. "Love leaves a trail."

Years later, that trail would lead Morgan Bennins-Alcott to Miss Lucy's halfway house, with her mother, Madison Jackson Winter, in tow.

A full-circle moment.

Not an ending.

A return to purpose.

Because the journey didn't end at Black Swan Lake.

It *began* there.

CHAPTER
FIFTY-TWO
AUGUST 22, 2017

Miss Lucy Halfway House
1:00 p.m.

TODAY, Miss Lucy stood on the porch of that house overlooking Black Swan Lake. The wind rolled gently off the water.

Smiling at the thought of her mother, she gently adjusted the hanging "Welcome Home" sign. It had been a gift from her mother, who had passed a few years ago.

Full of anticipation, she looked out at the driveway as a car approached.

Her first high-profile resident was arriving: Madison Jackson Winter, the woman being dropped off by the daughter she thought was dead. A woman the world knew through scandal, but who Miss Lucy could already see was something more.

Another soul trying to make it back.

Miss Lucy smiled as she approached the door.

"Come on in, baby. You're home now."

The next morning, Madison walked cautiously into the kitchen, where breakfast was already underway. The smell of coffee, cinnamon rolls, and turkey bacon filled the air.

At the kitchen table sat Mildred, a soft-spoken woman with deep-set eyes, and two other women.

Miss Lucy stood at the stove, flipping pancakes.

"Well, look who's joined us," she said, motioning Madison to a seat.

Sharice was the first to speak. "You're the preacher's wife, right? The one who got locked up for murder?"

Mildred shot her a warning glance. "Sharice."

Madison didn't flinch. "That's what they say."

Tina gave her a slow nod. "Cool. You want some coffee?"

The tension eased slightly. Madison took a seat, and Miss Lucy placed a plate in front of her. "Eat first. Then we talk about rules."

As they ate, Sharice kept glancing at Madison, as if she was trying to figure out if the woman in front of her matched the headlines. Mildred finally said, "Everyone here's got a story, sugar. This is a table, not a courtroom."

Madison nodded slowly, looking around at the women.

She wasn't sure where this chapter of her life would lead.

But for the first time in a long while, she didn't feel like she was walking into a war zone.

Maybe, just maybe, she was walking toward healing.

And maybe she wasn't alone.

As the conversation carried on, Madison quietly observed the other women at the table. Each of them, hardened by their battles, now sat with pancakes, mismatched mugs of coffee, and quiet laughter. Mildred, with her soft voice, had the steady patience of someone who had seen too much. Tina's sarcasm and headphones were armor. Even Sharice, with her tough talk and twitchy eyes, seemed more bark than bite.

And then it hit her, the contradiction.

These were the same women who, behind bars, had once walked the yard like warriors, whose reputations kept others at bay. But here, at this breakfast table, they looked like little girls trying to find a piece of peace.

Madison saw herself in them; how they leaned into the warmth of the kitchen, held their forks as if guarding something sacred, and listened for Miss Lucy's laughter as if it were music they hadn't heard in years.

They weren't just survivors. They were dreamers. Fractured. Brave. Trying.

And for the first time since stepping out of the prison gates, Madison felt something bloom in her chest.

Hope.

After Madison settled in the next morning, Miss Lucy sent word for her to come to the sitting room.

The hallway smelled of lavender and lemon oil.

Madison stood just outside the sitting room, fingers grazing the doorway, uncertain whether to enter. She could hear the low hum of jazz playing from the corner speaker, something old, full of trumpet and ache.

Miss Lucy sat in a high-backed chair near the window, her legs crossed, a worn book in her lap. She didn't look up when she spoke.

"If you're gonna hover, baby, you might as well come sit."

Madison blinked, surprised. Then, with a sigh, she stepped in and sank into the chair across from her.

Neither spoke for a while.

Outside the wide window, Black Swan Lake reflected the early morning sun, scattered like diamonds on the water. A blue heron skimmed the shoreline in slow, deliberate strides.

"Is this your quiet room?" Madison finally asked.

Miss Lucy nodded. "This is where I think. Where I forgive folks who never apologize."

That earned a small smile from Madison. A tired one. But real.

"You always this calm?" she asked.

Miss Lucy chuckled. "Only on the outside. On the inside? I'm still teaching the fire not to burn the house down."

Madison leaned back in the chair, arms crossed over her chest like a shield. She looked older than her age and younger than her sorrow. There were shadows in her eyes that sleep wouldn't erase.

"I can't seem to stop spinning," she whispered. "It's like I'm dizzy, but I'm not truly free."

Miss Lucy closed the book in her lap and set it aside.

"That's cause freedom's not a place. It's a process. Paperwork can't give it to you. And prison can't take it away."

Madison looked down at her hands. Still faintly shaking.

"Three years in, and I didn't feel half as afraid as I do now."

Miss Lucy leaned forward, resting her elbows on her knees.

"That's cause of there, you had a role to play. A wall to hide behind. Out here? You gotta be real again. That's the scariest part."

"Real?" Madison repeated. "I don't even know what that is."

The words came out like a confession.

Miss Lucy didn't rush to answer. She let the silence sit between them, soft and weighty. Then she said, "When I first got out, I used to look in the mirror and introduce myself. 'Hi, I'm Miss Lucy. I was a prisoner. I was a wife. I was a fool. I'm still figuring out what else I can be."

"Did it help?"

"Not right away. But I stopped jumpin' when I saw my reflection."

Madison, while looking out the window, asked, "Have you ever missed the version of yourself before it all fell apart?"

Miss Lucy smiled sadly. "She didn't survive. But she got me here."

They sat in the moment's hush. The wind carried a faint scent of pine. A car rolled by in the distance. A squirrel darted across the lawn and disappeared under the porch steps.

Madison let her eyes close.

"Sometimes I wonder if I was ever really her. The Bishop's wife. The community icon. The woman who smiled through it all. Maybe she was just another mask."

"Could be," Miss Lucy answered. "But even masks come from somewhere. What you built for others still counts. You just forgot to leave room for yourself."

"It's too late now."

"No, baby. Too late is when they bury you."

Madison chuckled, a dry, cracked sound that surprised her.

"You sound like Mister Mayor," she said, voice tinged with nostalgia.

Miss Lucy perked up. "Mister Mayor?"

Madison nodded.

"He was the only person who didn't try to fix me. He just… stood beside me."

Miss Lucy studied her for a long moment.

"Sounds like he saw the you that you're still trying to believe in."

"Yeah," Madison whispered. "He did."

There was a long pause. The kind that comes not from awkwardness but reverence.

Then Miss Lucy stood up, walked over to the windowsill, and picked up a tiny plant in a chipped ceramic pot.

"You see this here?" she said. "This little pothos plant? When I moved into this house, it was nearly dead. Brown, wilted. Just a limp stem in dry dirt. I almost threw it out."

She held it up to the light.

"But something told me to keep it. So, I watered it. Talked to it. Gave it sun."

Madison leaned forward, watching her.

"Now look at it. Still not perfect. Still a little crooked. But it's alive."

She set the plant gently on the table between them.

"Don't you throw yourself out, Madison Winter. You're still in the soil. And I see green in you."

Madison didn't respond right away. Her throat tightened. The back of her eyes burned.

"Do you believe people like us deserve a second chance?" she asked finally.

Miss Lucy smiled.

"I believe we deserve as many chances as it takes."

She reached out and took Madison's hand.

"Start here."

CHAPTER
FIFTY-THREE
AUGUST 25, 2017

Miss Lucy Halfway House
6:15 a.m.

IT TOOK Madison two full days to walk down to the lake.

Not because she didn't know where it was, it called to her the moment she arrived, visible from the back porch, just beyond a split-rail fence and a path worn into the grass.

But there was something about still water that scared her.

It listened too well.

That morning, before the other women stirred, Madison wrapped herself in an old gray sweater from the donation closet and made her way outside. With a gentle creak, she closed the screen door behind her. The grass was still damp with dew. Wildflowers leaned into the breeze, listening for secrets, as the path curved gently toward the shore.

As she stepped through the opening in the fence, the lake came into full view, wide, quiet, and perfectly still. It mirrored the early sky in soft blues and pale golds, as if it were holding a piece of morning in its hands.

Madison lingered for a while before settling on the wooden bench beneath a crooked cypress tree. A dragonfly fluttered close to her elbow, while a heron moved carefully along the edge, patient and exact.

She let her hands fall into her lap and stared out at the water.

"*So, this is where people go to think,*" she thought.

Her voice sounded foreign in the open air.

The wind picked up slightly, brushing her cheek like the back of a familiar hand.

For the first time in what felt like years, she exhaled fully.

She didn't mean to cry.

There was no trigger, no explosion. The tears came quietly and steadily, like a tide she couldn't fight. Her shoulders didn't shake. Her chest didn't heave.

It was the crying that belonged to exhaustion, not despair.

She pressed a palm to her stomach, grounding herself, as if trying to feel the parts of her body that still belonged to her.

How long had she been holding it all in? Too long, clearly.

There were no sounds but nature. No apologies in the wind. No lies in the trees.

And the lake... the lake didn't judge.

It didn't care who she used to be.

It just reflected. And listened. And waited.

Madison closed her eyes, recalling the diner, the gentle clink of dishes, the aroma of Harper's coffee, and how her name sounded when spoken with love. "*Autumn Storm,*" he'd say with a twinkle in his eye.

"*You're a whole damn season, you know that?*"

She smiled through her tears.

She missed him more than she thought she was allowed to.

She leaned forward now, arms on her knees, looking down at the rocks by the waterline.

She picked up one smooth, round, still cold from the night, and ran her thumb across its surface.

You ever just wanted to disappear?" she asked the lake.

Her voice was quiet, but it carried, stretching out over the stillness like a question thrown to the sky.

The lake didn't answer. But a ripple broke across the surface as if it had heard her.

She stood slowly, rock still in hand, and stepped closer to the edge. The breeze moved through her hair, short now, wild from sleep and untouched by pretense. She felt the weight of the stone, a smooth, solid thing, in her palm. It felt like the weight of her secrets, her guilt, her past lives all pressed into a single pebble.

"*I did once,*" she whispered, voice barely louder than the wind. "*I thought it would be easier to fade away. To shrink until no one could see me. To be silent enough, small enough, that maybe I could slip between the cracks of the world and vanish.*"

She glanced down at her reflection in the rippling water, shadowed and shifting, almost unrecognizable.

"*But that's not what I want anymore,*" she said, her throat tightening. "*I've learned it's better to appear. To stand in the light, messy, scarred, imperfect, but here. Alive. Visible. Real. Disappearing doesn't make the hurt go away. It just makes it easier for others to pretend you were never here.*"

A heron flapped its wings at the shoreline, startled into flight, and she watched it rise into the sky with long, graceful strokes.

"*I don't want to disappear,*" she said, more firmly now, to the lake and to herself. "*I want to be seen as I am. As me.*"

She lifted her arm and hurled the stone out across the lake. It skipped once, twice, then sank on the third. She smiled faintly.

"*Not bad,*" she murmured, with a tremor of pride in her voice.

Behind her, the house waited, quiet and still.

The morning light filtered through the trees like forgiveness. And for the first time in a long while, Madison felt the tremor of something rising inside her.

Not just survival. Not just endurance.

But an emergence from the ashes.

Later that afternoon, Madison sat with Miss Lucy on the back porch, sipping lemon tea in the fading warmth of late day.

"I've decided," she said.

Miss Lucy turned to her, the breeze lifting the edges of her scarf.

"I'm going back to Pine Ridge."

Lucy didn't speak right away.

"Because of Mister Mayor?" she asked finally.

Madison nodded. "He asked me to come back. He said the story isn't finished.

"And you believe that?"

"I believe I owe it to myself to see."

Madison looked down into her tea, watching the reflection of the sky ripple with each movement.

"I'm not the woman they remember. But I need to face them, not to explain, but to honor the part of me that was real there. That diner, that town… they gave me more than I gave back. And I don't want to be remembered only for how I left."

Miss Lucy reached over and patted her hand.

"Then go back with your chin up, baby.

Don't return to hide. Return to heal."

CHAPTER
FIFTY-FOUR
FEBRUARY 20, 2018

Miss Lucy Halfway House,
7:18 p.m.

THE LAKE WAS QUIET. It was always at twilight.

Madison stood at the edge, arms wrapped around herself, sweater sleeves stretched long over her hands. Watercolor, blush, gold, and lavender streaked the sky, settling into blue. The trees along the ridge whispered in the breeze, and the water caught it all like a mirror.

She didn't flinch when she heard footsteps behind her.

"What brought you back tonight?" Madison asked.

"I can't visit my mother twice in one day," Morgan replied.

Madison offered a tired smile. "Of course you can."

They stood side by side in the tranquility.

The water didn't rush them. Neither did the stars overhead.

"You remember the first time you saw me?" Madison asked.

"Of course," Morgan said. "Mugshot. Case file. All facts and no truth."

"And now?"

"Now I see a woman who survived things most people wouldn't talk about, let alone carry."

Madison's throat tightened. She looked down at her hands.

"I spent years playing different versions of myself. None of them ever felt... whole."

"You do now?"

"I feel closer."

Morgan exhaled. Her breath fogged just a little in the cooling night air.

"I've tried to imagine what it was like for you. Being locked up. Being alone. Everyone thinks they know who you are... and not being able to defend yourself."

Madison didn't respond right away. Then.

"It's the silence that hurts the most. Not the cell. Not the noise.

It's the knowing that you could tell your truth, but the cost would crush someone else."

She paused. "So, you bury it. And you carry it. And you hope that's enough."

Morgan looked at her. "You never said who you were protecting."

Madison met her eyes, steady and unflinching. "And I'm not going to."

"I figured," Morgan said. "But I had to ask."

They sat on the bench beneath the old tree, knees nearly touching, talking quietly as if the walls might still hear. They recounted the past six months in stolen moments, knowing it couldn't reclaim lost years. Madison loved each evening when Morgan picked her up from the bakery; each time was like Christmas. A gift that never faded.

They laughed about their weekend rituals: shopping, mani/pedis, and arguing over favorite foods. They remembered nights on the deck, watching the lake, trading stories, and discovering a shared stubborn streak that felt like home.

Now, on their last night in Pendleton, silence filled the space between them. It wasn't burdensome, just genuine. Six months weren't enough, but it was a beginning.

Morgan opened her palm, revealing a small velvet box.

"Janet, or as you know her, Sgt. Wallace sent you this," she said, smiling.

Madison took the box gently, her fingers brushing Morgan's. She opened it slowly, almost reverently. Inside was the delicate silver chain that Sgt. Wallace had always worn the precious dove charm, resting against the velvet lining, where it caught the light like a small, silent hope.

Madison gasped.

She gently traced the dove with her fingertip, finally grasping that Sgt. Wallace's stern words, unwavering gaze, and the quiet strength that once felt like rejection were not defenses against her but for her. It was a shield of truth, crafted to safeguard her from the brutal realities of prison life.

"When I finally explained everything to her," Morgan said, her voice hushed, "she wanted you to have this. As a reminder that you are never alone."

Madison's throat tightened.

She held the necklace like it might crumble if she let go, but she felt the weight of it, solid and light at once, like a prayer answered.

"She said you were stronger than you knew," Morgan added. "That even on the hardest nights, when it feels like no one sees you, you're still seen. Still loved. Still part of something bigger."

Madison closed the box gently, holding it to her chest. "I don't know if I'm ready for that kind of faith," she admitted, her voice breaking.

"You don't have to be ready," Morgan said, her own voice steady.

"Just willing to try."

Madison nodded, her tears falling silently. She slipped the necklace over her head, feeling the weight of the dove settle against her collarbone. It wasn't a burden. It was an anchor. A reminder.

"I'm willing," she whispered.

The two women sat in silence, each holding one end of the same weight.

"You leaving early?" Morgan asked.

"Before sunrise. I want the road to be quiet."

"Pine Ridge," she said.

Madison nodded.

"Back to the diner?"

"Back to whatever's left. If anything is."

"And if there's nothing?"

Madison looked at her. "Then I built it again. Just like he did."

Morgan stood, brushing dew from her skirt.

"If you build it... I'll come visit."

"You'd be welcome," Madison said. "Always."

Morgan hesitated, then leaned down and wrapped her arms around her.

It wasn't a perfect hug. A little stiff. But real.

And Madison held on just long enough to whisper: "Thank you... for finding me."

Morgan pulled back. "Thank you... for not letting them define you."

As Morgan turned to go, something in her footsteps slowed. She stopped just before the path turned toward the house.

A swirl of thoughts pressed behind her eyes.

All her life, she'd believed truth was clean, delivered in black and white, in facts and testimony. However, this woman's mother had shattered that illusion. Madison had revealed a truth unspoken, wrapped in silence and sacrifice.

Morgan had built her career around control, around knowing. But nothing about this felt orderly. Nothing felt sure. She wanted to ask for more. To press for names, for motives, for the whole picture.

But she knew what that would cost.

Madison stayed behind. Watching the lake.

Letting the quiet stretch one last time.

PART THIRTEEN
DUSTY AND MINNIE

CHAPTER
FIFTY-FIVE
MARCH 14, 2018

Miss Lovie's Home
10:30 a.m.

MISS LOVIE'S farewell wasn't a funeral; it was a gentle, private goodbye. Her handwritten will hid in a recipe book, nestled between the instructions for lemon chess pie and deviled eggs made with three types of mustard.

It named Morgan as the executor of her modest estate, which was not surprising. Miss Lovie had always said, *"The ones you feed are the ones you trust."*

Morgan arrived at Miss Lovie's house bone-tired, the exhaustion that sank deeper than her muscles. The week in Pine Ridge had drained her, hours of paperwork, tense meetings, and the unspoken responsibility of holding Madison steady. At the same time, they sifted through the pieces Mister Mayor left behind.

Still, she had promised Janet she'd help sort through Miss Lovie's house, and promises mattered.

But as she unlocked the door, a pang of guilt caught her. She hadn't attended the private home-going service. While others mourned, she'd been sitting at a table in Pine Ridge, watching Madison sign document after document, the weight of loss pressing on them both in silence. Now, stepping into Miss Lovie's quiet home, Morgan felt grief rush in, sharp and delayed, as though the house itself had been waiting for her to feel it.

The house was still. Too still.

No blues on the radio. No humming in the kitchen. No scent of cornbread rising in the oven. Miss Lovie had gone to glory in her sleep, just the way she said she would.

"When the time comes, the Lord won't need to knock loud. I'll already have the door cracked."

And now, Morgan stood in the back bedroom with the door half-cracked behind her, the light slanting in through yellow curtains. Dust caught the sun like gold flakes in the air.

She was here to assist Janet in settling the estate. Sort through a life.

What she didn't expect to find… was her own.

The box was unmarked.

Just a soft, square container lined with quilted floral fabric. Faded. Worn at the seams. Inside were a few tiny items wrapped in hospital linen: a baby gown, a pale-yellow bonnet, a baby bracelet with "Baby Doe," and two envelopes, aged and sealed with ribbon the color of dried lavender.

Miss Lovie addressed both envelopes to her.

Morgan sat on the edge of the queen bed, her knees suddenly weak. She slipped the ribbon off the first letter. The handwriting inside was firm, adult, with a tilt that suggested a nurse or a clerk.

Her fingers trembled as she brushed over the fragile paper, and suddenly she was back in the kitchen on those rare Sundays that Minnie allowed her to spend with Miss Lovie and Janet. The air was thick with the scent of simmering collard greens, candied sweet potatoes, and fried catfish. She could almost hear the old woman's voice, sharp and sure, as she set a heavy cast-iron skillet on the stove.

"Baby girl, Minnie always said you gotta get it perfect," Miss Lovie muttered, flicking her wrist to scatter salt over the sizzling pan. *"But lemme' tell you something, perfection ain't nothing but a fancy name for fear. Fear you ain't enough. Fear you'll get left behind if you ain't the best at every little thing."*

Morgan had stood at the kitchen table, licking the spoon from the lemon cake mix, while watching the way Miss Lovie moved, unhurried, confident, constantly tasting the food with her pinky finger like she trusted her senses more than a recipe.

"*You know why I don't keep a timer?*" Miss Lovie said, turning over a piece of fish. "*Cause food don't need a clock. It needs someone to pay attention.*"

The words had stuck with Morgan like gospel, far more potent than anything she'd heard in school. Now, in the quiet of the old house, she realized those moments had shaped so much of her. Miss Lovie's steady hands, her defiance of rules written by others, her insistence that life wasn't about performing, but about being present.

Minnie, with her starched shirts and sharp tongue, had always been trying to scrub herself clean of shadows. But Miss Lovie knew you couldn't wash away the truth. You had to carry it.

Morgan blinked hard, her hands tightening around the letters.

This wasn't just a goodbye. This was a map.

A map she hadn't known she needed.

Morgan's hands trembled as she unfolded the first letter, her breath catching in her throat. These weren't just old papers; they were keys to a story locked away for decades. The fabric-wrapped box held a time capsule from a silent day, the day Madison, a thirteen-year-old girl, gave birth alone in a sterile hospital room.

The truth was here, pressed between delicate lines of ink and the weight of a past no one had dared to speak aloud.

August 12, 1978

The Nurse's Letter

There are things I will carry to my grave. Things I cannot undo.

I did what I was told. I trusted the system. I followed orders because I was afraid.

And for that, I will never forgive myself.

That baby had a name before they erased it.

And that girl, the baby's mother, barely more than a child herself, deserved better.

The files were altered, the papers sealed, and I was told to sign.

I did.

But I will never stop hoping. Never stopped checking. Never stopped praying.

If someone ever finds this and the truth ever comes to light.

Please let that girl know: Her baby lived. Her baby was taken.

And it wasn't her fault.

And I am praying she is loved.

Morgan sat frozen, the weight of the nurse's words pressing down on her chest. The letter painted a clinical, detached portrait of a young girl too young to give birth, too young to understand what was being taken from her.

But there was more.

Her hands hovered over the second envelope, its lavender ribbon trembling between her fingers. This wasn't from a nurse or a clerk. Madison herself wrote this letter in the haze of loss and confusion, scribbling words as a little girl whose voice had been silenced for far too long.

Thirteen-year-old Madison's Letter

My baby, who won't know me. I don't know what your name will be.

I don't know if you are alive. They said you dead. Stillborn?

I think they lied cause I heard you cry.

I am thirteen and a half years old. They say I'm not ready to be anybody's mama.

I am sad, bleeding a lot, and shaking.

I didn't see your face, but I hope we look alike.

I'm sorry. This wasn't my fault.

I'm mad nobody listened to me.

If you are alive and get this someday.

Somebody hurt me really bad, and it made you.

But it hurts me more to lose you.

I didn't get to name you.

But if I did, it would be Willow Jackson Malone.

Because that was my Momma and Daddy's names.

If you grow up and people say you hard.

Tell them you were born of fire.

Tell them your mama survived things she was never supposed to survive.

And if you're reading this, then you are proof that I was right.

I loved you. Even if I never got to say it.

Maddie

Morgan sat there long after the letters slipped from her hands, her breath catching in her throat.

The sun through the curtain had shifted, casting long shadows across the faded quilt beneath her. The weight of Madison's words, raw, desperate, unfinished, melded with the nurse's quiet confession, forming a truth too heavy to bear and too fragile to let go.

For the first time, the pieces of her life, scattered like ash and memory, fit together.

But fitting them together didn't make them easier to carry.

Her chest tightened as a new ache pressed in: Miss Lovie's voice, Minnie's steady hands, Dusty's laughter. The people who had loved her, protected her, raised her to believe she belonged, had also kept this from her.

Not strangers.

Them.

Family.

The betrayal felt sharp and jagged. Did they believe she wasn't strong enough to handle the truth? Or were they too scared of what it might cost to let it come out? Her heart twisted with love and anger, grief and gratitude, unable to settle on just one. S

She closed her eyes, whispering into the quiet house,

"You knew. All of you knew."

CHAPTER
FIFTY-SIX
MARCH 18, 2018

Bennin-Alcott Estate
3:20 p.m.

THE DRIVE WAS EERILY QUIET, no music, no podcasts, just the hum of tires and the rush of wind. Morgan had taken this route countless times as a child, but today it felt like enemy territory. Every turn fueled a memory; every tree-lined block whispered things she'd tried to forget.

She gripped the steering wheel as the house came into view. For years, she had imagined this moment with fire, storms of confrontation, righteous fury. But now, all she felt was fatigue. Not the kind sleep could fix, but the kind truth demanded. Her chest tightened with something too tangled to name: grief, rage, the ache of something stolen. She had pictured this return as an eruption. Instead, it arrived as a sigh… low, tired, and final.

She paused with the engine running, staring at the pristine white shutters, the manicured hedges. This house had been her stage. A backdrop for a life carefully curated and color-corrected to avoid discomfort. It was where she first learned to smile when she wanted to scream, to apologize when she should have questioned. It was the house where questions went to die.

But it hadn't always been this way.

She remembered one night, when she was maybe seven, feverish and unable to sleep. Dusty had carried her downstairs, blanket and all, lit a fire, and made cocoa from scratch. They sat curled up in the den, wrapped in an old Afghan, while he read her favorite story aloud. She remembered the cocoa's warmth burning gently in her throat, and the way Dusty's voice wrapped around her like armor. That night, she felt safe. Loved.

Until Minnie came down an hour later, her face tight with disapproval.

"This isn't a campsite," she snapped, eyes on the mess of pillows and the half-empty mug. "We have rules for a reason."

Morgan had clutched the blanket tighter and said nothing.

She never asked for firelight stories again.

The memory surfaced now, uninvited, as she turned off the ignition.

She sat a moment longer, fingers resting on the key. Then she whispered, to no one, to herself, to the girl she used to be:

"You deserve the truth."

Then she stepped out of the car, heels clicking across the perfect stone walkway.

The house looked exactly as it always had, pristine, untouched by time. Every curtain hung without a wrinkle, every rug vacuumed into perfect lines, like rows of obedient soldiers. Even the roses, arranged with obsessive care, stood upright in a crystal vase, clipped just enough to obey. Not too full. Not too open. As if blooming too wide might break the rules.

Morgan stepped inside, and something in her chest clenched. A familiar knot tightened under her ribs, the kind that made her breath hitch, the kind she hadn't felt in years.

At thirty-nine, she was walking into the house she once swore she'd never enter again. Twenty years of distance vanished the moment the door closed behind her, as if the walls could breathe in memory and exhale guilt.

She hadn't come for reconciliation.

She hadn't come for tea.

She came to ask.

She came to know.

Thirteen and a half. That's how old Madison had been when she became a mother.

Morgan had turned thirteen here, catered party, white linens, sugar-dusted petits fours. She'd unwrapped ballet slippers and books while guests complimented how "graciously" she was growing. Her mother smiled through it all, poised and polished.

That same year, her birth mother was likely still wondering if the baby she'd been told was dead had ever taken a breath.

The contrast turned her stomach.

This house wasn't a home. It was a showroom. Wallpapered in silence, polished with denial. A place where questions cracked the paint.

The floor didn't creak. Of course it didn't. Creaks were imperfections, and this house didn't allow those.

Dusty appeared in the foyer first.

"My M&M," he said, voice still warm, soft at the edges. That familiar smile bloomed across his face, disarming, almost tender.

She let him hug her. He'd never shut doors.

But she didn't hug back.

Then came Minnie. Pressed blouse. Taupe lipstick. Watch flashing like a cuff. Her expression walked the usual tightrope; concern laced with control.

Morgan walked past her and entered the parlor without greeting or hesitation, saying, "I came for answers," and proceeded without waiting for an invitation.

Dusty followed, hands fidgeting. Minnie came in after, heels silent on the carpet. She didn't sit. Couldn't. She stood in her perfectly tailored silence, as if movement might unravel everything she'd built.

Minnie spoke first, voice like cut glass.

"Is this about that woman?"

Morgan turned.

"Her name is Madison. And that woman is my mother."

The words didn't echo. They landed like a dropped crystal.

Dusty sank onto the couch, stunned. Minnie stayed still.

"I found the birth records," Morgan continued. "Sealed illegally. Took three departments and a friend in the clerk's office to access them."

Her gaze locked on Minnie.

"Why did you lie?"

Minnie didn't flinch. Her voice came smooth, practiced.

"We never lied. We told you what we were told."

"That my mother was dead?"

"Yes."

Morgan's voice sharpened. "Then what about the letters?"

Minnie's mask cracked, just slightly. A flicker behind the eyes.

"You mean the ones Miss Lillie found in that old hospital bag," Morgan said.

Dusty blinked. "Minnie... what letters?"

"There were two," Morgan replied. "One from the nurse who helped deliver me. The other from Madison."

She took a breath.

"The nurse wrote: '*I wish I could've done more. But if you're reading this, know your mama loved you and never stopped crying for you.*'"

She faced Minnie fully now. "Madison wrote she thought she heard me cry."

Morgan's voice cracked. "But what I'll never forget is this: '*If you are alive and find this, please know, somebody hurt me bad and made you, but it hurts more to lose you.*'"

Dusty's hand covered his mouth.

"You read that, Minnie," Morgan said. "And still told me she was dead."

Minnie stayed composed. "You were a child. I didn't think you were ready."

"No," Morgan replied. "You never gave me the chance to be."

Minnie's tone grew sharper. "She was thirteen, poor, Black, and a nobody. You think I was going to let that story into your life? You had everything."

"There it is," Morgan said coldly. "You don't get to be 'the great white hope ' and act like saving me justified erasing her," she added, stepping closer. "You erased her to protect your image, not me."

"Morgan, you lost your Black card," Minnie snapped. "A white family gave you everything, Dior baby blankets, ballet lessons, Ivy League. Country clubs. Summers in the Hamptons."

Morgan's voice sliced. "I would've traded it all for one day with my real mother."

Minnie scoffed. "That's your elitism talking. You've never been hungry."

Stepping back and giving Minnie a look of disdain, "No, I was never hungry but never knew if I was truly wanted for me, or your agenda."

Dusty finally spoke, voice thick. "We loved you. From the moment we saw you."

"I know," Morgan said. Softer. "But love doesn't erase lies."

The room fell quiet.

She moved toward the door.

"So," she said, low but clear, "ever wonder what happened to that little Black girl you thought would amount to nothing?"

She let the silence hold.

She transformed into Lady Madison Jackson Winter. Starting with her marriage to a bishop, she built an empire, graced magazine covers, hosted galas, and raised millions for charity. The woman you deleted from history became someone the world couldn't ignore.

Minnie's spine stiffened.

"And the irony?" Morgan added. "You once gave her an award. Most Charitable Woman of the Year. Called her a pillar of grace. Never knowing she was the girl you erased."

Minnie paled.

"You shook her hand," Morgan laughed, "smiled for the cameras. Called her a role model. And you never knew."

Dusty buried his face in his hands. Minnie swayed, just slightly.

"She survived prison," Morgan continued, voice trembling. "She survived the scandal. Grief. She buried a son. And after all that... she still stands taller than anyone you ever introduced me to."

A pause.

"And she's mine. Not just by blood, but courage, survival, and choice."

Dusty looked up, broken. "What do you want from us?"

"Nothing," Morgan said. "Except to know you heard me."

A long silence.

"She only asked me one thing," Morgan added. "After I found her."

Minnie's voice was seemingly annoyed. "Well, what did she ask?"

Morgan's eyes filled.

"She asked, '*Did they love you?*'"

She held that line in the air like a verdict.

Morgan whispered, "I told her yes." It mattered to her, but not enough for me. She stepped back. "You gave me a good life," she said, "but you stole my truth." Turning, she walked out, her heels clicking on marble, her truth trailing like a shadow.

They were left alone in the silence.

The night air greeted her like a balm and a blade, cool, sharp, and freeing. She paused by her car, gazing up at the sky. The stars twinkled faintly, obscured by the haze of streetlights, yet still visible.

Still trying.

For the first time since reading that record, tracing her birth certificate with trembling fingers, and confronting the woman who brought her into this world... Morgan allowed herself to feel it, the sorrow, the release, and the ache where the lie had dwelled.

It was all hers now. As was the truth.

After the door closed behind Morgan, the house seemed even quieter than before, like it was holding its breath.

Dusty sank into the armchair in the den, elbows on knees, face in his hands.

"I didn't think it would feel like this," he murmured.

Minnie stood near the fireplace, arms still folded, but her posture had slackened. "Feel like what?"

"Like we failed her," Dusty said.

"We didn't fail her. We protected her. We gave her a life. A future."

Dusty looked up with tired eyes. "Did we? Or did we give her a version of life that only worked if she didn't ask too many questions?"

Minnie turned away. "It's more complicated than that."

"I know it is," he said, shaking his head. "But that doesn't make it right."

She was silent for a long time.

Then, in a voice that barely carried, she said, "I was afraid that acknowledging her past would ruin the life we built."

"Well, pretending it didn't exist did the same thing," Dusty replied.

He rose and moved next to her. "You made a decision and believed it was right. But now… we have to live with the consequences."

Minnie was silent.

And for the first time in decades, they stood side by side, not as parents with answers, but as people finally reckoning with the weight of the silence they had carried, and the truth that had always waited beneath it.

Later that evening, Dusty stood alone in the dimly lit parlor, lost in a quiet reverie. His eyes landed on Morgan's old ballet slipper, still resting on the dustless shelf where Minnie had kept it all these years, unable to let it go.

He reached out and picked it up gently, saying nothing.

His thumb brushed across the frayed satin, each thread whispering echoes of childhood recitals, grace, and all the unspoken dreams they'd curated in porcelain silence. He turned it once in his hand, then placed it carefully back where it had always belonged.

A quiet gesture.

A silent apology.

"We built her life on silence and told ourselves it was love."

Meanwhile, back at her condo in the city, Morgan stood in her living room, the familiar scent of home wrapping around her like a soft embrace. Her eyes settled on a framed photo, her law school graduation, smiles bright, arms linked with her parents, pride radiating from all three.

But that image felt distant now. A curated moment, eclipsed by all that had unfolded since.

She took the photo down slowly, her fingers trembling just slightly. Not from anger. From reverence.

In its place, she pinned a different picture, one snapped candidly by Miss Lucy at the halfway house. No formal poses, no forced grins. Just her and Madison, standing side by side. Not as prosecutor and defendant. Not as adversaries.

But as something more profound.

Survivors.

Women who had faced the fire and come out forged, not broken.

A quiet gesture. A silent reclamation.

This new image didn't represent success in the eyes of the world. It represented truth. Growth. The beauty born from unraveling, and the strength it took to rebuild.

And in that moment, Morgan knew this was who she truly was now. Not just a woman with titles and degrees, but one who had found her voice in the ashes.

And chosen to rise.

PART FOURTEEN
THE LEGEND

CHAPTER
FIFTY-SEVEN
FEBRUARY 21, 2018

Leaving for Pine Ridge
6:30 a.m.

AS MADISON LEFT the town of Pendleton, driving west toward Pine Ridge, her hands were relaxed on the steering wheel, and the landscape rolled by like a memory she couldn't quite grasp.

In the silence of the drive, her mind drifted back to the story Mister Mayor had once shared with her, late one night while the two enjoyed Cognac by the fireplace.

"You ever hear the real story of how this place came to be?" he asked, voice low and rough from years of whiskey and late-night conversations.

"I don't mean the version they tell tourists, or the one written in the town archives. I'm talking about the story, the real one. The one that isn't written down anywhere except in the bones of this land."

Madison shook her head, feeling the weight of his words settle into her chest. "I don't think I have."

Harper sat back, his voice low, steady.

"It starts with a boy in Alabama... 1957."

He didn't look at Madison as he spoke, just stared past her, like he was watching it all unfold again.

"My daddy was Reverend Lewis White. Everybody in our town respected him, or feared him. Depends on who you ask. He helped Black folks register to vote, even when it wasn't safe. Especially when it wasn't safe."

He exhaled slowly, eyes dark.

"That night, we were coming back from Bible study. Warm, thick air. My sisters were half asleep in the backseat. Mama was humming. Then the headlights. A truck behind us, speeding up. Ran us off the road."

He paused, jaw tightening.

"Daddy told Mama to keep us quiet. 'Stay in the car,' he said. He stepped out… and that's when they came. White robes. Hoods. Guns. Like something outta hell."

Harper's fingers curled slightly on the table.

"They grabbed him. Dragged him off into the woods. I was in the ditch, holding my sisters, trying not to breathe. I could hear everything: branches breaking, boots stomping, voices yelling. Then it got quiet. Too quiet."

He shook his head once, eyes wet but unblinking.

"Then came the light. Lantern glow. And that sound… that rope stretching under his weight."

He looked at Madison then. "You know what I remember most? They struggled. It took all of them to lift him. They cursed at how heavy he was. And I held on to that; he didn't go easy. Not even in death."

A beat passed. Neither spoke.

"He never begged. Never screamed. Just stood there. Silent. Defiant. And I carried that silence with me. My whole damn life."

Madison didn't say anything. She didn't have to. The silence between them was heavy, reverent.

Harper leaned back, the weight of the memory finally spoken aloud, still pressing on his chest.

Harper's voice dropped to almost a whisper. "Even now, I can feel the dirt under my nails. I dug my fingers into the ground to stop myself from screaming. Everything in me wanted to run, to fight, to throw myself into the fire. But his voice was louder than my fear."

He looked at Madison, eyes sharp with memory. "He said, *'Keep them safe.'* That was the last thing my father ever said. So, I held my sisters close, covered their mouths, made my body a wall between them and the worst thing I've ever seen."

He paused, the air between them thick.

"His body swung in that firelight, and I swear," Harper shook his head, voice steady but hoarse, "it never left me. That image. Fire, robes, smoke. His frame caught in the light like a warning... like a promise."

He exhaled. "And my mama... she didn't cry. Not once. Not when we drove away, not at the service. But she aged fast. Ten years in ten weeks. Her silence was heavier than mine."

He stared down at his hands. "We didn't leave the house for days. Fear sits with you, Madison. Stays in the walls. But word spread. Folks started coming. Some whispered. Others shouted. And by the end of that week, we were no longer hiding."

He leaned forward, elbows on his knees. "They held the memorial on the church steps. The same steps Daddy used to stand on with his Bible raised like a sword. But this time... hundreds came. From counties over. Suits. Veils. Their grief wasn't quiet. It was marching and music and anger braided with love."

His voice caught for just a moment.

"Dr. King came."

Madison blinked, caught off guard. "Dr. Martin Luther King?"

Harper nodded slowly. "Eulogized my father himself. Called him a martyr. Said, *'What was done in hate will not be forgotten, but neither will the light Reverend White carried into this world.'*"

He closed his eyes briefly, as if replaying it.

"I didn't cry. I couldn't. My jaw was locked. But when Dr. King placed that single white rose on my father's casket..."

A long pause.

"My hands wouldn't stop shaking. That rose burned into my memory. More than the fire. More than the rope. Because it meant something could still grow. Even after all that."

He looked up again, gaze steady.

"That's when I knew what my life was for. Not revenge. Not bitterness. But building something better. Something he'd be proud of. That rose," Harper said, his voice soft now, "was the beginning of that promise."

Harper went quiet again, not from sorrow this time, but from memory. Madison didn't rush him. She could see the weight still living inside him.

"I didn't speak for weeks," he finally said. "Not to my mama. Not to the preacher. Not to God."

He glanced down at his hands. "I wasn't angry yet. That came later. At first, I was just... hollow. Like somebody scooped everything out and left me walking around with air in my chest."

He paused. "I used to be curious, you know? Ask about stars, trains, birds, whatever passed me by. I used to sing. After he died, all that just... stopped."

His voice thinned but didn't waver.

"I'd sit on the back steps and stare at the trees he used to bless. Lay on the floor next to my sisters' beds just to make sure they were still breathing. Sometimes, I pressed my ear to the floorboards, hoping to catch his footsteps in the wood."

Madison's eyes glistened, but she stayed quiet.

"Mama never forced a word out of me. She just kept the house moving. Braided hair, cooked meals, swept silence like it was dust.

But at night, when she thought I was asleep, she'd rest her hand on my back and whisper, *"It's alright to come back now, baby. We still need you."*

He looked up, meeting Madison's eyes. "I didn't think I could. Not then. Not when hope could get a man killed. Not when trees looked like nooses. Not when even clean air smelled like fire."

He exhaled slowly. "But one morning, before the sun came up, I got up and went outside. Didn't know what I was doing. Just started digging. A trench, a garden, a hole, I didn't care. I needed something my hands could hold."

He gave a dry, quiet laugh. "Mama found me hours later. Blisters on my palms, dirt in my hair.

I looked at her and said, *'If I can't change what they did... I'll build something they can't burn.'"*

He leaned back, shoulders easing for the first time in the conversation.

"And that was the day I stopped being just his son. That's the day I became me."

Madison's voice was barely above a whisper. "A builder."

Harper nodded. "Not of vengeance. Of sanctuary."

"Last time I saw my mama, she was bedridden in the front room of her sister's house in Birmingham. Cancer hit her fast. Took all her weight, most of her voice. But not the fire. That never left her."

He paused, staring past the room for a moment before continuing.

"She reached out, took my hand, and pressed it to her chest. Her skin was paper-thin, but her grip still had something in it. She looked me dead in the eye and said, *'Don't let this be the end of us.'*"

His voice dropped.

"I leaned in close. Tears stingin'. Could barely look at her."

'You hear me, baby?' she said. *'You take this grief, and you make it mean something.'*

"I told her, *"I promise, Mama. I'll turn it into something good. Something that lasts."'*

Harper's jaw clenched slightly as he remembered. "She smiled, soft, like she knew, and said, *'Then I can go see yo' daddy in peace.'*"

He looked down at his hands.

"When she passed, I laid her right next to my daddy. Same red Alabama earth. Same soil their blood had soaked. No fancy headstones. Just the two of them, side by side."

A long silence settled before he added, "And that was it. I left Alabama and never looked back."

"First time I stepped off that truck in Northern Wisconsin, the cold stole my breath," Harper said, a wry curve at his mouth. "Wasn't just the air—it was the silence. Hit different from Alabama. No crickets, no hymns floatin' through windows, no voices across porches. Just wind. Pines. A sky so wide it made you feel like a speck."

He paused, hands resting on his knees.

"All I had was a duffel bag, two shirts, my Bible, a photo of my daddy… and a whole lot I'd never said out loud."

He met Madison's gaze, steady now.

"I didn't smile. Didn't speak unless needed. First one on site every day, swingin' that axe like I could split the ache outta' my chest."

"The fellas called me Preacher. Not outta' reverence, just 'cause I didn't cuss or chase women or laugh at their mess. Thought I was holy. Truth is, I was grieving."

He rubbed a calloused thumb against his palm. "Grief don't yell. It settles deep. Turns silence into a second language."

He looked up again. "At night, I'd lie there in the bunkhouse. Couldn't sleep. Sap in my nose, fingers twitchin', like they were reachin' for something soft… something gone."

"But I watched. Learned who barked and who bent. Where power lived. And where it leaked." A faint smile tugged at his mouth. "Found an old radio. Gospel outta' Chicago. Sunday mornings, I'd sit still and let the choir do what I couldn't."

Extending his glass to Madison for a refill, he continued as she rose to oblige his request.

One night, with frost thick on the windows, I stepped outside with a scrap of pinewood. Started carvin'. Just a little bird. Nothin' fancy. Just needed to shape somethin' instead of breakin' it.

He turned to Madison, voice lower now.

"That bird was the start of Pine Ridge. Didn't know it then. But I was searchin' for a place to plant my pain. Somewhere it could grow into somethin' that didn't burn."

He leaned back.

"I didn't set out to build a legacy. I just didn't wanna keep buryin' the good."

Madison returned, handed him the glass, and asked, "So, how did you get the land? What's the real story?" He laughed and said, "Slow down, lil girl, this story can't be rushed."

"Late November," he said. "They sent us further north, Walden family property. Overgrown. Forgotten. Just frost and brush and silence."

Didn't bother him.

"Foreman told us to split up. I took my tools and headed for the tree line."

He paused. "Didn't get far. Trees thinned. And then, gone. The forest just... gave way."

His voice softened.

"Land sloped down to a lake. Still. Holding its breath."

He looked toward Madison. "The breeze off that water felt older than pain. Trees leaned in like they were listening. And me?"

He gave a small laugh. "I stopped. Just stood there. No saws. No voices. Just my heartbeat. And the sound of pine needles hittin' earth."

He rubbed his chest. "Sky was pale gray. The lake mirrored it so clean, it felt like the world folded in half."

"A doe and her baby stood at the edge. No fear. Like they knew it was sacred ground."

He was quiet for a long time.

"Somethin' shifted. Not peace... but the shape of it. Like the land was sayin': *This don't have to be sorrow. Not forever.*"

He looked down at his hands.

"I knelt at the edge. Touched the water. Cold. Clean. Felt like truth."

He drew in a slow breath. "That's where Pine Ridge was born. No plan. No blueprint. Just a call in my chest."

He paused.

"Some places don't ask for permission to heal. They just invite you in and say:

Start here."

CHAPTER
FIFTY-EIGHT

DECEMBER 8, 1961

Walden Property Bunkhouse
9:30 p.m.

"FOR DAYS AFTER THAT LAKE..." Harper shook his head, smiling like the memory still surprised him. "I couldn't shake it. That hush, that feelin', like the land had laid its hand on my shoulder and said, *"You. You're the one."*

Wasn't words, just... knowin'. Like it had chosen me the same way I'd decided it."

He glanced at Madison, his tone softening.

Every time I shut my eyes, I saw that clearing. Felt that water again, cold, clean, full of promise.

So, when Old Man Walden started drinkin' too much and talkin' too loud one night, goin' on about land he didn't care to keep, braggin' how he'd dare anyone to take it...

Harper's voice dropped, low and even.

"I hadn't come there to play. But when he slapped down that challenge like a dare from the devil, I picked up the cards like I was answerin' a call. 'Cause that land was already mine. That game? How the world would catch up to what destiny already decided."

He leaned back, gaze steady.

"It started like any other night. Little stakes. A couple of jokes. A few coins passed hands.

But I was quiet.

Watched.

Learned.

Started winning.

First wages.

Then double.

Then folks stopped laughin'."

He paused. "Old Man Walden didn't like that."

"Drunk and red in the face, he slammed his glass down, pointed a crooked finger at me, and said, *'My land. Against your silence.'*"

Harper shook his head again, voice going flat.

"*'All of it,'* he said. *'You win, you walk away owning more acres than can be counted. You lose, you keep your damn mouth shut and work free the rest of the season, boy.'*"

The word *boy* hung in the air like smoke.

"Room got quiet," Harper said. "You could hear folks' breath catch. Nobody thought I'd take it."

He gave Madison a slow, knowing look. "But I did."

The memory sat between them for a moment before he continued.

Cards were dealt.

I won the hand, four-of-a-kind. Clean. Final. Righteous.

Old Man Walden didn't lay his hand down.

He stood up, shoved his chair back, and flipped the whole damn table.

"IT'S ALL YOURS, BOY!" he shouted.

Some folks say Walden had the better hand, folded on purpose. Said the guilt had been weighing him down for decades, taking a young Black man's life as part of the Klan, trying to square up with God before his number came.

Others say he did it to spite his kin, who he'd been feuding with for years. Didn't want them getting a single acre.

Harper exhaled, slow and sure.

"I don't care which version they tell. Truth is, I walked outta that room holdin' more than a deed. I walked out with a future."

He looked toward the window, as if he was seeing it all again, every inch of that land.

"Fifteen thousand acres of redemption. And all I had to do was say yes when the land called my name."

Then, softer: "Three days later, they found Old Man Walden dead in his home."

He didn't blink.

"Official story? Suicide. But the whispers flew. Folks said I forced his hand. Others blamed his family. Said they couldn't bear a Black man owning that kind of land, clean, legal, and untouchable."

He looked at Madison.

"Didn't matter. My name was on that deed. I had a key. And I wasn't givin' it back."

He leaned back in his chair, voice steady now.

"They came for me with lawyers, threats, and petitions. I stayed. I fought. I built."

Silence settled around him, solid as stone.

"A year later, once the courts signed off and Pine Ridge was mine for good, I went back to Alabama."

He smiled faintly.

"Not just to visit graves. I went to ask Jessie Mae Simmons to marry me."

He smiled, the memory softening his voice.

"She was the only girl I'd ever loved. Known her since grade school. Smart as a whip. Sharp tongue. Soft hands. She didn't say yes right away. Her folks were scared. Rightfully so. They'd buried too many Black boys with dreams. But I didn't beg."

He looked down at his hands, then back up.

"I just told her, *'I want to build something good. But don't want to do it without you.'*"

A pause.

"She came. Packed her bags. Rode north with me on the Greyhound bus, one hand on her Bible, one on mine."

Harper's voice thickened.

"She's the one who came up with the Christmas Wonderland. Said, *'Black children deserve winter magic too.'* So, we made it happen.

My hands. Her vision. White's *Christmas Winter Wonderland*. Still runnin' strong."

He nodded slowly.

"We had two boys, quick. Healthy and strong, like her. But our daughter came during a storm in December. Breech. No hospital within fifty miles would treat her. Black woman, middle of the night, snowy roads, they turned us away."

A long, bitter breath escaped him.

"The midwife did her best.

Baby girl made it.

Jessie didn't.

Bled out while I held her hand.

The only thing I could do was bury her beneath the cypress at the edge of the land she helped dream into life."

He rubbed his thumb across his palm, grounding himself.

"I wanted to burn the world down. But instead, I built."

PART FIFTEEN
THE LAST DAY OF NINA
AUTUMN STORM

CHAPTER
FIFTY-NINE
NOVEMBER 13, 2014

The Landing Diner & Bakery – Pt. 1
8:18 p.m.

THE LAST CUSTOMER left as Autumn switched off the open sign at The Landing Diner and Bakery.

"Finally," she muttered, the word a breath of relief more than sound.

Today's closing felt long overdue. The hours had dragged, each minute thick with exhaustion. Her legs ached, her back throbbed from stooping over tables.

The lights dimmed to their usual cozy glow, casting gentle shadows on the checkered floor. The lingering aroma of Chicken and Dumplings still clung to the air, warm and familiar.

She inhaled deeply.

"Smells like Mama Pearl's kitchen," she said aloud, her voice swallowed by the hum of the fan. "God, I'm tired."

This little diner was more than just a business. It was a sanctuary. Survival. The walls held pieces of her past she never spoke about, and parts of her healing no one could see.

"You've made it this far," she whispered, eyes scanning the empty booths. "Don't fall apart now."

She stepped into the kitchen, where chaos awaited: dishes piled high, prep lists scrawled in rushed handwriting. The infamous "PaPa's Pecan Pie" orders loomed large on tomorrow's to-do list.

She dropped the towel on the counter and exhaled. "Nope. Not tonight."

Even the pans appeared to sag under the weight of the evening.

Sadie's absence tugged at her mind again. That phone call, with its shaky voice and odd silences, was unsettling.

"*She's not okay,*" Autumn said to no one. "*Stomach cramps, my ass.*"

Not that she didn't believe Sadie was unwell. But there'd been more in the pauses than in the words.

"*She didn't want to say it,*" Autumn murmured. "*Just like I never did.*"

Her eyes drifted to the booth by the window.

The memory settled before she could stop it.

Three years ago...

The bell over the door had rung as it always did, cheerful and small.

A young woman stepped in, shoulders hunched beneath a too-thin jacket. Her hand gripped that of a little girl, maybe four, with hair in uneven pigtails. The child looked around the diner with wide, unblinking eyes.

Autumn had barely glanced up from wiping the counter.

"Help you with something?" she'd asked, trying to sound more hospitable than suspicious.

The woman hesitated, then nodded. "Could we just... get a grilled cheese?"

Autumn nodded, motioning toward a booth. "Sure. Sit anywhere you like."

They sat. Quiet. Autumn brought over the uncut sandwich a few minutes later.

The woman looked up. "Thank you."

Autumn noticed the way her fingers trembled when she picked up the knife to split it in half.

"Cute kid," she said casually.

"She's a good eater. Always likes cheese." The woman smiled, but it was a small, worn smile, as if it hadn't been used in a while.

"Name's Sadie," she said finally. "This is Sara Leigh."

Autumn paused. Something in Sadie's tone rang familiar, the practiced calm, the invisible weight.

"You staying in town?" She'd asked gently.

"Trying to," Sadie replied. "If we can."

No backstory. No excuses.

Just that: *If we can.* That had been enough for Autumn.

"Dishwashing pays under the table," she'd offered. "If you're looking for something."

Sadie blinked. "You serious?"

Autumn nodded. "Dead serious."

A sharp pain in her back snapped her to the present as she brushed past the edge of the booth. "Best grilled cheese I ever made," she murmured. The diner felt emptier without Sadie. Not just the workload, but the *absence* of her. Two women with secrets, stitched together by survival and small kindnesses.

She stared at the sink. Water droplets clung to the faucet, catching the low light like tiny stars.

"She reminded me so much of myself," she thought, fighting back a tear. "When I walked into this diner almost five years ago, my silence carried more than the ashes would ever tell."

Autumn leaned on the counter, the memory rising uninvited. Sadie's tired eyes, that quiet strength beneath fear. *"You looked like you'd been running for years,"* she whispered, the image still vivid. *"Just like I had."*

There was no one to answer, but the quiet had grown comforting until today.

At lunch, the chaos had been barely manageable without Sadie's help, and then in came Mister Mayor.

She smiled faintly. "That man. He is always my knight in shining armor."

He'd cracked jokes, poured coffee like a showman, and made the room lighter. His kindness had given her a second wind.

"Saved my ass today," she said, wiping a smudge from the prep counter.

The idea of a hot toddy and her bed, full of warmth, quiet, and sleep, made her heart race with excitement. She reached for the keys.

Then the bell above the door chimed.

She froze.

Not because she didn't expect someone. But because she had hoped, prayed, willed that no one else would come.

It was too late for casual drop-ins. Too dark for friendly hellos. Whoever had just stepped inside hadn't come for coffee.

Her body reacted before her mind did, heart racing, breath caught just behind her ribs.

A strange chill crept across the back of her neck like her bones had remembered something her brain couldn't place.

She didn't turn right away.

Instead, she closed her eyes for a beat, letting the hum of the fan and the smell of dish soap anchor her. The soft clink of the chime still echoed in her head.

The air shifted.

There was something about the way a man like him entered a room; you didn't need to see him to feel it.

He brought a storm with him. Always had.

The kind that seemed charming on the surface but churned with something uglier underneath.

Her fingers tightened around the towel she had grabbed by instinct.

Not a weapon. Not a shield.

Just something to hold. To anchor her to the present moment.

She glanced toward the emergency phone by the register. It may well have been miles away.

She squared her shoulders. Took a breath.

And then she turned around.

There he was.

Charlie

"Well, now," he said, voice slick as oil, "isn't this cozy?"

He entered as though he owned the space, his leather jacket slung over his shoulder, taking slow, unsteady steps, with a smirk tugging at the corner of his mouth. His movements had a jagged quality, reminiscent of a man who had been expecting a confrontation all day.

The comforting aroma of the daily special, "Chicken and Dumpling," was now overshadowed by the scent of stale alcohol and sweat.

He reeked of bitterness and bourbon, his eyes clouded with a glassy anger, unpredictable and dangerous. Sarcastically, he remarked,

"Who do we have here?"

Autumn grew tense. Her pulse raced.

"We're closed, Charlie."

"Don't worry, I won't be long," he said, circling the stools at the counter like a predator. "I just thought we should have a little... chat."

She backed up slowly and deliberately around the counter.

"Sadie's not here."

"Oh, I understand. I left her at home, which is why I came now. I didn't want her to interrupt us."

He smiled a rehearsed grin that didn't reach his eyes.

"That girl... she's got quite the spirit, doesn't she? But too fragile to carry all those secrets alone." He leaned closer, his gaze narrowing. "Unlike you."

Autumn narrowed her eyes but remained silent. Inside, her thoughts spiraled.

What does he know?

How long has he known?

God, please let this be another one of his games...

Clutching the towel, she silently urged herself, "*Stay calm. Don't let him see your fear.*"

Charlie's voice dipped into an almost gentle tone, false comfort layered in threat.

"You know, I'm not here to start trouble. I just think people should be honest. Especially about their truth."

He leaned closer, his voice soft and mocking. "You know, you excel at masquerading as someone else."

Autumn's jaw clenched. She reached under the counter to grab the gun she kept for security, gripping the cold steel handle but stopping.

"I don't know what you're talking about."

"Oh, come on. Don't insult me, Autumn... or should I say Madison Jackson Winter?"

That stopped her cold.

The name echoed through the space like a gunshot.

She hadn't heard her name in years. Not aloud. Not with accusation.

Hearing it from Charlie's mouth, slurred with malice and satisfaction, it sounded like a weapon. Like her past had clawed its way out of the grave she'd buried it in.

She stayed steady, straightened, and looked him in the eye, letting silence stretch, not from fear, but as a show of power. Let him guess what came next; she wouldn't give him the satisfaction of crumbling.

The version of Charlie that stood in The Landing Diner & Bakery that night was a far cry from the sought-after high school quarterback, voted "Most Likely to Succeed" and boyfriend of Sadie, the girl who made heads turn and hearts stutter, a cheerleading captain with soft blonde curls and bright green eyes that always looked a little lost.

Charlie had been her first everything.

First kiss.

First love.

First heartbreak.

They were high school royalty, the golden couple with crowns on prom night and scholarship dreams ahead of them.

When Sadie discovered she was pregnant, she was terrified. But Charlie had held her hand and promised it would be okay. Their families rallied around them; they quickly planned a wedding and rewrote their future.

What should have been their storybook beginning turned tragic the night of the wedding. Charlie's older brother, drunk and reckless, crashed the car that would forever change their lives.

The injury to Charlie's knee ended his football dreams. He blamed Sadie for the baby, the crash, and the life he lost. Once whispering dreams into her ear, he now shouted blame.

And worse.

By the time their daughter, Sara Leigh, was born, Sadie had become a shell of the girl she once was.

The bruises started small. The apologies are even smaller.

And then, one night, when the fear finally outweighed the shame, she ran.

Found sanctuary in Pine Ridge.

Found Autumn.

Found herself again.

CHAPTER
SIXTY

NOVEMBER 13, 2014

The Landing Diner & Bakery – Pt. 2
8:38 p.m.

THE AIR in the diner felt heavy, and the silence hung thick and charged between them. Autumn's heart pounded in her ribcage, a furious rhythm echoing in her ears. Charlie had crossed a line; he knew her secret.

Charlie circled the counter, smirking. "I did my homework. A friend checked the VIN of that pretty car you keep in the garage out back. Registered to Nina Autumn Storm. Interestingly, her license didn't match your face."

He continued, "But your face? It matched her former business partner, Madison Jackson Winter, the late wife of a prominent bishop in Hawks Landing, California, who died in a wildfire."

She didn't speak. She wouldn't give him the satisfaction.

Inside, Madison's thoughts unraveled. The sound of her real name, spoken so casually, so venomously, stabbed at her like ice down her spine. It was as if the walls of the diner closed in, not from fear alone but from the weight of everything she had buried. She could see her old life flashing before her eyes, the white-columned church, the news cameras, the bishop's voice echoing through the house she once called home.

Her carefully constructed world trembled on the edge of collapse.

It wasn't just about her secret being discovered.

It was about everything that secret had cost her.

The woman standing here in an apron, wiping down counters and baking pies, wasn't Madison Jackson Winter anymore.

That woman had died in fire and fear and silence.

And yet, here was Charlie, reaching into the grave, trying to resurrect what she had buried so deep it barely had a heartbeat.

"Oh, I struck a nerve, didn't I?" he said, voice low and gleeful. "Imagine what someone would pay to learn that you're still alive."

"What do you want?" Her voice was calm, but her hands shook beneath the counter.

Charlie's grin widened. "Fifty grand. By Friday. Or I talk."

She gazed at him, her heart pounding as her mind raced through unlikely options. Thoughts collided, each bringing doubt and uncertainty about what could happen next. Would she dare take a chance or play it safe?

The weight of the decision pressed on her shoulders as she searched for clarity amid the chaos.

Then came the final blow.

"You know that little bitch Sadie? She's got you wrapped around her finger. I tell you what, if I don't get my money, I'll make her life hell. And Sara Leigh's. Think about that. You want the little girl growing up without a mama?"

Her face twisted in disgust. "You're sick."

He moved toward her. Fast. Violent.

It felt like time slowed.

Autumn's instincts screamed at her to duck, to run, to defend, but her body froze. Charlie's hand cut through the air and struck her face with a deafening crack.

She stumbled backward, slipping and crashing to the floor. Her vision blurred, pain radiating through her jaw as she blinked against the stars in her eyes.

The diner swayed around her as her head throbbed.

Her breath caught.

She heard her own whimper echo in the emptiness.

Autumn's ears rang not only from the slap but from the silence that followed.

That awful, waiting kind of silence.

She was on the floor, cheek against the cold tile, breathing through her teeth. Her ribs screamed. The taste of copper spread across her tongue.

She blinked hard, trying to focus on the ceiling fan spinning above her like a lazy eye.

Is this it?

She'd been here before. Not on this floor. Not in this diner.

But in this feeling, this cracked-open moment where you wonder if the life you built is strong enough to hold you.

She heard her heartbeat more than she felt it.

Heard her own breath. The light buzz of the neon "Closed" sign in the window. The squeak of Charlie's boots on linoleum.

In another life, she would've screamed.

In this one, she waited.

Not for a miracle.

For a reckoning.

Then came a new sound: a sharp inhale followed by a whispered name.

"Autumn..."

Sadie

Sadie had come through the back entrance and stood frozen in the hallway, one eye swollen shut, the other wide with terror. Blood trickled from her split lip.

She had seen and heard everything.

She remembered the day she had walked into the diner with Sara Leigh, just looking for a quiet lunch. She had barely spoken two words before Autumn noticed the shadows behind her eyes, the bruises she didn't try hard enough to cover, and the way her daughter clung to her like a lifeline.

It had reminded Autumn of her own arrival in Pine Ridge, tired, scared, and clinging to the last scraps of dignity.

When Autumn offered her the dishwasher job under the table, and later wanted to promote her to waitress.

Sadie hesitated. *"I... I don't want to do the background check,"* she said.

Autumn raised an eyebrow. *"Why?"*

Sadie looked away.

"Because I'm hiding. And not from the law. From someone who knows too many people with access to too much information. I just... I need a fresh start. If that's not something you do here, I understand."

Autumn saw enough to know the truth didn't need to be pried loose.

She nodded slowly.

"We don't always need the details to know who someone is."

Now standing in this hallway, Sadie's heart was slamming against her chest, each beat thudding like a war drum. The terror was familiar, too familiar. But something shifted the moment she saw Autumn on the floor.

The woman who had given her hope, who had treated her like more than the broken shell Charlie had left behind. The woman was hurt and bleeding, and Sadie couldn't remain frozen.

In her mind, images flooded her: her daughter Sara Leigh's sleeping face, the bruises hidden by foundation, and the whispers she practiced before every phone call to keep anyone from knowing the truth.

She couldn't let this continue. Not again. Not this time.

She stepped inside.

Charlie turned.

"What the hell are you doing here?" he shouted, storming toward her.

Sadie backed into the door, hands raised. "Please... please, Charlie."

"You think you're better than me?" he roared, slamming her against the frame, one hand at her throat. "You think you can run from me?"

Autumn, still on the floor, pulled herself to her knees. Blood filled her mouth, but she didn't care. She threw herself at his back, fists flailing, trying to pry him off Sadie.

He roared and swung his elbow back, striking her in the ribs.

Autumn collapsed once more.

Sadie's breath was shallow and ragged as panic seized her. She recognized this sensation, having experienced it far too often before.

But this time was different. This time, she wasn't just scared.

She was furious.

The years of silence screamed inside her.

Charlie turned back toward her, fists clenched, and prepared for another blow.

Sadie slipped to the side and scrambled behind the counter. Her knees scraped the floor as she crawled toward the security shelf. Her hand met cold steel.

She turned. Her lungs were screaming.

She couldn't breathe, not because her throat still felt the choking of his hands, but because fear had taken hold from within.

Not again. Not this time.

Charlie's voice was a buzz in her ear; rage poured into syllables. But Sadie didn't hear the words.

She only heard Sara Leigh's laugh echoing in her memory, the laugh that only children who still believe in safety make.

She thought of tiny shoes by the door. School projects taped to the fridge. How her daughter asked, "Are we still safe here, Mama?"

And how she had nodded. Lied.

That lie was clawing at her now.

She didn't want to be brave.

She wanted to disappear.

But Autumn was on the ground. Hurt. Bleeding. Still trying to protect her.

And Sadie realized: *"No one is coming. There is no one else. This time… it must be me."*

Her feet moved. Her hand reached. The weight of the gun surprised her; it felt heavier than she thought it would. But her grip didn't falter.

Charlie turned.

She didn't aim with anger.

She aimed with love.

Love for the girl she used to be.

Love for the woman Autumn had helped her become.

Love for the child who still believed in her.

"Charlie!"

He hesitated, just long enough.

She raised the gun, arms trembling but steady enough.

He saw it.

"Sadie, no!"

The shot rang out, splitting the silence like a scream.

Charlie stumbled backward, the echo of the gunshot still reverberating through the walls like a ghost refusing to leave.

His mouth opened, but no words came. Just a sharp exhale, like surprise.

Blood spread slowly across his shirt, darkening the fabric in a widening bloom.

He looked at Sadie, not with rage, not even with fear.

Just... confusion.

Like he couldn't quite believe the story had ended this way.

One foot slid out from beneath him, and he hit the floor hard, limbs splayed at odd angles. A chair rocked nearby from the impact, then settled with a soft clack against the tiles.

His eyes didn't close.

They stared up at the ceiling, glassy and blank, reflecting the hanging light above like it was the last star in a sky he could no longer reach.

Autumn's breath caught in her throat as she turned her head toward the body.

In that moment, the diner, their sanctuary, felt like a crime scene, frozen in the echo of what had just been taken.

The kind of silence that followed wasn't peaceful.

It was judgment.

CHAPTER
SIXTY-ONE
NOVEMBER 13, 2014

The Landing Diner & Bakery – Pt. 3
8:57 p.m.

SADIE DROPPED THE GUN, sobbing. Her knees gave out, and she sank beside the counter, shaking violently.

Autumn crawled to her, pulled her close, whispered over and over, "It's okay. It's okay."

But it wasn't.

She looked across the diner to Charlie's lifeless form. Then she looked at Sadie, broken, traumatized, already consumed by guilt.

Sadie couldn't breathe. Her thoughts spiraled.

What would happen to Sara Leigh?

Would they take her away?

Had she just destroyed the fragile peace they had fought so hard to build?

Her body trembled as the reality set in. She had survived him, but at what cost?

Autumn no longer. *Madison* held Sadie tightly, her arms wrapped around the girl like a mother shielding her child from the storm.

Sadie was shaking, her breath fractured between gasps and sobs, the gun still warm where her hand had dropped it. Her mascara streaked like ink down her cheeks. She looked so young. Too young to carry a moment like this.

Madison looked at her, not as a coworker or friend, but as a mirror.

This is what they do to women like us, she thought.

They back us into corners. Make us feel small. Force us to fight for our lives and then punish us for the bruises we leave behind.

But not this time.

Madison shifted, rising slowly to her feet. Her ribs ached. Her mouth throbbed where Charlie had struck her. But her mind was clear.

She stepped over the shell casing. Past the blood. Past the man who once thought he could break her.

And something in her settled.

Not with fear.

With purpose.

She turned back to Sadie, her voice low, firm. "Listen to me. You didn't pull that trigger. Not anymore."

Sadie blinked. "What?"

"I did. You were never here. Do you hear me?

He attacked me. I defended myself. That's what the police will hear."

Sadie sobbed. "They won't believe."

"I'm not asking them to." Madison's voice cracked, but she didn't waver. "I'm not doing this for them."

She reached down and picked up the gun, wiped the grip clean, and set it on the counter with steady hands. Her fingerprints. Her blood. Her name.

"Go home to your daughter," she said. "Hold her. Let this be the last night she ever wonders why her mother is afraid of shadows."

Sadie clung to her for a moment, then ran.

Madison turned back to the body. Her heart was still hammering, but there was no panic now.

Only resolve.

She had spent her life being shaped by men, claimed, controlled, and silenced.

Tonight, she had reclaimed herself.

And this story, her final reinvention, would not be born in shame.

It would be born of choice.

Some women don't just protect.

They sacrifice.

Time of Two Deaths

The diner door slammed shut behind Sadie, leaving only silence and the low, persistent hum of the refrigerator.

Madison turned toward the far wall, where the old black-and-white clock hung crooked above the "Daily Specials" board.

The same clock that had ticked above her the first time she stood behind this counter.

The same one that had watched her wipe tables, pour coffee, and build a quiet, invisible life.

It read 8:57.

"Time of death," she thought.

But not just his. Hers, too. The last version of her, the woman who'd tried to disappear.

Slowly, she reached up and straightened the clock.

"That's enough pretending," she whispered.

Then she sat on the stool behind the counter.

And waited for the police.

PART SIXTEEN
THE LANDING DINER &
BAKERY RECLAIMED

CHAPTER
SIXTY-TWO
FEBRUARY 21, 2018

Pine Ridge, Wisconsin
6:08 a.m.

AUTUMN,

If you're reading this, then I've finally laid down my hat for good.

I made only one visit to that place where they locked you in, and I know you didn't want me to. But I had to look you in the eye one last time. I had to tell you I never believed the worst of you. Not for a second.

They called me "Mister Mayor" like it meant something. But I never built Pine Ridge by myself. You helped make it, too, with your pies, your stories, and that fierce heart of yours. You turned The Landing into more than a diner. You made it a town square.

I know the truth shocked the town when it came out. Hurt. Scared. Some judged you. But time has a way of softening sharp edges. They don't say it out loud, but they miss you. We all do.

So, I'm asking you to come back. Reopen The Landing. Rebuild what we started. Make this place sing again.

My attorney will be in touch. My will stipulates that all of my assets, except for $2 million each to my two sons and my daughter, are now yours. Bank accounts. Businesses. Land. Buildings. The red truck, too, if it still runs.

This place is yours now, not as a debt, not as charity, but because I saw you as mine, not as the daughter I never had, but as the father you missed out on.

Come home, Autumn. They say you can't go back.

But sometimes, you can start again from the same point where you left off.

Just... this time, with your real name: Madison Jackson Winter.

Always,

Harper, aka Mister Mayor

The air still smelled of pine and slow-burning wood, a scent she knew too well. It lingered in the quiet woods, clinging to memory like sap to bark. The trees stood in silent rows, their sturdy trunks a testament to the passage of time.

But she was no longer the woman who once drove this road in Nina's Jaguar.

Her heart felt like shattered glass; scattered pieces that might never fit the same way again.

This time, as she sat behind the wheel, anticipation pressed hard against her chest. Hidden beneath her coat, nestled close to her heart, lay a letter. And a key.

One comforted.

The other demanded.

The early morning hours cloaked Pine Ridge in stillness. Mist hovered low over the road, a veil between memory and present. In the distance, trucks from the nearby mill rumbled awake, the only sign of life as storefronts stirred. A golden hue kissed the rooftops as the sun rose behind the trees.

No aliases.

No masks.

Just Madison.

Or maybe Autumn, the name she had once worn like armor.

Perhaps she was both now: pieces of past and present, stitched together by survival and a kind of hope she no longer feared.

When she caught sight of the sign, her breath caught.

Pine Ridge. Black Owned.

The words hit her like a tide.

She reached instinctively for the edge of Mister Mayor's letter, folded deep inside her coat pocket.

His words had undone her; not because of the money or the land or the long list of things he left behind, but because he had *seen* her.

Truly saw her.

Stripped of pretense, of walls, of names.

That kind of recognition wasn't charity.

It was grace.

And it was terrifying.

With every mile closer to the town, the weight of his understanding settled heavier on her shoulders. Warm and thrilling, but threaded with fear.

Not everyone had forgotten.

Some had never forgiven.

Her past hadn't disappeared.

It had simply gone quiet.

And silence, she knew, could be deceiving. Somewhere out there, someone might still wait to remind her that redemption isn't free.

But this was her moment... a reckoning earned, not given.

She gripped the wheel tighter. The letter grazed her ribs like a heartbeat. Her breath trembled.

I'm ready.

Whatever waited for her in Pine Ridge, grief, grace, ghosts, she would meet it.

This town had once claimed her heart.

Now she was ready to reclaim it.

Then there it was.

The Landing Diner & Bakery

She didn't park right away.

She circled once, slowly and deliberately.

Madison eased her car through the main street of Pine Ridge like a whisper, like a prayer. The town hadn't quite woken up yet. Every storefront held a memory.

The barber's chair where Mister Mayor used to sit on Saturday mornings, laughing with the regulars.

The post office where she once mailed a letter she never dared sign.

The grocery store where a kind-eyed cashier used to slip extra eggs into her bag without a word.

A single porch light flickered outside the donut shop; its window was still dark.

One truck rumbled past, loaded with timber from the mill, tires crunching in a steady rhythm over gravel.

She passed the benches at the bus stop. The dark windows of Maxine's Beauty Parlor. Each one a ghost.

A newspaper thudded against a door, tossed by a boy on a bicycle; one of the only signs of life.

The silence wrapped around her like a question.

Would they welcome her back?

Would they even recognize her?

They hadn't changed much.

But she had.

She passed the mural painted after she left with the sweeping strokes on old brick: tall pines, pale snowflakes, and the word *RESILIENCE* in wide, curling script.

She wondered if they knew whose resilience they were painting. If her story had slipped into the mythos of Pine Ridge like so many others, Mister Mayor had quietly honored.

Or if she had simply become part of the silence.

She slowed the car, hands tightening on the wheel as it came back into view.

The windows were covered in dust. The sign hanging outside tilted a bit to the left. The flower boxes at the front were now empty, but the hooks still remembered when they held plants.

She pulled into the designated owner parking spot and made sure she was perfectly centered within the lines. After shifting into park and turning off the engine, a wave of nostalgia washed over her like a warm blanket.

Her thoughts drifted back to that long-ago day, etched in memory like paint on old wood.

The day she first arrived at this very spot. Mister Mayor had stood at the curb, beaming with joy. Her staff, her people, had gathered with balloons and applause, laughing, clapping, celebrating her dream made real. The bright sign had gone up with ceremony and cheer:

The Landing Diner & Bakery - Under New Ownership.

She had been the proud owner of a dream come true.

Now, in the stillness of the parking lot, she let her heartbeat slow. Each pulse was a quiet testament to the journey. The silence stretched out like a prayer, wrapping her in reflection and gratitude for everything that had unfolded since that golden morning.

She reached into the inside pocket of her coat and pulled out the letter.

She didn't reread it.

She didn't need to.

Instead, she pressed it to her heart, closed her eyes, and whispered: *"I'm not who I was. But I remember her. And I'm here to honor her."*

Then she stepped out of the car. The brick pavers welcomed her boots. A pine-scented breeze shifted through the trees. Somewhere down the block, a screen door creaked open... then shut again.

The town breathed.

And Madison Jackson Winter, no longer hiding, walked up the steps of *The Landing Diner & Bakery* like a woman who knew the ghosts wouldn't scare her this time.

She had survived the fire.

Now it was time to reclaim the light.

Standing at the door of the diner, her hand resting on the frame, Madison's thoughts were suddenly pulled back to that morning almost four years ago that they shared what was to be their last breakfast together.

The hush of dawn had settled across the polished counter and linoleum floor, too still, too soft, like the world was holding its breath.

Outside, the mist clung to the ground like a sleeping veil.

Inside, Mister Mayor stirred cream into his coffee with deliberate slowness, the clink of his spoon against porcelain a steady, almost metronomic sound.

Her apron was tied, clean, and ready to start the day. She poured herself a mug and slid into the booth across from him.

Their booth. *Their* ritual.

He didn't speak at first. Neither did she.

The steam rose between them in lazy spirals, like thoughts they rarely voiced. The quiet wasn't comforting this morning. It pressed. It listened.

Finally, Mister Mayor had broken the silence, his voice low and worn with age and knowing.

"Some days," he said, "the quiet feels louder than the crowd."

Autumn nodded, her hands wrapped around her mug, her shoulders tighter than she meant them to be.

"It's the silence that knows things," she mumbled.

Madison remembered how he had looked at her in that moment, saw her.

"You all right?"

She hesitated. Just long enough for the question to have meaning.

"Trying to be. I'm concerned about Sadie; she's not coming in today."

His brow creased. Sadie missing a shift was rare.

He offered a small, reassuring smile, but there was a flicker in his eyes, brief, but there.

"Try not to worry," he said. "God's got her and that baby."

The jukebox, silent for days, clicked on by itself.

A Sam Cooke ballad drifted through the diner, low and sorrowful, its opening notes falling like rain on a tin roof.

Mister Mayor's eyes softened, but his voice had a weight to it when he said, "That man had the voice of a prophet."

They ate quietly.

Two scrambled eggs. Toast. Simple. Steady.

But the steadiness felt brittle, as if it could splinter with the slightest push.

She didn't know it then.

That by nightfall, Charlie would be dead.

Sadie would run.

She would be on her way to prison.

And the next time she'd walk into the diner, Mister Mayor would be no more.

But, Mister Mayor, Harper Lewis White, a man who had lived long enough to know when a day wasn't sitting right.

Or maybe he only felt it, that unspoken knowing that creeps in on mornings like this, when the quiet won't sit still.

When it feels like the walls are listening.

When every clink of a coffee cup lands too sharp, and every breath feels like a held note that might never release.

She can still see him these years later.

The way he stirred his coffee was slower than usual.

The way his eyes kept drifting to the window, like he was waiting for something he couldn't name.

She didn't ask what he was thinking. She never did.

And now, that silence feels heavier than any word they might have said.

When he rose from the booth, he placed a folded napkin beside her cup.

"You already survived the fire," he said. "Now learn to live in the light."

The jukebox skipped, a hollow pop, a breath of static, and then the needle found its groove again, like even the music wasn't sure if it wanted to play.

She found that napkin months later, tucked in a drawer.

The ink had faded.

But the message hadn't.

The memory of that last morning pressed against her like a hand on her chest, Mister Mayor's quiet eyes, the napkin, the jukebox's hollow pop.

It shifted her.

She paused on the top step of the diner, her hand hovering near the door.

Not yet.

Not like this.

The thought wasn't loud, but it was final.

The shadows felt safer.

Her body moved before she fully decided, instincts stronger than intentions.

She turned. Slight pivot, felt like surrender, and retraced her steps, heading back down the porch.

Her footsteps echoed in the stillness, too loud, like they might wake something best left sleeping.

She walked fast, almost urgently, back toward the car.

Old habits die harder than most.

She drove to the rear of the diner, steering away from watchful eyes and lingering curiosity. Once behind the building, she parked in the shadows. A thin relief washed over her, fragile but real.

Her chest rose and fell in a shallow, uneven rhythm. Each breath felt like a warning. Or a prayer. The muffled quiet of the street lingered on the other side of the building, but here, in the hush of the back alley, she found the illusion of safety.

She was home.

But this time, the town would see her.

Not as a mystery.

Not as a fugitive.

But as Madison Jackson Winter.

She unlocked the back entrance of the diner. The hinges groaned as if they remembered her.

The smell hit first: dust, silence, and memory.

Flour. Coffee. A hint of Mister Mayor's old pipe tobacco.

She climbed the narrow stairs to the apartment above the diner, her first home in Pine Ridge, and the first place in her life that belonged only to her. The moment she crossed the threshold, the ghosts greeted her.

Not unkind. Just... waiting.

The sofa still wore the faded quilt Harper's sister had made.

The table still held the pen grooves from handwritten recipes.

The small window still looked out over the alley and the pine trees beyond.

She opened the drawer of the small desk in the corner, untouched since the night before her arrest.

Beneath a stack of papers and a dried rose, she found it.

The magazine featuring Bishop and her on the cover.

The one she'd discovered in the trunk of Nina's car.

The one she thought she'd destroyed.

It was glossy and over-staged; the kind meant for coffee tables and waiting rooms.

Bishop stood in a perfectly tailored charcoal suit, one hand in his pocket, the other resting lightly on her waist. She wore a cream sheath dress and pearls; her smile precise, practiced, the kind that didn't quite reach her eyes. Behind them, a blurred wash of chandeliers and marble promised elegance, hiding everything else.

Heading: *Bishop Winston Jacob Winter III and Lady Madison Jackson Winter, Most Influential Couple of the Year.*

Bishop smiled a careful, curated smile. Pride lit his eyes.

Not the kind that *saw* her, but the kind that admired how well she played her part.

Now she saw it for what it was.

A man more in love with power than with people.

Even so, once... she had loved him.

Deeply. Desperately.

Enough to lose herself.

She pressed the glossy page to her chest, caught between regret and release.

"You loved the stage," she whispered. *"And I accepted the shadows."*

On the nightstand, she found a drawing, one she'd almost forgotten. A crayon sketch, wrinkled at the edges. The diner, three stick figures. One labeled "Me." One "Mama."

And one: "Miss Autumn."

She traced the outline with her thumb, her throat tightening.

"She called me sunshine," she murmured. *"And I let the storm win."*

Bishop had built an empire on her silence. Sadie had escaped because of it.

One broke her.

The other, she had broken herself to protect.

Placing Mister Mayor's letter beside a framed photo of him, she exhaled. Then, for the first time in years, Madison stood at the window and whispered:

"I'm back."

CHAPTER
SIXTY-THREE
JUNE 4, 2018

Diner Opening Day,
8:00 a.m.

THE "*OPEN*" sign swung gently in the front window, still faintly smudged with fingerprints from the last time she had wiped it down.

The diner smelled of cinnamon, strong coffee, and Murphy's Oil Soap. The floors had been swept; the tables re-waxed, and the old jukebox in the corner glowed faintly to life, its lights flickering through half-lit colors as if it were still waking up.

Madison adjusted her apron, a soft linen one, the kind Mister Mayor always insisted gave the diner a *"home-cooked heart"* feel.

After three months of preparation, it was her first day open.

The first since the trial. Since the headlines. Since the silence.

And already, the air felt heavy with expectation.

She was halfway through rolling out dough for the first batch of PaPa's Pecan Pie when the bell above the front door jingled.

Her heart flinched.

A young man, probably in his early twenties, entered wearing an oversized jacket and carrying a nervous energy as if it were his second skin. He clutched a paper menu in one hand, as if it might bite.

She recognized his face vaguely. Maybe a cousin of someone who used to work at the mill.

He hesitated just inside the doorway.

"Is it okay if I sit?"

Madison wiped her hands on a towel and stepped out from behind the counter.

"Of course. Anywhere you like."

He took a seat at the counter, glancing around the diner like it was sacred ground he wasn't sure he still had permission to enter.

"I used to come here with my grandma, Loretta Hayes," he said. "Every Thursday. She loved your peach cobbler."

Madison smiled gently.

"I remember her. Tiny woman. Big voice."

A grin tugged at the corner of his mouth.

"That's her. You made her feel important."

She nodded, then turned and poured him a fresh cup of coffee. As she brought it over, he looked up again.

"Miss Autumn, right?"

She froze for a breath. That name, soft and worn, still carried the weight of survival.

But it no longer fit the woman standing in her own diner, on land left to her by a man who had seen her.

She met his eyes.

"I was. But it's Madison now. Madison Winter."

Thinking to herself: *"Autumn got me through. But Madison brought me home."*

The young man blinked once, then smiled again, warmer this time.

"Well… welcome back."

The bell rang again.

This time it was old Mrs. Ida from the church choir. She stepped in slowly, leaning on her cane, eyes narrowing as she scanned the space.

"You still serve real grits?" she asked, not unkindly.

Madison chuckled.

"If I ever stopped, Mister Mayor would come down and scold me."

Mrs. Ida sniffed, then nodded.

"I'll take a bowl, then. With sugar, no salt. Like the Lord intended."

Next came the Johnson twins, with their matching braids and glitter backpacks. Their mother whispered something as she ushered them in, an apology, maybe. Or just a truce.

Bit by bit, they came.

Quietly. Not all at once. Not with fanfare.

But they came.

Madison stood behind the counter, refilling mugs, flipping eggs, and folding napkins. Every move is as if an act of penance and power.

She signed her first delivery receipt just before noon, pausing over the line. Her signature, still unfamiliar yet confident, lingered in her mind. She pressed her palm flat against the page, grounding herself.

In the diner's corner, the jukebox clicked on again.

Sam Cooke. *"A Change Is Gonna Come."*

Madison glanced at the newly placed photo on the far wall...

Harper in his red truck, laughing like he knew something the world hadn't figured out yet.

She whispered, just for him: *"You were right. They came back."*

And this time, she wasn't going anywhere.

By late afternoon, the sun dipped low enough to stretch golden light across the sidewalk in long, lazy strokes.

The light made things look softer.

Forgivable.

Maybe time hadn't been so cruel after all.

Madison stood on the side porch of the diner, arms crossed loosely as the breeze tugged at the corner of her apron. The scent of fresh-brewed sweet tea mingled with the faint sweetness of a cooling pie crust on the windowsill.

The porch had once been Mister Mayor's favorite place in the world; the spot where he'd rock slowly, watch folks pass, and remind anyone who would listen that life had a rhythm if you paid enough attention.

She could almost hear him saying, *"Some people rush dinner. But the good ones? They linger on the porch awhile."*

Tonight, they lingered.

A few regulars pulled up folding chairs and stayed. Not because she asked.

But because it felt right.

Because some memories didn't live inside the diner, they lived out here, in the hush between bites and the stories people only told once the second glass of lemonade was poured.

Mrs. Ida settled into her rocker, humming an old hymn Madison hadn't heard since her first Sunday at Pine Ridge Chapel.

The Johnson twins knelt at the edge of the sidewalk, drawing loopy hearts and signing their names beside them, like love letters to the earth.

Someone brought a guitar. Someone else passed cobbler in Styrofoam bowls.

The porch light flickered on automatically, casting everything in a golden glow.

Madison stayed in the doorway, watching. Listening.

Not quite ready to sit, but no longer needing to run.

The crowd buzzed with laughter, clinking glasses, and the warm scent of cinnamon, pecans, and cornbread still drifting from the back kitchen.

The Landing was alive again.

For the first time in years, the diner hummed not just with music and motion, but with a kind of hope Madison hadn't dared believe would return.

She stepped back inside to check on the staff, making sure to-go orders weren't piling up.

Behind the counter, apron dusted with flour and pride, she sorted through slips when a familiar face emerged from the crowd.

He wasn't the same lanky boy who used to bus tables after school. Taller now, shoulders broader, but with that same wide grin, Daniel stood in line, holding a takeout box and looking more nervous than anyone else in the room.

Madison leaned over the counter, recognizing him instantly.

"Daniel. How's that syrup recipe coming along?"

He laughed, surprised. "You remember?"

"Some things leave a mark."

He stepped closer, the takeout box in one hand and a small bundle in the other.

"Takeout for Mama," he said, lifting the box. Then, offering the bundle, "And this is from me."

Madison unwrapped the napkin-wrapped gift: a small, well-worn wooden spoon. Her initials, *A.S.*, were still faintly carved into the handle.

The spoon had been a gift when Madison first started at the diner all those years ago. She had later passed it to Daniel on his last shift before he left Pine Ridge to live with his father and finish high school.

"This is for when you open that food truck," she'd told him back then.

Her breath caught.

"Wow... you still have it."

"My mom hung on to it," Daniel said. "She said it reminded her to keep you in prayer."

He hesitated, then added, quieter, "You were the first person to treat me like I had more in me than just being the help."

Madison met his eyes, voice low but steady.

"You had more than enough in you. I just reminded you."

Daniel's grin widened.

"I didn't get the food truck... but you'll be happy to know I got my culinary arts degree."

Madison froze for a heartbeat. Then, she stepped out from behind the counter and hugged him, tears catching in her eyes.

"I am so proud of you."

A beat passed, the kind that settles deep.

Daniel nodded toward the back kitchen.

"If you're looking for someone to sweep up tonight... I still remember how you like it done. Hot water. Two drops of lemon oil."

Madison smiled widely and truly this time.

"Grab an apron, chef. Forget the mop; get in the kitchen."

They both laughed.

He didn't hesitate.

As Daniel disappeared behind the swinging kitchen doors, Madison turned back toward the room, only to notice a shift in the air.

At the far end of the diner, the conversation dipped for just a moment, like someone had turned the volume down in the room.

A man had come in quietly, slipping into the last booth by the window.

He wasn't dressed like the locals, his jacket too sharp, his boots too new. He didn't take off his hat, just tilted it low over his brow.

He didn't order, either.

Just sat.

Watching.

Madison felt it before she saw it, that prickle at the base of her neck, the one that had kept her alive all those years ago.

She straightened the napkin stack by the register, forcing her hands to stay steady.

The man finally looked up, catching her eye for the briefest second before turning his gaze back to the window, as if he hadn't been studying her at all.

But Madison knew better.

There was no name to put to him yet. No reason to confront him.

Just a quiet reminder:

The past doesn't always knock. Sometimes, it just sits and waits.

PART SEVENTEEN
THE UNICORN

CHAPTER
SIXTY-FOUR

California
11:45 a.m..

THE PLANE TOUCHED down in California just before noon, the sun already stretching long, golden fingers over the tarmac.

Madison watched through the small oval window as the city came into view, familiar and foreign all at once. Ten years had passed since she'd set foot here, and yet the skyline still pricked at something deep inside her, like a scar pressed too hard.

She stepped into the terminal with her shoulders squared, her breath steady but shallow.

The terminal buzzed with activity, suitcases wheeling, voices rising and falling like the tide, but inside her, everything was still. Too still. Like the silence before a storm.

She didn't come to make a scene.

She came to sign her name.

Because technically, she was still married.

Being "legally dead" had complications. Now that she was alive again, at least on paper, there were documents to sign.

Paperwork that had been waiting for a decade.

Madison had expected lawyers. Maybe even reporters.

What she didn't expect was facing Bishop Winter himself.

She hadn't breathed California air in ten years.

Now, it hit her like a memory and a wave of mourning.

She rented a modest sedan and drove the familiar streets of her former life. The palm trees lining the boulevards swayed in the breeze like they had ten years ago, unmoved by time or scandal.

She passed the row of boutiques where she once hosted tastings and charity events. A slow, shimmering cascade sparkled in the afternoon sun at the fountain outside the museum mocked her, forever reminding her that life couldn't be curated and pristine.

She turned onto the wide boulevard that led to the courthouse.

At each red light, she wrestled to stare straight ahead, refusing to glance at the luxury shops or the church steeple where she'd once been the picture of grace and obedience.

Memories pressed in from all sides: lavish teas, whispered judgments, secrets that felt like silk and steel.

The courthouse loomed ahead, all modern glass and steel, wrapped in the cold air of formality. Rather than go inside right away, she detoured a few blocks and parked in front of *Jade Blossom Garden*, a small Chinese restaurant tucked into the corner of a plaza.

She and Nina used to come here, long before everything fell apart.

Back then, they were just two women trying to figure out how to breathe through the roles someone had cast them in.

The bell above the door jingled as she stepped inside.

The familiar scent of sesame oil, ginger, and steamed rice enveloped her like a memory.

She slid into the booth by the window. The same one they always chose.

The server, an older woman with kind eyes, smiled faintly at her, as if remembering her face.

"Shrimp egg foo yung," Madison said without opening the menu.

"And sweet and sour chicken for your friend?" the woman asked.

"Is she on her way?"

Madison shook her head slowly, a smile tugging at her lips, brittle.

"Not today."

As she waited for the food, she rested her hands on the table and closed her eyes.

The last time they were here, Nina had stirred her tea slowly, confessing in a whisper that she had fallen for a married man.

Madison had warned her gently, but Nina's eyes had been full of fire and hope.

"He says he's leaving her," Nina had murmured.

Madison had sighed, reaching for another dumpling. *"They always say that."*

They had laughed that day, a laugh that felt like rebellion.

They had clinked their teacups together and promised that whatever happened, they would hold each other's secrets.

Now, Madison sat in the same booth with that promise folded in her chest like origami; delicate and sharp.

The food arrived, fragrant and steaming.

She took a bite of the egg foo yung; the flavor was exactly as she remembered.

She chewed slowly, tears threatening but never falling.

She left a generous tip, paid in cash, and walked back out into the bright California light.

Inside, the hallways echoed with the sound of footsteps and murmurs. Madison stood before Courtroom 3B, exhaling slowly. Her reflection stared back from the marble wall, older, wiser, unrecognizable from the girl who once believed in fairy tales.

And then he arrived.

Bishop Winston Jacob Winter III.

A decade older, with slightly grayer temples, yet still exuding that practiced poise like a second skin. His tailored suit was flawless, and his shoes gleamed like fresh pennies.

His eyes. Those same commanding eyes flicked to her and softened just a fraction.

"Madison," he said, voice low, uncertain.

"Bishop," she replied. Not unkind. Just truthful.

He hesitated, and in that hesitation was the ghost of everything they had been.

As he looked at her, another memory came unbidden:

The day he'd walked into the hospital room and seen her cradling their newborn son, Coby. She had looked up, eyes radiant with innocence and awe, completely unaware that the man she loved didn't feel the same depth.

Guilt had pierced him then, sharper than any sermon he'd ever preached.

He had wanted to love her the way she deserved, but part of him had always belonged to someone else.

Time had suspended in that hospital room, each of them carrying a memory of that moment that was the same, yet opposite:

Madison, seeing his face soften, had dared to believe it was a turning point, that maybe, just maybe, he loved her.

He, seeing her glowing with new-mother joy, had almost felt guilty for not.

They entered the conference room together, where the lawyers sat waiting.

Neither of them spoke until the papers were before them.

She glanced at him once, offering the thing she had come to give. Not vengeance. No accusations.

Closure.

"I don't hate you," she whispered, pen in hand. "We were both playing roles. And I'm glad… that you finally ended up with the woman you loved."

His jaw clenched. A flicker of something passed behind his eyes. Shame, maybe. Or relief.

Bishop Winter sat across from her at the polished mahogany table; the divorce papers spread out between them like a last sermon.

The fluorescent lights above flickered faintly, casting a cold sheen on the table. Everything clinical, everything sterile.

A far cry from the pulpit and velvet-lined pews where he once ruled from a position of divine authority.

And yet here he was.

Small.

He used to preach redemption.

But Madison didn't need his doctrine.

She crafted her own truth.

He watched Madison quietly, noting the steadiness of her hand and the elegance still in her posture.

She had aged, yes, but the years had only refined her.

She looked like someone who had walked through fire and come out made of steel and silk. Not the naïve young wife he had once ushered down the aisle like a lamb to the altar.

He remembered that day too vividly now:

The feel of her hand in his.

The applause afterward was less for love, more for the optics.

Cora had chosen her.

Polished her.

Made her a symbol.

And he?

He had consented.

At first, it hadn't felt like manipulation.

It had felt like *calling*.

Like building a kingdom with a woman who made people believe in the brand of righteousness and charity he peddled.

But slowly, painfully, he'd realized what he loved most about Madison wasn't her heart. It was the way she made him look like a better man.

He hated that about himself.

He never questioned her disappearance into the fire.

And when the scandal came, when everything fell apart, he let her remain in the ashes.

It was cleaner that way.

He played the grieving husband, the devoted shepherd betrayed by a wayward wife.

And the church? The corporation?

It swallowed the story whole.

He looked at her now and thought: *"The ashes didn't tell your whole story."*

But he didn't say it.

Instead, he nodded once as she picked up the pen.

As if saying, *"Go ahead. Sign your way out of this."*

When she whispered, *"I don't hate you,"* something twisted in his chest.

Not because it felt untrue.

But it felt generous.

And he knew deep down he didn't deserve her grace.

She signed.

The ink curved into her name like a slow unraveling of history.

Madison. Jackson. Winter.

The name that had once elevated him now freed her.

He almost spoke her name aloud, but the moment passed.

As they walked toward the door, he felt the heavy echo of footsteps behind them, not just theirs, but all the versions of themselves they had once been.

The golden couple.

The public darlings.

The tragedy and the myth.

And now, just two people.

No pulpit.

No boardrooms.

No spotlight.

No script.

Just truth.

And silence.

"You deserved more," he whispered.

"So did you," she replied.

They left the ink to dry in silence.

And with it, the last tie to the life she had left behind.

As they exited the conference room, Madison walked slightly ahead, her mind beginning to quiet.

Until she saw her.

Cora.

She sat near the exit on a stiff wooden bench, her back perfectly straight, legs crossed at the ankle, gloved hands folded neatly over her handbag. The tailor had tailored the lavender suit she wore to within an inch of perfection. Tahitian black pearls at the neck. Not a single strand of gray out of place. Even now, especially now, she believed in appearance over apology.

When Madison stepped out into the hallway, the sound of her heels echoed like punctuation.

Not hurried.

Not hesitant.

Just assured.

She no longer moved like someone seeking permission.

She moved like someone who had outgrown the room.

Cora looked up and froze.

Something was terrifying in Madison's calm. Something unnerving in her elegance.

She wasn't angry.

She wasn't bitter.

She was free.

And Cora hadn't planned for that.

Their eyes met across the corridor. In that suspended second, no one else existed. Not the attorneys murmuring in the background. Not the clerks at their desks. Just the two of them and the screams of the past between them, sermons and secrets, teacups and betrayals.

Madison didn't flinch. Didn't blink.

Cora, for the first time in decades, didn't know what to say.

Then Madison spoke, her voice low and devastatingly clear.

"Thank you, Cora."

Three words. But they struck like thunder.

Not sarcasm. Not spite.

Just truth, delivered with a grace sharp enough to draw blood.

Before Cora could form a reply, Madison walked on.

Shoulders back. Chin high.

Leaving a faint scent of perfume and power in her wake.

For a long moment after Madison disappeared down the hallway, Cora stayed still. She felt the faintest quiver in her hand, the first crack in a façade she had perfected her entire life. She clenched her purse tighter, but it didn't help.

It was a strange and unfamiliar feeling.

Loss.

Not a daughter-in-law.

Not a family plan.

But of control.

She had chosen Madison once, for legacy, for image, for control.

And now, the legacy had turned its back on her.

Not out of rebellion.

She transcended.

Cora had depended on Madison to be loyal.

Instead, Madison had become legendary.

She had underestimated the girl.

And now she realized this woman had walked away through the fire without asking her permission.

"She won," she whispered under her breath to no one.

Not in court. Not on paper.

But in the only way that mattered.

She had walked back into the fire and come out sovereign.

And Cora sat there in her pressed suit, holding the ashes of a story she no longer controlled.

CHAPTER
SIXTY-FIVE
JULY 9, 2018

Hotel Suite
7:30 p.m.

THE SUITE OVERLOOKED the city skyline, glittering lights like distant stars scattered across the earth.

She kicked off her shoes and set down the designer handbag and designer dress she had bought earlier that afternoon. Both were sleek, elegant, and far too expensive.

She had laughed when she purchased them, not because of need, but because they felt symbolic. A full-circle moment.

The expensive bag was symbolic of Nina's black bag of money she had carried out of Hawk's Landing.

And the dress she wore, a deep emerald satin, soft against her skin, represented the cost she paid to dress up a new life.

Every thread sewn with survival. Every seam a silent scream.

Room service arrived: lobster bisque, calamari, shrimp cocktail, a slice of key lime pie, and Dom Perignon on ice. She ate cross-legged on the bed, flicking through channels on the muted TV, not watching.

This moment carried her back to that tiny upstairs bedroom at Mama Pearl's.

She and Nina, both barely teenagers, both barely surviving, lay side by side on a thin twin mattress, their backs pressed against the cool wall. The only light came from the flickering TV in the corner, a hand-me-down with the color washed out, stuck on Channel 13.

The soap opera played like scripture, sacred, dramatic, and not to be interrupted.

A woman in a satin robe paced across a marble foyer, weeping beautifully. Her husband was a senator. His secret child had just returned. There was a slap. Then a kiss. Then a vow to "start over."

Nina sighed like she was in church.

"I wanna live like that one day," she said, chin propped on her elbow. "With a house where the stairs curve, and you don't gotta ask permission to open the fridge."

Madison had smiled, arms tucked beneath her head. "I just want silk pajamas. And a name so long, they put it on envelopes."

They giggled quietly, careful not to wake the others.

Then Nina added, "And a man who holds my face when he kisses me. Not like he's tryna take, but like he's tryna stay."

That had quieted them.

Two girls in a borrowed room, dreaming of gowns and names and love that didn't hurt.

Now, decades later, Madison stood in a hotel suite with marble floors and silk pajamas. Her name was on legal documents and trust accounts. Despite that, the weight of that girl pressed gently against her ribs.

She whispered toward the glass, as if Nina might hear her: *"We made it."*

Rising from the bed, Madison stepped toward the floor-to-ceiling windows, the city glittering below like a thousand unspoken possibilities.

She placed a hand on the glass and whispered to herself,

"This... this is closure."

And for the first time in years, she smiled, not out of relief, but recognition.

CHAPTER
SIXTY-SIX
JULY 16, 2018

The Landing Diner & Bakery, 1:30 p.m.

A WEEK after returning from California, the bell above the diner door jingled gently, too soft to be urgent, too familiar to ignore. Madison looked up from the counter where she was folding napkins, her hands stilled mid-crease.

There, standing just inside the threshold, was Sadie.

It had been five years.

Sadie looked different, thinner, and paler, with a scarf delicately wrapped around her head. But her eyes... her eyes were the same. Wide, searching, carrying the pain that had aged her beyond her years and softened her in places that used to burn with fire.

Beside her stood Sara Leigh, now eleven, tall for her age and clutching a small backpack. She smiled shyly at Madison, a dimple appearing on one cheek.

Madison moved first.

She walked around the counter and reached for Sadie, her arms wrapping around her gently and mindfully. Sadie trembled in her embrace but held tight.

"Hey," Madison whispered.

"Hey," Sadie murmured back. "I heard you came home."

Madison pulled back to take her in. "You look... different."

Sadie gave a soft laugh. "So do you."

As they stepped deeper into the diner, a wave of memory hit Sadie like a slow, rising tide. Her eyes darted to the corner of the floor behind the counter, the place where Charlie had collapsed. They had scrubbed the linoleum clean long ago, but in her mind, she could still see the blood of that night.

The smell of blood and gunpowder still haunted her. She had stood frozen, with the memory of the gun slipping from her hand, her ears ringing with the echo of the shot. Madison had crawled to her, whispering it would be okay. That moment, wrapped in terror and sacrifice, was the last time she'd been in this place.

Sadie blinked and forced herself back to the present.

They sat in the back booth with a view of the mountains. Madison made tea; Sadie took hers with honey.

They sat quietly until Sadie whispered, "I'm sick again. It came back three months ago." Madison reached for her hand, and Sadie let her.

"I had both mastectomies and was in remission for years, but now it's in my bones. I have little time left."

Madison's breath caught. She hadn't known.

Not during her years in prison, nor during the silence that followed the night of the shooting.

Sadie disappeared after Charlie's death and left Pine Ridge the very next day, her name only whispered when locals discussed what had happened. Madison spent those years wondering and hoping she was safe.

But never knowing. Not until now.

Sadie gave a bittersweet smile. "I moved back in with my parents. Went through treatment. I didn't want to bring that pain back to Pine Ridge... or to you."

Madison blinked away tears. "Sadie... I didn't know."

"I didn't want you to. Couldn't. Not while you were in there."

"I would've written," Madison murmured. "I would've come."

"I know," Sadie said. "That's why I didn't tell you."

A long silence stretched between them.

Then Sadie continued, her voice steadier now. Making you cry was not the reason I came. The reason I came is… I have a favor to ask."

She looked over at Sara Leigh, who was busy playing a game on her mother's cell phone.

She doesn't know everything yet, not all of it. I'm unsure how to tell her. If something were to happen to me, I need to ensure she has someone who will love and protect her. Someone who looked after me when I didn't know how to defend myself.

Madison's voice was barely audible. "What are you asking?"

Sadie took a breath. "I want you to be there for her. Perhaps even raise her.

Madison froze, her heart suddenly loud in her ears.

"I've talked to my parents. They'll support it if you agree. I've already spoken to a lawyer. It's not official yet, but… if you say yes, we can start the process. I want her here. In Pine Ridge. With you."

Madison gazed out the window. The lake sparkled in the midday sun. Life flowed quietly like gentle waves.

"I don't know if I can replace you."

"You won't," Sadie said. "But you'll remind her of me. Of what survival looks like. Of what love can be."

Madison nodded slowly.

Then, she reached for Sadie's hand again and whispered, "Yes."

Sara Leigh looked up, her coloring paused, and caught the two women smiling through their tears.

In that moment, something shifted. The past lingered, the pain remained, but something more substantial took its place: hope, and maybe even healing.

One breath, one promise, one reunion at a time.

Six weeks later, Pine Ridge and The Landing Diner & Bakery still hummed with a quiet routine. But miles away, back at Sadie's childhood home, time moved differently.

Sara Leigh sat curled beside her mother on the bed. Sadie's skin was now pale and waxen, her energy fragile. But her eyes, the same eyes that had once burned with resolve, remained bright.

Madison entered the room quietly and took the seat at Sadie's bedside. She smiled at the girl first.

"Why don't you go grab the painting you made earlier? I think your mama would love to see it."

Sara Leigh hesitated, her small hand resting on her mother's. Sadie gave it a light squeeze.

"It's okay, baby," she whispered. "I'm not going anywhere in the next five minutes."

Once the girl was gone, Madison took her friend's hand.

Sadie spoke first.

Her voice was barely above a breath. "I still remember that first day at the diner. You hired me without even looking at my references."

"You asked me not to," Madison said, smiling faintly. "Said you wanted nothing to pop up that your husband's friend could find."

"I was so scared," Sadie said. "But somehow... I wasn't scared of you."

Madison brushed a loose strand from her friend's forehead. "You were brave then. You're brave now."

Sadie's eyes drifted toward the ceiling. "Is it wrong that I'm not afraid to go? Only that she'll forget me?"

"She won't," Madison said, tears in her eyes. "Because I won't let her."

Sadie nodded weakly. "Tell her I sang to her every night... that I loved her enough to stay... and enough to leave her with someone who could carry her through."

Madison leaned forward and kissed her friend's temple. "I promise."

As the last light of the afternoon fell across the bed, the two women sat in silence.

One holding on. One letting go.

When Sara Leigh returned, she climbed into the bed again.

And Madison sat nearby.

A witness to love.

A keeper of memory.

A guardian of what would come next.

CHAPTER
SIXTY-SEVEN
AUGUST 29, 2018

Flight Back to Pine Ridge
10:35 a.m.

SARA LEIGH PRESSED her forehead to the small, cool window of the regional plane, her breath fogging the glass. Below, the clouds rolled like waves. Beside her, Madison sat close, her hand resting gently over the girl's smaller one, a quiet reassurance, soft and solid.

For a while, the only sound was the hush of the engine.

Then, Madison leaned in slightly, her voice just above a whisper.

"Do you know how your mama picked your name?" she asked.

Sara Leigh turned, eyes wide and searching. A flicker of interest glinted through her sorrow.

Madison smiled, the memory warming her voice. "Sadie once told me that whenever something bad happened when she was little, your grandfather had a fix: Sara Lee pound cake, a scoop of vanilla ice cream, and a stuffed animal to hold."

Sara Leigh blinked. "Really?"

"She told me about the time her dog got hit by a car. She cried for days. So, her daddy brought out cake, ice cream... and a little stuffed puppy.

She named it Sara Leigh."

The girl giggled, just a little, and Madison felt something shift in the air, like the first breeze after a storm.

Reaching into her carry-on, Madison pulled out a cloth-wrapped bundle and carefully unfolded it. Inside was a small plush unicorn, white, soft, with a shimmering pink horn and a braided pastel mane.

"I wanted you to have this," she said. "Your mama loved unicorns when she was your age. Not because they were pretty, but because no one believed in them. Despite that, they showed up anyway."

Sara Leigh took the unicorn into her arms. Her fingers traced the soft curve of its horn.

"Unicorns don't cry when they're scared," Madison added, brushing a curl behind the girl's ear.

"They keep showing up anyway, like your mama did.

Like you are right now."

Sara Leigh leaned against her shoulder, hugging the toy tight.

"Was Mama magical?"

Madison kissed the top of her head, tears prickling her eyes.

"She was rare. Fierce. Gentle. She didn't wait for permission to shine. That's what magic is."

They sat like that for a long time, quiet, connected, held together by memory and something more.

As the plane descended and the hills of Pine Ridge appeared, Sara Leigh tightened her grip on the unicorn, as if it held a message only she could understand.

Madison whispered into her hair, "Your mama didn't just leave memories, baby girl. She left you. And that means her magic's still here."

The girl didn't speak. She didn't need to.

She held the unicorn a little closer.

The next morning, Madison woke up before dawn. Having gotten back to town late, the two stayed at the apartment above the diner instead of heading out to the cabin. The light in the apartment was dim and blue, brushing across the old wooden floor like a memory. She crept, folding the quilt at the foot of her bed and setting out two mugs instead of one.

A small gesture.

A new rhythm.

Downstairs, the diner waited, empty, still, and wrapped in the morning hush. But it didn't feel lonely anymore. It felt expectant. Like it knew someone new was coming home.

Sara Leigh was already awake, seated at the kitchen table in her pajamas, clutching the unicorn to her chest like a shield and a treasure all at once. Her legs swung under the chair, not quite touching the floor.

"You ready?" Madison asked gently, sliding a mason jar of orange juice across the table.

Sara Leigh nodded. "Do I get to wear an apron?"

Madison smiled, a slow curve of something settled. "Of course. But only if you're ready to earn your first tip."

They laughed together, bright, unguarded.

When they stepped downstairs, the bell over the diner door chimed, not for a customer but for them.

For the two girls, it was a welcoming home.

Madison knotted an apron around Sara Leigh's waist, looping the ties twice and tugging them snug. Then she reached beneath the counter and pulled out an order pad, placing it gently in the girl's small hands.

Sara Leigh looked up at her. "Do I get to write names?"

Madison knelt to meet her eyes. "You get to write stories. One plate at a time."

She rose and flipped the sign on the door.

Open.

And in that moment, the past didn't vanish. The grief didn't dissolve.

But it folded itself into something else, something lived in and laced with love.

The beginning of a new chapter.

One morning. One meal. One girl and her unicorn at a time.

PART EIGHTEEN
A KNOCK IN THE WOODS

CHAPTER
SIXTY-EIGHT
SEPTEMBER 5, 2018

The Landing Diner & Bakery
6:55 a.m.

THE LANDING WASN'T JUST a place to eat again; it had become the heart of something bigger. Morning light streamed through the tall front windows of The Landing Diner & Bakery, casting long golden slants across the freshly mopped checkered floor. The scent of cinnamon and warm butter filled the air, with preparations already underway.

Madison stood at the counter, wiping down a tray that didn't need cleaning. Her hands moved slowly, not out of habit but in reverence.

It had been only three months since she reopened The Landing Diner & Bakery, and already the town was humming with the same steady rhythm Mr. Harper Lewis White, lovingly known as "Mister Mayor," once stirred into it like sugar in his morning coffee.

"He'd be proud," she thought. *"But he'd probably scold me for still cleaning when I should be resting."*

Word had spread, not just about Madison's return, but about the quiet vision she carried with her. It wasn't loud or branded, nor was it printed on signs.

"I didn't need a slogan," she thought. *"I just needed a place where people could breathe again."*

It moved like a story too true to be written, shared in glances, gestures, and worn-out wisdom, stitched together from Mister Mayor's stubborn hope, Sadie's fierce grace, and Madison's redemption, earned like blisters on bare hands.

Every time the lumber trucks rumbled through town, echoing against the buildings, or when the diner door chimed with the soft patter of footsteps, she felt warmth bubbling inside her.

They came back, she realized, *not just for biscuits or coffee, but for her.*

During those times, it felt as if she could summon the comforting voice of Mister Mayor, echoing a deep truth: *"Start with love. Build from there."*

She smiled faintly. *"Still preaching at me, huh?"* she murmured under her breath.

Each word embraced her like a comforting hug, igniting hope and inspiration in her chest, reminding her that no matter the challenges ahead, her dreams must be rooted in love, nurturing growth, and connection.

Just before opening, Morgan arrived with a coffee carafe, signs of her weekly long drive, and updates on the zoning approvals for the youth center. Her visits had become more frequent since she became the town attorney, but it was more than just business that kept her in Pine Ridge these days. Their conversations had deepened, no longer strained or guarded, but easy, with the quiet rhythm of two women getting to know each other.

Today was the meeting of Pine Ridge's *Thursday Table of Four,* who gathered at the diner's round table for coffee, conversation, and the quiet business of holding a town together. Morgan naturally joined them, her presence settling into the space as if she'd always belonged.

"You're early," she said.

"I was already in town. Thought I'd stop in before court," Morgan replied.

"I spoke with the county. They're fast-tracking the zoning approval for the youth center," she said, eyes gleaming. "Guess they think someone in this town is worth investing in."

Madison smiled. "We all are."

Madison handed her a mug. "Coffee?"

"No, had enough," she chuckled. "Just a slice of PaPa's Pecan Pie, hot out of the oven."

"Always."

As Morgan slid into the corner booth, Miss Helen was the first to shuffle in, her cane clicking with authority on the tile.

"Morning, Miss Mayor."

The nickname had begun a week ago, mostly in jest. But it had a strange way of sticking.

"You made it; heard you weren't feeling well," Madison said, bringing over a steaming mug, "planned to stop by with chicken soup later."

Helen smiled, eyes sharp despite her age. "You think I'd miss the only meeting in this town with cinnamon rolls and good sense?"

Madison chuckled. "Fair enough."

Next came Lou, carrying blueprints under one arm and sawdust on both boots.

"Morning," he said with a nod, pulling out a chair with his free hand. "The mill's running late, so I've only got about thirty minutes before I need to wrangle a forklift."

"You always say that," Miss Helen said, "and then you sit here for an hour talking about nails and porch railings."

Lou gave a half-smile and poured himself coffee. "Only 'cause you keep asking for new projects."

Finally, Minister Denise swept in like a warm gust of purpose, head wrap bold, eyes brighter.

"Sorry, I'm late," she said, sliding into her chair. "Teen girls' Bible study turned into an impromptu group therapy session. We cried, we laughed, and someone confessed they were dating a boy from Mill Creek. It was dramatic."

"Bless her little rebellious heart," Helen muttered, sipping her coffee.

Madison sat last. She didn't open a notebook. She didn't need to.

Madison slid Morgan her slice of pie. "Payment for services rendered. Don't spend it all in one place."

Morgan arched a brow, fork hovering.

"One slice? For legal counsel and zoning miracles? I should bill you in peach cobblers."

They all laughed.

Four people.

Plus, Morgan.

One table.

Later, as they all left, Madison looked out the window while clearing the table, feeling a familiar swell of pride, like Mister Mayor's sunlight in his eyes.

Across the street, the county had approved renovating the old post office. Soon, the neighboring storefront would be Pine Ridge's first community learning center. Volunteers stopped by the diner daily, offering their time, donations, and muscle.

Too good to last? The thought flickered uninvited, but she pushed it away.

Heading back to the kitchen, the door chimed, and Caleb, the high school quarterback, entered, gleefully asking, "Can I leave these flyers about our car wash on Saturday?"

"Sure." She smiled.

"Hey, was that your grandpa or something?" he asked, pointing to the framed flyer of Pine Ridge's first White's Christmas Wonderland festival, with Harper Lewis White's picture looming large.

Madison laughed low. "Not by blood," she said. "But by choice."

Caleb nodded, like he understood something bigger than the words. "Kinda feels like he's still around."

Madison glanced up at the picture and whispered, "Yeah. He is."

As Caleb slipped back outside, Madison watched him go. Sunlight caught the wet brushstrokes on the mural being painted across the street, bold colors stretching upward.

Imperfect, but full of intention.

But as she turned back to the counter, the bell above the door gave the faintest jingle; then stopped.

Nobody came in.

The silence afterward felt heavier than it should have.

Madison's gaze lingered on the door, then slid to the booth by the window, *that booth.*

The one where, on the diner's opening day, a man had slipped in without a word.

Not dressed like the locals. Jacket too sharp. Boots too new.

He hadn't ordered.

Hadn't stayed.

Just sat. Watching.

Madison felt the same prickle now she'd felt then, a whisper at the base of her neck that refused to leave.

She pressed her palm flat to the counter, grounding herself.

Probably nothing.

But even in Pine Ridge, she knew better than to ignore the feeling that the past might not knock. Sometimes, it just sits and waits.

By evening, the eerie feeling faded as the diner filled with activity. Old-timers played dominoes in the back. A small band strummed blues on the side porch with their chords wrapping laughter and soft conversation like smoke.

The night wound down. Chairs flipped onto tables. The last customer slipped out.

That's when she noticed him. A man stood at the window, observing silently with hands in his pockets, eyes obscured by shadow. His face was unfamiliar to Madison, yet somehow familiar. He locked eyes with her for a moment, gave a single nod, and then turned away.

Detective Perry adjusted his coat collar on the sidewalk and vanished into the night. He hadn't planned to return to Pine Ridge, only to find a ghost, maybe his own. Years ago, Charlie had hired him to find Sadie, and he had succeeded.

Then Charlie vanished.

And Detective Perry went looking again until the night everything changed.

He was at the diner's window. File in hand. Ready to collect.

And he saw it all.

The fight.

The gun.

The fall.

He left without a word.

Watched the trial from a distance.

Watched Madison take the fall. Not because she was guilty, but because the truth had no clean edges.

The system wouldn't have understood.

Maybe he didn't either. Not fully.

But now, something else had called him back.

Not guilt.

Not revenge.

Just a favor.

And the only woman with the power to grant it was the one on the other side of the window.

That night, as Madison turned the lock and stepped onto the diner's front porch, she stared out across the square, reminded of quiet nights at Black Swan Lake beneath the stars.

In her coat pocket, Harper's letter rested like a heartbeat. Always there. Creased, soft at the edges, but never forgotten.

She didn't look back.

She looked forward.

Brick by brick.

Bruise by bruise.

And in the night's hush, she whispered: *"Miss Mayor has a ring to it."*

CHAPTER
SIXTY-NINE
SEPTEMBER 6, 2018

One Harper Way Road
8:50 p.m.

DETECTIVE. Perry parked a half mile down the gravel road from the log cabin Madison inherited from Harper Lewis White. The tires crunched over frost-covered stones, loud in the quiet of dusk. The home sat nestled between thick rows of pine trees, its wooden beams silvered by time and twilight. Warm light glowed faintly through the windows, like a heartbeat tucked in the woods.

Detective Perry didn't want to be seen. This wasn't diner business. This was private.

She opened the door, wearing a faded denim work shirt over soft, comfortable faded jeans. It was unremarkable; her appearance didn't hint at a woman fleeing from ghosts or past traumas. Instead, she looked like someone who had faced her challenges and come out stronger, having endured the metaphorical fire of her experiences. Her posture and demeanor exuded the quiet confidence of a woman who had survived significant trials, yet she did so without the lingering smell of smoke, both literally and figuratively.

Previously, she may have recoiled at a sudden knock like the one she heard. But now, she merely tilted her head and stated, "You'd better come in."

Her eyes, sharp yet unreadable, revealed a focus that suggested she could discern more profound truths amid the surrounding chaos, like a keen observer able to sift through the dust to find what was real and vital beneath the surface.

She stepped aside without a word, letting him in like a woman who knew the house was hers, and so was the story.

"I need a word," he said. "It's about something I saw. And someone I found."

Inside, Madison led him to the den. The scent of cedar and Harper's old pipe tobacco lingered faintly in the walls. Detective Perry sat down in a deep armchair, and Madison perched on the edge of the hearth, arms folded.

"I'll get right to it," Detective Perry said, voice rough like gravel.

Madison's fingers tightened around her coffee mug, knuckles paling against the porcelain.

"Back when Charlie hired me to find Sadie," he began, "I was also working another case. A young woman in California, adopted by a prominent family, was trying to find her birth parents. Her sealed birth records raised some red flags."

Madison arched an eyebrow, but didn't speak. Her thumb traced the rim of the mug, a slow circle.

"The young woman was persistent," Detective Perry went on. "Smart. And rich. I tracked down the original hospital and... a name. Then another. And the trail led to Bishop Jacob Winston Winter, III."

Madison blinked once, twice, her throat suddenly dry.

Her voice came out hoarse.

"What?"

Detective Perry didn't soften it.

"He and the woman he's married to now, Elise. They had a child back in 1990."

Madison's heart slammed against her ribs. A single, sharp thud stole her breath, then another, faster, harder, as if her own body were trying to pound its way out. Heat rushed to her face, her vision narrowing until the room felt like it was closing in.

"But... I never heard..." Her voice cracked, more exhale than words.

"Because Cora Winter paid the girl's family to put the baby up for adoption," Detective Perry said.

The name alone gutted her.

Cora. Always Cora, calculating, smiling, pulling strings from behind velvet curtains.

His words landed like body blows, each syllable knocking the air from her lungs.

"It was quiet, legal, and buried," Detective Perry continued, his tone measured, almost apologetic. "She threatened the family, said she'd destroy them if they didn't comply. Paid enough to make them disappear. Bought silence for years."

Madison's breath stuttered, catching high in her chest. She pressed her palm hard against her thigh, nails digging into the fabric of her jeans until she felt the bite through her skin. The pressure was the only thing anchoring her, a desperate attempt to ground herself while the room tilted. A cold sweat beaded at her temple.

Her mind flooded with questions. *Who? Where? Could it be?* But her throat was paralyzed, unable to produce any sound.

Detective Perry paused, letting the weight of it settle. His gaze stayed fixed on her, steady, waiting.

And Madison sat frozen, the world tilting beneath her, torn between the terror of hope and the raw ache of betrayal.

"The mother never knew where her baby ended up. The bishop never looked because he didn't know.

And that young woman? She only recently found out the truth."

Madison's mind reeled, the pieces snapping together too fast: Cora's cold manipulations. Bishop not knowing. The long shadow cast over her marriage.

Her stomach turned.

Her voice was a rasp.

"Why the hell are you telling me this now?"

"Because she wants to meet her birth father," Detective Perry said.

He leaned back, but his eyes never left hers.

I believe you're the only one who can get past Cora and convince him to show up. She doesn't want any press or drama, just closure.

Madison leaned back too, slowly, as if glass formed her body, her breath catching in her throat.

"And you?" she asked, eyes narrowing.

"Just want the money I'm owed, and walk away from this clean," he said.

"No secrets. No leverage. Just... done."

Madison studied him, her gaze sharp, unyielding. She rose and crossed to the sideboard, where an unopened bottle of cognac waited like an old secret. Her fingers tightened around the glass as she poured, the amber liquid catching the lamplight. Heat rose in her chest before she even tasted it, her hand trembling slightly as she lifted the drink, more for something to hold than to swallow.

The silence stretched long enough to feel like judgment.

Detective Perry's jaw shifted.

His gaze dropped for the first time.

Then he said it.

"There's something else."

Madison's spine stiffened, but she didn't speak. She watched him the way a woman watches the weather, trying to guess if it's about to turn.

Detective Perry looked down at his hands, rubbing his thumb over a callus that had been there since before he retired. He exhaled slowly.

"You're not gonna like it."

Madison's eyes narrowed, her breath steady but shallow. "Then say it anyway."

He nodded once. A beat. Then another. His jaw tightened, as if forcing the words through stone.

"I was there," he said quietly. "The night Charlie was murdered."

The words detonated. Madison's stomach dropped so hard she thought the floor might open beneath her. Her grip faltered on the glass; amber liquid sloshed against the rim before she caught it.

A jagged flash tore through her mind, the sticky linoleum floor of the diner, Sadie's trembling hands wrapped around the gun, Charlie's body crumpling against the stool as the echo of the shot split the air.

Madison had tasted the gunpowder, smelled the iron tang of blood, and stepped forward to carry the blame.

The air in the room shifted, not louder, but quieter. The kind of silence that pressed against the skin, heavy, unrelenting. Like the cabin itself had inhaled and was holding its breath, waiting for her to shatter.

Detective Perry didn't look at her. "I came to collect payment. Had the file in my hand. But when I got to the window...I saw you. Him. The fight."

A beat.

"I saw the gun. And I saw her run."

Madison didn't move. Didn't blink.

"I didn't call the police. Didn't step in. I left."

Her voice, when it was heard, was soft and deliberate. "You watched it happen."

"I did." He finally met her eyes. "And I saw why it happened. I know the difference between murder and survival, Madison. I saw the difference that night. But the courts wouldn't have."

"And you just...disappeared."

"Because I thought letting the truth breathe might do more good than choking it with process."

A long, blistering silence.

Madison turned away, pressing her palms into the mantel as if to hold herself upright. Her voice was quieter, edged with steel.

"You saw the truth and chose silence."

Detective Perry stood. "Sometimes silence is its own kind of judgment."

The room went still.

"So, you'll help me reach Bishop Winter?" he asked.

Madison nodded once. "I'll see what I can do. No promises."

At the door, Detective Perry hesitated. "You're a good woman. You didn't deserve what happened."

Madison's smile was soft, tired, but genuine. "Neither did Sadie."

He nodded, then stepped into the night. Over his shoulder: "I'll be in touch."

Madison stood in the doorway for a long time, staring out at the trees. In the distance, moonlight shimmered off the treetops, quiet, patient, and full of secrets waiting to surface.

Madison waited until Detective Perry's car headlights disappeared beyond the trees before locking the door behind her. The house felt vast and silent, filled with the whispers of Mister Mayor's memory and the weight of everything she'd just learned. She pressed her back to the door, eyes drifting to the cold heart. The fire was long gone, but the ashes remained mute, unyielding, holding truths they would never tell.

CHAPTER
SEVENTY
SEPTEMBER 6, 2018

One Harper Way Road
10:15 p.m.

AFTER A QUICK SHOWER, Madison moved on autopilot, as if each task might keep her from unraveling. She made a sandwich she barely tasted, set a bottle of water on the nightstand, and refilled her snifter, though her hands shook pouring it. Collected Detective Perry's file from the table, silent and damning, its weight pulled at her like an anchor.

She brought it with her into the bedroom, retreating to the spot in the cabin she thought could comfort her. Sadly, the quilt, the pillows, and the light cedar scent in the walls, which were usually familiar comforts, offered little solace tonight. She sat in bed, the glass sweating in her hand, and stared at the file as if it might open by itself.

Every instinct told her to tear into it, but still she hesitated. Once she opened it, there would be no taking it back. No more ignorance, no more silence. For a long moment, she breathed, counting the seconds, the air thick with the echo of Detective Perry's voice.

Then, with a sharp inhale, she set down the glass, reached forward, and pulled the file into her lap.

Her hands trembled slightly as she opened the file.

Inside were copies of hospital records, a redacted adoption certificate, an old yearbook photo of Bishop Winter's now-wife, the same smile, the same defiant tilt of the chin.

She turned the page, and there it was.

A photograph.

The slightly grainy color suggested someone had taken it on a college campus or during a work retreat.

The girl wasn't older than twenty-five; maybe even younger.

She wore a pale blue blouse, her black bob cut falling just below her chin, one hand mid-gesture, as if she had just finished laughing.

It was the smile that undid her.

Not wide. Not forced.

Just the quiet, crooked kind that came from someone who didn't yet know how much the world could hurt her.

Madison felt the breath rush out of her chest.

She scanned the bottom of the photograph.

A name handwritten in blue ink: *Grace.*

The girl had Bishop Winter's chin.

His cheekbones.

But the eyes?

They weren't his.

They were someone else's, Elise, entirely open, searching, like she was still hoping to be claimed by something... or someone.

Madison's hand moved to the edge of the page, fingertips trembling. Her voice cracked when it came, barely more than air.

"You had a daughter," she whispered. "While I was holding our son."

The room tilted, not with dizziness, but with the sudden weight of seeing what she hadn't realized she'd been bracing for. Not jealousy. Not even betrayal. Just the sorrow of knowing what people had buried for decades.

The file lay open in her lap as memory clawed its way back.

She was in the hospital room again. The smell of antiseptic. Coffee gone cold.

Bishop stood by the bassinet, no tie, collar unbuttoned, and sleeves rolled. His hand hovered above Coby's head like a priest's blessing, never touching.

Madison had reached first, lifting their son to her chest. "Here," she'd whispered. "Hold him."

Bishop had hesitated, then taken the baby like an offering from an altar, reverent, careful, almost afraid.

Coby's tiny fingers curled around one of his. And for one breathtaking second, Madison had believed: *This is the start. This is when he sees us. This is when we become a family.*

The image shattered.

The file in front of her interrupted the thought.

Bishop's hands had held their son, and somewhere else, silence had erased his daughter.

Madison blinked hard, throat tight. Her fingertips brushed the photo of Grace again, slower this time, almost tender. She thought of the letters she had written in prison, the ones to Coby that never got mailed. Thought of Sadie's dying request. And now this girl, this child born in shadow, wandering her whole life in the fog of someone else's shame.

Her voice trembled, but the words were steady.

"You deserve more than truth," Madison murmured. "You deserve to be known."

It felt like both a promise and a warning.

She turned the page. Notes. Ledgers. The payoff in black and white.

Cora Winter's signature in looping, arrogant ink. Everything was there.

The lie. The cover-up. The child lost.

A sob rose sharp in her chest. She swallowed it down. She wasn't crying for herself. She was crying for that girl. For the truth that had cost too many people too much.

Closing the file, she rested her hand on it. And a single thought burned clear.

The ashes have covered long enough. This ends now.

CHAPTER
SEVENTY-ONE
SEPTEMBER 7, 2018

One Harper Way Road
5:18 a.m.

MADISON BARELY SLEPT.

She'd risen before the sun, unable to stop replaying Detective Perry's words in her mind, the weight of his confession, the buried daughter, the truth he'd carried like a quiet curse. Shadows stretched long across the floor as the early light filtered through the blinds, turning the cabin into a museum of memory.

She brewed coffee, but it tasted like ash. Her stomach was a knot.

Every creak in the walls felt louder.

Every tick of the clock rang with foreboding.

She paced the living room barefoot, Mister Mayor's photo still on the mantle, watching her like a silent guardian.

What haunted her most wasn't what Detective Perry had seen, but what he had insinuated.

Exposing her secret.

Revealing a truth that could undo so many careful lies?

She reached for the file again, her fingers trembling. Pages that last night felt clinical now screamed with betrayal: names, numbers, and secrets.

Cora.

Bishop.

The child.

And now, a request.

She found herself at a crossroads, being asked to reconnect with a figure she had deliberately buried deep in the recesses of her memory.

This wasn't just any man.

This was the man she had just seen again, after almost ten years apart, to sign the official divorce papers a few months earlier. On the outside, she had been present, poised, and almost gracious, strong enough to let forgiveness steady her hand. But inside, she fought to cage the volcano threatening to erupt.

She had rehearsed their meeting for days beforehand, scripting each glance, each word, the way she once did in Paris when she studied how silence itself could be a weapon of power. And she delivered it. A flawless performance.

Until she saw Cora.

Not at the table, not part of the proceedings, but sitting on a wooden bench just outside the courthouse doors. Waiting. Watching.

Cora, a sentinel of everything Madison had to surrender.

When Madison walked past, their eyes met. She summoned the last of her composure, her voice steady but laced with exhaustion.

"Thank you," she breathed.

Cora's smile was thin, confused. And in that moment, Madison felt the echo of every battle she'd fought in silence.

He embodied her past; his very presence intertwined with the secrets she had tried so hard to forget. He had played a significant role in her erasure from her own life, whether out of an unwillingness to confront the truth or sheer cowardice.

The thought of reviving those memories sent shivers down her spine, as every thought of him conjured a swirl of emotions: longing, betrayal, and perhaps an unquenchable curiosity about the mysteries between them.

Why had she buried him so thoroughly?

What truths had she hidden away, and could facing him lead to the answers she desperately sought?

She shut the folder sharply, her fingertips grazing its frayed edges as if attempting to hold onto its hidden secrets. Letting out a deep sigh, she sat on the edge of the sofa, her eyes locked on the phone, which appeared to vibrate with unexpressed potential.

This call would reopen every wound she'd painstakingly stitched, and awaken the ghosts she thought she'd buried. But deep inside that dark tangle, something else shimmered: a chance at truth.

A sliver of hope.

However, within the shadows of her past, a tempting chance emerged that could reveal something valuable. Something deserving of preservation. Something pure that might change everything she understood, drawing her back into a maze of feelings she believed she had long fled.

She dialed the numbers carefully, feeling the weight of each ring resonate in the silence around her. Her breath was held hostage, trapped in a moment of tension, as she waited.

Finally, the mechanical sound of voicemail greeted her.

A single beep echoed, breaking the stillness.

"It's me," she said, her voice steadying, and a quiet fire ignited within her.

"Call me. You know it must be important."

The urgency in her tone was unmistakable; it conveyed a message that went beyond the simple request for a return call.

After a brief pause, she hung up. Not with certainty, as doubt lingered in the back of her mind. But with purpose, a sense of determination fueling her next steps, she knew that this could be a turning point, no matter how uncertain the outcome might be.

A few days later, the Landing Diner & Bakery was just calming down after the lunch rush during the break between lunch and dinner. The only sounds were the hum of the fridge, the gentle clinking of stacked plates, and the conversations of a few lingering customers.

Suddenly, the bell above the door rang.

Madison glanced up slowly.

An elegant man in a charcoal pinstripe suit stepped inside, removing his sunglasses.

She straightened. Without stiffness. Without fear.

Just... ready.

He stepped forward, the faintest gleam of silver cufflinks catching the low light.

The left one sat slightly crooked, like always.

Madison's breath eased out, one quiet, steady stream, and her shoulders squared, a gesture she didn't have to think about.

She didn't invite him to sit. She didn't need to.

Some storms arrive unannounced.

Others are right on time.

PART NINETEEN
ASHES DON'T TELL EVERYTHING

CHAPTER
SEVENTY-TWO
SEPTEMBER 11, 2018

The Diner
2:45 p.m.

THE CHIME over the door at The Landing rang out like a bell before a storm.

It was early afternoon, and the diner was settling after the lunch rush. Madison stood behind the counter, wiping menus that didn't need wiping. The hum of conversation and clatter of dishes filled the space like music until it stopped.

Bishop Winston Jacob Winter III stood in the doorway.

Sunlight framed him in soft gold, a halo too poetic for a man bringing storms with him. He looked older. Thinner. Gray threaded his once-perfect hair. The suit still fit like money, but the eyes held something else.

Regret.

Madison's hands froze on the menu.

Not because she wasn't surprised, but because she'd rehearsed this moment, on sleepless nights, in the mirror of her mind.

Poise wasn't peace. It was armor. And she'd worn it for years.

She hadn't heard a word after leaving that voicemail. No call. No text.

Now, a week later, here he was. Walking in like the past decade hadn't shattered them both.

This wasn't the first time she'd seen him since she'd come back.

They'd sat across from each other at the courthouse, signing the divorce papers, pretending it was all just paperwork. He'd brought Cora. She'd brought silence.

That day had been legal. Guarded. Cold.

But this?

This was different.

Bishop moved further into the room. The conversations picked up again as people turned away from him, leaving a deep silence behind.

At the counter, a customer whispered, *"Isn't that the husband from the trial?"* Another nodded. Recognition rippled. Faces turned. Forks paused mid-air.

Madison met his gaze.

"Bishop."

"Madison."

The air between them thickened, unspoken words pressing in from every side.

Finally, he moved toward the far booth, Mister Mayor's booth, the corner seat where truths had been told and secrets had been kept. He slid into it like he knew he didn't belong but needed the cover, anyway.

Madison followed, a cup of coffee in her hand. She set it down gently, like sliding a peace offering across a line neither of them had agreed on.

She sat. The weight of years dropped between them like an invisible wall.

"I didn't expect to hear from you," Bishop said.

"I wasn't sure I'd ever want to hear your voice again," she replied.

"But something came up."

He nodded, eyes flicking to the counter where customers pretended not to stare.

"You didn't bring Elise," she said, more observation than question.

"No." A beat. "She doesn't know I'm here."

Silence again, but this time it wasn't empty. It was loaded.

Madison's voice cut through it.

"Sophie," calling to the waitress. "My bag, under the counter."

Sophie moved quickly, but Madison's fingers stayed still on the table, flat, steady, because her pulse wasn't.

Sophie returned and set the bag on the table.

Madison slid her fingers inside, found the file, and pulled it out slowly. The envelope felt heavier than it should have.

She opened it and laid a single photograph on the table, then a stack of documents.

"Bishop," she whispered, eyes steady on his.

Each page whispered a truth long buried.

"She's your daughter."

His hand froze halfway to the photo. The words hung between them, sharp as broken glass.

A thousand questions flickered behind his eyes, but he stayed silent.

"Elise had a baby the same year Coby was born," Madison continued. "Your mother made sure you'd never know."

Bishop's jaw tightened.

"Cora paid Elise's family to convince her to put the child up for adoption. She threatened to ruin them if they refused."

He closed his eyes.

"She never told me," he murmured.

"She didn't need to," Madison replied. "I lived with her. I know what Cora was capable of."

He reached for the documents.

Birth certificate.

Adoption record.

A photograph of a young woman with Elise's eyes.

His fingers lingered on the picture. Trembled.

He traced her cheek with his thumb, careful, like he was afraid she'd disappear if he blinked too long.

He read the name written underneath: *Grace Ann Wooden.*

Not his name. Not just someone's child.

His.

"I never had a chance to love her," he whispered. His voice cracked on the last word, and for a moment, he looked younger.

Smaller.

"And yet..." Madison leaned in. "She's out there. And she wants to meet you."

Silence settled.

Not empty silence.

A silence thick enough to carry all the things neither of them had ever said.

Finally, Madison spoke again, her voice low but sure:

"As I said at the courthouse, I'm not mad at you. Not anymore."

His eyes lifted. A flash of surprise.

"After everything... you don't hate me?"

"I did. For a long time."

She let that truth sit there, then breathed out.

"But that woman died in prison, Bishop. This one... she's just trying to finish the story."

Their hands brushed as she gathered the papers back into the envelope. The heat of that touch felt like the only thing tying the past to the present.

Bishop looked back at the photo, voice breaking: "Maddy... what should I do?"

"You meet her," she said. "You tell her the truth. You let her see that not all ghosts stay buried."

He nodded slowly.

"And why did you call me?"

She gave the faintest smile.

"Owed someone a favor. And because it was the right thing to do."

Outside, the autumn wind rattled the diner's window.

Inside, the air went still.

Two people, once bound by pain, sat in its ashes...

And maybe, just maybe, ready to build something new.

CHAPTER
SEVENTY-THREE
MAY 22, 1989

The Winter Family Foundation Offices
10:35 a.m.

YEARS EARLIER, Bishop sat in shock on the edge of his office couch, clutching a mug of coffee that had long since gone cold. The chill of the ceramic barely registered against the ice spreading through his chest.

Across from him, Elise stood stiff, her hands clasped too tightly in front of her, knuckles pale.

"I lost the baby," she said, the words breaking apart as they left her mouth.

The air left the room.

"What?" His voice cracked, as if someone had pulled the floor out from under him.

Her lips trembled, but her eyes never quite met his. "I... I had a miscarriage," she managed, each syllable scraping its way up her throat. "While I was away in Denver with my sister. That's why I stayed longer than expected. I needed time. I couldn't tell you right away and didn't want to see you. I had to... process it. I'm so sorry."

The explanation fit the timeline. She *had* been gone, nearly six months, in fact, supposedly helping with her sister's new baby. She'd written sparingly, called even less. At the time, Bishop chalked it up to distraction, to the everyday chaos of a household with an infant. But now, sitting here, the distance felt deliberate, as though she'd orchestrated her absence to make her story more believable.

He set the coffee aside, head falling into his hands. The word "miscarriage" echoed like a tolling bell.

Elise turned away quickly, but not fast enough to hide the flicker in her eyes.

It wasn't grief. Not entirely.

Because deep down, Elise carried a different truth. Her pregnancy hadn't ended in tragedy. It had ended in a quiet adoption, one her family orchestrated under Cora Winter's unwavering watch.

A secret purchased with threats.

Sealed with shame.

Bishop's fingers tightened around the mug.

He stared at the floor, his voice a whisper.

"*I would've loved them.*"

The tears on his face weren't dramatic. They slid silently, uninvited, a slow betrayal of his own composure.

Elise stood there, her own grief a mask, holding his sorrow like a stage prop while her own boiled beneath the surface, sour and unspoken.

Every time she saw the pain on his face, it felt like he was unknowingly accusing her, as if he could *sense* the truth pressing at the edges of her silence.

She never told him.

Not when he said he would have loved the child.

Not when the tears kept coming.

Not even when his voice cracked, raw with loss, and the space between them turned into a chasm.

Some lies weren't just spoken.

They lived in the air between two people, sharp as broken glass, waiting for someone to bleed.

Madison startled him out of his thoughts.

"I've got to prep for the dinner rush. Depending on how long you're in town, we'll have to finish this conversation later."

He hesitated. "I've got a flight out tomorrow."

She nodded. "Then tonight. I'll close early. We can talk more at my house. Seven?"

He agreed.

"I'm at One Harper Way," she said. "You won't miss it, it's the cabin on the edge of the woods."

As she gave the address, a flicker of memory crossed her mind, the first time Harper had shown her that house.

Years earlier, Harper had stood barefoot in the doorway of what was once the old Walden homestead: two bedrooms, a drafty roof, and a kitchen that sagged with memory. When he brought Jessie Mae there, he promised her more than land. He promised her a future.

She had looked at the cabin and rolled up her sleeves.

Brick by brick, Jessie Mae transformed that decaying shell into a log masterpiece with vaulted ceilings, a wraparound porch, and every inch touched by her hand.

"She built it so I wouldn't be alone," Harper once told Madison over fried catfish and hot water cornbread one lonely Thanksgiving. He'd sipped his Cognac, eyes misting.

"And I never was. Not with her in the bones of this place."

Minutes later, outside the diner, Bishop strolled with the envelope, its heaviness more apparent than previously. On Main Street, the Pine Ridge air hit him like a stranger's handshake, familiar yet distant.

He passed the hardware store, the post office, and a barber shop with its old red-and-white pole still spinning. A child on a bike waved. He didn't wave back.

The town didn't wear its history; it wore resilience. Mister Mayor's fingerprints were on every stone, every story.

Bishop's gaze drifted back to the diner window, where Madison stood framed in the light.

What was it about Mister Mayor, he wondered, that he managed to do in four years what he couldn't in twenty-three?

Turn her into a woman who loved herself.

He feared the answer might be everything.

Back in his car, he rested his hands on the steering wheel, the envelope in his lap, a photo of Grace on the seat.

The engine idled.

"Is it too late to be the man I should have been?" he thought.

The question lingered, heavy as the silence, but somewhere beneath it pulsed another truth he wasn't ready to name, because naming it might set everything on fire.

CHAPTER
SEVENTY-FOUR
SEPTEMBER 11, 2018

One Harper Way Road
7:25 p.m.

BISHOP WINTER ARRIVED at the cabin as the last light faded behind the pines. The air smelled of damp moss and chimney smoke, the kind of quiet that made you hear your own thoughts louder.

The cabin stood at the woods' edge, windows glowing, smoke curling from the chimney. Madison opened the door. Calm posture. Cautious eyes.

She stepped aside. "Come in."

The cabin smelled of cinnamon and cedar, welcoming, but not soft. Bishop paused just inside, eyes taking in the heavy beams, the photos along the mantel.

"I invited someone," Madison said.

Bishop's brow lifted.

"Detective Perry," she added.

Detective Perry appeared from the side hallway, sweater gray, voice sharper than his clothes.

"Let's get to it," he said. "I've been in Pine Ridge too long, chasing this case longer than I planned."

Bishop frowned. "What case?"

Detective Perry sat, lacing his fingers. "I was outside the diner the night it happened. I saw more than what made it into any report."

Bishop's voice tightened. "You saw the murder?"

"Detective Perry." Madison's voice was low, sharp, and warning.

Their eyes met; a flash of steel between them.

Madison's gaze drifted briefly around the cabin, the place Harper had built with Jessie Mae, a house meant to be safe. This wasn't supposed to be a battleground. And yet, even here, old ghosts found their way in.

The memory crept in like smoke, anyway.

Charlie bleeding on the diner floor.

Sadie's hand on the gun, steady. Her own hoarse voice whispers promises she can't keep.

Three years of her life, *gone*. Despite that, these two reached for that night like it belonged to them. Detective Perry's voice snapped her back. "I saw enough to know that sometimes silence is survival."

"And leverage," Bishop muttered.

Bishop's jaw tightened. "What does this have to do with me?"

Detective Perry reached into his jacket and laid two photos on the table.

"Because I wasn't working for you, Bishop. I was working for someone else."

He tapped the photos, "For her."

"I am sure Madison informed you that this young woman is your daughter and wants to meet you."

Bishop nodded his head.

Detective Perry continued. "She's not angry. She wants to meet you."

Bishop's hand clenched on the table. "Why go to Madison? She's not..."

Detective Perry cut him off. "Because your mother keeps you unreachable. So, I went to the one person you *would* hear."

Bishop's eyes shifted to Madison. She stood by the fireplace, arms crossed, and something shifted inside him, sharp, quiet, undeniable.

He'd always thought Madison was just a footnote, but now he saw her clearly.

Cora built walls that trapped him, and Madison was the door.

Detective Perry leaned back. "And for the record, I didn't threaten anyone. I told her the truth. Her voice could open a door; mine couldn't."

Bishop turned to Madison. "And you agreed?"

Her voice was even. "Looks like he was right. You're here."

Silence. Heavy.

Bishop finally asked, "And what did he offer you in return?"

Detective Perry smirked faintly. "Nothing. Well, maybe I implied I knew things about the murder. But I just wanted one thing. A chance. For her."

He tapped the photo.

"She deserves that."

Madison moved closer, voice low. "He used me. But only because she deserves better than silence."

Bishop let out a slow breath, one that sounded more like surrender than agreement. His hand hovered above the photo, then dropped flat against it, covering his daughter's face.

"Alright," he said at last, voice rough. "Arrange the meeting."

Perry nodded, pushing back from the table. "I'll call her tonight."

As he stood, Perry's gaze flicked once more to Madison, lingering just long enough to sharpen the air between them. It wasn't triumph, exactly. More like a warning: doors, once opened, don't always close again.

Bishop didn't look up. His hand stayed pressed against the photograph as if keeping something dangerous from slipping free.

And in the silence that followed, Madison understood, this wasn't just about Grace. Whatever came next would test them all.

Madison walked him to the door. Stopped him with a hand on his arm.

"I said yes because of her," she said. Voice calm. Firm. "Don't confuse that with approval."

Detective Perry's mouth twitched. "Didn't mistake it."

And then he was gone.

The door shut. The room fell quiet.

Bishop stood by the fireplace.

Madison didn't move.

For the first time all night, he realized this wasn't just her house.

It was her line in the sand.

PART TWENTY
YOU HAD ME AT SALMON CROQUETTES

CHAPTER
SEVENTY-FIVE
SEPTEMBER 11, 2018

One Harper Way Road
Minutes Later.

AS THE DOOR closed behind him, she turned back to Bishop, standing at the fireplace.

"You sure you're ready?"

He looked around the room, then back at her.

"I'm not sure of anything anymore," he admitted. "But I know it's time to stop running."

Madison nodded, small but certain, and turned toward the kitchen.

"You want to stay for dinner? About to whip up a batch of salmon croquettes."

He trailed behind her slowly, almost able to smell the aroma of salmon and herbs wafting through the air as he thought about them.

"You had me at salmon croquettes," he said with a half-smile. "You know, Coby and I loved your salmon croquettes."

She smiled over her shoulder. "Good."

He sat at the counter while she moved around the kitchen, grabbing ingredients, lighting the stove, and pulling out a cast-iron skillet.

"Why are you just sitting there?" she teased, handing him an apron.

It was familiar, almost painfully so.

They cooked side by side, falling into a rhythm they didn't know they remembered. She handed him the seasoning without asking. He flipped the croquettes with practiced ease. When the food was ready, they sat at the small breakfast nook near the window.

They poured wine.

They talked, not about the past pains, not about the mistakes, but about Coby. They traded memories of fundraisers and argued playfully over collard greens versus spicy cabbage, his favorite.

For a fleeting moment, time folded in on itself. The weight of years, the emotional bruises and silences, eased. Freedom didn't feel like fireworks; it felt like this: a quiet shift in their hearts, a breath they hadn't realized they'd been holding.

They shared wine and warmed glances that held both longing and understanding. The world outside disappeared, and in that pocket of stillness, they were simply two people, scars and all, finding something real. Maybe not perfect. Maybe not permanent.

But for tonight, enough.

The next morning, sunlight spilled through the bedroom window, casting a soft golden glow across the sheets. Madison stirred, eyes blinking open to the red numbers on the alarm clock: 7:15. She thought. *"I must have slept through the alarm."*

She stretched, with an ache in her muscles both familiar and strange. Her hand drifted across the sheets, half-expecting warmth.

But the bed was empty.

She sat up slowly, her heart dipping into that old hollow. "Nothing changes," she whispered to herself, more sigh than speech.

The silence and empty bed carried her back.

Hawks Landing.

The years of waking alone. Nights when her husband brought wine, laughter, warmth, and mornings when all of it dissolved with the dawn. It was a rhythm carved into her: comfort, then absence.

Last night returned in fragments: wine, laughter, salmon croquettes, the hum of music, the almost-dance, and the long hours spent tangled in memory and each other's bodies.

But now?

Gone.

She slipped into her robe, intent on coffee, and trying to shake the ache in her chest.

Halfway down the hall, she stopped.

Whistling. Low. Off-key.

She rounded the corner.

Bishop stood by the stove, apron on, bare shoulders exposed, spatula in hand, flipping pancakes with a sense of contentment as if he truly belonged in this moment.

Her breath caught, sharp, involuntarily.

He turned just enough to see her in his peripheral vision.

"Morning, beautiful," he said, voice rough with sleep.

She leaned against the doorway, blinking, disbelieving.

"You're still here," she whispered, afraid the words might break the spell.

He smiled faintly, eyes on the pan.

"For once... I didn't want to run."

CHAPTER
SEVENTY-SIX
SEPTEMBER 13, 2018

Denver
12:30 p.m.

TWO DAYS LATER, Madison and Bishop boarded a quiet flight to Denver.

Neither spoke much, both caught in their swirl of memories and what-ifs. Bishop stared out the window for most of the flight, hands clasped tightly in his lap. Madison sat beside him, the envelope from Detective Perry tucked in her purse.

Grace was 28, married to an NFL MVP quarterback, and a mother to twin boys. She had gone back to med school after taking time off to start a family.

Her photo, with its soft smile and guarded eyes, had haunted Bishop since the moment he saw it. Now, as they pulled up to her home in a tree-lined suburb, something deeper stirred.

They sat in silence, staring at the house.

White porch. Blue shutters. A porch swing swayed in the breeze.

"Hawks Landing," Madison said quietly.

He nodded. "Burned to the ground. Nothing left of who we used to be."

Neither moved.

Then the door opened.

Grace stepped out, petite with her hair in a loose bun, barefoot, wearing jeans and a sweater. She didn't hesitate; she ran down the steps and immediately embraced Madison tightly. Madison held her, stunned by how familiar her scent was, vanilla, lavender, the same mix she'd worn herself when Coby was small. Her throat tightened. Not because Grace hugged her, but because it felt like being found.

Then Grace turned to Bishop. Her eyes glistened.

"You looked taller in my imagination," she teased, as if to lighten the moment.

She swallowed, voice trembling but clear.

"I don't need answers. Just your time."

Bishop nodded, his eyes wet.

"I can give you that," he whispered.

That afternoon, in that house, devoid of cameras, titles, and lies, three lives, long separated by silence, started to reconcile.

One truth at a time.

Madison gave them space. She sat on the floor of the twin boys' room, playing with them until they dozed off in her lap, their tiny breaths syncing like twin lullabies.

She stroked their backs, her heart tender with the weight of borrowed joy.

She thought of the last few days with Bishop, watching him sit in the diner booth, making calls, reading, and even helping with the dinner rush. But her mind kept drifting to the evenings: cooking together, talking until sleep pulled them under, falling asleep in each other's arms, and holding tight like neither one wanted to let go.

Not once in all that time did they speak of the past.

Except for Coby.

"Miss Madison, sorry to wake you," Grace whispered, scooping the boys from her lap.

Madison blinked, startled out of her thoughts.

"Oh, I wasn't asleep, just thinking."

They smiled at each other, an unspoken understanding passing between them.

Back downstairs, Bishop and Grace laughed like old friends. The normalcy of it made Madison's chest ache.

Father and daughter embraced, and Bishop kissed her forehead. "I'll be back for Christmas," he promised.

Outside, as they buckled in, Bishop spoke.

"I'm going to tell Elise," he said, quiet but certain. "Grace is comfortable letting her decide if she wants to meet."

Madison nodded, then slid closer, their shoulders brushing, a solid, grounding presence.

She didn't speak. Neither did he.

In that moment, Madison felt it: an undeniable bond, the kind that words would cheapen.

A connection born not just of shared history, but shared loss.

Two people whose daughters had been hidden and erased by others, who believed they knew better.

For the first time, Madison realized this man, complicated as he was, knew the taste of grief that didn't come with funerals; the grief that leaves you alive, but missing pieces you'll never get back.

She laid her hand over his.

Not claiming.

Not demanding.

Just being.

Bishop turned his hand under hers and laced their fingers together.

No promises.

No explanations.

Just presence.

"I'll stand with you," she said with a ring of promise. "However it plays out."

They held hands as the car pulled away.

The September sky over Denver shifted restlessly, clouds breaking apart to reveal a fragile blue, as if the season itself was caught between holding on and letting go.

CHAPTER
SEVENTY-SEVEN
NOVEMBER 22, 2018

One Harper Way Road
8:20 a.m.

THE KITCHEN at One Harper Way Road was alive with the quiet sounds of Thanksgiving morning. The soft clinking of mixing bowls, the rustling of apron fabric, and the low hum of an old jazz playlist drifted from a Bluetooth speaker on the windowsill.

Madison stood at the counter, hands dusted in flour, rolling out crusts for PaPa's Pecan Pies. The scent of brown sugar and toasted pecans wrapped the room in warmth.

Across from her, Bishop wore an apron, sleeves rolled, carefully de-stemming collard greens at the sink. Steam curled from the kettle on the stove, catching in the morning light that spilled like honey across the floorboards.

Over the kitchen door hung Mister Mayor's plaque:

Some people build their lives with bricks. Others with bruises.
I built mine with both.

Madison smiled to herself.

So much had vanished. Yet, in this kitchen, they had created this moment together.

Bishop hummed tenderly as Marvin Gaye's smooth and low voice drifted through the room.

"You still remember that one?" she asked.

He looked over his shoulder. "I used to sing that to you when the family did karaoke night."

She grinned. "You did."

She paused, chuckling. "Gracie called this morning. Wanted to make sure you got everything for the mac and cheese. That girl thinks she invented it."

Bishop's mouth curved. "Really? Sweetheart, don't get smug. I overheard Morgan reminding you not to be too hard on the guy she's bringing. You know, the one who is still married and hasn't filed yet. That should make for some dinner conversation."

Madison smirked. "Okay, so we both have daughters we didn't know we had. But somehow, they feel like they've always been here."

The cabin already felt full, laughter sneaking in before the guests even arrived.

"You happy?" Bishop asked quietly.

She didn't answer right away. She finished fluting the pie crust, rinsed her hands, and walked to where he stood.

He turned, wrapping his arms around her waist.

"Most days," she said, resting her head on his chest.

He nodded, tenderly running his fingers through her gentle curls. "Me too."

They stood there, just breathing, the stillness as steady as the smell of pecans and cinnamon.

Then, tires crunch over gravel. Madison turned to the window, heart hitching slightly.

"They're early," she said, though neither of them moved.

Bishop gave her a quick kiss on the forehead before heading to the window. "You'd better get those pies in the oven."

She smiled, pouring the pie filling.

"That's just Hank," Bishop added, squinting through the window. "Dropping off the fresh catfish for the fry."

Madison laughed. "He's as dependable as the sunrise."

What felt easy in this moment had its roots in a moment three weeks earlier, in a Denver hotel where nothing seemed certain.

Silverware clinked softly against porcelain, a low hum of conversation weaving through the elegant restaurant in downtown Denver. Madison sat across from Bishop near the fireplace, her plate of salmon and asparagus half-eaten, her posture composed but her thoughts anything but.

Bishop had barely touched his food.

She could feel the weight of something unsaid pressing between them. For a moment, she thought he might ask what everyone else had asked.

Did you kill Charlie?

But when he finally spoke, it was different.

He looked at her, eyes heavy.

"Why did you leave?"

Her answer came firm, not cruel.

"I had no reason to stay."

The words lingered in the air, not sharp but empty. They ended their dinner with polite small talk, each wrapped in silence. As they got up, Madison gently touched his shoulder.

"Have their best bottle of champagne sent to your room," she said, her tone light, more peace offering than promise.

He blinked, puzzled. "Why?"

"For surviving your first meeting with Grace," she said with a playful smile. "And for being brave enough to ask me the question that mattered."

Some answers were behind them now. Others waited just ahead.

Thanksgiving morning, back at One Harper Way Road, Madison pulled the first pies from the oven. Bishop leaned in to take a whiff.

"Don't even think about it. You'll spoil your appetite," she warned.

"Not possible," he said, grinning.

Their laughter filled the kitchen.

Quiet, comforting, and healing.

Whatever occurred that night two months ago in Denver, and the truths they were still processing, they faced it together.

This wasn't just a second chance; it was their first real one.

Their first chance... on their terms.

That morning, they had arrived early, weaving through TSA lines in quiet ease. Madison checked the departure screens, eyes searching for their gates, though part of her attention kept drifting to the man just behind her. Traveling beside Bishop after so many years apart felt both strange and oddly familiar, as if muscle memory had carried them into a rhythm her heart wasn't sure it trusted yet.

"Your flight's out of Concourse B," she said. "Mine's..."

She didn't finish.

Bishop stepped behind her, close enough that his breath warmed her ear.

"I'm not going back to California," he whispered.

Madison turned, brow crumpled. "Why aren't you going home?"

He held her gaze, voice steady now.

"Because I'm leaving."

"Leaving?" she echoed. "Why?"

He shrugged, soft but resolute. "I have no reason to stay."

Her eyes searched his face, her heart thudding.

"Then where are you going?"

"The place people go when they're ready to start over."

He didn't hesitate. "Pine Ridge."

She stared at him, the air between them charged. And for a moment, in the middle of a crowded terminal, time held still, as if something destined had quietly shifted.

She didn't ask what it meant. Didn't ask if it would last.

She just smiled and took his hand.

Even now, slicing the pie, she wanted to pinch herself and make sure this was real.

Bishop leaned against the counter, apron still tied crookedly, watching her slice into the first pie.

"You ever think about how quiet it was, all those years?" he asked, voice low.

Madison didn't look up, just smoothed the crust with the back of the knife.

"Quiet isn't the same as peace," she said.

"No," he agreed, shaking his head. "Quiet's heavy. Like if you moved wrong, the whole damn thing would crack."

Finally, she met his eyes. "We lived with that weight, Bishop. Carried it so long we forgot we could put it down."

He held her gaze for a beat, then nodded, almost to himself.

"So… what now?"

Madison glanced toward the door, where voices were gathering outside, along with laughter, footsteps, and the sound of family drawing close. She looked back at him and gave a small, confident smile.

"Now?" she said. "We let the silence break."

The door opened, and Sara Leigh ran in excited. "Gracie's here with the twins!"

Noise spilled in warm and bright, filling the kitchen like sunlight.

For years, silence had been Madison's shield, her punishment, her survival. But in this moment, with the clatter of voices and the chaos of family pouring in around her, she realized something startling.

Silence hadn't protected her.

It had starved her.

And now, for the first time, she wasn't afraid of the noise. She welcomed it. She leaned into it.

She met Bishop's eyes once more, and without speaking, they both understood.

What came next, their story, their truth, wouldn't be written in silence.

It would be written here, in the noise, in the living, in the breaking open.

The fire had taken so much. The lies had buried more.

But ashes don't tell everything.

EPILOGUE

THE HOUSE WAS FINALLY QUIET.

Laughter still clung faintly to the walls, but now only the low hum of the refrigerator filled the kitchen. Madison lingered at the table, her hand resting on the pie knife, crust crumbs scattered like confetti from a celebration she wasn't ready to end.

She should have felt content.

The noise of family.

Bishop's steady presence at her side. Grace's smile softening, inch by inch, into something that looked like trust.

For the first time in years, the silence inside her had broken.

Upstairs, Bishop's laughter drifted faintly as he helped tuck the twins into bed. Sara Leigh played video games in the den, while Morgan and her gentleman friend shared wine in front of the fireplace.

Madison closed her eyes, letting the sound wrap around her—safe, domestic, ordinary.

The life she had once believed was lost.

Then the buzz came.

A sharp vibration against the counter.

She startled, gaze snapping to the phone Bishop had left charging by the fruit bowl. The screen lit up, casting an eerie glow across the dim kitchen.

A name stared back at her.

Elise.

Madison's breath caught.

Her first instinct was to look toward the stairs, but Bishop's voice was still drifting down, warm, and unguarded. He had no idea.

The phone buzzed again.

Insistent.

The name burning on the screen like a brand.

Madison's fingers hovered above it, her pulse pounding in her ears.

She didn't answer.

She didn't have to.

The message was already clear: *Elise wasn't gone.*

She was calling.

And one way or another, she would be heard.

Madison set the knife down, the air around her tightening like a fist.

Because this wasn't an ending.

It was a pause.

And the worst secrets are the ones that survive the flames.

ABOUT THE AUTHOR

Norma Jean Richards is the pen name of *Norma J. Washington*, psychologist, pastor, spiritual advisor, podcast host, and author of several acclaimed self-help books on women's empowerment, marriage, and healing. Known for her compassionate voice, profound teaching, and bold storytelling, she brings emotional depth and cultural insight to her fiction.

With a social media following of over 145,000, Norma has spent years helping women rediscover their voices. Now, through fiction, she's telling the stories that haven't yet been told.

Ashes Don't Tell Everything is her debut novel, written under her maiden name to honor her roots, her voice, and the stories passed down through generations.

Learn more and connect with Norma Jean at:

Next Chapter Life Press Author's Page

www.coachnextcchapter.com/norma-jean-richards

norma@coachnextchapter.com